THE WYATT BUTTERFLY

'*Chain of Evidence* deserves a fanfare...Multilayered and multistranded...written in vivid and uncompromising prose.'
Sue Turnbull, *Sydney Morning Herald*

'Disher is one of Australia's very best crime fiction writers and this is a compelling read.' *Sun Herald*

'A must-read mystery.' *Woman's Day*

'Another powerful statement from one of Australia's top crime writers.' *Courier-Mail*

'Gains extra frisson if you read it on the Peninsula; Disher strips away the glamorous views to reveal desperation, deviants and depressives...and that's just the police force. The plot twists like a back road short cut and pulls like the rip.' *Sunday Age*

'His best novel yet in what has been a distinguished career, he propels us methodically yet elegiacally, the past impending on the present and setting the future into sometimes quite astonishing motion...Now on the same procedural shelf as international greats such as John Harvey, Tony Hillerman and Ian Rankin, Disher brings crime fiction back to simple facts, the painful themes that churn beneath banal surfaces. No one works the flat, elided plains of realism better.' Graeme Blundell, *Australian*

'Intelligent, atmospheric...Fans of such gritty yet cerebral crime novelists as Ian Rankin and John Harvey should be well pleased.' *Publishers Weekly*

'Challis is a fine creation: strong and resourceful, yet with enough human frailty to satisfy the tastes of readers raised on Connelly, Rankin, or Patricia Cornwell. This is intelligent, well-crafted fare, enlivened by a sharp awareness of society and the dark undercurrents beneath it.' *West Australian*

'A slick, fast style that's delightfully free of filler and extraneous plotlines. Once the hook is set, he just lets the story pull you along... Disher is definitely not to be missed.' *Toronto Globe & Mail*

'Disher is delivering the best crime fiction around.' Peter Corris

GARRY DISHER grew up in South Australia, travelled extensively and now lives on the Mornington Peninsula in Victoria. Awarded a creative writing fellowship to Stanford University in 1978 and a full-time writer since 1987, he is the author of more than forty titles—crime and literary novels, children's and YA fiction, anthologies, and history and creative writing textbooks. His Wyatt thrillers and his Challis and Destry police procedurals have garnered acclaim worldwide, winning awards in Germany and appearing on best-books-of-the-year lists in the USA. *Chain of Evidence*, the fourth Challis and Destry novel, won the 2007 Ned Kelly Award.

His other highly-acclaimed novels include *The Sunken Road*, shortlisted for the NBC and South Australian Festival awards, *The Divine Wind*, winner of a NSW Premier's Award, and *The Bamboo Flute*, a classic of children's fiction and winner of the CBC Book of the Year award.

www.garrydisher.com

THE
WYATT
BUTTERFLY

GARRY DISHER

TEXT PUBLISHING MELBOURNE AUSTRALIA

The Text Publishing Company acknowledges the Traditional Owners of the country on which we work, the Wurundjeri people of the Kulin Nation, and pays respect to their Elders past and present.

The paper used in this book is manufactured only from wood grown in sustainable regrowth forests.

The Text Publishing Company
Wurundjeri Country, Level 6, Royal Bank Chambers, 287 Collins Street,
Melbourne Victoria 3000 Australia
textpublishing.com.au

Port Vila Blues first published by Allen & Unwin 1995
Fallout first published by Allen & Unwin 1997
This omnibus edition published 2010 by The Text Publishing Company
Reprinted 2021

Cover design by WH Chong
Page design by Susan Miller

Typeset in Baskerville 12/16pt by J & M Typesetting
Printed and bound by Griffin Press

National Library of Australia
Cataloguing-in-Publication data:

Disher, Garry, 1949-

The Wyatt butterfly / Garry Disher.

ISBN: 9781921656262 (pbk.)

Robbery--Australia--Fiction. Criminals--Australia--Fiction.

Disher, Garry, Port Vila Blues.

Disher, Garry, The fallout

A823.3

PORT VILA BLUES

1

Carlyle Street, Double Bay, 7 a.m. on a Tuesday morning, the air clean and cool. Behind closed doors in the big houses set back far from the street, people were beginning to stir, brewing coffee or standing dazed under showers. Wyatt imagined the smell of the coffee, the sound of the water gurgling in the pipes.

But not at 29 Carlyle Street. According to Jardine's briefing notes, the house would be empty for the next few days. It was the home of Cassandra Wintergreen, MP, Labor member for the seat of Broughton, currently in Dili on a fact-finding mission. 'Champagne Marxist and ALP head-kicker from way back,' Jardine had scrawled in his covering note. That meant nothing to Wyatt. He'd never voted. If he read the newspapers at all it was with an eye for a possible heist, not news about political tussles. His only interest in Wintergreen lay in the fact that she had $50,000 in a floor safe in her bedroom: a kickback, according to Jardine, from a grateful developer who'd asked her to intervene in a planning dispute regarding access to a strip of shops he was building in her electorate.

Wyatt continued his surveillance. Whenever he staked out a place he noticed everything, no matter how trivial, knowing that something insignificant one day can be crucial the next; noticing in stages, first the general picture, then the finer details; noticing routes out, and obstacles like a rubbish bin or a crack in a footpath that could bring an escape undone.

There were two gateways in the long street frontage, indicating a driveway that curved up to the front door then back down to the street. Shrubs and small trees screened the front of the house from the footpath and from the houses on either side. It all spelt money and conviction.

Conviction. Wyatt had grown up in narrow back streets. His mother had never spoken about his father and Wyatt had no memories of the man. Wyatt had earned himself broad convictions on those narrow streets. Later he'd read books, and looked and listened and acted, refining his convictions.

Jardine's floor plans revealed a hallway at number 29, two large front rooms on either side of it, and a range of other rooms at the back and on the upper level. Jardine had marked three possible hitches for Wyatt's attention. One, the house was patrolled by HomeSecure once a day, usually around midnight; two, the alarm system was wired to the local cop shop; three, he'd not been able to supply the cancel codes for the alarm system but the combination for Wintergreen's safe was her birth date: 27–03–48. Jardine built his jobs on information supplied by claims assessors in insurance companies, the tradesmen who installed security systems, surveillance reports and bugged conversations collected by bent private detectives. A word dropped here and there by real estate agents, chauffeurs, taxi drivers, bank clerks, casino croupiers, clubland boasters.

Wyatt watched for another five minutes. It was the variable

in any situation that kept him on his toes. Without the habit of permanent vigilance he knew that he'd lose the edge, and that might mean a final bullet or blade or at the least steel bands manacling his wrists. There was always the unexpected change in layout or routine, the traffic jam, the flat battery, the empty safe. But these were things you could never fully prepare for, so you hoped they'd never happen. If they did, you tried to absorb them as you encountered them and hoped they wouldn't trip you up. The innocent bystander was often the worst that could happen. Man, woman or child, they were unpredictable. Would they panic? Stand dumbly in the line of fire? Try to be a hero? Wyatt hated it if they got hurt or killed—not because he cared personally but because it upset people, particularly the police.

Satisfied that the house was empty, Wyatt crossed the street to number 29, a brisk shoe-leather snap to his footsteps. Dressed in a dark, double-breasted coat over a collar and tie, swinging a black briefcase, he might have been the first businessman up that morning. Soon cars would be backing out of driveways, white exhaust gases drifting in the air, but for the moment Wyatt was the only figure abroad on the long, prosperous streets of Double Bay.

He paused at the driveway. A rolled-up newspaper was lying in the gutter nearby. Wyatt had dropped it there unseen in the dark hours of the morning, but anyone watching from a nearby window now would have seen him bend down, pick up the newspaper and stand there for a while, looking indecisively up the driveway at the house as if he were asking himself whether or not he should take the paper in or leave it there where it could be damaged or stolen. They would have seen him decide. They would have seen him set off up the driveway, a kindly passerby, banging the paper against his knee.

The front windows could not be seen from the street or the

houses on either side. Wyatt swung the briefcase, smashing the sitting room window. At once the blue light above the front door began to flash and Wyatt knew that bells would be ringing at the local police station. He had a few minutes. He wouldn't rush it.

The newspaper was tightly rolled in shrink-wrapped plastic. It had the stiffness and density of a small branch. Wyatt dropped it under the window and walked unhurriedly back down the driveway and onto the footpath again.

In the next street he took off the coat and tie, revealing a navy blue reversible jacket. There was a cap in the pocket. He put that on and immediately looked as though he belonged to the little Mazda parked near the corner. Dark, slanting letters on each side spelled out 'Rapido Couriers' and he'd stolen it from a service depot the night before. Couriers were as common now as milk vans in the old days, so he wasn't expecting questions and he wasn't expecting anyone to be looking for the car in Double Bay. He climbed in and settled back to wait, a street directory propped on the steering wheel—an old ploy, one that worked.

He fine-tuned the police-band radio on the seat next to him in time to hear the call go out. He heard the dispatcher spell the address slowly and give street references.

'Neighbour call it in?' a voice wanted to know.

'Negative. The alarm system at the premises is wired to the station.'

'A falling leaf,' the patrol-car cop predicted. 'Dew. Electrical fault. What do you bet me?'

Another voice cut in: 'Get to it, you two.'

It was as though the patrol-car cop had snapped to attention. Wyatt heard the man say, 'Right away, sarge, over and out,' and a minute later he saw the patrol car pass, lights flashing behind him on Carlyle Street.

The toothache didn't creep into his consciousness, it arrived in full, lancing savagery. Nerves twitched and Wyatt felt his left eye flutter. He couldn't bear to move his head. It was the worst attack yet, arriving unannounced, arriving when the job demanded his full attention. He tapped the teeth on his upper left jaw, searching for the bad one as though finding it would give him some comfort. It was there, all right.

He snapped two paracetamol tablets out of a foil strip and washed them down with a bottle of apple juice. Then he took out a tiny jar of clove oil, shook a drop on his finger, rubbed it into his jaw and gently over the tooth. He'd been doing this for five days now. He didn't know if the painkillers or the clove oil did much good. They didn't make things worse, so that was something in their favour.

Wyatt blocked out the pain and concentrated on the radio. It was good to be working alone, the appeal of the planning and the execution—and, if he cared to admit it, of the anticipated and actual danger. He thought for a moment about these jobs Jardine was blueprinting for him. In one instance, three months earlier, a millionaire had hired them to get back the silverware collection he'd lost to his ex-wife in the divorce settlement. In another, a finance company had paid to have a bankrupt property developer who owed them two million dollars relieved of two undeclared Nolans and a Renoir.

The radio crackled. The patrol car came on the line: 'False alarm.'

'Explain, please,' the dispatcher said.

The voice might have been writing a formal report. 'Constable Wright and I approached the premises. We observed that a front window had been broken. On closer examination, we discovered a rolled-up newspaper lying on the ground under the window. Constable Wright obtained entry to the premises through the broken window. The premises are furnished but empty and intact. We await further instructions.'

The sergeant came on the line. 'Knock off the fancy talk. You reckon the paper boy got a bit vigorous?'

'Looks like it, sarge.'

'Okay, go back in, turn off the alarm, and shoot over to the highway. There's been a pile-up.'

'Right, sarge.'

'Meanwhile I'll give the security firm a bell and get them over to seal the window.'

'Right, sarge.'

Wyatt continued to wait. When he saw the patrol car leave along Carlyle Street, he reversed into an alleyway, got out, and pasted HomeSecure transfers over the Rapido name. Finally he pulled on overalls stencilled with the name HomeSecure and drove around to number 29, spinning into the driveway with a convincing show of urgency. Pulling up at the front door, he got out, cleared the remaining shards of glass from the window frame with his gloved hand and climbed over the sill and into the house.

He made straight for the main bedroom. It was a curiously flattened room: a futon bed base and mattress at ankle height, low chest of drawers, squat cane chair in one corner, built-in closet, no pictures on the walls. Only curtains existed above waist level and they admitted the blurry light of early morning onto the bed. It was also an asexual room, as though Wintergreen spent all of her passion brokering deals somewhere else, for her profit or for the profit of those who might one day help advance her career.

The safe was under a heavy Nepalese rug at the foot of the bed. Wyatt lifted the floorboard panel, keyed in the combination, heard a hum as the electronic lock disengaged.

He opened the door and looked in on a cavity the size of a

small television set. There were papers and files stacked in there, but not the fifty grand that Jardine had promised. Wyatt emptied the safe and knocked against the sides and base with his knuckles. He snorted. The bottom was false.

Wyatt pushed experimentally at the corners. The base lock was a simple push-pull spring-loaded catch. He swung it open.

The fifty thousand was there all right, bundled in twenties, fifties and hundreds. Wyatt stacked them into slits in the lining of his overalls. Twenty-five for Jardine, twenty-five for himself.

He paused. There was something else down there in the darkness, a small, soft, black velvet bag. Wyatt reached down, pulled it out.

The object that tumbled into his palm gleamed softly in the light of his torch. It was a butterfly, 1930s Deco style, with an eight-centimetre wingspan. The body consisted of 2-carat diamonds set in gold. The wings were also gold, set with flowing rows of baguette diamonds in channels alternating with rows of round diamonds. He turned it over. A thin line stamped in the gold read Tiffany & Co.

Wyatt added the butterfly to the fifty thousand dollars. Jardine would know someone who'd know what to do with it—sell it overseas as it was or melt the gold setting and sell the stones separately. A local buyer was out: the larger stones could be identified and traced too easily—they'd be on record somewhere, able to be matched to an X-ray or a photograph.

He was out of the house and easing down the driveway five minutes after he'd gone in. He paused for a moment at the gate, then eased the Mazda onto the street. There were more people about now: children walking to bus stops, men and women heading to work in glossy foreign cars. They looked scrubbed clean and well fed, that's all Wyatt knew or cared about them.

2

Wyatt's tooth was giving him hell by the time Ansett's early breakfast flight from Sydney touched down in Melbourne on Wednesday morning. He always travelled light, knowing that if anyone intended to grab him it would be while he waited around for his luggage to tumble onto the carousel. He had an overnight bag with a change of clothing in it, wrapped around the Tiffany and the fifty thousand dollars. And where possible he avoided leaving a paper trail, even with fake ID, so he walked past the hire-car booths and caught a taxi.

Thirty minutes to Brunswick Road, and even on the exit ramp it was bumper to bumper. He checked the time: 8 a.m. They should be awake in the Coburg house.

The cab driver turned left off the exit ramp and headed east along Brunswick Road.

'I'd like to give Sydney Road a miss,' he said, 'if that's okay by you?' Wyatt nodded his assent. Sydney Road was the most direct route into Coburg but he knew that it would be bad, locked with peak-hour trams and heavy transports. The driver turned left a couple of streets before Sydney Road and wound his way deep into Coburg, a region of hot little streets and weatherboard houses, finally delivering Wyatt at the entrance to a dead-end strip of asphalt ten houses long. Wyatt got out, paid the man, let his senses register that he was safe, then headed for the white weatherboard where Jardine was maybe slowly dying.

Jardine's sister opened the door. She was careworn, thin, a spasm of emotion pulling her mouth down at one corner when she saw it was Wyatt at the door. It was a look Wyatt knew well, so he said her name carefully, softly, barely murmuring it: 'Nettie.'

Sourness became exasperation and she said, 'Why don't you leave us alone? We're managing. You're just bringing back bad memories.'

'Did he say that?'

She looked away stubbornly. 'It doesn't do him any good, seeing you.'

'Let him be the judge of that, Nettie.'

Jardine's sister bit her lower lip. Then she shrugged, closed the screen door in Wyatt's face and disappeared down the gloomy hallway to a room at the back. The house was in need of restumping and the interior smelt of cooped-up humans and dampness. The house was rented. The wallpaper, carpets, light fittings and laminex benches were left over from the dismal end of the 1950s, and Wyatt looked forward to the day when he could rescue Jardine and the sister and place them somewhere better.

Nettie materialised from the shadows, hooking limp strands of hair behind her ears. She resembled an Oklahoma dustbowl survivor, etched cheekbones and eyes wide, dark and long-suffering. 'I just want you to know,' she said, opening the screen door to admit Wyatt into the house, 'he doesn't blame you but the rest of us do.'

Wyatt stopped and stared at her. His voice was cold, factual and remote, with no detectable emotion in it: 'Nettie, he knew the risks.'

Jardine came from a family of half-bent secondhand dealers and back-of-a-truck merchants. They were careful and stayed out of trouble. Jardine's getting head-shot six months ago on a job with Wyatt had been unaccountable, the kind of thing that could have happened to anyone, but it was a first for Jardine's family and Jardine was the only one who wasn't blaming Wyatt for it.

'He knew the risks,' Wyatt repeated.

What Wyatt wasn't admitting was that he did feel some responsibility—not for the fact that he'd put Jardine at risk, but for what had happened since. When he'd first seen Jardine again after the job, Wyatt had been shocked by the change in the man with whom he'd pulled a dozen successful jobs over the years, a man he liked and trusted—as much as Wyatt liked and trusted anyone. Six months earlier, Jardine had come out of retirement as backup on the hit on the Mesic compound looking fit and alert, a man with a slow-burning good humour, but they'd been ambushed after the Mesic job and Jardine had been head-shot, a graze above one ear. Wyatt had paid Jardine his fee, taken him to a doctor who didn't ask questions, and gone to ground in Tasmania, a base where the wrong people would never find him.

He'd assumed that Jardine had gone back into peaceful retirement, but the Jardine he'd seen in Sydney a few weeks later was partly paralysed along one side, kilos lighter, a few IQ points slower and duller. Jardine tended to forget things. He owed two months rent. Pizza cartons and styrofoam coffee cups littered his pair of rooms at the Dorset Hotel in Newtown, and it was clear that he wore the same clothing for days at a time.

Wyatt had hauled his old partner off to a 24-hour clinic, fabricating a cover story to account for the wound which still showed as a raw slice in Jardine's scalp. 'Stroke,' the doctor diagnosed. Probably brought on by the injury. Jardine needed professional care. Was there someone who could look after him for the next few months? A friend? Family? A live-in nurse, if that could be afforded?

Wyatt contacted the family in Melbourne. For two days he let himself be tongue-lashed by them. Finally Nettie said she'd take Jardine in. Wyatt had known someone would. All he'd wanted was for them to say so. 'I'll pay the bills,' he told them.

Nettie had never married. She'd had a job in the Kodak factory but lost it a year ago and didn't like her chances of getting another. She found the Coburg house, a dump with enough room for two adults at a monthly rent that wouldn't cripple Wyatt, and Jardine moved in with her. All their needs—medical, domestic—Wyatt paid for.

He knew it was temporary and he looked forward to the time when he could score big and set Jardine and Nettie up for life.

Get that unwanted weight off his mind, his back.

'I promise not to upset him,' he told Nettie now.

Nettie had made her point. She turned away from Wyatt in the hallway and opened the door to one of the front rooms. She jerked her head: 'He's out the back.'

Wyatt clasped her arm gently and gave her a package. 'To keep you going,' he said. 'Twenty-five thousand.'

Nettie didn't look at the money, didn't count it. The money disappeared with her into the front room and Wyatt's final contact with her that morning was the sensation of her thin arm in his fingers and a sound that might have been a muttered 'thanks' hanging in the air between them.

He walked through to the back of the house, a fibro extension with a low, buckled ceiling and dust-clogged louvred windows. The only good thing about it was the morning sun striking it through a fig tree in the yard outside. The air was warm, a little streaked and blurry owing to the dust motes stirring in the angled sunlight, and smelling only faintly of illness, privation and cut-short dreams.

Jardine clawed a hand over the old bakelite smoking stand next to his lumpish armchair. His mouth worked: 'Mate,' he said at last, smiling lopsidedly. 'Where did you spring from?'

'The Double Bay job, remember?'

Wyatt spoke harshly. He hated to see the weakness in Jardine. Jardine seemed to exist in a fog a lot of the time now and he wanted to cut through it. 'The MP on the take, Wintergreen.'

Jardine looked across at him, wavering, trying to draw back the spittle glistening on his lips. His left hand rested palm up in the threadbare brown blanket in his lap. The left half of his face was immobile. A strange, inappropriate expression formed on his face and Wyatt realised that his old friend was frowning, trying to recall the briefing session, the job itself. Then Jardine's face cleared. A smile of great sweetness settled on it, and his voice was clear: 'Got you now. No hassles?'

Wyatt shook his head. 'I gave your share to Nettie.'

Jardine shook his head. 'Mate, I don't know how to thank you. Me and Net—'

A lashing quality entered Wyatt's voice. 'Forget it.'

Jardine straightened in the armchair. His right hand fished a handkerchief from the pocket of his cardigan and he wiped his chin defiantly. 'Okay, okay, suit yourself.'

Wyatt unbuckled his overnight bag. 'I found a piece of jewellery hidden with the money. Valuable, Tiffany butterfly.'

'Nice.'

'We need someone who can offload it for us.'

Jardine laboured to his feet and shuffled into the adjoining kitchen. A short time later, Wyatt heard his voice, a low murmur on the telephone.

He stared across the room at the little computer perched mute on a card table. Jardine used it to cross-reference jockey weights, track conditions, blood-line and other horse-racing factors. In five years he claimed to have won $475,000 and lost $450,000 using his system. What people didn't know was that Jardine had also spent the past few years selling burglary and armed holdup plans to professionals like Wyatt. Wyatt didn't know how many jobs Jardine had on file, but he did know that they were all in New South Wales and that all would grow rapidly out of date the longer Jardine stayed in Melbourne with his sister.

Jardine came back. 'A sheila called Liz Redding, eleven this morning, a motel on St Georges Road.'

Wyatt watched Jardine carefully. Jardine's face had grown more elastic in the past few minutes, as if his mind worked well if he had something to stimulate it. Wyatt even recognised an old expression on Jardine's face, a mixture of alertness and absorption as he calculated the odds of a problem.

'Fine.'

3

They took a taxi to meet Jardine's fence. Wyatt wound down his window and leaned into the wind. Every after-hours lapse and misery the car had ever seen was leaking from the seats into the confined space behind the driver. Jardine, foggy in the head again, leaned back into the corner and appeared to sleep. It irritated Wyatt. First the vicious, jabbing pain in his upper jaw, and now this, his friend well under par when he needed him to be sharp with the woman who would be fencing the Tiffany for them.

'What's she like?' Wyatt had asked, before the taxi arrived.

'Never met her.'

A chilling kind of dispassion was Wyatt's style, but this time he'd given in to his impatience and his throbbing tooth. 'Mate, how do you know she's any good?'

'I checked around. Mack Delaney trained her.'

'Mack's dead.'

'Yeah, but he was one of the best.'

Wyatt conceded that. He'd used Delaney once in the old days to move stolen gear. Delaney had specialised in ransoming silverware, paintings, watches and coin and stamp collections back to the owners or to the insurance companies, but now and then he'd forge the provenance of a painting and sell it at auction overseas. As he'd explained it to Wyatt, art thieves had it good in Australia. Insurance premiums were prohibitive, meaning galleries and private owners were often not insured, relying on cheap security systems to protect their paintings. They also tended not to keep good photographs of the items in their collections, or at best only kept handwritten descriptions. An international magazine called *Trace* tackled art theft by maintaining a computerised recording system, but subscription costs were high and there were on-line compatibility problems, and, as a result, few of the Australian galleries, dealers, auctioneers or private collectors had joined. Many paintings stolen in Australia were shipped overseas to private buyers. Mack had explained that in Japan it was possible to gain legal title to a stolen art work after only two years; in Switzerland, after five years. Then there were the buyers who had no interest in aesthetics. They used the paintings to finance drug deals. In Wyatt's eyes, everything boiled down to that, these days.

Wyatt peered at the motel as they passed in the taxi. There always was a motel, in Wyatt's game. He hid in motels, outlined hits in motels, divided the take in motels. Motels made sense. The other guests left you alone, coming and going just as you did. If the truth be known, half of them were probably up to something illicit or illegal anyhow. Unfortunately motels were also easy to stake out and potential traps. They were stamped from the same mould: layout, carpet, paintwork, bedding, decor, prints above the fat beds.

They got out of the taxi a block past the motel and walked

back. It was called the TravelWay and it faced St Georges Road. One lane of cracked and buckled asphalt had been cordoned off by plastic ribbon and witch's hats, and boggy holes had been carved out under the tram tracks in the centre of the road. In the late morning light the street was a wasteland, still and lifeless.

Wyatt viewed it sourly: this wasn't a place with a quick exit. The motel itself was a simple building, a one-storey block parallel to the street, with rooms facing St Georges Road and an identical number of rooms backing on to them, facing suburban back yards at the rear. Most of the cars in the lot were Falcons and Commodores, commercial travellers' cars, white station wagons with sample cases and cardboard displays stacked behind the front seats. Wyatt automatically examined the interior of every car in the lot and on the street outside, then watched the door to room 14 for a few minutes while Jardine sat on a bluestone block in the sun.

Satisfied that they weren't walking into a trap, Wyatt knocked on 14 and stepped to one side. That was automatic, too: he'd been shot at through spyholes; men had come at him through doors or bundled him into rooms through doors much like the red door to room 14.

Jardine, hearing the knock, blinked and limped to join him. A woman's voice, pleasant and inquiring, the voice of a faintly puzzled legitimate guest, said, 'Who is it?'

'Frank Jardine,' Jardine said.

The door opened. Nothing happened. When hands didn't seize Jardine and men didn't scream at him to drop to the ground, Wyatt stepped into view behind him.

The woman's eyes flicked over them, assessing their faces, where they had their hands, finally checking the motel forecourt and the torn-up street behind them. Until she'd done this she said nothing, expressed nothing but wariness, but then she smiled, a

16

flood of warmth in the poky doorway. 'Come in,' she said, stepping back, one hand indicating the room, the other holding the door fully open.

As they edged past, Wyatt saw her glance at his overnight bag. Aware of his eyes on her, she looked up and grinned. He smiled a little, despite himself. She had a cheery vigour that he liked, an air of someone good at her job but not about to let it button down the atmosphere. She wore sandals and a billowy cotton shirt over patterned tights. A faint scent of soap and shampoo drifted around her head. Her hair was fine, dark and dead straight, parted in the middle, framing her face. There was a faint asymmetry about her features: one eye seemed to stare out a little, one cheekbone sat a fraction lower than the other, giving her an air of sceptical good humour and quick intelligence.

Wyatt entered the room cautiously. Apart from the standard fittings, it was empty. Jardine checked the en-suite bathroom and came out again, nodding the okay. So he hasn't completely lost it, Wyatt thought, setting the overnight bag on the bed and unzipping it.

'Straight down to business,' the woman said.

'He is a bit obsessive,' Jardine agreed, catching her mood. Together they watched Wyatt.

'Does he talk? Drink tea or coffee?'

'Been known to,' Jardine said.

Wyatt had few skills at this sort of thing, but he made an effort. 'I won't have a drink, bad tooth, but you two go ahead.' His palm floated automatically to his cheek.

The smiling sympathy in Liz Redding's face and manner was genuine. 'Abscess? Old filling?' She came close to peer at his face. 'It does look swollen on that side,' she said. 'You'd better get it seen to or your performance will suffer.'

She could have meant anything by that. He felt an absurd

17

desire to embrace her. 'I'm fine.'

'Sure. Tough guy.'

'Look, can we get down to it?'

'Suit yourself.'

Wyatt stepped back from the bed and leaned his rump on the leading edge of the television bench under a painting of junks on Hong Kong harbour. Jardine swung the room's only chair around and sat in it. Both men watched Liz Redding fold back the tissue paper until the Tiffany sat in the palm of her hand.

'Nice,' she said at last.

Taking a jeweller's glass from her pocket and holding it to her eye, she examined the Tiffany stone by stone, turning the piece occasionally, allowing for light refraction. Finally she took a small set of scales from a box in her satchel and weighed it. 'It's the real thing, all right.'

'How much?' Wyatt asked.

'He does like to get down to it, doesn't he?' she said. 'Depends on whether or not it's sold as is or broken up, the gold and the stones sold individually.'

'Be a pity to do that,' Jardine said. He took the Tiffany from her hand, placed it above her right breast, angled his head to gauge the effect. 'That's where it belongs.'

Liz Redding grinned, pushed his hand away. 'Yeah, right, once a year I draw the curtains, remove it from its hiding place, admire myself in the mirror.'

Jardine grinned back at her.

Wyatt's jaw was burning. All the strain of his chosen life seemed to erupt in him and he snarled, 'Cut the crap, you two. I want to work out where and when so we can get the hell out of here.'

It might have been Wyatt's anger, or it might have happened anyway, but Jardine's treacherous body failed him again. He seemed suddenly to fill with shame, shifting in his chair and moaning softly.

Wyatt frowned at him. 'What?'

Jardine, his face contorted, said helplessly, 'Mate, I've shit meself.'

Wyatt stared at him. 'Oh, Frank,' he said.

He lifted Jardine out of the chair. Jardine was a tall man, once quick and strong like himself, but now he was skin and bone. The chair seat was smudged watery brown and Jardine reeked of his own waste.

'Come on, pal. I'll take you to the bathroom.'

Jardine shuffled with him across the floor. 'I'm sorry about this. I'll—'

'Shut up,' Wyatt said. He felt a kind of tangled anger. He didn't want thanks, he didn't want to clean shit off his friend, he had no room for feelings he'd never had before, yet he knew all of it was unavoidable and necessary.

'Sometimes I just—' Jardine said.

'For Christ's sake, shut up.'

Then Liz Redding was on the other side, helping him support Jardine. 'Quit that. You're upsetting him.'

For a moment, Jardine was the instrument in a tug of war. 'I'm taking him to the bathroom,' Wyatt said uselessly.

'No you're not. I'll do it. You haven't got the touch.'

'I'll call a taxi.'

'Forget it. Just leave, okay? I'll get him cleaned up and I'll drive him home myself.'

Wyatt released Jardine. Jardine's shame eddied around the three of them. By now it was an intimate thing to Wyatt, not strange or repellent. He said, 'Take care, Frank.'

He turned to Liz. After a moment he said, 'Thanks.'

She sighed, nodded, smiled sadly. 'Give me twenty-four hours to put out some feelers, here, Amsterdam, maybe New York.'

'Okay.'

She led Jardine into the bathroom, saying, 'Tomorrow morning suit you?'

'Southbank,' Wyatt said.

'Fine.'

Wyatt left the motel. He liked to be the first to leave. If you left first, the others couldn't wait around the corner and follow you.

4

The bank was a 'feeder'. The largest branch in the largest town in the upper reaches of the Yarra River Valley in Victoria, it 'fed' the smaller branches in the smaller towns. Fair enough—except that a cool half million was in the vault, twice the normal amount, and if they didn't hit the place tonight, all that money would disappear into the wallets and paypackets of the locals tomorrow.

There was twice the normal amount in the vault because this was Wednesday and tomorrow was Thursday, payday and also the first day of the Upper Yarra Festival. According to the blueprints supplied for this hit, over the next four days wineries would be flogging raw whites at twenty bucks a pop, every village showground in the valley would stage a handful of run-down ghost trains and shooting galleries, and it all added up to a lot of people needing a lot of spending money, starting tomorrow morning.

Niekirk glanced at his watch. The town clock had struck midnight ten minutes ago, but the eight-to-midnight disc jockey was still inside Radio 3UY, next door to the bank. The midnight-to-dawn announcer had arrived, but until the other man clocked off and went home, Niekirk, Riggs and Mansell had to sit tight and wait.

Not that the waiting would be a problem. The three men sat in the van like clones of one another: silent, watchful men in their thirties, dressed in black balaclavas, black overalls. The van belonged to Telecom, stolen an hour earlier in Eltham. If anyone asked questions, Niekirk, Riggs and Mansell were tracking down a cable fault. They also had a stolen Range Rover with tinted windows stashed in Warrandyte. The Range Rover was Riggs' and Mansell's way out of the hills. They were wearing dinner suits under their overalls and if anyone stopped them later, they were a couple of winemakers celebrating the start of the festival.

Niekirk had his own way out. He'd be carrying the money and he didn't want Riggs and Mansell to know where he was taking it. And once he'd made the delivery, Niekirk didn't know where the money was going. De Lisle, the man who put these jobs together, wanted it that way, and Niekirk was in no position to argue, not when De Lisle could put him in jail for a long time, and especially not when De Lisle controlled the purse strings. Disappear with the money himself? Forget it. De Lisle would find him in five seconds.

Mansell went tense suddenly. He was in the driver's seat, a headset clamped to his ears, a police-band radio in his lap. He fine-tuned the radio, listening intently. 'I'm getting something.'

Neither Riggs nor Niekirk spoke. If they had something to worry about, Mansell would soon tell them. Even so, they relaxed visibly when Mansell grinned. 'Kid ran his car into a tree near Yarra Junction.'

Niekirk nodded. That was good: a car smash would tie up the local boys in blue for a while. He watched Mansell. Mansell

22

disliked being the driver and radio man. But, as Niekirk continued to point out to him, Riggs was needed to open the safe, himself to oversee the job, leaving Mansell to keep watch.

Niekirk spoke. 'Here he comes now.'

A man had come through the side door of Radio 3UY. He wore a denim jacket and jeans and his shaved skull gleamed in the moonlight. The three men saw him stretch, yawn, shiver, then climb into a sad-looking VW and clatter down the hill and out of sight.

Niekirk glanced at Mansell. 'All clear?'

Mansell nodded.

'Let's go.'

Riggs and Niekirk slipped into the darkness and across the street to the metre-wide alley that separated the bank from the radio station. The bank's rear door was flat and implacable, a dark steel mass in the wall. There were two locks, and Riggs knelt before the lower one, took a set of picks from the breast pocket of his overalls, and went to work. Niekirk watched him, training the narrow beam of a pencil torch at the lock.

A half minute later, the lock was open and Riggs started on the upper one. He breathed heavily as he worked, audible sounds of effort and concentration. Then the second lock fell open and he seemed to deflate, the tension draining away from him.

Niekirk folded back a flap of his overalls, where he'd stitched a tiny radio into a pocket above his breastbone. He depressed the transmit button. 'We're going in.'

He heard Mansell's acknowledgement, a crackle of static, and pushed open the steel door. According to the briefing notes, there was minimal security inside the bank. There had never been the need for it—you didn't get bank raids in these little hill towns, where lives were modest and every road was crippled with S-bends. But Niekirk hadn't lived as long as he had by accepting

23

the things he was told without checking first. He paused in the doorway and played the torch beam over the interior walls, floor and ceiling. Nothing.

He put his mouth to the radio, said, 'It's clear,' and led the way into the bank.

Behind him Riggs shouldered a canvas bag of tools and closed the door in the rear wall, sealing them off from the cloudy moon.

The briefing notes consisted of floor plans, a description of the security system, external patrol times, notes on staffing levels and the size of the take, and an estimate of the minimum time elapse before cops might be expected to arrive if they happened to trip a hidden alarm. There was also a number to call if they were arrested. As with the other jobs they'd pulled for De Lisle, the groundwork and backup were impressive. Someone had done his homework. But Niekirk didn't know who the someone was, and that was the big weakness in this job. All he knew from De Lisle was, they had a green light as far as the local armed-holdup squad was concerned.

The vault was in a room adjoining the staff toilets along the far wall of the bank. Veiling the torch beam with his hand, Niekirk led Riggs along the main corridor, past a storeroom and the manager's office, and across an open area where desks and cabinets squatted like outcrops of granite on a wintry plain.

A heavy steel grille barred the entrance to the vault. The briefing notes hadn't said anything about that. Niekirk murmured into the radio: 'There's a grille we weren't told about. I'll keep you posted.'

The radio crackled.

Again Niekirk trained the torch while Riggs probed with his set of picks. The steel grille gave him no more trouble than the door to the bank itself, and a minute later Niekirk was saying into the transmitter: 'Final stage.'

Riggs unzipped his canvas bag. First he removed a heavy-duty industrial drill and rested it at the base of the vault. He followed that with a weighty metal device shaped like an ungainly handgun. It was an electromagnetic drill-stand and it hit the vinyl tiles of the floor with a thud. Finally he reached in and wordlessly handed Niekirk a small fluorescent camping lantern, two coils of thick black rubber power leads and a double-adaptor.

Niekirk flicked a switch on the lantern. A weak, localised glow illuminated the door of the vault. He searched the walls and skirting board. There was a power point in the corridor outside the grille door. He plugged in the two leads, switched on the power and said softly: 'Ready.'

Riggs pulled the drill trigger experimentally. The motor whirred, muted and powerful. He rested the drill on the floor again then heaved to his feet, holding the drill-stand in both hands. He eyed the combination lock assessingly for half a minute, then pressed the leading edge of the electromagnet against the vault door. Metal slammed against metal, clamping the drill-stand to the face of the vault like an ugly handle. Finally he fitted the drill with a diamond-studded bit.

Neither man said anything for the next fifteen minutes. While Niekirk watched and listened, Riggs drilled three holes through the Swedish steel door of the vault. Guided by the electromagnetic drill-stand, he was assured of being accurate to within five millimetres of the crucial point in the locking mechanism, just above the tumblers. Metal filings curled to the floor, smoke wisps rose from the hot tip of the drill, and even with wax plugs in their ears the sound seemed to tear each man open.

After fifteen minutes Riggs unclamped the drill-stand and rested it on the floor. He glanced at Niekirk, who said into the radio: 'Anything?'

Mansell's voice crackled: 'All clear.'

Riggs fished in his bag for a small tin. It held powdered chalk, which he rubbed into the palms of his hands, the sound dry and satisfied. Then he took out another of his special tools. This was an aptoscope, used by urologists to examine the human bladder. He crouched at the drill holes, positioned the aptoscope, and began to examine the tumblers inside the lock. After a while he breathed, 'You little fucking beauty,' and started to poke and probe with a lock pick. Two minutes later, he had the door open.

Niekirk bent his mouth to the radio. 'We're in.'

They worked quickly. Riggs repacked his bag while Niekirk stepped into the vault and began to empty it. Their first job, back in February, had involved hitting the safety-deposit boxes of a bank in suburban Brighton, seizing bonds, cash, jewellery; this time the orders were clear—take the money only. The money was in small plastic containers similar to margarine tubs, stacked neatly along a shelf. As Niekirk piled them outside the vault, Riggs carried them away to the rear door of the bank, next to his tools.

Then things began to go wrong. Mansell came on the air and said, 'A security patrol van just pulled in behind the bank.'

'He's early,' Niekirk said.

'I'll keep you posted.'

Niekirk joined Riggs at the steel door. They heard a handbrake crank on just outside, heard a car door slam, and footsteps approached the bank. A moment later the door was rattled experimentally and they heard a faint slither as the patrolman slipped a calling card under the door. They expected the man to drive away then but instead he seemed content to wait there for a while. They heard him urinate against the wall, farting once with a sharp brap, and then a second vehicle arrived.

Niekirk and Riggs heard whispers, a giggle or two, and knew they were stuck there inside the bank for the time being.

Niekirk walked back along the corridor to a point where his voice wouldn't be heard outside the bank. 'Looks like his girlfriend has just turned up. We'll go with the other plan.'

'Right,' Mansell said.

This was their third heist. The newspapers had begun to call them 'the magnetic drill gang', stressing that they stamped their raids with efficiency and professionalism. Part of that was being ready whenever a situation reversed itself. That's why they always had a backup plan to put into place. They'd each studied the bank earlier in the week, defining the likely problems. How could they get out if their planned route was blocked? The front door was no good—it faced the main street. They couldn't burrow out or blast a hole in the wall, so that left the roof.

Working swiftly and silently, Riggs and Niekirk dragged desks and chairs to the centre of the main room and built a tower. Four desks placed together formed the base; two desks stacked on top of them formed the second tier; a single desk formed the third. Niekirk climbed to the top and reached up. His fingers brushed the ceiling, white acoustic battens. He called Riggs to bring him a couple of chairs. Now he could slide the battens away, giving him access to the space under the roof.

With Riggs passing to him from below, Niekirk stacked the money in the ceiling. Then he climbed down and both men ranged quickly through the bank, flashing the pencil torch at all the doors. They chose the storeroom door; it was long and sturdy and lifted free of its hinges as though it had been oiled for just that purpose. They went back to the desk tower. Niekirk climbed to the top, took the door from Riggs and slid it up into the ceiling.

It was warm and airless under the roof. Using the rafters for support, and working with the aid of the camping light, the two men carted the money and the door to the wall opposite the side wall of the radio station. The roof was steeply pitched here and they had to carry out the next stage doubled over. Removing the terracotta roof tiles one by one, stacking them silently, they opened a gap to the sky. Cool air poured in; clouds drifted across the face of the moon.

The roof of Radio 3UY was a little lower and less than two metres away from the roof of the bank. It was also flat. Niekirk saw a tarred surface, an airconditioning shack and a manhole cover. Using the storeroom door as a bridge, he crossed to the other side. For the next two minutes he stacked the money as Riggs slid the containers across to him. He could feel vibrations under his feet. Radio 3UY was blasting the night away.

They took the disc jockey with .38s in their hands and balaclavas over their faces. The DJ was playing an early Animals track, running his fingertips over an imaginary organ keyboard. He gulped when he saw the two men. He moved to cut the song and yelp into the microphone but Riggs moved first, smashing the edge of his gun across the DJ's throat.

It was hard and vicious and unnecessary. 'Steady,' Niekirk said.

That was all he said. He had electrical tape in his pocket. He bound the man to his studio chair, then tipped man and chair onto the floor. The song finished. Both men froze. But it was an album. Another song started.

Songs had been short in the sixties and seventies. Niekirk guessed that he and Riggs had about two and a half minutes. He put his mouth to the radio: 'Come and get us.'

Mansell backed the Telecom van onto the radio station's forecourt. Parked like that it obscured the foyer doors from the street. The three men worked quickly, forming a chain, Riggs passing the money to Niekirk at the doors, Niekirk passing to Mansell, who stacked the containers in the rear of the van.

Another song started, 'Sky Pilot', droning from a speaker mounted to the wall above the reception desk. Good, a longish song, seven minutes at least. Niekirk kept the money moving, knowing there was no guarantee that the DJ wouldn't free himself. There was no guarantee that loyal listeners wouldn't investigate when 3UY went off the air soon, either.

Then they were loaded and Mansell was driving them out of there, Riggs in the passenger seat, Niekirk with the money in the rear of the van, just as 'Sky Pilot' ended, nothing following it, only a speaker hiss like a mute presence at the end of an open phone line.

Mansell turned left onto the main street, accelerating smoothly. A late cruising taxi cut in around them but otherwise the town was dark and deserted. Voices murmured on the police band: a domestic in Eltham; suspected prowler in St Andrews.

They'd parked the Range Rover at the rear of a used-car lot in Warrandyte, 'sale' stickers plastered across its windscreen. The entrance to the yard itself was a simple driveway with a hefty padlocked chain across it. Niekirk picked the lock, waited while Mansell drove in, looped the chain across the driveway again, and followed on foot to the rear of the lot.

Mansell parked in shadows next to the Range Rover. The three men got out and then stopped still and stared at one another. There was always this moment of uncertainty. If there was going to be a cross, this was the time and the place for it. They each carried guns and they stood with their gun-hands curled ready to snatch and fire, a standoff that could collapse into pain and blood.

Mansell broke it. He moved next to Niekirk and said, looking levelly at Riggs, the risky one: 'We've been paid. It's time we weren't here.'

Riggs studied both men narrowly, then suddenly grinned. Moving carefully, he took out his gun and handed it to Mansell, butt first. Mansell was the quartermaster. The gun hadn't been fired; he would issue it again, issue it for job after job until the time one of them fired it, and if that happened he would dump it in a river.

Then Mansell collected Niekirk's gun and after that they loaded the money into a pair of small gym bags. Finally, still watching one another warily, the three men stripped off their overalls, gloves and balaclavas, Mansell bundling the clothing into a garbage bag, ready for burning. The clothing was evidence against them. When you went into a place you left part of yourself behind, and when you left a place you carried part of it with you. The forensic boys knew that, too.

The job was done. Mansell and Riggs were ready to leave but still Niekirk was wary. If Mansell and Riggs had the opportunity to drive away with half a million, why should they be satisfied with the twenty-five thousand dollar fee that De Lisle had paid into their accounts?

The silence stretched between them, Niekirk at ease with it, Mansell beginning to show signs of strain. It was always like that. There didn't seem to be an end point to Niekirk's eyes, only darkness, and no one ever endured his stare for long. Mansell turned and got into the driver's seat of the car.

But Riggs seemed to think that he had something to prove. He winked at Niekirk, an expression edged with contempt. 'See you on the next job,' he said, climbing into the passenger seat.

Mansell fired up the engine. The Range Rover began to creep across the car yard. Niekirk watched it burble away, on to the road and into the darkness.

5

Springett and Lillecrapp worked the surveillance using a pair of Honda 750s, not cars, wanting speed, ease and concealment on the tight mountain roads. They maintained contact on a little-used emergency band, restricting themselves to clipped commands that might almost have been static, and kept well back, lights off, when they tailed the Telecom van from the bank to the car yard.

Lillecrapp went on ahead to an unlit service station with instructions to tail the Range Rover. Springett watched Niekirk, Riggs and Mansell make the transfer with night binoculars, stationing himself on rising ground behind the car yard.

So far, he'd seen nothing iffy—but that didn't mean anything. Niekirk and his men could easily have been skimming off some of the money while they were in the bank itself, let alone in the van. Surely the temptation was there. No one had known to the last dollar how big the take would be, after all. As soon as Springett had got word that the money would be in the bank he'd briefed De Lisle in Sydney, and De Lisle had arranged the hit. Niekirk, Riggs and Mansell were De Lisle's men, not his.

If they were crooked—and someone had to be, given that the Tiffany brooch had suddenly shown up again—then Springett wanted to be sure of his facts.

He took the glasses away from his face, blinked and rubbed his eyes, focused on the yard again. The Range Rover was leaving. Lillecrapp would pick it up farther along the road and tail it. Springett's instructions had been clear: 'Stay with the vehicle until you get an idea of where it's headed. There's no need to follow it all the way to Sydney. What I'm interested in is if they stash something somewhere along the way, meet with someone, unaccountably double back, that kind of thing.'

Lillecrapp had blinked uncertainly, brushing his ill-cut fringe away from his forehead. 'You don't want me to stop them? Heavy them?'

'Christ, no. Just do what you're told.'

Niekirk stayed behind after the Range Rover left. Springett watched him. The man was thorough, giving the van a final check. Springett knew there'd be no joy there for forensic technicians. The three men had worn gloves, so there'd be no prints to give them away. They hadn't smoked; they hadn't had anything to eat or drink. They might have left clothing fibres or shoe grit behind at the bank, but soon there wouldn't be any clothing or shoes available for a match, only ash somewhere. These guys were pros.

Finally Niekirk wheeled out a big motorcycle that had been stashed behind a rubbish skip and packed the gym bags into the panniers. It was one-thirty in the morning when he left the yard. Springett stayed well behind him. The roads out of the hills and down onto the coastal plain were fast and quiet, yet Niekirk kept to the speed limit all the way.

There was probably half a million dollars strapped to the bike. As Springett had informed De Lisle, it would be in new bills, consecutive serial numbers, therefore easy to trace. But that was De Lisle's problem. Springett had no intention of ripping off the money himself. There were fences around who would give him twenty cents in the dollar, but that would take time and effort and leave him exposed. It was better to take the one-third cut De Lisle was offering him to identify the hits. Only De Lisle was in a position to get the full return on half a million, a haul that would be like hot potatoes to anyone else.

Springett tailed Niekirk down to the Doncaster freeway and along it to the Burke Road exit. The traffic was sparse, the lights in their favour. A sweet setup, he thought. De Lisle sends in a contract team from across the border, men who aren't known to the local boys in blue and who can fade back to Sydney after every hit. The foot soldiers like Riggs and Mansell get paid a decent flat rate. I get a retainer plus the promise of a one-third share of the take once the heat has died down and De Lisle has laundered everything. Ditto Niekirk. And if Niekirk and his men get arrested, there's a number they can call, a green light to get them out of that kind of trouble.

Sweet, Springett thought, except De Lisle has some serious dirt on us, we have to wait for our money, and already someone has fucked up with that Tiffany.

Springett followed Niekirk onto the south-eastern freeway and toward Carlton, keeping below the speed limit, the heavy bike burbling under him. At Faraday Street he stopped and got off the bike, watching Niekirk make two sweeps of the street and finally make for a taxi parked halfway along. There were a dozen taxis just like it nearby, all operated by Red Stripe, a small suburban outfit housed in a narrow tyre-change and service depot on the next corner. Taxis moved in and out of Faraday

Street twenty-four hours a day, shift drivers clocking on and off at irregular intervals.

Springett nodded to himself. No one was going to look twice at a man wheeling up on a bike and transferring his gear to a taxi. He guessed that the taxi light, meter, radio and Red Stripe decals were authentic but that the car itself, a Falcon, was simply Niekirk's transport when he was in Melbourne to pull a job or do the groundwork for one. He could go anywhere in it and no one would question his right to be there.

Springett watched from the shadows. The boot lid up, his body screening the boot well, Niekirk transferred the money from the bike's panniers to the car. Two-thirty. He got in and started the taxi. Springett kicked the Honda into life and tailed him again, out of the parking space and across Carlton toward the southern edge of the city, eventually rolling down La Trobe Street and turning left into Spencer Street.

As far as he knew, this was the final stage for Niekirk. A courier would be coming to collect the money and take it to De Lisle. The operation was protected in part by safeguards and circuit breakers. De Lisle remained as far as possible in the background, activating the members of his team separately and by message drop. In turn, Niekirk and his men met only when they were planning and pulling a hit. Springett and De Lisle stayed in touch via a couple of post office boxes.

It worked, but still, De Lisle had a hold over each of them and Springett hated it. He liked to stay on top of things when he could. So far he trusted De Lisle. He had to. But he had no reason to trust Niekirk, Riggs, Mansell or the courier, who'd all been hired by De Lisle.

He braked the Honda. Niekirk parked the taxi and fetched a tartan suitcase from the boot. He was outside a place called U-Store, a self-storage warehouse a few hundred metres west of the big rail terminal on Spencer Street. It was a long, single-storey building with a roof and a verandah of red corrugated iron like a colonial style farmhouse. It looked no more or less out of place than anything else in that part of the city.

Springett cruised past, U-turned, parked the bike and waited. He had a fair idea of what the building looked like inside: windows and doors fitted with sensors and alarms; a couple of security guards patrolling the corridors; the guard on the front desk taking a while to get with the flow of the midnight-to-dawn shift, holding a half-full mug of coffee just beneath his chin, yawning in Niekirk's face, stretching and swallowing a few times as he checked Niekirk into the warren of lockers beyond the security door, camera monitors flickering silently behind him.

A few minutes later, Niekirk emerged without the suitcase. Springett watched him get into the taxi and pull away from the kerb. Bye bye, Niekirk, he thought, and settled back to see who would come for the money.

But Niekirk surprised him. He steered the taxi into the Spencer Street bus terminal, which was just a block away and on the opposite side of the street. Interesting. Maybe Niekirk and the courier were working the skim.

They were muted hours in the city, between 2 a.m. and 6.30. A couple of taxis, slow between the lights, their drivers shoulder-slumped inside, dreaming over the wheel; delivery vans stacked with the midnight print run of the *Age*; lone cars using Spencer Street as a conduit between west and east of the river. Dew dampened everything and Springett got cold sitting there, watching for the hand that would walk out of the U-Store, carrying a distinctive tartan suitcase.

By 6.30 the station was starting to breathe again. Springett imagined the echoing chambers underground, the shoe snap of early commuters streaming from the trains, walking stunned and

35

staring into the grey light above. He saw them bunch at the pedestrian crossings and choke the Bourke Street trams. A pub opened its doors to the men hawking phlegm into the gutter outside.

A man was stacking newspapers and magazines on the footpath outside the station. Springett saw him stand a box on its side, wrap himself in a blanket, and sit there morosely, scarcely acknowledging the commuters who bought their morning papers and pressed money into his hand, held palm up like a dead creature. But the man did have a styrofoam cup in his other hand and steam was rising from it and Springett felt a hollowness in his gut.

He was curious to see a parking officer rap on the window of Niekirk's car. She exchanged words with Niekirk, all the while looking toward the rear of the car. An interstate coach was heaving off Spencer Street and into the parking station, road-grimed, snarling, top-heavy with surly, fatigued passengers. Then exhaust smoke from another big motor shot into the air and an airport transit bus rattled into life. The terminal was waking up and Niekirk was getting in the way.

Springett watched Niekirk head the taxi toward the street. He grinned to himself. Niekirk didn't want to miss connecting with the courier, but at the same time he didn't want a ticket for parking illegally. A ticket started a paper trail, placing a driver and a vehicle at a particular place at a particular time.

Springett saw him judge a break in the traffic, swing onto Spencer Street and head two blocks away from the station, to an unoccupied parking meter diagonally opposite the U-Store. He reversed in, shunted a few times until the car was angled for a quick exit, and settled back to wait again.

It was 7 a.m. Springett was buffeted as a number of big trucks gusted past him. It was a convoy, cranes, boilers and massive preformed cement slabs and pipes heading for a building site somewhere across the city. They filled the air and Springett might not have seen the tartan suitcase knocking against a blue-uniformed knee if he hadn't trained himself in twenty years to ignore the things that had nothing to do with the job.

Fortunately the lights changed and the crosstown traffic was stalled long enough for him to watch the progress of the man carrying the tartan suitcase. He was about thirty-five, medium-sized with a forgettable, smooth-cheeked face that might never have been scraped by a razor. The only hair on his head was an inadequate scrape of brown, blending at the edges with pink skin. A pilot or a cabin steward, Springett guessed, judging by the blue peaked cap under the man's other arm.

That made sense, if the money was going straight to De Lisle in Sydney. It was easy for flight crews to avoid baggage checks, and no one questioned their right to be in an airport or on a plane.

The man walked back along the footpath opposite Niekirk. Springett watched, expecting him to make contact with Niekirk, but he darted across the street and boarded the airport transit bus.

That made sense, too. The courier wouldn't risk using his own car for this job, and he wouldn't risk letting a taxi driver log the journey, one fact among the many that map who we are, where we've been, that can be used against us one day. The driver of the transit bus, driving this route many times a week, wouldn't remember the courier.

It all helped to give Springett a better fix on De Lisle, a man who ensured that everyone who worked for him took pains and covered himself and muddied any trail that might lead back to the top. Which probably explained why Niekirk had stopped behind to see who was coming for the money. Working on a need-to-know basis didn't suit Springett, either. Knowledge was power.

But now Springett knew that he was no closer to knowing who might have pocketed the Tiffany brooch after the Brighton bank job in February. Time for a bit of push and shove. Niekirk was staying at a motel in St Kilda. He'll keep, Springett thought. First I need to know from Lillecrapp if Riggs and Mansell pulled anything after they left Niekirk in the car yard.

6

After leaving Niekirk and the money, Riggs and Mansell had driven north, Mansell winding the Range Rover through farming land beyond the hills of the Yarra Valley, Riggs hunting through the FM bands on the radio, filling the vehicle with gulps of sound. Where 3UY should have been there was nothing, only a faint scratching. He switched off and settled back in his seat. 'Done the locals a favour tonight, no more golden oldies.'

Mansell slowed for a hairpin bend. 'What'd you do to him?'

'Clobbered him, tied him to his chair.'

Mansell shook his head. 'Jesus, Riggsy.'

'What?'

'It looks bad. It's the sort of thing that gets the local boys bent out of shape.'

Riggs could feel anger rising in him. 'You weren't there, pal. He was going for the microphone.'

'What if you'd killed him?'

'That crap he was playing,' Riggs replied, 'I should've

finished the job.'

Despite himself, Mansell sniggered. He said what Niekirk was always telling them, mimicking Niekirk's flat tones: 'Quick, clean, that's our trademark. We appear out of nowhere, pull the job, disappear without a trace.'

Riggs laughed harshly. 'Niekirk, writing headlines in his head.'

Mansell said soberly, 'If he falls, we fall with him, and for blokes like us that's a bloody long drop.'

Riggs snaked his hand out, clamping his fingers around Mansell's lower jaw. 'But it's not going to happen, is it, old son? Eh? It's not going to happen.'

He stared at the side of Mansell's head. After a while he released him. Mansell jerked away, hunching his shoulders. For the next hour, neither man spoke. Riggs gazed sourly out at the blackness beyond the shapes at the road's edge and Mansell concentrated on throwing the Range Rover through the switchback curves of the road.

They had far to go. The airport was closed for the night and they knew that morning flights, and bus and train departures, could be monitored. The best option they had was to drive—not all the way back to Sydney but as far as Benalla. Here they would dump the Range Rover, change into casual clothes and catch a coach to Sydney. 'No jobs on our own turf,' as Niekirk put it. Mansell could see the sense in that. Three times now they'd slipped down into Victoria, robbed a bank, slipped back again, netting themselves $25,000 each time. He only wished he felt free to pick and choose, come and go, like your average holdup man.

They drove for three hours in silence. Mansell broke it first. They were far north now, the Hume Highway stretching across the sodden plains of central Victoria. Feeling he could relax a little, he said: 'What do you make of Niekirk?'

Riggs stirred in his seat. 'Arsehole.'

Mansell grunted his assent. 'What do you think he does with the stuff?'

'Spends it for all I know.'

'Come on, be serious. Someone's behind him, right?'

'Like a cracked record, this conversation. We get paid.'

'Yeah, twenty-five grand a job. Not much considering the risks involved. You can bet Niekirk's getting more.'

They lapsed into silence again. There were a couple of traffic lights in Benalla, an oddly comforting sign of civilisation after the high country where Ned Kelly had once ranged and stolen horses and eluded the troopers.

Mansell parked the Range Rover behind a block of flats in a side street and they changed into casual clothing. The street lights were far apart. There were no clouds this far north. The river had flooded and receded again a few weeks earlier, leaving the little city mud-smeared and damp, smelling of wet carpets and rotting, fecund spring weed growth. Mosquitoes attacked them.

They set out along the broad, flat back streets. 'The thing is, Manse,' Riggs said, 'where's he getting his information? Shit, this time last year all Niekirk had us pulling was the odd burglary.'

'The thing is,' Mansell flung back over his shoulder, 'how much are we dipping out?'

Riggs nodded. 'That, too.'

They continued in silence. When they reached the lighted part of town they watched for a while from the shadows. No uniforms, no patrol cars, no unmarked cars bristling with aerials. When the bus pulled in, thirty minutes later, Riggs and Mansell were stationed several metres apart and could have been mistaken for strangers.

7

Wyatt looked at his watch: she was early. He made room for her on the bench.

She sat, shifted a little, looking for an opening. Finally she said: 'I spoke to Frank on the phone. He sounded stronger.'

Wyatt nodded. But he had to make an effort, so he said, 'Liz, I want to thank you for helping him yesterday.'

'It was nothing.' She said it mildly, looking away at the river.

They talked, growing easier with one another. Most people couldn't read Wyatt and it rattled some of them. There were others, like Jardine from the old days, who had long since adjusted themselves to the fact of his stillness. To them, Wyatt was constructed of silence, a single unadorned look for all emotions and a suspicious mind. But he could be trusted, so they accepted that it was not necessary to know anything more about him. Along the way Wyatt had also run into some who found his self-containment an affront and a challenge. Men got cocksure and women tried to draw him out. Wyatt would do nothing to encourage it, but he might show a faint irritation finally, and act swiftly, irritated because he could not see the point of anyone's interest in him.

That's why he began to experience a forgotten pleasure, the uncomplicated company of a quirkily attractive woman, as the sun warmed his bones and broke into shards of light on the river behind a cruising pleasure boat. Liz Redding wasn't questioning him, wasn't wanting to know him better, wasn't playing any games that he could detect. He relaxed marginally, crossed his legs at the ankle, tipped his face to the sun.

They were on Southbank, the stretch of the Yarra that had been reclaimed from the old industrial grime for the sake of tourists and postcard photographers. A bike path, plenty of close-cropped grass, flagpoles, cafes, Cinzano umbrellas, the Melbourne central mile growling across the water.

Wyatt was starting to like the sun and the view and the company of the woman next to him, but he also liked the fact that he had all the exits he'd need if this were a trap. He could even swim away if he had to, and he'd toss the Tiffany butterfly into the river rather than allow cops to tie him to it.

'No motel this time?'

'I don't like to repeat myself,' Wyatt said, then clammed up a little, not wanting to talk about himself, not wanting to sound self-satisfied.

Liz Redding smiled. It wasn't an issue. He saw her look away. Her eyes were drawn to the river as if it were a flame. His, too, though he was also drawn to Liz Redding, an unaccustomed fascination with her body and quizzical face. And he seemed to want to breathe her in, as if her skin and hair were reacting to the sun, maybe even to him.

She said, 'Have you got it?'

43

Wyatt had a small gift box nestled in tissue paper on the bench between them. He was conscious of her long thigh, sheathed in a skirt this time, as he leaned to open the box. She seemed to watch his hands, big hands snarled by veins, as he prised off the lid. To anyone walking by, he might have been opening a gift from his lover.

He watched her. He would not have registered the brief intensity and concentration that passed across her face if he'd not been looking for it. 'Lovely,' she murmured at last.

But that wasn't it, the loveliness of the brooch. She hadn't responded like this yesterday. There was something else, and he'd have to wait for it.

She glanced left and right along the bicycle path and then behind her. They were alone for the moment. He saw her move the Tiffany to her lap and turn it over twice. Then she checked the path a second time, put her jeweller's eyepiece to her right eye and bent her head over it. Wings of straight black hair swung about her cheeks, concealing her scrutiny of the diamonds. The movement also bared the back of her neck and Wyatt found himself touching her there.

She took it for a warning. Within a second she had whipped out the eyepiece and crammed it and the Tiffany into the gift box. She turned to him, smiling, getting close, part of a charade of lovers on a park bench. But Wyatt went tense at her touch so she looked around, saw that they were alone, and moved until she was a fraction apart from him again. She looked at him oddly, and Wyatt shrugged, to give himself time and something to do.

In the end, she behaved as though nothing had happened. Wyatt felt his edge of embarrassment recede. Suddenly the world seemed to be full of possibilities. But he said nothing, did nothing.

Liz Redding drew in air. 'We won't be cutting this up, by the way. It'll remain intact.'

Good. She'd found a buyer. Wyatt wondered if he wanted her because she was like him or because he wanted her to be like him. The moment he met someone, he could spot the flaw in them, which was often the same thing as the trait that defined them. It was a blessing and a curse and had rarely let him down. Beneath the professionalism, Liz Redding was excited by the Tiffany and all the risks involved, his risks and hers.

Some kids went by arm in arm bawling out: 'Rolling, rolling, rolling down the river.' The year Wyatt had served in Vietnam, refining skills he'd learned on the street, every American GI he'd encountered had been singing that song. The Americans had terrified him. They blundered across the landscape, doped to the eyeballs, inviting an ambush. Wyatt made it a rule to stay well clear of them. The only good thing about the dope was that they all seemed to use it, including security guards at the US bases, and it made them slack and careless. Wyatt had snatched his first payroll in Vietnam. It bought him a year's travelling in Europe when he finally quit the army.

Then Liz Redding said, half to herself, 'Yep. This is the one. I'd been wondering when this little beauty would show up again.'

At once Wyatt went cold. His face was mostly flat cheeks, bones, unimpressed eyes and a mouth that could look prohibitive if it didn't occasionally turn up in a smile. There was no smile now and he saw her flinch. His voice was tense and quiet: 'Turn up? I've only just acquired it.'

'I mean—'

Wyatt was hard and certain. He made each word sound like a slap. 'You mean the Tiffany's got a history. When you saw it yesterday you recognised its description from a stolen valuables list.'

She winced, angry with herself. Wyatt had seen women cure

45

themselves of him quickly, and expected that of Liz Redding now that he'd caught her out, but she didn't do that. Instead, a certain defiance came back into her face. 'So what? I assumed you'd been hanging onto it, that's all.'

'I haven't, so tell me about it.'

She cocked her head and watched his face carefully. 'Are you on the level? You only just got your hands on it?'

'Just give me the history.'

'You've heard of the so-called magnetic drill gang, right? Some time ago they hit the safety-deposit boxes of a bank in Brighton. The Tiffany was among the stuff reported stolen.'

That was an irrelevancy. Wyatt brushed it aside. 'The thing is, how do you know?' He stared at her. 'You're no fence.'

He stood, pocketing the Tiffany, and began to walk away from her, not hurrying it, but not wasting time either. His nerve endings were wide open, expecting clamping hands on his shoulders, his arms, but no one called out or stopped him. In a minute or two he would be an anonymous face in the crowd and a minute or two was all Wyatt ever needed.

Then she was swiftly and silently matching him step for step. 'There's a reward.'

He walked on. 'Forget you ever met me.' He said it quietly, not bothering to look at her.

'I mean it, Wyatt, there's a reward. That's my job, I negotiate rewards on behalf of the insurance company, okay?'

She grabbed his arm angrily, jerking him to a stop. 'Twenty-five thousand, all right? No questions asked. But it will take a couple of weeks to line up.'

Wyatt considered the odds. It takes a very heavy, very professional team to hit the safety-deposit boxes of a bank successfully. Who were they? And who had given—or sold—the

46

Tiffany to Cassandra Wintergreen, the woman he'd stolen it from? Wyatt felt that he was on the edge of something better left alone, a sixth sense he relied upon to keep the odds working his way, but Liz Redding was also very close and alive in front of him. If he set the rules he would be all right. He stayed long enough to tell her how to get in touch with him, then faded away among the strollers thronging Princes Bridge.

8

Pacific Rim flight 39 from Melbourne and Sydney touched down at Port Vila International Airport a few minutes past the scheduled arrival time. Late Thursday morning and Lou Crystal unbuttoned his uniform jacket and went down the steps to the tarmac. The tropical air seemed to sneak up on him, warm, humid, smelling of aviation fuel and ripe, rich fruit, so that he was perspiring before he reached the terminal building. Over one shoulder he carried his usual stopover bag; in the other hand he carried the tartan suitcase that had been stashed in the U-Store locker in Melbourne. Crystal's instructions were clear each time: attach an address label reading 'Mr Huntsman, Reriki Island Resort' to the tartan suitcase and lodge it with the driver of the Reriki Island Resort minibus.

The passengers from flight 39 were lining up at the immigration counters. Crystal eyed them as he walked through, wondering if one of them was Huntsman, but all he could see were backpackers, honeymooners and middle-aged Australians and New Zealanders spending their superannuation payouts. They looked tired and pasty-white, impatient to get to their resort hotels and try on neon yellow and green shorts, T-shirts and sunblock. Crystal despised them. He loathed their noisiness and ignorance and simple pleasures.

Pacific Rim Airlines had been flying in and out of Vanuatu since Independence in 1980. Crystal himself had been stopping over in Port Vila for five years. Everyone knew him and he nodded left and right as he slipped through immigration and customs and onto the main concourse. Here, clones of flight 39's passengers were queuing up to pay their departure tax. They were noisier, a little more sunburnt, overburdened with cheap local handicrafts, but essentially no different. Crystal walked past them, still carrying the suitcase and his weekender bag, out to the taxi and minibus ranks outside the terminal building.

A misty rain was drifting in, obscuring the tops of the mountains, leaching brightness from the green of the lower slopes. Banyans, coconut palms, pandanus and a handful of tree ferns and milk trees bordered the airfield and lined the nearby roads. Creepers and orchids choked some of them. There were leaves like shields and swords everywhere in Vanuatu and in the rainy season they dripped water on to Crystal's head. In the mornings sometimes he'd see spiders the size of his hand waiting motionless at the centre of huge webs strung between glossy trees.

There were half a dozen people waiting in the Reriki Island minibus. The driver was leaning against the canopied luggage trailer, smoking a cigarette. He smirked at Crystal, took the proffered suitcase and stored it on the covered trailer. Then he went back to smoking and waiting and forgot about Crystal. For his part, Crystal was glad to be rid of the case. He was guessing drugs, and drugs were bad news, even in this backwater.

Pacific Rim pilots and cabin crew on stopover were obliged

to stay at the Palmtree Lodge, a small collection of motel units on a crabbed, featureless lagoon south-east of Port Vila. Fifteen minutes by car, a fare of eleven hundred vatu, and that's where Lou Crystal should have been going when he climbed into the dented Toyota taxi.

'*Yu go wea?* Palmtree Lodge?' the driver asked, recognising Crystal as a regular and addressing him in Bislama.

Crystal shook his head. 'Malapoa Restaurant.'

The driver started the engine. He nodded cannily. 'Good coconut crab.'

'That's right,' Crystal said.

The drive took ten minutes, past small houses and flat-roofed cement-walled shops set amongst cyclone-stripped palm trees. Crystal had been on Vanuatu when the last cyclone had hit the islands. He'd been unnerved by it, a ceaseless wind that bent palm trees almost to the horizontal, tore apart coral reefs and dumped ships hundreds of metres in from the water's edge. He'd seen flying tin cut a woman's arm off and his balcony furniture at the Palmtree Lodge had cartwheeled across the coarse cropped lawns between the motel units and the coral beach.

The taxi pulled off the road and stopped. 'Nine hundred vatu,' the driver said.

Crystal paid him and got out. The Malapoa Restaurant was on a tiny spit of land jutting into Port Vila harbour. Crystal had eaten excellent coconut crab there. If it hadn't been for the patrons—idle yachting types from all over the world, shouting at one another—he would have eaten there more often.

He let the driver see him walk into the Malapoa courtyard. When the taxi was gone, Crystal re-emerged and walked fifty metres to a public toilet block. He went into one of the cubicles, his head reeling from the urine-thick atmosphere, and stripped off his uniform, exchanging it for shorts, T-shirt and sandals that he'd packed in the top of his weekender bag.

The toilet block was set on the edge of a narrow carpark attached to a small concrete wharf. Water taxis and harbour-cruise boats used the wharf. So did the Reriki Island ferry, and that's all Crystal was interested in.

He stood under a corrugated iron shelter to wait. Reriki Island dominated Port Vila harbour. It was a humped, jungly lump of land in a small bay, the shore lined with airconditioned, balconied huts on stilts. It was a resort island; the manager lived in a red-roofed house among palm trees on the highest point of the island. There were three restaurants, a swimming pool, boats for hire and a tiny wharf. You did not have to be a resident to visit the place, and that's what Crystal was banking on now.

He saw the ferry leave the island. It made the harbourside run every few minutes, twenty-four hours a day, a two-minute trip each way. Crystal watched the ferry skirt around a couple of two-masted yachts. One looked worn and hard-working. A bearded man was pegging towels and T-shirts to a rope above the galley. The words 'Miami Florida' were painted across the stern. The other yacht was tidier and more seaworthy by about a quarter of a million dollars. It came from Portsmouth and Crystal was betting the owner was one of the loudmouths in the Malapoa Restaurant.

The ferry docked and Crystal got ready to board. It was a long, low, flat-bottomed aluminium craft fitted with a canopy roof. The sides were painted in bright splashes of colour: words, symbols and shapes that reminded Crystal of the sanctioned graffiti he'd seen on railway underpasses in Melbourne.

One person got off. Three got on with Crystal. He eyed them briefly: two kids with slim brown legs and a local man dressed in a white shirt and a black cotton wrap-around garment like a skirt. The words 'Reriki Island Resort' were stencilled on the top

51

pocket of his shirt.

The ferry drew away from the wharf. Crystal looked back at the receding harbour shoreline, the mixture of waterfront businesses, rusting warehouses and tattered inter-island cargo ships. At the midway point he saw the resort's minibus pull into the carpark. He'd beaten it by only a few minutes. The driver and passengers got out and he saw the driver begin to stack the luggage next to the ferry landing.

The ferry docked at the island and Crystal alighted with the other passengers. Steep paths led up to the main buildings. The grounds were carefully landscaped: neat palms, pandanus, small banyans, orchids, coral-edged walking tracks, close-cropped grass in between.

Crystal sat on a bench at the centre of a patch of grass. The clouds cleared suddenly and he was drenched in late afternoon sunlight. There were several tourists nearby, doing what he was doing, enjoying the sun. He half closed his eyes, waited, and saw a Reriki Island bellboy wheel a trolley-load of suitcases up to the main office. The tartan suitcase was unmistakeable among them.

A few minutes later, Crystal followed. There were plenty of people about: visitors, people staying at the resort, resort staff. No one looked twice at him.

The main building was constructed to resemble an oversized jungle village meeting place: a high-ceilinged roof, exposed beams, open sides, a suggestion of bamboo fronds and rattan. It housed a bar, a dining room and the reservations desk. Crystal sat at a small cane table in a shadowy far corner of the vast room. He had 20—20 vision. The sky remained clear and he could see every detail of the harbour, the yachts and the distant rocky beaches smudged with mangroves and casuarinas. He could also see the bar clearly, and the reservations counter where the new arrivals' luggage was being stacked by a porter.

Half an hour later the tartan suitcase was the only one not claimed or delivered to any of the cabins. Nursing a beer, Crystal maintained his watch over it. He grew drowsy. A small drama at the bar woke him, shouts of *bonjour* as a middle-aged white man came into the bar and clasped several of the black staff. He seemed to be a great hit with them. '*Bonjour*,' they said, and he beamed, and asked after their kids.

Crystal headed for the cover of a cane screen, fear and hate hammering in his heart. The man himself, centre of all his recent misery. Crystal peered around the screen. There was no mistaking De Lisle: aged about fifty, starting to go plump and soft, wearing a white shirt, white trousers, and a straw hat with a red band around it. The humidity seemed to be affecting him. He was pink in the face and mopped his forehead and neck with a blue handkerchief. He twinkled a lot, a hot, damp man in the tropics, surrounded by admirers. At one point he took an asthma spray from his pocket and sucked on it frantically, closing his eyes for a moment afterwards, his fleshy chin tipped back, rising to the tips of his neat tasselled shoes as though preparing to levitate, then returning with a smile to the people circling him, calling *bonjour* to the bartenders, who were all grinning.

Lou Crystal took in every hated detail about the man. Then he took in how De Lisle left with the tartan suitcase, carrying it down to the jetty, where a waiting water taxi took him to a little dock under a cliff-top mansion on the other side of the harbour.

9

The house was on a cliff top two kilometres from the post office in the centre of Port Vila. It had been built for the director of a French bank a couple of years before Independence in 1980, and that fact accounted for the two features that De Lisle had been looking for when he bought the place. One, the house was luxurious, the plunging grounds beautifully terraced, with harbour frontage and views across the blue water to Reriki, the island resort in the bay; two, the nervous French colonist had erected a steel-mesh security fence around the perimeter to keep the rebels out. Now Vanuatu was a republic but the fence was still there. In fact, De Lisle had also upgraded the alarm system inside the house. All that cash and jewellery coming in was making him nervous.

De Lisle stepped off the broad verandah and climbed down the steep steps to the little concrete dock at the bottom of the property. He'd once thought of putting in a small funicular to run between the house and the water's edge—the climb back up the steps was a killer—but that would have been inviting trouble. He pictured thieves beaching silent canoes and swarming up the cable into his house and cutting his throat.

At the bottom he checked that no one was lying in wait on the other side of the perimeter fence and unlocked the steel gate. He'd bought the house three years ago, soon after the first of his tours through the Pacific as a circuit magistrate. Now he had an ocean-going yacht as well, the *Pegasus*, a two-master gently bumping against the truck tyres along the edge of the little dock. De Lisle had crewed in a couple of Sydney to Hobarts a few years back and knew he could sail the *Pegasus* around the world if he wanted to. Depending upon his work schedule, he often sailed it between Port Vila and Suva. He kept the yacht fully stocked with food and equipment. In fact it was his way out of Port Vila if anything should go wrong. He had a second set of papers: in five minutes the *Pegasus*, Coffs Harbour, could be transformed into the *Stiletto*, registered to a company in Panama.

De Lisle's various bank accounts were also in company names. It was all a smokescreen, and as necessary as food and water, now that he was moving large amounts of money into and out of Vanuatu. Being a tax shelter, the country offered security provisions and confidentiality agreements protecting his banking and other activities. No income tax, no capital gains tax, no double taxation agreements with Australia. No exchange controls or reporting of fund movements. And he was able to deposit money in whatever amounts he liked, in any currency, no questions asked.

There was nothing to excite the attention of the police in his apartment in Sydney or his house in bushland behind Coffs Harbour. He kept anything like that here in Port Vila, in safes and safety-deposit boxes.

He stepped onto the yacht, removed the security shutters,

unlocked the cabin door and went below. The interior was teak-lined and when he opened the curtains it glowed a rich and satisfying colour in the morning sun.

The safe was concealed behind a small bulkhead wall oven. De Lisle unlocked the oven, pulled until it slid forward on rollers, and reached in. There were documents stacked on the bottom shelf, duplicates of the information he'd passed on to Niekirk for the next heist, the Asahi Collection of precious stones: floor plans, a map of the alarm system, staffing level, the size of the take, the best time to hit, the expected delay before the cops would respond to an alarm, what number to call in the event of an arrest. De Lisle took out everything from yesterday's Upper Yarra job now, and fed it to the garbage compactor under the galley sink.

He leafed through the material he had on Riggs, Mansell, Niekirk, Crystal, Springett—as far as he was concerned, the only useful outcome of all those inquiries and royal commissions he'd sat on over the years. All those names: paedophiles, bagmen, cops running protection rackets or moonlighting as burglars and receivers, perjurers, officials with their fingers in the till. It was pervasive and as natural to the running of the world as mothers' milk.

The thing was, all those names had something to hide and all were potentially useful to De Lisle. In some instances he'd had to wait. He hadn't had a courier until Lou Crystal's name had cropped up during an investigation into Australian sex tours to Asia, for example.

After the Asahi job he would quit. He would retire from the bar and come here to Vila to live. He'd had retirement in mind for the past year, but he was also prompted by the fact that he couldn't count on Springett and Niekirk remaining patient for-ever about getting their cut of the action. And they could see with their own eyes what each hit was worth. They didn't have the resources De Lisle had for moving the stuff, but they were men, they'd get greedy sooner or later, despite knowing that De Lisle had dirt on them that could put them away for a very long time. How serious was he about using that dirt, anyhow? They'd name him for sure, if he did. That option would be at the backs of their minds. So, time to quit while he was ahead, finish liquidating the cash and jewels from the bank raids, pay them off.

De Lisle locked the safe, secured the yacht and started up the steps to his house. He took them slowly. Only 27 degrees but 90 per cent humidity and his breathing was ragged, his shirt and underwear soaked, before he'd reached the halfway point.

He paused to catch his breath. Work tomorrow. Vanuatu lacked lawyers and judges, particularly in the north. The Public Prosecutor's Office and the Public Solicitor's Office were there to get cases ready for court, but they were understaffed and the day-to-day court staff were overwhelmed with demands from jungle bunnies and expatriates wanting help with forms and claims. So, several times a year, De Lisle sat on the Supreme Court of Vanuatu to help ease the strain. He was funded by the Australian Government's Staffing Assistance Scheme, and he loved it. He got to hear evidence in open-air courts half the time, just bamboo and palm tree fronds between him and the blue sky above. Mainly British law, with a bit of French and a bit of jungle bunny thrown in. Last time he was in the little republic he'd been obliged to turn a blind eye to a spot of police brutality. The police had been called in by a council of chiefs to warn off a man believed to be practising witchcraft, but things got out of hand and the man had died of injuries. Still, no loss to anyone.

And the trips to Vanuatu provided the perfect cover for moving the stuff that Niekirk and his crew had liberated from those Victorian bank jobs. The world was going to blow one day—corruption, erosion of values, mobs in the street—and De

Lisle wasn't about to be caught without a hedge against that kind of collapse.

He put one foot after the other again and continued up the steps. Deep breathing, that was the answer, deep breathing to control the heart, deep breathing to concentrate and clarify the mind. To centre himself, in the jargon of a fuckwit who'd insisted on making a statement to the court back in Sydney last week.

Deep breath. If he didn't watch it he'd die of a heart attack on the job. He snorted—'on the job' was right. The last time he'd been in the cot with Cassandra Wintergreen she'd leaned on one elbow and grabbed the spare tyre around his waist, pinching tightly, grinning cruelly: 'Here's a little fellow who loves his tucker.' De Lisle had batted her hand away: 'Quit that, Cass,' he'd said, wishing now that he hadn't given her that tasty Tiffany brooch from the safety-deposit hit Niekirk had pulled for him in February.

He put Wintergreen out of his mind. Half a week's work here in Vanuatu, then spend two or three days sailing the *Pegasus* to Suva. A spot of Supreme Court work in Fiji, then fly back to Sydney, leaving the *Pegasus* moored in Suva. A quick turnaround in Sydney this time. He'd arranged his workload so that he could be in Vila to collect the Asahi stones.

Grace, De Lisle's hi-Vanuatan servant, was waiting for him on the verandah. White cloth on the cane table, martini in a steel jug beaded with condensation, chilled glass, a plate of oysters. De Lisle stood close to her, rotated his bulk a quarter turn, fitting his groin against her thigh. Her brown skin felt cool beneath the hairline. Then cotton, a series of bumps along her spine, then her wonderful arse.

De Lisle rested the folds of his chin on her bare shoulder. He watched her stare out across the water, very still except as he began minutely to move against her.

10

It was eight o'clock on Thursday morning before Niekirk got back to his motel. He crawled into bed, exhausted from the bank job and the long hours staking out the U-Store building.

He slept long into the day, then showered in scalding water, needles of heat easing the strain in his neck and shoulders. He dressed, caught a tram into the city, walked the arcades. 'The Asahi Collection, on show from Monday 9' said the discreet card in the window of the Soreki 5 department store. Niekirk mapped the area in his mind, then sat in a coffee shop opposite, watching the security men change shifts. Groundwork. He would spend another day doing this, then fly back to Sydney, wait for word from De Lisle.

Late in the afternoon he returned to his motel. He was turning the key and pushing the door open when a man came through the door behind him, crowding his back. Another was already in the room, smiling humourlessly at him from the edge of the bed. If Niekirk hadn't been exhausted he might not have been bushwacked. They wore suits and he knew that was bad news.

He turned to the suit behind him, half inclined to fight his way free, but stopped when he saw the gun, a police issue .38 revolver, stopped when he heard the giggle, high and mad.

'I wouldn't if I were you.'

The guy leaned back against the door, a gun-happy light in his eyes, tongue tip sliding once over his upper lip. 'Don't make me,' he said, giggling again, jerking his head in a nervy spasm, tossing hair away from his eyes. It was a ragged fringe of hair, cut haphazardly by someone once a month—wife or girlfriend, but maybe even mother for all Niekirk knew—over an eager killer's face.

So Niekirk turned to the suit on the bed, who said immediately, smiling all the while: 'A few matters to discuss, Sergeant Niekirk.'

So they had his name. Niekirk forgot about offering his fake ID. He reassessed the smile of the man on the bed. It was a reflexive, all-purpose smile, the kind used to express rage, pain, pleasure, hope, bonhomie to the media, ingratiation to the men upstairs who outranked him, and often nothing at all. The other guy had the .38 but this was the one Niekirk had to watch.

'What matters?'

The smile. 'This and that. Missing items.'

The voice was deep-chested, a sonorous baritone that liked to listen to itself. Niekirk said, 'I'm entitled to a phone call.'

The senior man got to his feet. He was tall, a little stiff. He made a flowery gesture at the bedside telephone with one long, well-shaped hand. 'Be my guest.'

Niekirk had memorised the number he was to call if the local boys in blue nabbed him. He stood rather than sat, and faced the room, the telephone cord clumsily draped across his chest. He waited for the dial tone and punched in the number. At once he heard the ringing tone on the line and a soft burr in the room. Smiling one of his smiles, the elegant senior man fished a small black fold-up phone from his pocket.

Niekirk replaced the handset. 'You're our green-light cop.'

The austere face kept smiling. 'I suppose I must be.'

'Got a name?'

The smile faded a little, deciding. 'Springett.'

'You'd have rank,' Niekirk observed.

The smile came back. 'Inspector.'

'Who's the cowboy on the door?'

'Lillecrapp.'

'Jesus Christ.'

'It is a mouthful. Sit down. The bed.'

Niekirk complied. Springett remained standing, every hair in place, a neat, perfect knot in the bright, chaotically patterned tie at his throat. The suit itself was sombre, the shirt crisply white.

Niekirk said, 'What missing items?'

'Cast your mind back to your first hit, that bank job in February.'

'What about it?'

'You'll recall there was a small gold butterfly encrusted with diamonds?'

'Think I'm a philistine? I know what it was, a Tiffany.'

'A Tiffany, exactly. Well, it's turned up again.'

'How do you mean?'

'I got word yesterday afternoon that a small-time character here in Melbourne is trying to fence it.'

Niekirk raced through the possibilities. He knew that Riggs and Mansell hadn't pocketed anything from the safety-deposit boxes, for he'd packed everything himself. They couldn't have

61

dropped it in the alley behind the building. There couldn't have been two Tiffanies. De Lisle wasn't stupid enough to offload it to a small-time fence. 'The courier,' he said.

'Now I wonder how come I knew you were going to say that?' Springett said.

'I handled the transfer. My men didn't take the Tiffany. I didn't take the Tiffany.'

Springett was watching him. Behind the smile he was guarded, sceptical. 'You sound very sure of yourself.'

'Fuck I'm sure. I'd check out the courier.'

Springett said nothing for a while, as if weighing up possibilities. 'I take it that you know a man called De Lisle?'

Niekirk grinned. 'Now we come down to the nitty-gritty. Yes, I know him.'

'I thought so. De Lisle's setup works in theory, separating your side of things from mine, separating the courier from both of us, like a circuit-breaker arrangement in case one of us takes a fall. But what happens when one of us starts acting solo, know what I mean?'

Niekirk watched him carefully. 'You don't like it that the left hand doesn't know what the right is doing. Nor do I. I especially don't like it that you knew my name but I didn't know yours. Did De Lisle give it to you?'

'I insisted on knowing. I had to be ready to cover up if anything happened, like your name appearing on an arrest report.'

'Fucking lovely. An imbalance of power between us right from the start. So, if I pull the jobs for him, what do you do?'

Reluctantly, Springett said: 'I put the jobs together—identify the target, supply photos, floor plans, maps of the alarm system.'

Niekirk looked at him cannily. 'For a fee?'

'Now *that's* the nitty-gritty,' Springett said. 'I get a cut of the action. Exactly a third.'

'Same here. It's my blokes who get a set fee.'

'But have you been paid your third yet?'

'A retainer.'

Springett nodded. 'Sounds familiar.'

'The rest when the heat's off and De Lisle's moved the stuff.'

'Trusting pair, aren't we? A retainer to keep us sweet. Not many men would put up with that.'

'Fucking spit it out, Springett. He's got you over a barrel, same as he's got me. If we don't play ball he puts us away. If we do his dirty work, we stay out of jail and pocket a few hundred thou. Am I right or am I right?'

Both men relaxed, feeling a common ground between them. Lillecrapp continued to loll against the door, bored, too absorbed in cracking his knuckles to feel envy or interest in what they were saying.

Niekirk said suddenly: 'What's De Lisle got on you?'

Springett's face shut down. 'Now you're stepping over the line.'

'Suit yourself.'

'It's no longer a factor.'

'Sure.'

'It's strictly business now.'

'Sure. So you've told him the Tiffany's shown up?'

'Not exactly.'

'Meaning no. Going to tell him?'

'What's your feeling?'

'Don't. If there's been a fuck up, a rip off from our end of the operation, I say we deal with it ourselves. We don't want him pissed off. Or there's another possibility: he's moved all the stuff and is conveniently not paying us what he owes us.'

63

'Using small-time fences? Unlikely,' Springett said. 'Plus he said he'd wait a few months.'

'De Lisle hasn't said anything about the Tiffany not showing up in the original haul?'

'That doesn't mean anything,' Springett said. 'He didn't know what was going to be in those safety-deposit boxes in the first place, so why would he be worried if it didn't show up in the stuff the courier delivered? I didn't know about the Tiffany myself until the owner and the insurance company provided my people with photos and a description. Either it was ripped off by the courier *before* Di Lisle took delivery, or De Lisle's sold it already to someone who's trying to sell it again. I like the first scenario, myself, and I say we deal with it ourselves. I'm not ready for De Lisle to get an attack of the nerves and shut us down. I can't afford it.'

'The mortgage,' Niekirk said. 'School fees.'

'Exactly.' Springett rubbed his jaw. 'So I say we lean on the courier.'

'You've convinced me.'

They were silent for a moment. Springett said: 'I watched you watching him.'

Niekirk snorted. 'And the rest, arsehole. You knew what the job was, and when, so you watched me and my blokes pull it and then you followed me, right? So much for De Lisle's fail-safe method.'

Springett shrugged. 'If the stolen Tiffany hadn't shown up I wouldn't have had to shadow you last night. *You* were watching the courier, don't forget.'

'So we're all suspicious of one another. So what?'

Springett stretched tiredly. 'Keep your shirt on. I'd've watched him in your shoes. What did you make of him?'

'He probably works for an airline.'

Springett began to nod his narrow, well-tended head. 'Travel all over the country, no questions asked.'

'There's another job going down in a couple of weeks' time,' Niekirk said.

'The Asahi Collection. What of it?'

'We grab the courier before he delivers to De Lisle. Put the hard word on him, see what he admits to.' Niekirk paused, looking hard at Springett. 'How did the Tiffany turn up, anyway?'

In reply, Springett took out a photograph. 'This is from the files. This guy and another guy we know nothing about recently had a meeting with a local fence.'

'Frank Jardine,' Niekirk said at once.

Springett let some surprise show through the smiles. 'You know him?'

'He was never active and we never had anything on him in Sydney,' Niekirk said, 'but the whisper was he blueprinted the odd payroll snatch or townhouse burglary.' He looked up. 'He's in Melbourne now?'

'Turned up six months ago. Not a well man, from all accounts.'

'But still working.'

'A few weeks ago he handled some paintings stolen from a house in Sydney. The insurance company paid to get them back.'

Niekirk snorted. 'Always do, piss-weak cunts. If they'd let us do our job…'

'Same thing's likely to happen with the Tiffany.'

'So, lean on Jardine, find out who gave him the Tiffany. Save a lot of running around.'

Springett glanced away at a point on the wall. 'Can't do that. The Tiffany's only just shown up, and I'd rather sniff around than risk scaring these people off.'

'No pictures of this other guy?'

'Not yet.'

'You're letting the deal go through?'

'Yes.'

'No questions asked.'

'That's right. We can't risk an official investigation. We don't want the Tiffany being traced back to its source, because that could turn up your name, my name, De Lisle's name. De Lisle would shop us to save his neck, count on it. I don't fancy ending up in Pentridge. I put too many hard cases in there who'd love to have a crack at me. We need to let the Tiffany fall out of sight again but meanwhile ascertain how and why it showed up, and make sure we fill the hole in De Lisle's operation, if there is one. That way, if there ever *is* an investigation it will come to a dead end.'

Niekirk grinned. 'If you were to delete one or two of these characters, you'd have your dead end, no problem.'

'Worth keeping in mind,' Springett agreed.

11

The tortoiseshell frame was fitted with broad, elliptical lenses which lightened the dark cast of Wyatt's face and softened its hard edges. He wore grey trousers, black shoes, a sports coat over a white shirt and a tweedy, out-of-date tie. The ID card clipped to his belt suggested that he spent his life shuffling forms or drafting regulations that said no to everything.

So no one was looking twice at Wyatt, but Wyatt, preternaturally wary, was going home the long way. After leaving Liz Redding he had driven to Moorabbin Airport, on the flat lands south-east of the city. Cessnas, Pipers, a couple of helicopters and one Lear Jet were parked near the hangars, fuselages and wings reflecting the late-morning sun. There was a handful of student pilots in the air, circling the field, touch landing and taking off again. Wyatt watched for a couple of minutes then entered the terminal building.

Island Air was a desk front three metres long, staffed by a young woman wearing a polka-dot dress. According to her name tag she was called Nicole and she smiled at Wyatt. 'I hope you're Mr White.'

Wyatt agreed that he was.

'We thought you weren't going to make it. The others are just boarding now.'

Wyatt looked at his watch, then at the clock on the wall behind her. The difference in time was twenty minutes and that meant his watch was faulty.

Nicole was all smiles. 'Battery?'

'Must be,' Wyatt agreed.

It wasn't the kind of mistake he could afford to make. It wasn't the kind of mistake he'd normally anticipate, either. He gave Nicole his ticket and watched her fingers on the VDU keyboard. Island Air flew to King Island twice a day, at 11.30 a.m. and 3.30 p.m. He was booked on the eleven-thirty, timed to connect with a TasAir flight from King Island to Wynyard. It was a long way home, costly and tedious, but Wyatt liked to avoid showing his face in the terminal building of major airports. He had a car at Wynyard. From there to the flat he rented in Hobart was a three or four hour drive.

Nicole's smile was a wide seam of white teeth. She leaned on the counter and pointed to double-glass doors at the side of the terminal. 'Through there, Mr White.'

Island Air flew twin-engine, ten-seater Chieftains on the King Island route. The flight took fifty minutes and Wyatt ignored the other passengers and read about the magnetic drill gang's raid on a bank in the Upper Yarra region outside Melbourne. The *Age* gave it a bare, three-sentence outline. The *Herald Sun* police reporter gave it ten sentences and was inclined to be hysterical. She finished the story with a quote from a man in the street: 'It certainly makes you think.' If that's a gauge of the ordinary Australian's powers of reflection, Wyatt thought, then he deserves everything he gets.

King Island looked green and hilly in the water below, dairy farms stitched together in irregular patterns by narrow roads. The Chieftain touched down at twelve-twenty; ten minutes later, Wyatt was aboard a fifteen-seater Heron. He was offered sandwiches and coffee but his first hesitant bite of the sandwich fired up his bad tooth and his first sip of the coffee made it worse. He swallowed two paracetamol tablets and closed his eyes, the thin planes of his face drawn together in strain and exhaustion.

He awoke, senses dulled, when the Heron bounced down at Wynyard. On the drive south, Wyatt judged that he had about another twelve months with Jardine. They wouldn't have a falling out, they wouldn't get caught—Jardine would simply run out of good jobs for him. What then? Wyatt couldn't see any big scores on the horizon, he couldn't see himself doing contract work for organised people like the Sydney Outfit, he couldn't see himself putting teams of unknowns together again. The old ways were gone, it seemed. Men like him—private, professional, meticulous— were anachronistic in a world given over to impulse and display.

A great deal was at stake. Ten, fifteen years ago, Wyatt had been able to pull just a few big jobs each year, living on the proceeds, spending weeks or months at a time in places where no one knew him. He liked having a safe haven, a place where he was unknown and overlooked, a place he could slip home to between jobs. He'd had it once, a comfortable old farmhouse on fifty hectares on the Victorian coast south-east of Melbourne, bought with the proceeds of a bullion heist at Melbourne airport. His windows had looked out over the sea and Phillip Island, and for Wyatt living there was like a rest from running.

Then everything had gone wrong and he'd been forced into a life of mistakes and betrayals and looking over his shoulder for the man carrying a gun or a knife or a badge. For three years

69

he'd felt hunted, on edge. But now he had a chance to regain the things he'd lost and control the strings that had pulled him into risks he should never have taken. He had sufficient money to live on, no one in Tasmania knew who he was and, once he'd paid his debt to Jardine, he would buy an end to his running.

He crossed the Derwent at five o'clock. Traffic was mounting up but that didn't mean anything in Hobart. He followed a minibus past the Government House lawns and looped down through the streets of the city. Tomorrow he'd go back there and find himself a small downtown dentist who ran a busy practice and get his tooth filled. The old sandstone buildings looked soft-edged and warm, glowing softly in the last hour before the sun settled behind the mountain. Below him, on the left, there were the same masts in the yacht basin, the same timber workers' vigil outside the Parliament building. Then he was climbing again, curving up and left into Battery Point.

The apartment block was a squared-off, three-storey beige brick construction from the 1960s, set into a steeply pitched part of the Battery Point hillside overlooking the Derwent. According to tourists, environmentalists and people living on the hill behind it, the building was a blight on the landscape, but it suited the tenants, who could see the water and the mountain. Wyatt had a one-year lease on a street-level flat—street level to cut down on his escape time if anyone with arrest or death in mind for him came snooping around. The rent was low, he could walk everywhere, the neighbours left him alone. There was no one to notice or care if he should slip away for a day, a week, a month. No letters came, the phone never rang, no one looked at him with interest or emotion.

In fact, if any of those things *were* to happen, Wyatt would hit the ground running.

12

Two weeks after his meeting with Springett, Niekirk was back in Melbourne. Riggs arrived that evening, Mansell the following morning. Both had taken rostered days off work. They made it a rule never to fly in together. They met in a motel room in St Kilda Road, and Niekirk had to wait while Mansell gabbled away about his flight down from Sydney. Mansell was like most people, governed by a set of conventions that said you wasted a few minutes kicking pleasantries around before you got down to work.

When Mansell was finished, it was Riggs who spoke first. 'What's the target?'

Niekirk wordlessly tipped floor plans, photographs, a security-system map and a page from a street directory onto the double bed. Mansell bent to pick up a photograph, then straightened, groaning, stretching his back, making a show of it.

Riggs, as stolid and featureless as a slab of rock, crossed to look at the plans. 'Jewellery heist?'

Mansell peered again at the photograph. 'Lovely bit of rock.'

Niekirk picked up a second photograph, a necklace, white gold catching the light softly, emeralds, rubies and sapphires hard and sharp against the gold, like ice splinters in the morning sun. 'The Asahi Collection,' he said, 'on loan from Japan.'

Valued at $750,000, according to the newspapers. Niekirk had calculated his return if he were to try fencing the stones himself. Ten cents in the dollar? He knew he wouldn't do it. There was no one he could trust, and De Lisle had a long reach.

He watched Riggs and Mansell. Riggs was examining the plans now, giving them a grave scrutiny as if he were putting the hit together himself. He had still, capable, long-fingered hands, his body loose in grey cords, a check shirt and a heavy yachting pullover. He could have been anyone—thief, cop, car mechanic—but someone who kept himself calm and ready, and someone with an unpredictable, vicious streak. Sensing Niekirk's scrutiny, Riggs said, 'Where?'

'We're going there now.'

Niekirk took them into the city, to a region of tiny arcades bounded by major streets. Satisfied that they hadn't been tailed, he led them into a snack bar. They sat on stools at a bench that ran the length of the front window of the place. The air smelt of vinegar and superheated oil, shaken apart by a radio tuned at full volume to an easy-listening station. Niekirk's elbow was stuck in a smear of tomato sauce but he ignored it and pointed to a raw new building across the street from the snack bar. It was a narrow, black glass department store, six storeys high, called Soreki 5. Japanese, and it had only just opened for business. There were branches like it all through the Pacific. This one had a gallery on the first floor, and management intended to show fur, porcelain, painting and jewellery collections month by month.

Under cover of the shouted conversations around them, the radio and the thick smacking of cafeteria crockery behind the stainless steel counter, Niekirk said, 'Their first-ever exhibition starts tomorrow morning, and will be here for the next month, so we go in tonight.'

Tonight, when security wouldn't be up to scratch. 'Any questions?'

'We won't need the drill this time?'

'Correct.'

'Maybe the local boys will think there's a new crowd at work.'

'Maybe.'

They rested during the afternoon and were stationed in the alley by 2 a.m., in a white van marked 'Food Transport Vehicle' this time. Niekirk sat in the driver's seat, Mansell next to him, Riggs in the back. Now and then while they waited to go into operation, Mansell fine-tuned the police band radio. Niekirk listened with half an ear as the dispatcher's voice, ghosting with signals from the atmosphere, reported burglar alarms, broken glass, a knifing near the clubs in King Street.

Shortly after two o'clock, Riggs got out and walked away from the van toward the Soreki 5 building. The department store sat black and glassy on the street facing the alleyway. Riggs passed from the alley into the lighted street. He wore a security patrol uniform, gold cloth badges, black trousers, brown shirt, black peaked hat, and Mansell said softly, 'All he needs is a pair of jackboots.'

Niekirk ignored him, intent now as Riggs crossed the street and stopped at Soreki 5's heavy glass doors. He saw Riggs rap on the glass with the base of a torch. A moment later Riggs switched on the torch and illuminated a fistful of documents in his other hand.

Soreki 5 employed its own security guards. They watched for shoplifters during the day and yawned over skin magazines at night. They were trained, but men like that got soft on the job and knew that they were Mickey Mouse guards compared to the men who worked the big contract patrol firms, who regularly got shot at or beaten up and generally led a riskier life. That's how Niekirk had explained the psychology behind Riggs' ploy at the briefing session, and now he fastened a set of headphones over his ears and began to monitor Riggs' conversation with the Soreki 5 guard.

The voices came through sharply, transmitted by a pickup in Riggs' lapel:

'Come on, pal, I haven't got all night.'

Sounds of disengaging locks, then a muffled voice growing less muffled: 'What's your problem?'

'Medicare.'

The Soreki 5 man was slow. He didn't say anything and Riggs repeated, 'Medicare. You know, on the top floor.'

'Everything's jake here. I've got it covered.'

Riggs said, barely patient: 'Maybe so, but the thing is, Medicare isn't one of yours, right? We've got the contract for that, even though they rent space in the building.'

'I don't know. Nobody said anything to me.'

'Well, that's your problem. So how about it, going to let me in?'

'I don't know. I better just—'

'Look, pal, they had ninety grand delivered there today, to cover the next week. If anything happens to that money and it comes out that you refused to let my firm in for a look-see, then your head's on the block, not mine. If anything happens to that money and you *have* let me in for a look-see, then it's my head on the old chopping block. Right? So do us a favour, just sign me in,

I'll be out of your hair in two shakes of a dog's dick, no problem.'

'More than five minutes and I'm calling my supervisor.'

'No problem.'

'And I come with you.'

'No skin off my nose.'

Niekirk saw Riggs go in. Then he heard the big locks smack home and heard Riggs say, 'After you.'

The Soreki 5 guard worked some contempt into his voice. 'We can't just barge upstairs. I've got to activate some bypass switches on the alarm system first, you know.'

'You're the boss.'

Niekirk heard nothing for two minutes after that. But plenty was happening inside the building and he ran it through his head like a film strip: Riggs waits for the guard to deactivate the alarms on the stairs and the lifts. Riggs tickles the man's ear with his automatic pistol. Riggs pulls a hood over the man's head and cuffs him to a display case. Niekirk's instructions had been clear: 'We don't need a hero on our hands and we don't need a panic merchant. Keep him calm, tell him he won't be hurt so long as he does what he's told. If the guard is hurt, I'll want to know the reason why.'

Niekirk looked at his watch, thinking that Riggs should be giving the all-clear about now. He waited, still and silent, a shutdown so absolute that he might have been one of the living dead. The city streets were deserted. There was a hint of dampness in the air, a sheen of moisture glistening on the silent cars, on a beer can in the gutter, on the Elizabeth Street tram tracks. Thirty seconds later, Niekirk heard the heavy main door being unlocked, Riggs saying simply: 'It's a goer.'

Niekirk nudged Mansell. 'Anything from the boys in blue?'

'Not around here.'

'Let's go.'

They got out, walked to the end of the alley and across the street to Soreki 5, as unhurried as men who did this sort of thing every night of the week. Riggs was waiting for them in the foyer. The guard, his head hooded, was on his back, one wrist in the air, bracketed to the rim of a fire hose. He was as rigid as a dead man and Niekirk looked hard at Riggs. Riggs stared back unwaveringly, shook his head in denial.

Niekirk left it at that. There was no point in asking the prone guard how he felt. That would only risk giving the man another voice to describe to the cops and it would certainly irritate Riggs.

He jerked his head. Riggs led the way to a narrow door set flush into the wall behind the foyer desk. He opened the door with the security guard's keys and leaned forward to examine the bank of switches behind it.

Niekirk watched Riggs. The big man ran his finger and eyes rapidly across and down, seeking the isolation switches to the alarms in the little gallery on the first floor. He identified three, murmuring as he deactivated each one: 'Gallery door...electric eye...pressure pads in the display cases...'

Then he looked at Niekirk. 'All clear.'

Mansell went back outside to the van. Niekirk led Riggs up the staircase in the corner of the building. There were lifts, but Niekirk considered a lift to be a potential trap. You can fight or run in a stairwell. The only way out of a lift is up, into another trapped place, a shaft narrow, dark and deep and smelling of stale air and grease-slicked cables.

The stairwell door on the first floor released them into a vast room of women's dresses, mannequins and fashion displays, all of it shadowy, the irregular shapes like islands in a dark sea. Niekirk turned over a couple of price tags with his gloved fingers as they passed through the room: $999, $1,200.

The gallery was a glassed-off area at the far end of the first floor. He pushed the twin doors experimentally: they swung open and no alarm that he knew about sounded or flashed where he could see it.

They went in. The rings, necklaces and bracelets were displayed on black velvet-covered blocks under heavy glass domes. Niekirk and Riggs lifted off the first dome, revealing a pressure switch under the rim. No lights, no sirens, no metal grilles sealing them off from safety.

They were out of there in three minutes. Niekirk carted the Asahi collection out of the building in a photographer's camera bag. Seven hundred and fifty thousand dollars worth, and it took up no room at all.

Mansell picked them up at the entrance to the alley. He was mild, silent, grinning a little to see them. He swung the van onto Elizabeth Street, then left into Flinders Street. At the top end of Flinders Street he turned left again, past the Windsor Hotel, past the solitary policeman on the steps of Parliament House, and finally away from the city centre.

Relieved now, Riggs and Mansell started to congratulate themselves. Niekirk had nothing to say. In his mind he wouldn't be safe until he was alone again and the jewels were in the U-Store locker. He asked Mansell to stop at the junction of Nicholson Street and Johnston Street and watched the van drive away. A few minutes later he was in his cab, turning toward Spencer Street and a date with the courier.

13

'Go all right?'

'Piece of cake,' Niekirk said.

'Your boys off home?'

Niekirk nodded. 'They took a rostered day off work for this. They're on duty again tomorrow.'

Springett grunted.

Niekirk leaned forward in Springett's unmarked car. It was five-thirty in the morning and the city was beginning to stir. 'That's him, bloke in the blue uniform.'

Springett murmured into his radio and started the car. Niekirk saw Lillecrapp uncoil from the doorway of a building adjacent to the U-Store and block the courier's path, grinning inanely, showing crooked teeth, jerking his ill-cut hair out of his eyes. The courier halted, turned to bolt, but by then the car was gliding to a stop beside him, tyres scraping the kerb, Niekirk opening the rear door for Lillecrapp to bundle him inside.

Then Springett was accelerating along Spencer Street and

Lillecrapp had cuffs on the man's bony wrists. Niekirk fished inside the uniform jacket and pulled out a wallet.

'Louis Crystal, Pacific Rim Airlines. Well, Lou, guess why we're here.'

'I've kept my nose clean.'

'Sure you have.'

'Why don't you bastards lay off. I do my job, I stay at home, I've stopped all that other business.'

'Makes a bloke wonder what sort of other business and how De Lisle got to hear about it,' Niekirk said, and saw Crystal's spirit wither a little at the name.

Springett was racing the car toward the docklands. He found an asphalt wasteground and parked between a rusty shipping container and a weed-choked cyclone fence. He turned around, stared at Crystal over the back of his seat. 'You must be feeling pretty sour at De Lisle. Is that why you ripped him off?'

Crystal opened his mouth, closed it again, searching for the trap. 'Don't know what you mean.'

'Cards on the table, okay, Lou? Three times since February you've picked up a tartan suitcase at the U-Store and delivered it to De Lisle in Sydney. Today's delivery will be the fourth.'

Niekirk took over. 'So, what went wrong? De Lisle not paying you enough? Felt you'd like to get back at him? Or maybe you just got greedy?'

'I don't know what you're talking about. I swear—'

'Don't swear, Louis, it's not nice.'

Crystal squirmed, looked desperately at his watch. 'My flight goes in an hour. I'll lose my job—'

'You won't need a job, way you're going, skimming a bit here and there so De Lisle won't notice, flogging it on the sly.'

'I wouldn't know how. Drugs leave me cold.'

Niekirk glanced at Springett. The cringe, the shudder, the

79

heartfelt denial seemed real.

'Drugs, eh?'

Crystal stared miserably at his hands. 'Look, I just deliver the cases, all right? We do it all the time in my line of work. How am I supposed to know what's in them? You can't pin trafficking on me.'

'Tiffany's more your style?'

Again Crystal looked for the trick in the question. Giving up, he said, 'Never met her.'

Springett laughed. 'Good one, Lou. Must remember that one.'

Bewildered, Crystal said, 'I'm going to miss my flight.'

'Assuming for the moment that you haven't been pinching stuff from the cases, how do you work the delivery?' Niekirk demanded. 'Does De Lisle meet you in Sydney face to face? Maybe you put the suitcase through with the other luggage and he collects it himself?'

'Not Sydney. Never Sydney.'

Springett was surprised. 'Here in Melbourne? Bit risky.'

'No, no,' Crystal said, deeply agitated. 'Vanuatu.'

'Vanuatu?'

'I put the case among the luggage for one of the resorts, Reriki. De Lisle picks it up, takes it to his place.'

Springett frowned at Niekirk. 'His *place*, Lou?'

Crystal, sensing that he was being let off the hook, said, 'Yeah. This mansion, kind of thing, overlooking the harbour in Port Vila.'

'Mansion.'

'Yeah. I asked around; he's retiring there.'

'You've made every delivery to Vanuatu?'

'Yes.'

'You suspected it was drugs?'

'Wouldn't you?'

'I want you to look at some photos,' Springett said.

They watched Crystal examine the file snap of Frank Jardine and the blurry surveillance photograph of the man they now knew was called Wyatt, with a woman on a park bench, the Arts Centre behind them. Crystal looked up anxiously. 'Never seen these people before. Should I know them?'

Springett smiled a wide smile of apparent warmth, reached over the seat, slapped Crystal's knee. 'Lou, it's time you were gone. Wouldn't want you to miss your flight.'

As Crystal got out at the U-Store, visibly relieved, Springett said: 'A word to the wise, old son. Keep this to yourself, all right? If I get the slightest hint that De Lisle knows you've been talking to us, I'll be down on you like a ton of bricks.'

Crystal swallowed, nodded, glanced agitatedly at his watch, disappeared into the U-Store to collect the case.

They watched him go. Niekirk said, 'I let you play it as you saw it, but I would've held onto the case, used it to bargain with, find out what De Lisle's up to.'

'One,' Springett said, 'we don't want to alert him. We don't want him closing down and shooting through on us before we get what's owed to us. Two, I for one don't want to be stuck with a suitcase load of hot jewellery I haven't got a hope in hell of moving. I think we agree Crystal's in the clear? He wouldn't have the nerve to dip his hand in.'

'You're saying De Lisle's been converting the stuff all this time, right? He should have paid us by now?'

'Think about it. Vanuatu's one of those places, no tax, no-questions-asked banking. He's even got a house there. I mean, what a set-up. We can't touch him.'

'Yeah, but he is a circuit judge in the area.'

'Perfect cover, right? Bastard.'

'Okay, you've made your point. So what do we do?'

'Tread very carefully,' Springett said. 'He could put me away for ten years, don't know about you.'

'Me, too,' Niekirk said.

'What's he got on you, out of interest?'

'About three years ago he came to see me during an inquiry into police corruption, waving a deposition in my face.'

'And you were mentioned.'

Niekirk nodded. He could almost remember the text of that deposition word for word:

'My name is Bratton, I'm a senior constable with the New South Wales Police and I work with Sergeant Niekirk. During the past three years we have used the police radio network and code names to mount and coordinate break-and-enter operations against private homes and small businesses around Sydney. We often use department equipment to force entry. If necessary we manipulate fellow officers and the courts to our advantage. A number of known burglars have owned up to our burglaries in return for sentence consideration. The extent of our burglaries has therefore been concealed, and at the same time the force appeared to have a good clear-up rate. The system worked because we were eager to prove our loyalty and toughness to one another.'

And Niekirk could remember what De Lisle had said:

'Looks like the culture of secrecy and protection in the force doesn't extend to you, eh, my little mate?'

Then De Lisle's face had sobered. 'Okay, you don't need to be an Einstein to know you're fucked if I decide to table this before the Commission.' He cocked his head. 'Come on, Niekirk. This is the point where you're supposed to ask: "What do you want?"'

Niekirk had said it flatly: 'What do you want.'

'That's better,' De Lisle had said. 'In return for my not tabling this document, I want you to do the occasional little favour for me.'

And that's how Niekirk explained it to Springett. 'I did bugger-all for him, really,' he concluded. 'Couple of small jobs. Information about a few people. Until now.'

'He paid well?'

'Yep.'

'In effect, you never felt threatened. It felt like a working relationship, not blackmail.'

Niekirk curled his lip. 'Springett, the psychiatrist. Yeah, that's how it worked.'

Springett turned one of his smiles into a rare laugh. 'What happened to Bratton?'

Niekirk shook his head. He'd sent Riggs after Bratton, a nasty accident, but he wasn't about to tell Springett that. 'Your turn.'

'Same kind of thing. I was working Vice. A fair number of the Melbourne brothels are run by the Sydney Outfit. You could say I was on a retainer and De Lisle found out about it.'

'What did you do for him?'

'Like you, information, leaned on a couple of people, that type of thing.'

'He must have creamed his pants when you joined the Armed Robbers. His very own green-light cop.'

Springett's smile widened. 'Steering my team away from your team.'

Lillecrapp giggled. He was so stolid and obliging that Niekirk had forgotten he was there.

'Okay, so we don't tackle De Lisle. What do we do?' He picked up the surveillance photographs of Wyatt and Jardine. 'What if these characters shoot their mouths off about where they got the brooch? What if they're arrested and start making deals?

83

I don't want to wake up one morning to find the toecutters on my doorstep. I don't want to wake up knowing I've been ripped off.'

'You go on back to Sydney, keep an eye on De Lisle,' Springett said easily. He glanced at Lillecrapp. 'Meanwhile I'll plug a few holes down here.'

14

Shaken by his encounter with the men outside the U-Store, Crystal said stuff it to De Lisle's stipulation about no cabs. He collected the tartan suitcase from the U-Store, walked back to the station and hailed the first taxi on the rank.

The driver was a woman and she sniffed slowly, deliberately, when he got into the back seat, not the front. Barrel-shaped, a sparse pelt of carroty hair on her fleshy head, no one was going to take her for granted. 'Plenty of room up front.'

'I'm tired.'

Her voice was a nicotine-riddled croak. 'So am I, Sunshine, so am I, but I say we're only on this earth once.'

Crystal tuned her out. He stared at the dewy cars streaming both ways along Spencer Street, his arm protectively around De Lisle's suitcase against his thigh on the seat beside him. He itched to open it, but it had been locked and he didn't have a key.

'What are ya? Pilot? Cabin steward? You know what they say

about cabin stewards,' and she began to wheeze, a version of a laugh.

Crystal focused on the driver. Her head was a hazy balloon shape spotlit by the low morning sun. He held the suitcase closer to his hip.

'I asked what you did,' she said.

Crystal looked away from her. She hadn't washed recently. He opened the window a couple of centimetres.

'Cat got your tongue?'

The taxi had stopped for the King Street lights. There was a luggage tag attached to the tartan suitcase: black leather with a clear cellophane window. Crystal fished a name card from his pocket, reversed it and printed the words 'Mr Huntsman, Reriki Resort' on it, then slipped the card into the leather tag.

Huntsman. What crap. Crystal was tempted to remove the card and write De Lisle down instead. But that would let De Lisle know he was onto him.

'I'll say it again—cat got your tongue?'

Crystal didn't know why he had to be subjected to this and he told the woman so.

'Some people, they think their shit doesn't stink.'

Crystal admonished himself. Don't say anything, don't give her an edge of encouragement. He felt the cab's tyres slap over tram tracks. A few minutes later he lurched gently against his door. The woman had turned left with a faint tyre squeal and was accelerating along William Street. He mentally plotted their route: skirt the Vic Market, merge right onto Flemington Road, right again onto the Tullamarine Freeway.

He stared at the cars and buildings without seeing them. All of Crystal's grief led back to De Lisle, starting with an interview room that was like any interview room anywhere: functional, sparse, close and sour, as though every falsehood, craven emotion and confession ever heard in it had become a permanent part of the air and the fittings.

There had been others there in the room with De Lisle: a senior federal policeman, a senator, a shorthand typist, a couple of sour faces in suits. De Lisle had started the questioning: 'Like the tropics, do you, Louis?'

At once Crystal had known what this was about. He looked at De Lisle, looked him full in the eyes, small eyes behind a protective squint. 'My job takes me there.'

The Fed leaned forward. He was a charmer, full of smiles, only they were the professional smiles of a cadaverous undertaker. 'We're not talking about your crappy job. We're talking about other sorts of trips. Holidays, kind of thing.'

Crystal said: 'Sorry, was that a question?'

The Fed ignored him. He flipped through a file on the desk in front of him. 'You're single?'

Crystal said nothing.

'I beg your pardon—I see here that you were married once but divorced several years ago. No kids, I take it?'

Crystal shook his head imperceptibly.

De Lisle said, 'You've got a girlfriend though.'

Crystal shrugged. 'Is that a crime?'

'A single mother, I believe. Two boys, six and eight.'

The Fed leaned back, folded his arms across his chest. 'Some blokes have trouble relating to women. I'm not saying they're queer or anything—they switch their attention to little kiddies.'

'By befriending single mothers,' said one of the suits.

'Look, if you lot are going to charge me with anything, charge me.'

'This is only an inquiry, Mr Crystal,' the senator said.

De Lisle cut in: 'Some men seek attention in other ways, like hanging around in public lavatories, slipping porn under the door to kids,' shrugging as if all this were regrettable but understandable. 'Kids are curious. I know I was at that age. They want to find out more, so it's only natural some of them will follow through.'

The senator had looked on, appalled and fascinated. The nameless faces in suits smiled a little. De Lisle and the Fed watched Crystal shift in his seat. There was a cast in one of the Fed's eyes, giving him a look of permanent scepticism. 'But you'd think the toilet block approach would be pretty dicey. There'd have to be easier ways of getting kids to come across for you.'

'I wouldn't know.'

'So you just *amble* your way through life, not thinking about sordid things like that,' De Lisle said.

Crystal stiffened. He had caught the man's word stress.

'Funny you should say that, your worship,' the Fed said. 'AMBL is an acronym.'

'Is it?'

'Association for Man-Boy Love.'

'Huh,' De Lisle said, full of wonder. 'Better than Australian Paedophile Support Group. You can't get an acronym out of that.'

The seconds ticked by. De Lisle turned the pages in Crystal's file. 'Well there's a coincidence.'

'What?'

'Our friend here has been to Thailand and the Philippines six times in the past three years.'

'Go on.'

'Yep. I asked him just now if he liked the tropics but I don't think I caught his answer.' De Lisle bent forward, trying to look up into Crystal's face. 'Where do you like best? Thailand? Maybe Jontien? I hear it's got a fantastic white beach. Or maybe you prefer the Philippines? I hear Batangas is nice.'

One of the suits said: 'A bloke who was so inclined could pick himself up a kid for ten bucks in one of them places.'

'Those places,' De Lisle corrected automatically. 'You know what they say, Lou, "Sex before eight, or it's too late". Would you say that, Lou, old son, old pal, old sport?'

Crystal remembered turning on De Lisle, snarling: 'I don't know what you're on about. Whatever it is, you're barking up the wrong tree.'

The Fed said coldly, 'Quit the bulldust, Crystal. You're a rock spider. Think what the hard boys in Pentridge will do to you when they find out. They hate guys like you even worse than they hate cops. All those hard men, sexually abused by blokes like you when they were little kids. They'll cut off your cock and make you eat it.'

The senator gasped. Crystal said, 'You can't prove anything.'

'Yeah?' The Fed leaned down, fumbled in a briefcase, came up with a videotape. 'We found this in your ceiling this morning. You seem to be having more fun than the kid. What is he, Thai? About eight years old?'

Crystal had let a sob rip from his throat. 'Children seduce too. It's not only the adults.'

'But they're still children,' the senator said. He grimaced. 'People like you, you give Australia a bad name in Asia.'

There was silence. To fill it, Crystal found himself saying, 'I want to make a deal.'

'A deal?' De Lisle said. 'You haven't been charged with anything. This is an inquiry, that's all, a fact-finding exercise.'

An hour later, Crystal had been out on the street, sweating, drained, pale, but a free man. Free until De Lisle got in touch with him that evening with a proposition.

Unvarying red tiles and powerlines were slipping by now as

the taxi jockeyed for a clear run along the freeway. When the airport came into view, Crystal leaned forward and said, 'International terminal.'

'Oh, *International* terminal, whoopy doo,' the woman said.

Crystal gave her the exact fare, told her to keep the change, and got out. Inside the terminal he reported for duty, stashed the tartan suitcase in his staffroom locker and helped get the airbus ready. It was a day like any other.

So far.

But knowledge was power and forty minutes before takeoff Crystal made his way to the airline's supply room. Among the airsickness bags, spare pillows and blankets, plastic suit covers and aircrew badges and caps there was a bunch of keys. He'd once counted them: forty. Suitcase keys, hanging on a brass ring like ranks of tiny flattened people. The airline had collected the keys over many years. There was always a passenger who'd lost the keys to his luggage. There was always one key that would fit.

He waited until he was alone in the locker room and went to work on the tartan suitcase. The sixteenth key sprang the lock and he found neatly packed but cheap shirts, underwear and socks. Disappointed, he began to rummage, and that's when he found the stuff. He gaped, felt the surface of his skin tingle: brooches, necklaces, earrings, pendants, rings. Something about the weight and density of the metal, the way the stones caught the light, told him that De Lisle was no traveller in costume jewellery.

15

In the way that he obsessively aligned the edges of knives and forks with the weave pattern in a tablecloth, or stacked firewood according to size, Wyatt walked once a day, every day. This walk took him in a loop around the high streets of Battery Point, then down onto Salamanca Place and past the yacht basin, and finally up again into the steep slopes of North Hobart. If he ever varied his route it was to cut down the Kelly Steps instead of through the park, or circle the moorings clockwise instead of anticlockwise.

Two weeks since the Double Bay job and this morning there was blossom on the fruit trees in the Battery Point gardens. Wyatt paused to stare at a house on the park overlooking the water. A climbing rose clung to the verandah posts and there was old glass in the windows, thick and irregular, so that the massive sideboard and silver candlesticks in the room behind the glass seemed to swim in and out of shape. A widow's walk went right around the house and Wyatt could imagine sitting up there, watching the big ocean-going yachts tacking up the Derwent. He wondered if a woman had ever paced the boards of that widow's walk a hundred and fifty years ago, watching for returning sails or waiting for a knock on the door.

Wyatt decided to go by way of Kelly Street. He plunged down the Kelly Steps, hearing the clack of a typewriter in the tiny whaler's cottage at the head of the steps, then slowed. There was a man below him, mounting the steps, and at the bend he stopped and looked up. Wyatt tensed, gauging the danger in front of him, listening for footsteps behind him. When he was putting a hit together he made it a point to avoid lifts, undercover carparks, stairwells. He never let himself get boxed in. Instinct and caution had got him through forty years on the planet but this time he'd allowed his guard to relax.

He stopped and began to crouch, as though to tie his shoelace. At the same time he turned his head and glanced back toward the head of the steps. Clear. He glanced down again and relaxed. There was fury on the man's face, directed at a daydreaming child, a small boy trailing his fingers on the stone and singing softly to himself. 'Jesus Christ, get a move on,' the man snarled, reaching down to yank the boy's arm.

Wyatt straightened and continued on down the steps. Who would come for him here, anyway? All the old scores had been settled.

He strolled the length of Salamanca Place, keeping to the grass islands, avoiding the spill of tourists and drinkers outside the cafes and bars. After a moment's confusion about traffic flow at the end of the walk, he circled around to the right, past a restored ketch and on to the main dock area. More tourists, queuing for ferry rides, reading menus outside one of the restaurants, gawking at the yachts.

Wyatt gawked, too, but with a more critical eye. For the past six weeks he'd been paying an old yachtsman to take him out in the man's two-master and teach him how to work the sails, navigate, look after himself at sea. When he had the money, when he had cleared his obligation to Frank Jardine, he would buy a boat and live on it. A boat made sense, given the life Wyatt had chosen to lead, was forced to lead. He didn't think that fate would let him live in one place year after year again, and he didn't want to stake everything on a house and land if the police or some death-dealer from the past managed to find him and force him to abandon it all and run again. If he lived on a boat he'd be mobile. He could follow the big jobs around, or move on whenever the local heat got too much for him. Plenty of people lived on boats. There were globetrotters moored in every marina and yacht basin in the world. No one would ask him to justify himself, no one would notice him. And although he wouldn't have the rolling open hills of the place on the coast he'd been forced to abandon three years ago, he'd at least have the vast sea and sky.

Wyatt left the waterfront and headed inland along Argyle Street, the climb steep and steady toward the top of the mountain behind the city. He was tempted to buy a boat now and live on it here—until something went wrong and he was forced to run again. Something would go wrong, that he didn't doubt. If he were to rely only on himself, Wyatt would be wealthy, known to no one, bothered by no one, as close to a perfect life as he could want. But he never could rely only on himself. There was always someone to please, bully, coax or manage, and inevitably one of them let him down. They made mistakes or got greedy or didn't like the way he wouldn't have a beer with them afterwards. Their life stories padded the daily newspapers, notable usually for some act of viciousness or stupidity that ended in a remand cell or on a slab at the morgue.

Wyatt stopped at a flyspecked barbershop half a block west

of Argyle Street. The sun-bleached ads inside the glass were fifteen years out of date and dust clogged an old pair of clippers set alone on a crepe-papered hatbox in the centre of the window. Wyatt had never seen any customers in the chairs or waiting along the wall inside, but he'd learned that the place had been there since the 1950s and the sort of men Wyatt had to deal with from time to time swore that it had been a successful maildrop for all of that time.

The man reading the *Hobart Mercury* in the barber's chair wore a white shirt with the sleeves rolled up and a fat paisley tie tugged free of the collar. He had plenty of slick black hair combed back from his forehead as if pasted there with grease. The face he turned to Wyatt was tired, worn and grubby, like his business. He recognised Wyatt and said at once: 'Just the one item.'

The barber climbed down from his chair and walked half-bent to a room at the rear of the shop. He came back with a large padded envelope. The address on it was a box number and the name was Carew, another name Wyatt was using at the moment.

Wyatt handed the man twenty dollars and wordlessly left the shop. The envelope had been inexpertly prised open and sealed again. That wouldn't have helped the barber, for Jardine had simply passed on a message from Liz Redding, but any level of curiosity on the part of the barber was intolerable and so Wyatt went back into the shop.

The man knew and backed away, stammering, 'Something else, mate?'

Wyatt's eyes locked on him dispassionately. There were several ways he might play this. The most obvious involved a degree of risk. If he were to hurt the barber, damage his property, or take back the twenty, the little man would notch up another injustice and look for a way to collect on it—the police, some minor thug mate with ambitions.

Some sort of physical payback was what the barber expected, he was born and bred to it, so Wyatt's stillness baffled him. Then he grew aware of Wyatt's cold gaze. He began to splutter, close to tears: 'I didn't mean to. The flap was—'

A mistake. If the barber had admitted opening the envelope and stopped there, Wyatt would have nodded and left him in the jelly of his fear. But the little man was trying for an excuse.

Very slowly then, with chill deliberation, Wyatt raised the bony forefinger of his right hand. It was a slender, sunbrowned finger and the barber shut his mouth and stared, fascinated, as it seemed to float across the gap between them. His eyes tracked the finger. Wyatt stopped when it made contact. It was no more than a whispering brush against the tip of the man's nose, but the effect was dramatic. The little barber seemed to spasm and smoke like a man in an electric chair.

Wyatt left. He still hadn't spoken, and by the time he was out of the door and crossing the street he was thinking only of the next day, meeting Liz Redding in the ranges east of Melbourne and exchanging the Tiffany for twenty-five thousand dollars cash.

16

This time they drove through the night, dumped the van on the outskirts of Sydney, and collected Mansell's Toyota. They entered the fuming traffic again, the spine of the Harbour Bridge an impossible distance ahead of them.

Mansell yawned. They'd been on the road for ten hours. He needed a shave. They both needed a wash and a change of clothing. He felt constipated and his eyes were prickly. They sat there in the creeping lanes of cars and buses, approaching the city in short, weak spurts between traffic lights.

After a while Mansell said, 'What are you working on at the moment?'

'Me? Same old shit,' Riggs said indifferently, as though the night behind him had never happened. 'Solicitors milking their trust funds, bank clerks ripping off cheques. There's this one case, a bloke sets up a dummy company, gets his mates to invest in it, promising them it's going to merge with a bigger company, meaning the shares will rise, only it's all bullshit and his mates lose the lot. He's into them for five million.'

Mansell shrugged. 'Throw the book at him.'

'Not that simple—he disappeared swimming off Palm Beach last month.'

Mansell looked at him briefly. 'Faked it?'

'A gut feeling.'

'Follow the paper trail.'

'Yeah. Piece of cake.'

For a while then they stared ahead. They were tired, their necks stiff with tension and hours of sitting. Riggs said, 'What about you?'

'Glebe doctor runs a hose from the exhaust pipe of the family car parked in the garage at the side of the house into the spare room where his wife's sleeping—a room the size of a shoebox, the door and window easily sealed—then when she's dead he carts her out to the car, runs a shorter hose into the car itself. Bingo. Verdict suicide.'

'Will you get him?'

'He left her too long on the bed. Her blood settled where it wouldn't have settled if she'd died sitting upright, like we found her. We're pulling him in this morning.' He rolled his shoulders. 'Shit I wish I'd rostered myself two days off instead of one.'

Riggs grunted.

They reached the harbour tunnel and the white car slipped like an oiled pellet past the slick tiles, drawn by the curving lights. Mansell tried to picture the metres of sludge above their heads, composed of mud, plastic bags, hubcaps, guns and skeletons, then metres of harbour water, all of it pressing down, down.

The light quality began to alter and the car climbed toward the sunlight. The sun was weak in the grey sky but Mansell was glad to see it. He took the North Sydney exit, winding automatically through the little streets. They had nothing to say to each other.

Until Riggs stiffened in the seat next to him. 'Did you see that? Pull over, back up. Something's going down in that side street.'

'Riggsy—'

'Just do it. There's a punk down there about to get the shock of his life.'

17

'The weather in Sydney today will be fair and mild, light winds, with an expected top of twenty degrees. All you peak-hour crawlers out there in radio land, stay tuned for today's Rego Reward. If your plates are announced, you could win one thousand dollars.'

Baker stayed tuned, but they didn't call his rego number so he slid in a cassette of Jimmy Barnes and lit a smoke. Then he took his foot off the brake, moved one car length along with everyone else, braked again. Judging by the scream-scrape whenever he braked, it was metal against metal on all four wheels. Still, it wasn't his car. The cow had a job—let her fix her own car. He helped in plenty of other ways.

Baker twisted around on the collapsed springs of the driver's seat. The brat was standing on the back seat, bumping his skinny rear against the torn vinyl of the seat upright, the same movement over and over again. Mouth open, shoelaces already trailing, vacant look on his pinched face. Baker's arm, thick and gingery, shot out and grabbed a pitiful wrist. Skin and bone. 'What'd I tell you? Eh? What'd I tell you?'

The brat seemed to wake out of a trance, showing confusion and fear. He stopped the bumping motion but wouldn't look at Baker.

'Fucking can't keep still. I told you. What'd I say?'

Troy wouldn't meet his gaze, just looked down at the UDL cans, parking infringement notices and McDonalds cartons on the seat and the floor. The cow was on early shift this week, so Baker had had to dress the brat himself: jeans, skivvy to hide a couple of fresh bruises, cornflaked windcheater, runners that wouldn't stay tied. Baker stabbed a finger into the boy's collarbone. He did it again. He hated the way the kid's face would just shut him out. Never any gratitude, never acknowledgement of any kind. Like his flaming mother that way. Seven years old and Troy screened Baker out of his life as though Baker didn't exist, was no part of the family at all.

Then the cars moved again and Baker turned back to the wheel. Why couldn't the brat walk to school? He'd done that at that age. Hadn't hurt him either. No geezer ever tried to snatch him off the footpath and play with his dick, and he'd grown up knowing how to look after himself. But oh no, not our precious Troysie Woysie.

Baker wondered who the father was. He bet Carol didn't even know herself. Claimed he was an American naval officer, but that was more of her bullshit. Liked to say how she'd struggled for seven years, not easy bringing up a kid by yourself, blah, blah, blah. Which meant that Baker had a dream run when he first showed on the scene. She was starved for sex, just crying for it.

Now the rot was setting in. Wanted to know his job history, like she was his fucking dole officer or something. Kept looking in the employment pages, circling jobs for him in red biro. Told him it wouldn't hurt to get out there and look, no job was going to come knocking on the door. Just lately she'd get pissed off over little things, like if he hadn't cleared up or done any shopping by the time she got home. And she was really getting on his back about his *addiction*, as she called it, to dope and booze. Said he had a problem. Said he was getting worse, more unpredictable, his fuse shorter. Fucking bitch. Baker's hands tightened on the steering wheel, as he thought of her scrawny neck.

He turned around. 'Fucking keep still, will ya?'

Turned back to the wheel again. She was starting to get prune-mouthed about the brat, too. It was okay at first, told him she knew Troy could be a handful, encouraged him to use a bit of discipline, but now she'd turned a hundred and eighty degrees and last weekend she'd ordered Baker into the bathroom and pointed a quivering finger at the brat: 'Those marks weren't there yesterday, he's my son and I'll deal with him,' etcetera, etcetera.

The traffic was stalled again. Baker cranked down his window, letting in a blast of Sydney traffic fumes. It cleared his head but he badly needed a hit of something, speed for preference. He could try that bloke in the side bar of the Edinburgh Castle; he was generally holding.

That's if Carol had put forty bucks in the kitty, like she'd promised. He'd check when he got home.

Which would mean doing the shopping at some no-frills supermarket, generic tins of spaghetti and meat sauce for dinner, and another tirade when she got off work this arvo.

Baker flicked the turning indicator as he approached the next set of lights, signalling a left turn. He had to hold the lever in place or it would jump out. He couldn't actually hear the ticking sound so he had no way of knowing if the thing was working or not. Just another item in the list of little helpful things Carol thought he might get around to doing for her one day, along with taking Troy to school all this week.

Something made Baker glance in the rear-view mirror. Some bitch in a Volvo was behind him, flashing her headlights. She had a pointing finger pressed to her windscreen and she was mouthing things at him.

'So, the turning light doesn't work,' he muttered. 'So fucking what?'

Still she kept shaking her finger at him. 'Well, what?' Baker said, talking to her image in his mirror. He shrugged elaborately, lifting empty hands in the air, signalling *what?* to her. Fucked if he knew what she was on about. As for Troy, he'd turned around and was looking out through the rear window at the woman in the Volvo.

'Hey, Troy, whyn't you give her the old finger?' Baker said, little puffs of amusement escaping him as he accelerated toward the corner, yanked on the wheel, and steered the barrelly Kingswood into the street where Troy went to school.

The thing was, the Volvo woman stayed with him. Now the bitch was tooting her horn, stabbing her finger at him, flashing her lights. Her face was twisted with outrage and after only a few seconds of that Baker thought: Right, slag, I'll fucking have you.

There was no one about. This part of the street had a deserted factory on one side and a wrecker's yard the size of a football ground on the other. The school was another kilometre away. Baker pulled over to the kerb. The Volvo pulled in behind him. He stayed where he was: let her make the first move.

In the wing mirror he saw the woman get out, close her door carefully, stand watching him. After a while she seemed to make up her mind. She walked toward him, her image growing in the mirror: plenty of bouncy hair, Reeboks, red tracksuit. Baker knew her type. Young mother, plenty of money, full of fucking opinions.

He got out and leaned on his door. 'Got a problem?'

She actually stamped one foot and stood there shaking in the grip of a powerful emotion, bent forward at the waist. 'That child should be properly restrained.'

Restrained? 'Speak English, lady. What are you on about?'

She pointed. 'Your son—'

'Not my son.'

'Your ward, then. He should be strapped into a seatbelt.'

'So?'

'What if you have an accident? What if you have to stop suddenly? He could be seriously hurt.'

Baker uncoiled from the door. 'Any of your fucking business?'

That got to her. Her little fists were clenched and her eyes were fiery. 'Yes, if you like, it *is* my business. When a child is at risk it's *everybody's* business.'

Baker closed the distance a metre or two. 'Listen, slag.'

The woman retreated a couple of steps but wasn't backing down. 'It's against the law for a child to be unrestrained like that.'

'I'll give you unrestrained,' Baker said, and he hit her hard, just once, dropping her like a stone.

He watched her. She shook her head as if to clear it. When she touched her mouth and saw blood on her fingers, she yowled and scrabbled away from him, dragging her backside along the street. Baker imagined that she wasn't wearing much under the tracksuit. He caught up with her. Surprisingly, she curled into a tight ball. He hesitated, weighing it up.

'Who gives a shit,' he said.

He stepped over her. Yeah, he knew it. There was a little kid in the Volvo, strapped in the back seat, singing to herself. Little satchel, dinky little dress and socks and shoes. 'Precious koochy koo,' Baker said. 'Daddy's princess.'

He opened the driver's door of the Volvo and grabbed the woman's purse. Eighty bucks, wacky doo. Enough for a hit, plus he could treat Carol and the brat to Pizza Hut tonight.

He folded the money into his back pocket and that's when a car came out of nowhere and two guys in plain clothes pinned him against the flank of the Volvo. One of them, a blocky character in need of a shave and a mouthwash, got in a few punches before cuffing him. 'You're nicked,' he said.

18

Wyatt walked down through the mall, heading back to Battery Point. He glanced about him as he went, automatically looking for the face, the gait, the conjunction of person, place and body language that would tell him he'd been found. But the little downtown streets were benign in the sun, so he went on half-alert and did what he sometimes liked doing, visited the place as if for the first time.

He noticed the school-leavers in the mall, kicking their heels and shifting place constantly but never going anywhere. They had nowhere to go. There were no jobs for them. Wyatt looked beyond them to the pedestrian traffic. No Asian or Indian faces; no blacks, no Pacific Islanders. It was a mono-featured city.

He saw plenty of young men wearing beards, jeans, walking boots and red, green and blue check shirts, and guessed that they had a four-wheel-drive or a utility parked nearby. And there was another kind of male, stamped with old money and long breeding. They walked tall along the streets, braying and impervious, fathers and sons with straight backs, costly English tweeds and an air of entitlement radiating from them. They would have been out of place and out of joint anywhere but on the streets of Hobart.

But, more than anything, the city breathed wholesomeness and conviction. Perhaps that was the central factor—everyone here knew their place, except the kids in the mall.

He kept walking. The dental clinic was in a lane off Elizabeth Street. He was five minutes early and was kept waiting for twenty. At eleven o'clock he walked out with a new filling in his jaw.

That afternoon he was on a bus to Devonport, and by evening he was on the overnight car ferry to Melbourne. He slept badly: a bunk bed in a steel tomb below the waterline; young men, intoxicated to desperation point, stumbling in from the discotheque; all the unknowns ahead of him.

At dawn he showered, got dressed and climbed the stairs to an upper deck. He ate breakfast in a dining room in which the carpet, curtains and fittings were the colour of the vomit that streaked the iron steps outside. Toast and coffee, as bad as any he'd ever had. After that he stood in the open air, choosing a point near the bow where he could watch the ferry's progress toward the narrow entrance to Port Phillip Bay. He could see land on either side: hills, flat country, white beaches and a couple of fishing towns. Then a lighthouse and the ferry was pitching through The Rip.

Wyatt remained on deck, breathing the cool air, as the ferry skirted the Bellarine Peninsula and cut up the centre of the bay. A year ago he'd travelled these waters alone in a stolen motorboat. Having shot a man who'd sold him out, he'd been on the run. He usually was, in those days.

The ferry berthed at 8.30 a.m. and Wyatt filed off with the passengers. As usual, he swept the docks, looking for men standing featureless and still in the background. There were men like that in every port in the world, waiting to nab someone in particular or simply watching to see who was new in town, intelligence they might later tie in to a robbery or a killing.

There was no one, but Wyatt had altered his appearance again anyway, this time with a wad of chewing gum in his cheek, a baseball cap on his head and a football-club scarf trailing from his neck. Not that Wyatt knew or cared about football. Everything about football was collective, and Wyatt had never joined or wanted to join or feel part of the herd—a trait that had kept him free and more or less unknown, unreachable and uncorrupted for all of his life.

He caught a taxi. Thirty minutes later he was at the Budget car rental place in the centre of the city, mapping out a route to the little town of Emerald in the hills.

19

The day began badly with a female duty lawyer at the Magistrate's Court calling him Terry. Not 'Mr Baker', 'Terry', as if he didn't deserve the respect of *Mister*. Then again, in Baker's experience of the court system, the only people ever to call him Mr Baker had been the beaks who'd sat in judgement of him.

'Sit down, Terry,' she said. 'That's the way.'

Baker pulled up a pouchy vinyl chair, orange, scabbed with cigarette burns, and leaned back in it, giving the Legal Aid bitch the once-over. Her name was Goldman, that made her Jewish, and Baker peered at her face for confirmation. Given that your Jew is fond of cash, what was she doing Legal Aid shitwork for? Baker pondered on that for a while, then he had her: classy dresser, sharp brain, the type who likes to slum it once in a while. He grunted, satisfied with his analysis, folded his arms and waited. But he felt twitchy. He badly needed a hit.

The Goldman woman turned the pages of the charge sheet. 'Assault, theft, threatening behaviour...'

'You know how they like to throw the lot at you, hope some of it sticks,' Baker said.

She looked up at him. 'So, what are you saying, Terry? You're denying all of it? Is that how we plead you, not guilty?'

Baker rolled his shoulders around, searching for the right words. 'I was aggravated, wasn't I?'

'Aggravated?'

'Yeah. She come at me.'

'She attacked you?'

'Sort of, yeah.'

'So it was self-defence?'

'Yeah,' Baker said.

He watched Goldman pick through his file. Now and then she pursed her lips, made a clicking sound with her tongue, as if she didn't like what she saw there.

'Terry, according to your record, you have a drink problem, correct?'

'I've been known to down the odd coldie. Why?'

'And drugs.'

'You know,' Baker said, 'recreational.'

'According to a previous assessment, made just six months ago, you were on a downward spiral.'

Downward spiral? Baker stared back at Goldman. 'What the fuck does that mean?'

'It means your psychological and physical conditions were deteriorating, Terry. You were obliged to seek treatment at a clinic. According to the clinic, you dropped out after three visits.'

'I wasn't sick,' Baker muttered.

The lawyer clutched the edge of her desk with both hands, leaned toward him across the paperwork. 'Terry, I'm looking for our line of defence, okay? It's called mitigating circumstances. A history of drug and/or alcohol abuse can be taken into consideration, helping to account for your actions.'

Baker bristled. 'What do you mean, abuse? I'm fucking not an alky, not a junkie. Fucking watch it, lady.'

Now she did call him 'Mr Baker'. Temper up, the bitch spat at him: 'Mr Baker, I'm appointed by the court to help people who cannot afford a lawyer and who do not wish to conduct their own defence. I'm not deciding guilt or innocence—that's the court's job. You've got to meet me halfway here. The police prosecutor is going to give you a very hard time. I've seen Sergeant Day in action many times. He'll try to rattle your cage, get you worked up so you look bad in the eyes of the beak. Is that what you want?'

'No.'

'No. So why don't you help me work out a line of defence?'

'Suit yourself.'

'Not suit myself. Not suit myself at all. I want you to meet me halfway here.'

Baker frowned at her. 'It's a committal hearing, for Christ's sake.'

'So? Are you saying you don't want me to try to find grounds for a dismissal first?'

Baker shrugged.

Goldman pushed on. 'And if I can't find grounds for a dismissal, don't you want a good defence mapped out for when trial time comes around?'

'I can always shoot through.'

Goldman regarded him coldly across her desk. 'Do that and you won't get bail next time you're picked up.'

'Maybe there won't be a next time.'

Goldman's voice softened. 'Terry, listen to me. Look at your history: in homes from the age of eleven, juvenile court at fourteen and again at fifteen and sixteen, six months suspended for possession, a community order for going equipped to burgle…At this rate you'll be the next chicken in the yard at Long Bay, Bathurst or Goulburn.'

Baker flushed. 'People like you, think you're so great.' He wanted to explain what it had been like for him, but the words wouldn't come, only pictures in his head and hot shame and anger choking in his throat. His father had started fiddling with him on his fifth birthday. Fiddled with his twin sister, too. When they were eleven the old man and the old woman had taken them to Penang, supposedly for a holiday, except they hadn't stayed long and on the way back he and his sister had worn condoms packed with smack taped to their waists, little angels who wouldn't arouse the suspicion of customs officers. There had been other trips after that, a lot of the smack finding its way up the old man's arm—him *and* his mates—putting them in the mood for a bit of kid-fucking, the old man happy to oblige his mates, two kids already in the house. Baker felt a lot older and wiser than any Legal Aid bitch fresh out of law school, who couldn't understand why he was wasting himself on dope and booze. If Baker had the words, he'd explain to Goldman that the world looked a lot better skewed than it did real, that the dope and booze blunted the pictures in his head. The seconds went by. He swallowed, caught his breath. He tapped his chest. 'Think I couldn't handle the yard? Piss it in, lady.'

She gazed at him calmly. 'You almost sound as if you welcome the prospect.'

'Lady, when I go to prison it's going to be for a fucking good reason, not some pissweak assault charge, theft, whatever.'

They watched each other for a few moments. Some of the heat had leaked away now, as though Baker had stated his case and the duty lawyer hers and the result was a stalemate, maybe mutual regard.

111

Goldman moved first. 'Okay, Terry, we'll do our best with what we've got. You're on the slate for two o'clock. Don't be late, don't wander off. Now if you'll excuse me, I've got another dozen people to counsel this morning.'

Baker stood. The action was sudden, the chair crashing over behind him. That embarrassed him—he hadn't meant it to happen and it must have seemed like aggression or disappointment. He righted the chair, all of his movements contained and careful, and saw only one way of retrieving the situation. He stuck out his hand. 'Thanks. Much appreciated.'

The duty lawyer was occupied with the papers on her desk and didn't notice his hand. He made her notice it, leaning completely over the desk and wagging it at the level of her breasts. 'Mrs Goldman? I just want to say thanks.'

She blinked. '*Ms*, not Mrs.' Then she shook with him, her hand small, dry and firm, and Baker suddenly felt that the day was on the mend.

He walked down the corridor, past other duty lawyers in other offices, and came to the waiting room. Nowhere to sit. It was a place of writhing children, fat women striking out suddenly, junkies chewing their nails to the gristle, bewildered parents, young car thieves and break-and-enter merchants leaning like James Dean on the walls. Baker looked around in disgust. Behavioural problems, medical and physical disabilities, tears, ethnics in their best suits, not to mention the uniforms, cops and court officers.

Too much for Baker. He checked his watch. Almost noon. Time for a few quick belts.

The pub across the road had Castlemaine on tap. Baker had a schooner, a vodka chaser, a schooner, a vodka chaser. He patted his pockets. He'd had a Serepax prescription filled just the other day. He found the tablets in the same pocket as the car keys. He swallowed one, then threw back another vodka. Another beer would have been a big mistake: 'Just nipping out for a leak, your worship.' Baker sniggered, imagining the look on the beak's face.

The guy behind the bar gave him a wink on the way out. 'Good luck, mate. Keep your head.'

'Thanks,' Baker muttered.

Keep his head? What did the guy mean? Baker crossed the road. On the other side he put one foot after the other up the steps of the courthouse. In through the swinging doors and then a double-check of the computer printout on the notice board. There it was: Baker, Court 5, 2 p.m. He looked at his watch. Holy Christ, five past two.

'Where have you been?' Goldman hissed outside number five court. She reeled back. 'Oh, Terry, you haven't been drinking?'

'Settles the nerves,' he told her.

'Well, come on. Victor De Lisle's the beak today and he doesn't like to be kept waiting.'

It became apparent to Baker during the twenty minutes that followed that he might have made a miscalculation with his cocktail of beer, vodka and Serepax, especially on top of the downers he'd popped that morning. He was aware of the police prosecutor droning away: guy in a suit, solid build, a moustache like you see on nine out of ten coppers. Then Goldman had a go, and Baker heard her suggest to the beak that they settle his case now, save some strain on the court system. Baker yawned a lot. He beamed. He was required to stand through all of it and that was the hard part.

Then the fog cleared a little and Baker felt the eyes of the magistrate fix on him. Baker twitched at the man, halfway between an open smile and a respectful nod.

'Ms Goldman?'

'Your worship?'

'Is Mr Baker inebriated? Have you been drinking, Mr Baker?'

'If the court pleases, Mr Baker is an alcoholic, a disease he is currently doing his best to overcome.'

'That's not what I asked, Ms Goldman. I asked whether or not he has taken upon himself to appear *in my court* in a state of intoxication. Mr Baker, perhaps you would care to honour us with an explanation one way or the other?'

Baker frowned, picking his way through the heavy language. 'Pardon?'

'You're a bit of a *loafer*, eh, Mr Baker?'

A cop at the back laughed out loud.

De Lisle went on: 'When's the last time you did an honest day's work, Baker? Maybe you're not a loaf, maybe you're a sponge. Soak up the welfare system, do you, Baker? Got some poor woman at home supporting you?'

'Your worship, I really must protest—'

'I'm not interested, Ms Goldman.' De Lisle's face twisted. 'I see his type over and over again. Useless. A drain on the community. Repeat offenders too stupid to learn from their mistakes.'

'Your worship, really—'

'Not now, Ms Goldman.'

Something was going on. Baker concentrated, hearing the sneer in De Lisle's voice, registering the contempt. De Lisle? What kind of a wog name was that? He saw a short, pink, fattish kind of character, self-satisfaction written all over him. I'll get you, pal, Baker thought. Calling me useless. Calling me stupid.

Meanwhile De Lisle was all professional again. He overrode Goldman and began gabbling a legal summation in a recitative voice, to the effect that Baker did have a case to answer and was bailed on his own recognizance to appear in the District Court on a date to be fixed.

Baker wasn't interested in that. He barely listened. He was encouraging a picture in his head: De Lisle thrashing about in pain, begging, *pleading* with Baker to spare his worthless life.

20

Wyatt slowed for a traffic bottleneck in Ringwood, the hills clarifying in the distance, and considered just how murky this deal with the Tiffany had become. If Liz Redding were simply a fence, he'd be wary out of habit, knowing that the only other factor to take into account was the ripoff factor: you can't get rid of the goods yourself, fences can, so you're forced to rely on them, knowing they'll always rip you off a few per cent. But at least you also knew that neither you nor the fence wanted the law involved.

But that kind of certainty didn't exist when it came to someone who walked the murky ground between the insurance companies and lawless professionals like Wyatt. The insurance companies were ostensibly on the side of the law. The only thing in Wyatt's favour here was their well-known reluctance to fork out the full value on any claim. They would rather fork out a few thousand dollars to get the Tiffany back intact, no questions asked, than pay the full replacement value—which didn't mean they wouldn't also work with the law if it suited them to do so.

With that in mind, Wyatt did what he could to stack the odds in his favour. He hadn't been carrying for months—too much metal, too many airport metal detectors, and Jardine's burglaries hadn't warranted a gun. But today he had Jardine's unused, untraceable .32 automatic in the waistband at the small of his back. Not his preferred handgun, but it would do if the shooting were close and fast.

Next was the handover place itself. If there'd been more time and if he were dealing with a buyer or a fence, then he'd have insisted on meeting in the safety-deposit vault of a bank. He'd have a safety-deposit box, the buyer would have a box. He'd have the Tiffany, the buyer would have scales, pincers, jeweller's eyeglass and purchase cash. They'd complete the trade in complete privacy and neither would be tempted to pull a cross, not with so many guards, cameras, witnesses and steel doors around.

But there wasn't the time, and Liz Redding wasn't a simple buyer or fence, so he'd suggested a Devonshire tea place near Emerald. It was taking him over an hour to get there, but the hills offered escape routes and boltholes. He could slip away on one of the back roads or hole up in a weekender cabin or even perch up a tree for a few hours. He'd be hard to track from the air and hard to follow in the dense ground cover.

He thought through the getaway alternatives. If this were a trap he was walking into, he'd run and keep running, assuming he had the initiative to begin with. If not, then he was left with holing up in Emerald until the heat was off, or holing up a few kilometres away until it was safe to leave. He thought he knew how the cops would work it. They'd block the roads out first. If he didn't show, they'd move the search closer to Emerald. Clearly the answer was, if he got away in the initial confusion he'd hide where he could watch the roadblocks. When they came down for the cops to narrow the circle, that was the time to run and keep running.

Assuming the cafe itself wasn't being staked out, the interior crowded with cops posing as customers, waiters, cashiers, cooks.

Finally, Wyatt had worked on himself, doing what he always did before a hit. He'd eaten a modest breakfast, enough to give him energy but not slow him down. He had a train timetable in his pocket, and reserves of cash to buy his way out of trouble. And he was wearing a useful, quick-change disguise if he needed one: the jacket was reversible, there was a beret folded into an inside pocket, he wore sunglasses. Change all three factors and he might change his appearance sufficiently to get away unnoticed.

The cafe offering Devonshire teas was on the northern edge of the town, separated from the first of the shops by a belt of gums, tree ferns and bracken. Wyatt parked the car in a bay outside a milkbar, went in, bought an icecream, came out again. He set off down the street, heading away from the cafe. He strolled for four blocks, not hurrying, taking tiny smears of the icecream into his mouth to make it last. Then he crossed the street and came back, pausing now and then at the window of a craft shop, a nursery, a display of New Age crystals and self-help books. The crystals and the books were incomprehensible to Wyatt.

The sweep was smooth, methodical, made with the steady, quiet competence with which he stamped all his jobs. He didn't let the tension of his situation work on his nerves. It helped that he didn't see anything that he hadn't expected to see. There were a few tourists like himself, a few local merchants, housewives doing the shopping, a couple of horticultural types in Land Rovers and here and there a stoned-looking sixties' counter-culture throwback, probably from a hovel back in the hills somewhere. Wyatt preferred the pure, peeping bellbirds to any of them.

By now he had a clear picture of the Devonshire tea place. It had a first floor balcony with umbrellas open to the sun, but he wasn't about to tree himself there. He'd meet Liz Redding on the ground floor: plenty of doors to the open, and plenty of windows if it should come to a dive through the plate glass, his jacket over his face and arms for protection. Otherwise there seemed to be a basement, a rose arbour at the side, a couple of shadowed porches and alcoves of greenish, weathered boards. He'd stay clear of places like that, just as he stayed clear of any place where he might find his exits blocked in front of him and some final threat coming hard behind him.

So, he was as safe as he could make himself. That left only the negotiation itself. Wyatt had no doubts about his strength there: he had the Tiffany, Liz Redding wanted it.

What else did she want? He wanted her, but that didn't mean he was going to act on it. Then he stopped thinking those things and watched a car pull into the small asphalted area in front of the cafe. Liz Redding was driving but it was not the car she'd been driving the day he and Jardine had met her at the motel in Preston. No sticker of any kind in the rear window.

She got out. Plenty of loose material hanging on her slim frame today: baggy pants, a billowing white T-shirt reaching to her knees. She swung the strap of a black purse over one shoulder and strode into the cafe. He went in after her, knowing that he wouldn't feel any more or less safe five minutes from now.

21

Baker trailed Ms Goldman back to her office, and the moment he pulled the ugly vinyl chair up to her desk he blurted it out: 'You know what he bloody well called me? Stupid, useless, lazy.'

She took some time to respond, his file spread open in front of her. He'd noticed that about her before. Getting her attention was like trying to turn a ship at sea, you had to allow plenty of room and time. Well, she was Legal Aid, the government was paying her, so he wasn't going to get top priority. If he had plenty of dough, she'd be all over him. Finally she dragged her eyes away from the file, saying 'Hmmm?' absently, looking more or less past his right ear, not into his eyes.

'Useless,' Baker repeated. 'He said I was stupid and lazy.'

'I don't recall that.'

'That's what he said. Shouldn't be allowed. I mean, fair go, there's a recession on.' Baker waved his hand to indicate the masses huddled in the corridors and waiting rooms outside. 'I bet fifty per cent of the poor bastards who come here haven't got a job, so why have a go at me?'

'I remember he asked if you were a loafer,' the Goldman woman said, twinkling a little.

'See? Like I said, he called me lazy.'

'Oh, Terry, that's just his little joke, a play on words. Your name is Baker, right? Bakers bake loaves, hence loafer.'

Baker wasn't about to let her mollify him. He felt obscurely ashamed and bitter. 'What about calling me stupid and useless? Anyhow, what kind of name's De Lisle? Wog name, not even Australian.'

The lawyer refused to answer that. She was looking into his face now, all right, so he knew he'd hit a nerve. She held his gaze, cool and blank, and he looked away, trying to make it casual, masking it with a cough, a scratch, a realignment of his limbs in the orange chair.

Maybe the Goldman woman was relenting, for she said, 'It was the luck of the draw that we got him today, rotten luck in fact. He does have a reputation.'

'Tell me about it,' Baker muttered. He looked into the distance to show that he didn't give a shit.

'But he's highly regarded and he does his bit, which is more than you can say about a lot of others.'

'Yeah? How?' Baker demanded.

She shrugged. 'Well, he's a circuit magistrate in a couple of Pacific countries.'

Baker grunted. 'Let's hope a shark gets him.'

He added the shark to the fall off a cliff, the shorting light switch igniting built-up gas, the smacking front of a Mack truck, the sort of thing he could set up so it looked like an accident.

Ms Goldman laughed, a genuine laugh, as if they were on the same wavelength when it came to De Lisle and what he deserved. Maybe the guy had squeezed her one day without being asked, Baker thought, gazing at her, thinking he'd like a piece of that himself.

She read it in his eyes and something in her shut down again, her shoulders hunching forward, her forearms on the desk, effectively closing her body off from him. 'Now, Terry, your defence,' she said.

'She had it coming,' he said promptly.

The Goldman woman took that seriously, jotting something down in her notes. 'In what way?'

'Well, I mean, she come up behind me flashing her lights, blasting me with her horn. I mean, how was I to know she didn't have a carload of skinheads on board, like, you know, an ambush or something?'

'But, Terry, you stopped the car. You wouldn't stop if you feared for your life. I have to ask this—were you high at the time? Had you taken anything, alcohol and drugs together perhaps?'

'Jesus Christ, I thought you were my fucking lawyer.'

'I'm not fucking anything,' Ms Goldman said, and it was like a slap across the face to Baker.

He put up his hands. 'Okay, I apologise. I just want to know how come you're, like, taking this woman's side.'

'Terry, I'm simply doing what the prosecution will do to you in the courtroom.'

Baker considered that for a while. 'All right, how about we argue self-defence?'

'But you knocked her to the ground. A chipped tooth, lacerations, a mass of bruises. How do you explain that, except as an overreaction? The kind of overreaction one might expect from someone under the influence of drugs or alcohol, I might add.'

Baker closed his eyes, tightened his fists. A wave of blackness and heat swept through his head, sparks popping behind his eyelids. He fought it down. 'Fucking lay off about the booze and drugs, will ya? Please? Just lay off?' His voice was high, pained. 'Everyone on at me, all the time, I've fucking had enough.'

He'd scared her. He didn't want that. He waited for his heart to stop thumping, then took a deep breath. 'Like I said, she come up behind me flashing her lights, tooting her horn, so naturally I thought I had a flat, or maybe the boot was open. Then we both stop and she gets out of her car and comes at me, sounding off about the blasted kid should be *restrained*, whatever. Like I said, self-defence.'

'It's you who should have been restrained, Terry.'

He looked at her and it was full of hate. 'So that's how it's going to be, you're all gunna have these digs at my expense, turning everything I say around. Yeah, thanks a lot.'

'Terry, did she actually assault you?'

He shifted in his chair. 'Sort of.'

'How do you mean? Did she hit you, spit on you, threaten you with anything?'

'If I'd've been closer I would've felt the spit coming off her. She was good and toey.'

'Did she threaten you verbally?'

'How do you mean?'

'Did she say she'd do something to hurt you if you didn't restrain the child—what's his name? Troy?'

'Troy, yeah, little brat. Well, she reckoned I was careless, kind of thing, letting the kid ride around without a belt on.' He showed her his palms apologetically. 'I know, I know, I should've strapped him in, but you know how kids are, all over the place, can't keep still.'

'Terry, I'm trying to work out if you were provoked in any way, and, if so, whether or not you were justified in striking out at Mrs Sullivan. Mitigating circumstances, in other words.'

'Talk English, can't ya?'

She leaned forward. 'We may be able to obtain a fine and a suspended sentence if we can show that your striking the woman—though to be deplored—was understandable given the nature and degree of her provocation.'

Baker muttered, 'We should get the bitch to back down.'

'I didn't hear that, Mr Baker.'

Baker put his head on one side. 'But you'd have her address, right?'

'Terry, I'm warning you.'

But Baker was lost in staging another revenge and his mind drifted. Wait till the Sullivan woman was in a multi-storey carpark somewhere, shove a spud up her exhaust pipe so she can't get the car started, then jump her, get her to withdraw all charges, maybe put her out of action somehow.

That's if he could find her. Christ, the Sydney phone book was probably chocka with Sullivans.

He became aware of a snarling exhaust note outside the building. When it didn't let up after half a minute, Baker went to the window.

He liked it, oh he liked it very much. Some bloke was parked across the street in a hotted-up panelvan, brrrapping the motor, letting the vehicle hunt and rock a little as if he were slipping the clutch, ready to take off. But it wasn't the panelvan that interested Baker, it was what it stood for. Clearly the poor bastard had been given a bum's rush in court and he was shouting his grievances to the world through a megaphone: 'Men and women are not equal...Justice for women, injustice for men...Modern justice, keeping a father away from his kids.'

'Go for it,' Baker muttered.

The lawyer joined him at the window. 'Oh, God, not him again.'

Baker laughed. 'Got lumbered with De Lisle, did he?'

'If anything, De Lisle would be on his side. No, he's been hassling us for months.'

She had her mouth open for more but just at that moment the traffic cleared and the panelvan screamed and leapt smoking and snaking away from the kerb, across the street and through the main glass doors of the courthouse.

They heard the crash. The screaming started a couple of seconds later. 'He's hurt someone,' Ms Goldman said, and she hurried out.

Baker left, too, but he paused for a moment at her desk first. He spun the file around. There it was, Diana Sullivan, an address in St Leonards.

They were all moaning and wringing their hands at the front of the building. The panelvan had come right into the foyer and buried itself against the front desk. Baker saw blood and glass, a lot of it. If he'd been a different kind of a person he could have lifted the occasional wallet and handbag in all the confusion. As it was, he saw Ms Goldman helping a woman into the Ladies'. She saw him. 'I'm sorry, Terry,' she said, harried, pale-looking. 'Ring me tomorrow?'

'No worries.'

'Great.'

Baker slipped away through a side door. Carol's Kingswood was in a K-Mart five blocks away. It took him a while to find the street directory under the UDL cans and toys and other crap on the back floor. St Leonards.

But when he got to the address, no one answered his knock, and when he went around the side of the house, a woman from next door poked her head over the fence, demanding to know who he was and what he wanted.

He waved the classifieds section of a newspaper in her face. 'I've come about the VW.'

'I think you must have the wrong address. Diana doesn't own a VW.'

Baker was perplexed.

'Besides,' the woman went on, 'someone assaulted her and she's gone to stay with her mother till the trial.'

Then, conscious that she'd said too much, the woman frowned and reached a fleshy arm over the fence. 'Let me see that ad.'

Baker backed away. He said, 'It's okay, no worries, my mistake,' and other unconvincing things as he backed out of there.

In the Kingswood again he planted his foot. If the nosy cow was calling the cops right now he'd better track down some mates who'd swear he'd been on the piss with them all afternoon.

So, forget the Sullivan woman.

Fix De Lisle instead.

22

'Just coffee,' Wyatt told the kid waiting on them at the corner table, near a door, next to a window.

Liz Redding looked at him across the table, a faintly amused expression on her face. What he read there said that she thought him abstemious, and not only because he hadn't ordered anything to eat, so he said, 'And an apple danish,' seeing her mouth stretch into a grin.

'Now I don't feel so bad about ordering scones and cream,' she said. 'It's been a while since breakfast, and it's a long drive up here.'

This was small talk. Wyatt didn't try to look interested. Liz Redding wasn't someone who'd indulge in it for long, anyway.

He nodded pleasantly, looked around. He was sitting where he could see the room, each door, part of the strip of asphalt outside. Liz Redding had her back unconcernedly to the room. That was a good sign, it said she wasn't expecting trouble. Then he realised that she could see all she needed to see reflected in the mirror behind him. He decided that that was a good sign, too.

There were no other customers. The cafe was the kind of place that did plenty of business on weekend afternoons, a little on weekday afternoons, virtually none before lunch. All that glass on three sides admitted plenty of warming sunlight into the room. Wyatt could detect coffee in the air. The waitress had passed their order through a serving hatch behind the cash register and was perched on a stool now, chin down, frowning over the split ends in her hair. A radio murmured on a shelf behind her, too low for him to isolate one word from another. No music, so he guessed it was a talk show. Crockery clattered in the distant reaches of the kitchen.

The tables, chairs and benches gleamed with a honeyed, piney light. It was a restful place for a transaction outside of the law. Wyatt scratched one fingernail across the tucks in the check-patterned gingham tablecloth and saw Liz Redding's hand there, long-fingered, elastic, appealingly knuckly. They were good hands to look at and he imagined the rest of her.

One hand seemed to twitch in reaction to him, lift, fall to the cloth and pick at the material. She said, 'They want me to check the stones.'

He'd expected that. He passed her the Tiffany but then their orders arrived. Liz Redding's eyes were avid, full of appetite. 'Just in time. I could feel crankiness coming on.'

Wyatt watched her spoon the chocolatey froth of her coffee into her mouth, take the first sip, lick away the residue from her upper lip. She leaned toward him across the table and he thought for a moment that she wanted to kiss him, but she propped her chin in her cupped palm and said, 'What's the waitress doing?'

Wyatt looked past her to the cash register. 'She's gone out the back.'

'Good.'

Liz sat back, fastened her jeweller's glass to her eye, examined each of the stones intently. Wyatt watched her hands, the clean, healthy pores like pinpricks speckling the brown skin. She looked up. 'So far so good. You haven't substituted pieces of cut glass for the stones. Now to see that you haven't substituted cheap diamonds for expensive ones.'

She was twinkling, enjoying herself. She handled the Tiffany again, peering for telltale scratches around the settings. Satisfied, she rummaged in her bag and brought out a tiny set of scales. Wyatt watched carefully, but her hands were quick and covert this time and he glimpsed nothing of what else she might have in the bag.

'Still all clear?'

He nodded.

She placed the scales on the table, effectively concealing them among the cups, plates, sugar bowl and a tall, matched pair of salt and pepper shakers.

'She's back.'

Liz froze. Her hands crept around the scales.

'It's okay. She's staring off into space.'

Liz used a small tool to prise out a couple of representative stones. She picked them up with tweezers, weighed one and then the other in the tiny bowl of the scales.

'*Women's Weekly* seal of approval,' she said. 'Each stone weighs in as the real thing. Sorry,' she said, meaning the rigmarole.

Wyatt was unconcerned. 'It's business,' he said.

He had no appetite, for the transaction was not complete, but picked up the danish anyway and bit into it. The pastry was thick, binding, and it dried the inside of his mouth. The apple was too chunky. He drained part of his coffee, ate more of the danish.

It was then that Wyatt's mouth seemed to fill with grit. He

grimaced, tongued the stuff to his lips, removed it with his fingers.

'What's wrong?'

Wyatt placed the offending sludge onto his plate and separated pastry and apple from a jagged chip of tooth and new amalgam. His tongue automatically ran along his upper teeth, registering a rough hole and a loose fragment, all that remained of the tooth that had been making his life hell for two months.

'I've lost a filling.'

Fascinated, Liz Redding stared at the chip on his plate. 'More than that. Your tooth's split. Is it the tooth that's been bothering you?'

He nodded.

'A new filling on top of old ones?'

'Yes.'

'It split open,' she said. 'They'll do that. Which one is it?'

'Top. Back,' he said, his tongue busy.

'That's not so bad. It won't affect your chewing and you won't need a false one in its place.'

'You seem to know all about it.'

She was still leaning across the table, her upper body straining toward him. Unconsciously he leaned toward her. They seemed to be joined by this humble human catastrophe.

That's why they failed to notice the junkie with the gun. He came in through the main door and a moment later Liz blinked and murmured, 'Behind me.'

Wyatt looked past her shimmering black hair to the doorway. The man who stood there, a little rocky on his feet, wore scuffed boots, a torn T-shirt, greasy jeans and denim jacket. He needed a shave and a haircut. Wyatt expected to catch a whiff of him, a smell compounded of unwashed skin and clothing, oil and petrol, and something else, a rotten intestinal system leaking cheap alcohol and costly, impure chemicals bought in alleys and brewed in backyard amphetamine factories.

The man hadn't seen them. He wiped the back of his hand across his nose, tried to focus, jerked the gun as if waving crowds of people aside. Wyatt watched carefully, following the gun. The size told him it was a .357 and it seemed to have the weight of a genuine .357, not a disposal-store replica. Then he saw the man stop wavering and focus on the waitress. She was rooted to her stool, uselessly opening and closing her mouth. The man giggled insanely and shuffled toward her. 'Gimme,' he was muttering, 'gimme,' showing a mouthful of healthy teeth, and that wasn't right.

Liz Redding had her bag in her lap, bent over it protectively. She had the Tiffany in there, and Wyatt's reward money. 'We should do something before he hurts her,' she said, beginning to turn her head.

Wyatt stopped her, his voice low and even, not wasting itself on unnecessary words or useless inflections: 'Don't move. Don't attract his attention.'

They waited there, frozen, watching the junkie. Wyatt saw him push the waitress off the stool. 'Gimme. Gimme.'

The shove seemed to wake her. She stumbled to the register, opened it, shrank back against the serving hatch. No one in the kitchen had noticed her. Wyatt heard dishes rattling, a cheerful whistle, water rushing into a sink.

The junkie crammed a few notes from the till into his back pocket. He was sniggering, maybe imagining the next fix. Wyatt saw him swing away again toward the door, then stop, greed showing on his face.

Liz breathed, 'Oh God, he's seen us.'

Wyatt watched as the junkie approached them slowly, keeping behind Liz Redding but beginning to circle so that he would soon be coming in on their flank.

Wyatt's left flank. It seemed to be deliberate. Wyatt had the little .32 in his lap but the angle was bad. He'd have to shoot across himself, across the table, and, unless the man widened the circle, he'd have to place his shot close to Liz Redding's shoulder.

So far the junkie was mostly bleary and unpredictable, as if he'd targeted them as a soft touch who'd hand over their wristwatches and spare cash and not kick up a fuss about it. But then the muzzle of the .357 came up, the man spread his legs and crouched, and he began to raise a steadying hand to the gun. He was clean and cool and focused suddenly, snapping out of his chemical trance more quickly than any junkie Wyatt had ever known.

All these things registered with Wyatt and he swung the .32 into view, catching his knuckles under the lip of the table, wasting a precious fragment of time.

He would have been too slow. It was Liz who shot the man. She didn't do what amateurs do, turn her head first to find the problem then bring her gun to bear on it, but swung everything around—trunk, arms, eyes and gun—cutting the delay time, tracking the target, firing the instant she had him placed.

She shot the junkie twice, one a doubling-over punch to the stomach, the other straight into the crown of his head. This second shot blew the man back against a table. He rolled off, tangled with a chair, and fell, leaving a red smear on the tabletop. Wyatt saw that he was dead. The interesting fact about the dead man was his crooked wig.

23

'Oh no, oh no.'

It was Liz Redding and her face was white, dismayed.

Wyatt reached over, took her gun, turned her to face him, her chin clamped in his hand. 'Liz, snap out of it.'

'I've killed him.'

'It was a setup. We can't stay here,' he said.

He had the voice of a convincer, flat, exact, experienced. Liz came with him into the sunlight and let him drive her out of there in her car.

He barrelled down the first side road, a winding channel between overhanging trees. Three hundred metres down he spotted a narrow parking bay and a pipe-and-glass bus shelter. He pulled in. 'Take off your T-shirt.'

She looked at him numbly then nodded. She was mute, everything closed down now, but he was banking that elation and relief would flood in soon—and anger, and questions.

He was already taking off his jacket and reversing it, tan

corduroy outermost, the plain weatherproof cotton now the lining. He stripped off his buttoned black shirt, pulling it over his head to save time.

Beside him, Liz Redding's head and arms were briefly lost to view as she bent forward and removed the big T-shirt. He saw her flexing stomach, her breasts beneath her raised arms, squeezing together briefly, the brownness very brown against an unfussy white cotton bra. Wyatt felt a powerful urge to pull her against his chest. It was as much a symptom of his lonely state, a memory trace of friendly, uncomplicated intimacy with a woman again, as a need to feel her bare skin against his. Then she was shaking hair out of her eyes and swapping shirts with him. He also gave her the jacket and the sunglasses and seconds later was peeling the little rental car away from the parking bay, snaking down the road as he accelerated.

A short time later, he began to double back, turning right at each intersection until they were on an approach road to Emerald again. He slowed as they entered the town, looking left and right as he cruised past the side streets. Liz Redding was looking with him. 'There,' she said.

It was a small, high-steepled church with room for parking under a box hedge at the rear. No one would spot the car there for a few hours, maybe even for a couple of days. They got out, walked unhurriedly back into the town. Wyatt sensed the change in Liz Redding, an electric charge in her step. She was waking out of her shock and misery, engaging with the world and him again. Her arm went around him and he felt a ripple of energy in her flank.

They ambled to his chunky rental Commodore, got in. By now there were sirens in the distance, an awareness of high drama telegraphing itself from person to person along the street. Wyatt started the car, signalled, U-turned slowly and took them out of there.

He was looking for somewhere to hole up overnight. Motels and hotels were out. So too—to a lesser extent—were guesthouses and places offering bed and breakfast. Wyatt and Liz Redding no longer resembled the couple who'd fled from the cafe, and their car was different, but the police would eventually begin a check of all accommodation addresses in the area and want to talk to all couples.

He found it outside the next town. The sign read 'Expressions of interest invited for this outstanding commercial opportunity', the hype referring to a half-built holiday lodge consisting of a mud-brick reception area and half a dozen mud-brick cabins. Weeds grew hard against the walls and plywood had been tacked over most of the windows. Here and there tin flapped in the wind. There was a lock-up garage at the rear of the property. The lock was flimsy. Wyatt forced it and drove in. Nothing inside but dusty drums and a stack of floorboards. They closed the door again, hurried across to the lodge, and began to check each of the buildings, keeping to the back walls. The cabins were empty but two rooms behind the main office had been set up as accommodation for a caretaker or nightwatchman in the days when the developer still had hopes for the place. They found a tiny kitchen with tins of Irish stew and peaches on a shelf, a gas burner, a kettle, three enamel mugs and half a packet of stale tea. In the other room there was a foam mattress on a lightweight tubular metal camping cot, two thin khaki blankets folded at the foot of the bed.

They stood there, turned, and contemplated one another gravely. Since fleeing the cafe, Wyatt and Liz Redding had scarcely spoken, communicating in snatched murmurs, a kind of shorthand that worked because they each wanted the same thing, each faced the same odds. Now they didn't need to talk at all. Wyatt eased the reversible jacket away from her shoulders. He

135

unbuttoned the black shirt. Liz Redding fixed her gaze on him, eyes dark in her strong, dark face. When the shirt was on the floor, Wyatt leaned his bony nose to the dark cleft between her breasts, kissed each upper slope, reached around to unfasten the strap. He was clumsy and she laughed once, quietly, not minding.

Then Wyatt was unbuckling the belt at her waist but he felt her hands on his, pushing him away with a queer, embarrassed kind of modesty. She finished the act for him, watching his face as she let the pants fall to the floor, weighted heavily by something, the belt, then slid her briefs to her ankles and stepped out of them.

When it was her turn to strip him she started slowly but grew impatient, all the constraint gone as if it were pointless. She was full of charging energy, and Wyatt was infected by it. He fell back with her onto the bed and let her straddle him.

She began. He saw her close her eyes tight in concentration, head tilted to one side as if she were listening for a voice. Then a little later she'd remember him, and grin and buck and lean down to bite his lip.

At the end of it, she dozed. Wyatt waited. Finally her eyes snapped open. 'You were right, it was a setup.'

'Yes.'

'He was acting the junkie. Someone hired him to kill us.'

'Or only one of us. Me,' Wyatt said.

She stiffened in his arms. 'Or me. I didn't set you up.'

They fell silent, playing out the possibilities.

'You're good with a gun.'

He felt her shrug against him. 'It pays to be. In this game you've got to be prepared for any contingency.'

Queer, formal wording. Wyatt rolled away from her.

She was alarmed, a little hurt. 'Where are you going?'

He leaned back to kiss her. She smelt and tasted humid and salty from their lovemaking. He heard her murmur, the words unintelligible but affection and desire clearly there in them. He disengaged. 'Handkerchief,' he said.

She watched him, lazy-looking and tousled, propped up on one arm. That changed to alarm when she saw him reach for her trousers. 'I haven't got—' she said, stopping when he uncovered the little revolver concealed there.

She seemed to slump, then rallied. 'So? So what if I carry two guns?'

All the tenderness was gone from Wyatt. He fixed on her like a pin through a butterfly. 'A crotch holster? Come on.' He gestured with the little gun. 'This is your backup piece. If you were wearing boots I'd also expect to find a gun there. But it was the way you handled yourself in the cafe. You've had training. And look at this, no front sight, thumb-bar filed off the hammer so it won't catch on anything.'

'Mack Delaney trained me,' she muttered, mouth sulky.

'Bullshit,' Wyatt snarled, a slow hard rage building in him, narrowing his face and filling it with colour. 'Delaney's dead. You knew I couldn't check on you.' He gestured with the gun. 'Get up.'

When she was standing before him, tall and bare and defiant, he said, 'Pick up your shoes.'

He saw it in her face at last, confirmation, a sense that she knew he had her. 'Let's talk about this.'

'The shoes.'

He watched her pick them up. She half drew back one arm sullenly, as if she might smack him down with a shoe, but stopped when he ground the tip of the gun against her throat. 'Let's see it.'

She removed it from beneath the lining of her left shoe. She held it out, propped between thumb and middle finger so that he could read it. He read 'Victoria Police' and 'Senior Constable' and that was enough.

'How long have you been working undercover?'

She shrugged. She wasn't going to say, but then seemed to think that it wouldn't matter what she said now. 'A few months.'

'If you knew the Tiffany was stolen, why didn't you have me arrested at Southbank that day?'

'Too soon.'

Wyatt stared at her fathomlessly until she said, 'I thought you were part of the magnetic drill gang. I wanted the whole gang.'

'Who knew you were meeting me today?'

'That's my problem.'

'I'd say it was a problem for both of us.'

'Let me handle my side of it. The cash is there in the bag. That part's real enough. The insurance company wants the Tiffany and was prepared to pay to get it back. Take the fucking Tiffany too, for all I care.'

'A deal's a deal,' Wyatt said. 'You figured I belonged to this gang?'

'I did. I don't now.' She paused. 'At least tell me where you got the Tiffany.'

He smiled his brief vivid smile. 'No. This way we find out who tried to kill us from separate ends.'

'Vengeance is mine, sayeth the Lord,' she said, then seemed to wonder why she'd said it.

There were nylon restraining links in her bag. He let her get dressed then cuffed her to a corner of the iron cot. 'I suppose you could always drag it down the road with you.'

She bit her bottom lip. 'So you knew I was a cop before you had sex with me. That was pretty calculated of you.'

*

He touched her cheek with the flat of his hand, a tender gesture for Wyatt. 'Calculation had nothing to do with it.'

She stared at him carefully for a few seconds. 'I guess I believe you. Thousands wouldn't. How did you know about the ID card in my shoe?'

'I thought my way into your skin,' Wyatt said, as fanciful as he'd ever got with his language. 'I'd carry ID if I were working undercover. I'd want it for a situation like this. I'd want it if I had to bargain for my life.'

He saw the alarm in her face. 'I'm not going to kill you,' he said, moving to the door. 'You helped Frank Jardine.'

'You're sparing me because I helped your friend? Is that what you're saying?'

Wyatt couldn't answer that.

24

Springett checked his watch. Unless there'd been a balls-up, Lillecrapp should be on his way back from making the hit about now. He pictured it, Lillecrapp's wet teeth bared, a mad light in his eyes, that falsetto giggle he was always coming out with, roaring down out of the hills, two more bodies to his credit. As the saying goes, a natural-born killer. Springett pondered upon that as the traffic ahead of him shunted forward two car lengths and stopped again, trapped by a Sydney Road tram. Lillecrapp had been useful; now he was a liability. Springett wondered if paying him off would work. Unlikely. Lillecrapp would want more, or he'd brag to someone when he was in the sack, or grievances would begin to eat away at him. Maybe Niekirk's boys could arrange an accident for him?

The conductor appeared in the open door of the tram, jerking his thumb at the line of cars, signalling them to pass. Greasy hair, in need of a shave, runners on his feet: How did someone like that keep his job? Springett accelerated, sticking his middle finger at the man as he passed the tram.

He was in a big Falcon from the divisional motor pool. He liked to drive with both feet, one riding the accelerator, the other the brake, a kind of edgy dance that made his blood race. That was the beauty of your automatic transmission.

He found his landmarks, a furniture barn opposite a mosque, and turned off Sydney Road, into a system of narrow streets. The red light in the Falcon's rear window winked as he surged, braked, surged, braked, steering a course between beefy cars parked outside the tiny houses neat as pins, new cladding on the walls, wet cement gardens, Middle Eastern smells and music hanging in the air.

Springett felt hungry. He would eat soon, but not before he was finished with Jardine. He needed that margin of irritation you got when hunger creeps in.

According to Liz Redding's notes, Jardine lived in a rented house with an unmarried sister. He rarely went out. He was ill; the sister looked after him. Springett gnawed at his bottom lip. A shame about the sister. She wasn't involved. Jardine himself had said so—it was in Liz Redding's notes. A shame to have to knock her as well as her brother.

Springett slowed for Jardine's street, prowled along the row of houses in the car. No numbers on the front doors or gates, of course, so he was relying on Redding's surveillance photographs. There: the white weatherboard, a sorry-looking ruin sitting in a patch of onion weed. He drove past, turned around, drove out of the street, looking for the laneway that ran behind the houses. Redding's photos showed a back gate fashioned from a sheet of iron, held shut with a twist of wire. Every house had a high laneway fence and there were no flats overlooking the lane. He could go in that way unobserved, catch Jardine and the sister with their pants down, maybe literally.

Redding was thorough, at least Springett could say that about her. Pity she had tunnel vision. Pity it had to be her that Wyatt and Jardine contacted, instead of a real fence, for the Tiffany would have disappeared again by now. But it was her, and it got her thinking that she was onto the famous magnetic drill gang. Tunnel vision. 'No worries, boss,' she'd said, 'I'm going to follow this through to the bitter end.'

Bitter was right. A bullet between the eyes from Lillecrapp. And an end that was sooner than she'd expected.

Springett got out, locked the car, crossed the street into the lane. If Liz Redding had been allowed to arrest Wyatt and Jardine, been allowed to process them and stick them into interview rooms, then there wouldn't have been a lot that Springett could have done about it. One of them would have talked, seeking a deal, and sooner or later De Lisle's name would have come up as the main man in the chain of people who'd handled the proceeds of the Brighton bank job.

Springett had said it himself to Niekirk: De Lisle will talk to save his neck, count on it.

Springett had a break-and-enter-gone-wrong in mind for Jardine and the sister. He wanted it to look like one of those random, messy, everyday tragedies that you find in the poorer areas of the cities of the world. He didn't want the homicide boys scratching their heads over an atypical shooting; he didn't want neighbours reporting gunshots; he didn't want to have to get rid of a gun afterwards. He didn't want to get rid of a knife, either, or risk blood fountaining over his clothing.

So he was carrying a baseball bat.

Springett came to Jardine's skewiff laneway gate. He unfastened the wire, edged into the back yard. No dog—Redding's notes would have said if there was a dog.

Not much cover, either, apart from a fig tree, a clothesline and a couple of dead tomato plants in plastic pots. And according to Redding, Jardine liked to sit at the back of the house, where the sun penetrated, and watch his hopeless hours pass by. No time to waste. Springett charged across the yard, jerked open the screen door, shouldered through the inner door, and found himself two metres away from Jardine on a daybed.

There was a tartan rug over Jardine's legs, a form guide on his chest. Jardine opened his mouth and Springett saw fear crawl in him, literally claw its way through his body. Jardine jerked, tried to speak, rolled back his eyes, tugged at his collar, and died.

For a long moment, Springett gaped at the body. He closed his mouth, swallowed, looked nervously over his shoulder, then back at Jardine again.

Jesus Christ, a stroke, he thought. But where was the sister? He jerked into action, running into each of the other rooms, swinging the bat. Nothing. The sister was out.

He went back to Jardine and felt for a pulse. The guy had definitely carked it. What a fucking piece of luck. No investigation.

Springett tucked the baseball bat under his jacket and left through the front door, onto an ordinary street of the struggling class, everyone indoors in front of the TV or hanging out down the DSS.

Springett whistled, bounced on his toes a little. Almost time to go to the public phone near the high school in Princes Hill, wait for Lillecrapp to call in that he'd plugged another two holes in this operation.

Leaving just one big hole.

25

Would he call someone to say where she could be found? Would he come back for her? Liz Redding had wanted to be able to answer yes to either question, but she had seen the transformation in Wyatt, and told herself no. Life for Wyatt was not a matter of expansive gestures, throwing care to the winds for the sake of desire, but of tactics.

She had rotated her bound wrists uselessly after he'd disappeared through the door. Nylon restraining cuffs, lightweight, a little flexible, but nevertheless tough and effective. She'd have to cut them somehow. If a caretaker had lived here, maybe he'd left tools behind when he'd moved out?

She glanced at the mattress, now sad and dusty-looking. What would it be like to sleep regularly with a man who was mostly silent, who lived in some private reserve of the mind where you could never reach him? Whose face—as soon as the striking smile faded—was cruel rather than appealing, the contrast swift and unsettling?

She got to her knees, lifted the little cot onto its side, and tumbled the mattress into the corner. The tubular frame sat on U-shaped fold-down legs, one at each end. By hooking with her feet she was able to close the legs flush with the frame. The cot was more manoeuvrable now; Liz lifted it off the floor and waddled with it into the depressing kitchen.

She hadn't realised how much she relied upon independent action in each arm. With her wrists manacled together around the metal frame of a camping cot, opening drawers and cupboard doors required great patience, strength and dexterity. And a sense of humour, for the cuffs chafed her badly and the cot knocked painfully against her shins. Once when a drawer fell out her hands fell with it before she could stop herself, which dropped the bottom edge of the frame with a solid smack across the toecap of her shoes. She jerked so fiercely on the cuffs in response that the nylon broke the skin and blood began to leak stickily over her fingers.

'Eureka,' she muttered, opening another drawer. A little tenon saw, the blade rusty, the handle held together with black electrical tape. Raising her right foot to support the weight of the cot while she worked with her hands, she flicked aside a file and a packet of nails, then propped the tenon saw blade upright, its teeth outermost, and nudged the drawer home until it clamped the blade in place. This gave her a twenty-centimetre cutting edge. She began to raise and lower her arms, running the nylon link along the saw teeth, the metal cot knocking the cupboard, her thighs. When the link finally snapped open, the bed dropped like a stone, falling from her supporting foot and onto the other again. The pain and regret and humiliation brought on blinding tears.

She recovered, freed her wrists, gathered her things. Wyatt had left both guns, including the little revolver he'd found in her crotch holster. It was a .22 Colt Cobra weighing fifteen ounces, with a six-shot chamber and two-inch barrel. It had weighed slightly more before she'd filed down the hammer and front sight. She put it in her bag. She would have to lose the other gun now that it tied her to the shooting—or at least lose it until she knew who the dead man was and who had sent him and until she had her story right. Then she washed her hands and forearms, getting rid of any telltale powder residue that might be detected by a paraffin test.

There was a heating-oil tank growing out of weeds at the rear of the building. Liz prised open the lid, dropped the gun, heard a dull slap as it landed in sludge at the bottom.

One minute later she was out on the main road, flagging down a bus. In Belgrave she caught a train, express to the city. She should have gone in and reported to someone then. Instead, she went home and made herself a drink. She was in the mood for rebellion and proud lament. She clacked through her CDs, the Chieftains, Sinead O'Connor, the Dubliners, settling on Clannad. She'd have some explaining to do to Internal Investigations and her boss when this was over but, until she knew who she could trust, she wouldn't be going by the book.

Not for the first time, Liz wondered how much the job had changed her, how much she'd lost. Working undercover meant that she sometimes had to remind herself that she was a cop, after all. She rarely spent time at the police complex in Elizabeth Street, and then only entered by way of an underground corridor from a building around the corner. She tended to meet other coppers in pubs, parks or restaurants. The rest of the time she played a drug dealer, a fence, a street girl. It was a nervy double life and it took its toll on her. She was resented by some elements inside the force and only trusted outside it after painstaking groundwork. She encountered cops who didn't like her because

146

she was young, female, got results, had letters after her name, and she encountered crims who would want her dead if they knew what she did for a living. The ID in her shoe had saved her life twice in drug deals that had gone haywire; she'd flashed it, and hard men had put up their guns and backed off rather than kill a cop, but that didn't mean there weren't also hard men walking the streets who had too much to lose or wanted a payback or simply hated cops too much to care about an ID card.

Liz could feel the scotch burning away the tension. At least by working burglary she had a margin of safety that hadn't existed when she'd worked for the drug squad. Dealers, buyers, they feared ripoffs, not cops, and always went armed. They were jumpy people to deal with and the days were long. She'd often worked eighteen-hour days, from 4 p.m. to 4 a.m., setting up a deal and an arrest, then paperwork until 10 a.m.

Not that the drug element didn't exist behind the city's burglaries. All crime flowed to and from drugs these days. The street scum burgled TV sets to buy drugs. White collar addicts committed fraud to feed their habits or pay their debts. The profits from armed robberies and stolen car and art rackets were used to buy into drug distribution networks. And the stakes were so high, the profits so great, the effects of the drugs themselves so destabilising, that crims now were more vicious, more unpredictable than they'd ever been.

Liz Redding sipped her scotch and thought of Wyatt and Jardine. They represented an older, cleaner time and were rapidly going out of date. Jardine's ill-health, Wyatt's sharkish grin and urgency with her on the dusty mattress—she felt an ambiguous regard for each man, she felt closer to them than to her colleagues, her dirty double life. She didn't want to see them caught or hurt. All she'd wanted was to trace the Tiffany, trace it back to the magnetic drill gang.

She guessed she'd taken this latest assignment as far as it would go. Springett had arranged crash courses for her in fencing jewellery and assessing the weight and worth and provenance of precious stones and metals, and had told her to go around the pawnshops, certain pubs and clubs, seeing who was flash, who had money, cars, clothes, who the party animals were. All it had got her were a couple of small busts until finally a whisper that Frank Jardine, poor, sick sod, was the man to see.

It occurred to Liz then that she might be making a bad mistake about Wyatt and Jardine. Never romanticise these bastards: she'd had that drummed into her at briefing sessions often enough. It was entirely possible that Wyatt had ripped off Jardine and Jardine had sent a killer after him. Or that Jardine had discovered who she was, sent a killer to get both of them and keep the Tiffany and the reward money for himself.

She glanced at her watch. Three o'clock. Still a lot of the afternoon left.

She took her own car this time. First, she called on Pardoe, her contact in the insurance company. He was pleased to get the Tiffany back. He smiled at her attentively across his desk, a pale, watery man with red lips and fingers he liked to steeple beneath his chin.

'We're very pleased. The question remains, is this gang getting its information from one of our employees? Have you been able to establish that one way or the other?'

Liz didn't return the smile. She felt jumpy and trusted no one. 'Your people are clean. As far as anyone knows—in here and out in the street—I am a fence who can be trusted, so I'd have heard something by now. Besides, the Asahi Collection wasn't insured by your firm.'

Pardoe nodded gravely. 'Fortunately. That little lot won't be seen again. So, who? I'm not asking for police secrets, you understand. I'm merely curious.'

Her expression neutral, Liz rose to leave. 'We're still working on that.'

She left the building. According to the files, a crowd using an electromagnet and a drill had been active in Victoria way back in the seventies, hitting office safes, banks, jewellers and credit unions. Those men would be almost twenty years older now. Maybe they were back in action. Maybe they'd passed on their know-how to a younger crowd. Even so, they were getting their information from someone with inside knowledge of the alarm systems, holdings and security weaknesses of a range of places.

Her second visit was to Jardine's house in Coburg. The skinny, harrowed, bitter sister opened the door and told her that she was too late. A hard man had come calling at about the time Wyatt was gliding inside her. The sister had been visiting the house across the road, sitting in the front room drinking tea, and seen the man leave her house. The thing was, she hadn't seen him go in, so she'd excused herself and hurried across.

'I found my brother dead,' she said. 'Stroke. He had this look of fear on his face you wouldn't believe. He was literally frightened to death, I don't care what anyone thinks.'

Liz was prepared to believe her. She asked for a description of the man.

'Sort of tall, neat, wore a suit, had this smile on his face.'

'Not Wyatt,' Liz muttered, half to herself.

Jardine's sister sniffed bitterly. 'Ultimately Wyatt,' she said, slamming the door.

Next stop, headquarters.

26

Wyatt had gone looking for Frank Jardine first, on the premise that even a trusted friend, a child, or a nun in a habit could do him harm. If it had been Jardine who'd sent the hired gun to the cafe in the hills, Wyatt was prepared to kill him.

But it hadn't been Jardine. Instead, Wyatt found the grieving, angry sister, who talked about a visitor, about a stranger who'd literally frightened Jardine to death. All Wyatt could do now to find the man behind all this was backtrack the Tiffany, see what names he came up with. He grieved a little, felt a twinge of guilt, gave the twenty-five thousand dollars to Nettie, and flew to Sydney.

He didn't tackle Cassandra Wintergreen at her house, knowing how spooked she'd be there after the burglary. Using information supplied in Jardine's original briefing notes, he staked out her electoral office, half a ground-floor shop, 'Cassandra Wintergreen, Member for Broughton' in a broad, thick-lettered arc across the window glass. Between it and the other ground-floor tenant, a Radio Shack outlet, was a foyer sealed from the street by sliding glass doors.

He waited until late afternoon, went in, looked at the list of tenants: five floors of accountants, dentists, osteopaths and firms with names like Allied Exports Inc.

He looked at his watch: 5.45 p.m. According to Jardine's notes, the nightwatchman would be locking the sliding doors at six-thirty, and Wintergreen always worked late and would let herself out—small pieces of knowledge, but Wyatt and Jardine had built all of their jobs on an accumulation of small details. Wyatt crossed to the stairwell, climbed to the fourth level, found a men's room and prepared to wait.

After the groundwork there was always the waiting—for Wyatt a kind of self-hypnosis in which his senses registered only the essential: the foreseeable dangers, the wild cards, the variables, the job at hand. He knew how to let part of himself disengage while the other part remained wound tight and watchful. He knew how to sit, rest his limbs, and still keep a part of his mind sufficiently stimulated to stop himself from shutting down.

Not that his tooth would have let him drift into sleep. He'd swallowed painkillers and had others in his pocket. According to the pharmacist at the airport, they wouldn't make him feel drowsy, but, just in case, he'd also swallowed a five-grain, heart-shaped Benzedrine. Now he was on edge a little, but he figured that was better than the searing pain in the rotting stump of his tooth.

At six-forty-five Wyatt turned off the power to the ground floor, let himself in the rear passageway door to Cassandra Wintergreen's suite, and went straight to the inner office. Wintergreen, fiddling with the light bulb on her desk lamp, looked up, startled, mouth opening to cry out.

Wyatt clamped his hard, dry palm over her mouth. 'I won't

hurt you, I want information,' he said softly, staring fixedly at her until something in him convinced her to nod and go slack.

He removed his hand.

'About what?' she asked.

'The Tiffany butterfly stashed with your fifty thousand.'

She jerked against him. She smelt musty, stale with old perfume. 'You lousy bastard. Give it back. It was a gift, great sentimental value. And it might interest you to know that that money represents the hard work of my constituents, a downpayment for a shelter for—'

There was only one way to reach a mind like hers. He slapped her left and right and told her that he didn't have the time or the patience for this. 'You are bent,' he said slowly, his face close to hers. 'The Tiffany was stolen from a Melbourne bank in February and there's no way you can account for it legitimately. Your only choice is to tell me who gave it to you. If you don't, I'll hurt you and later tell the media where the kickback came from. Someone will listen.'

He knew that much about how her world worked. He watched her, saw the rapid calculations behind her eyes, still caked with mascara, and finally learned about De Lisle's apartment in Woollahra, his house on the northern New South Wales coast, his yacht, his work in Fiji and Vanuatu.

27

After leaving Nettie Jardine, Liz drove back to her flat in Parkville. 3LO had the Emerald shooting on their four o'clock update. She locked the car and took the Elizabeth Street tram to headquarters, staring out at Daimaru on one side, then the Vic Market on the other. It came down to one thing: who knew she was meeting Wyatt? Pardoe at the insurance company, but he didn't know where or when—unless he'd had a tail on her for the past few days. And why do that if it meant he'd risk losing the Tiffany?

Wyatt and Jardine, but it was clear that they'd had nothing to do with the shooter.

Her skin began to creep. That left someone she worked with in the Armed Robbers. They were often asked to advise on security in banks and building societies.

Superintendent Montgomery? Somehow she couldn't see it. He'd moved to Burglary from Traffic and was dotty about his grandkids. It was with a great deal of reluctance that he sanctioned undercover work, its grey areas, the necessarily blind-eye approach. He would have been entirely happy for his officers to pull in a series of small fish, not hang out for the big ones.

Her creeping flesh would not let her alone. How could she go to Montgomery with her suspicions? She'd shot a man dead and left the scene without reporting it or declaring who she was. Even soft Grandpa Montgomery wouldn't save her from the toecutters once he knew that. She'd be stripped of all rank, suspended, maybe face charges. It wouldn't help that the man she'd shot was probably a hired gun, a potential cop killer. She'd killed him *and* fled the scene, and that just wasn't on.

She mused about the risks involved in this job. There was always plenty to bring you down when you worked deep cover, submerged in a role for weeks at a time. Liz had known young male cops to confuse their roles, get hooked and start sleeping with the women who were always on the fringe of the drug scene, even fall in love with them.

Alcohol. It always flowed freely when crims were putting a deal together.

Money. Pocket a bit on the sly? Tell the Department's paper pushers that your buy money got lost between the crime scene and the evidence safe, blew away in the wind, got unaccountably soaked in blood?

And the danger itself, getting your kicks out of walking a knife edge day after day after night.

And there were plenty of other risks beyond your control: cover blown by a corrupt colleague, cover blown by an incompetent colleague, cover blown by little old ladies who, recognising you, inquired after your mother and asked why you weren't in uniform today.

Liz stepped down from the tram and dodged blatting horns to cross the lanes of traffic and enter the police complex at the top end of the city. She made her way to Homicide, waited for

Ellie Shaw to catch her eye, then mouthed: 'Coffee?'

Ellie was looking harassed. She glanced worriedly at her watch, the clock on the wall. The detectives around her were doing a lot of murmuring into telephones. They looked harassed, too.

'It will have to be quick,' Ellie said, joining her in the corridor. 'We've got a real flap on this afternoon.'

They took the elevator to the cafeteria. Liz paid for coffees and danish and for a vivid moment pictured Wyatt, his hawkish face and his dismay when his tooth fell out.

'You do look a bit tense. What kind of flap?'

Ellie leaned forward. 'That shooting in the hills.'

Well, this was falling into her lap. Liz said casually, 'What about it?'

Ellie leaned forward. 'It was a cop.'

Liz froze, believing her friend was saying that a cop had done the shooting. Her voice caught: 'How do you know?'

'We ran the guy's prints. Lo and behold, he's known to the police, only not as a crim, as a cop. Can you believe it?'

It wasn't difficult for Liz to say wow and widen her eyes. 'What was he doing there?'

Ellie shrugged. 'You tell me. I assumed he was working Burglary because your boss came in to our department to ask about him.'

'Montgomery?'

Ellie shook her head. 'DI Springett. You're on his team, aren't you?'

'Huh,' Liz said.

She hadn't wanted his name to crawl into her mind. He was too close. Springett, a man she didn't like but admired all the same, cold as a fish, utterly detached, a man who asked questions for a living and expected nothing back but lies and evasions. He hadn't seemed to hold her youth, her sex or her education against her. Rather, he'd promoted her, put her in charge of the challenging cases.

Like the magnetic drill gang, guiding and encouraging her every step of the way.

Guiding, that was the key word. Guiding her so that she'd never find them, and if she did get too close he was in a position to head her off or give warning.

Ten minutes later, Liz was watching Montgomery reddening behind his desk. 'You're kidding me.'

'No, sir, I checked. Lillecrapp used to work with Springett on the Vice Squad and—'

'You actually shot him dead and left the scene without reporting it?'

'Boss, listen, there's only one way Lillecrapp could have known about the meeting, and that's if Springett told him and he tailed me.'

But Montgomery was still overcome, holding his plump cheeks between plump, desk-work hands. 'Christ Almighty. How the fuck do I explain this?'

Liz paused, a little puzzled. 'Explain it as it is, sir. A senior officer's been feeding information to crims, sending a killer after a fellow officer.'

Montgomery snarled, looking ugly now, no longer kindly: 'Fuck that. I'm talking about the shooting. The press are going to have a field day when they hear how it happened. You say this Lillecrapp character was about to shoot you? I suppose we can say it looked as if he'd gone off the rails.'

Liz leaned over until she was centimetres from his face. 'And fuck you, sir.' She saw Montgomery blink, make a wide O of dismay with his mouth, and she went on before he could reclaim the advantage. 'A policeman in plain clothes tried to kill me. I'm not making it up. This man can be connected to Springett. This afternoon Springett's been asking questions about the shooting. How did he know so soon?' She stood back again. 'Springett gives security advice to business firms, right? Visits their premises, all that kind of thing?'

Montgomery still looked ugly, his face flushed and sour, but he was listening. 'This had better be good.'

Liz mapped it out for him, how Springett came by his inside information and passed it on. 'He's still in the building,' she concluded.

A weary kind of resolve powered Montgomery out of his swivel chair. 'At least he should be allowed to have his say. Come with me.'

She backed away. 'Why? Where?'

'We're going to see what his reaction is. Every man has the right to face his accusers.'

'Sure. I accuse, he denies, leaving us deadlocked. I say we tread carefully. I mean, he ordered me *killed*, boss.'

'That's your version. Isn't there another reading? For all I know, you're behind it. Maybe Springett and Lillecrapp were getting close to you and that's why you shot Lillecrapp. See what I mean? Come along.'

Liz stared at him bitterly. There was nothing grand-fatherly about Montgomery now. 'Thanks a lot. Stick up for your own, right? Stick up for a senior officer. Stick up for the boys.'

But she went out with him, conscious that she was sounding like a child. On their way to Springett's office she told herself that she needed facts and figures to throw in their faces, not supposition. Who did she know in Records who owed her a favour?

Another thing she told herself: maybe Montgomery's involved.

157

28

It had been sweet while it lasted. Now things were slipping away from Springett, De Lisle fucking them around, Lillecrapp fouling up in that Emerald shooting. He'd made appropriate noises of shock and bewilderment around the Department but soon the suits upstairs would want a word with him about Lillecrapp, and he'd just seen Redding in the building, looking grim.

Better to run than wait for confirmation that they suspected him. Fly out before they could alert the airlines. Find De Lisle before the little shit ran with everything. Get Niekirk to help him.

Springett had documents in his desk that related to each of the magnetic drill robberies. It wasn't incriminating—he was in charge of the investigation, after all. What he shredded were his notes on the alarm systems, security patrols, staffing levels, timetables, the photographs of Wyatt, Jardine and Redding, material that was innocuous on the surface but which he'd be asked to account for if he were arrested.

He had money, false passport and a change of clothes in a gym bag in the bottom drawer of his desk. There was a gym on the top floor; everyone knew that he exercised there once a day, so his walking down the corridor with the bag wasn't going to excite anyone's attention.

Too bad he couldn't risk going home first. There was nothing to incriminate him there but it was a shame he couldn't take his Glock pistol with him. Austrian, 9mm, constructed mostly of ceramic material, it could pass through a metal detector and not set off the alarm. Now it would sit forever under the floor in his study, or at least until developers demolished the house and erected a huddle of townhouses on his block, something that had been happening up and down his street in the past couple of years. The world was full of arseholes.

Springett hadn't gone five paces before Redding and that old fart, Montgomery, stepped out of the lift and began heading toward him. Montgomery raised an arm: 'A word, Inspector Springett.'

Springett knew what about. He slipped his free hand inside his suit coat, wrapped it around the butt of his service .38 and approached them with a friendly bounce in his step, trying to read their faces. But something in him spooked Redding. She shouted a warning and ducked back into the lift. Too bad—she would have made the better hostage. He snatched out the .38, roared: 'Montgomery. I want you. Stop there.'

Instead, the stupid fool turned to run. He wore shoes with flat, gleaming soles. Springett saw a flash of newish leather as the soles failed to gain purchase on the highly polished linoleum, pitching Montgomery face first into a fire extinguisher and then like a sack of potatoes to the floor.

Fuck. Now he had no hostage at all.

Springett ran back the way he'd come, past his office, into a region of dark storerooms, filing cabinets and spare office furniture. He found a corner and waited and thought.

Springett didn't actually hear or see anything, but within a couple of minutes he began to register a shift in the atmosphere. He knew how they'd work it: first, activate the one-way staircase locks on each floor, meaning there'd be no way out if he were to try the stairs; second, man all the exit doors; third, lock each elevator at the bottom of the shaft; finally, make a sweep of the building.

They wouldn't have locked the elevators yet, not this quickly. Springett chose the service elevator because it ran in an unfrequented corner of the building and might be overlooked in the early stages of the hunt. According to the indicator above the doors, it was in the basement. This was the 9th floor. He pushed the button to bring it up to the 9th, then ran down to the 8th floor doors. No one saw him force the safety doors open and step onto the roof of the elevator as it passed the 8th floor and went on up to the 9th.

He waited for five minutes before the elevator was sent to the basement and locked there. He heard the elevator doors being opened. He heard voices and footsteps beneath him as men checked inside the elevator and then through the basement itself, before heading upstairs to continue the search.

Five minutes later, Springett shoved aside a batten in the roof of the elevator and dropped through to the floor. No one saw him cross to the corridor leading to the street at the side of the building. It was only used by undercover officers. People often forgot it was there.

29

Vincent De Lisle was at the courthouse by eight-thirty on Tuesday morning, pushing through the door marked 'Magistrates', saying *bonjour* to everyone.

Saying *bonjour* was an idiosyncrasy he had, something quirky and appealing. He said it fifty times a day and it earned him a grin from those who knew him and alerted those who didn't to look twice and remember.

But this time a woman he privately referred to as an ethnic dyke from the Women's Refuge Referral Service accosted him in the corridor, scowling at the *bonjour*. He knew she was a dyke from the short hair and dangly earrings, and he knew she was ethnic from the ID on her lapel, Toula Nikodemas. 'I want a word,' she said.

'Not now, Miss Nikodemas.'

'It concerns your attitude, Judge.'

'Magistrate. And there's nothing wrong with my attitude,' De Lisle said, sweeping past her. He sniffed the air: furniture polish, sweat and fear. Up ahead he could see a crush of defendants, their families, their briefs.

Toula Nikodemas was at his heels like a harrying dog. 'Last week you put one of our clients in jeopardy when you dismissed her case. One could be excused for thinking you take the view that if a woman is from a non-English-speaking background, she's less deserving.'

De Lisle halted in his tracks. He stopped being a reasonable man with work to do and became a crowder, instinctively pushing into the space around Toula Nikodemas. 'Are you saying I'm biased, racist?'

She backed away and he pursued her, a warning finger in her face. He had small, clean, mild hands that would never pull a trigger or turn on a current, but that did not stop them from being hands that would sign a death warrant if capital punishment were still in force.

'Are you? Because if you are I'll sue you so fast you won't know your hairy arse from your hairy elbow.'

The Nikodemas woman took a deep breath. 'I banish your negativity from my presence. I shall not let you or anyone like you drain away my essence.'

Jesus Christ, De Lisle thought. He turned his back on her and strode into his office.

'Morning Mr De Lisle,' his new clerk said.

De Lisle glanced at her in fury, the incident in the corridor threatening to spoil his day. What was the clerk's name? Sally Something, a bright young thing, and wearing a skirt and blouse, thank Christ. The one before her would turn up in trousers half the time. She saw his fury, and went pale. Oh, hell, De Lisle thought, mustering a smile. 'Well, Sally, your first "Ladies' Day".'

Sally Something smiled dutifully at the old joke. 'I put the intervention orders on your desk, sir.'

It was a massive desk, solid oak, topped with ink-blotched green leather. A spill of pink-ribboned briefs, reports and folders hid the top from view and De Lisle curled his lip. 'You might live like that at home but not in my chambers, missy.'

Sally rushed to the desk. De Lisle saw the heat rising in her face, staining her cheeks and ears red. 'Sorry, sir, I'll just—'

She bent over the desk, tapping everything into order with the flats of her hands. De Lisle eyed her calves, lovely bike-riding muscles tensing under her dark stockings. He eyed her rear and the shape was perfect, but the smack he gave her was carefully avuncular as he moved immediately clear of her with his forgiving wink. 'Not to worry. But in this business, appearances matter, remember that. One of my colleagues has been known to throw a case out of court simply because a barrister appeared before him wearing brown shoes with a blue suit.'

The blush was still there. Sally finished straightening his desk and edged away from it. De Lisle wondered if she was a bra burner. No way was he going to let her get uppity in the job. He recalled that she'd gone to a state school. Her law degree was from ANU, so she'd come a long way, meaning she was probably grateful, unlike some of the private school snots he'd had in the past, who saw everything as their birthright. De Lisle himself was the son of French immigrants. He'd put himself through law at the University of Sydney. He'd also come far, but it hadn't been easy and now he was making up for it in ways young Sally Something couldn't even begin to guess at. The grin was splitting his face and Sally smiled back nervously, without a clue in the world what he was thinking.

'Right,' he said. '"Ladies' Day". Perhaps you could brief me?'

This put Sally on firmer ground. 'Yes, sir. First up is a—'

'Sit down, girlie.'

Sally sat and De Lisle sat and they faced each other across his heaped desk. 'First up is a North Ryde woman whose husband—'

De Lisle spat the word. 'Nationality?'

'Turkish.'

De Lisle shook his head but didn't speak. He scribbled '#1, Turkish' on his pad, then looked up again. 'Skip the next part, I know it by heart. She in some refuge at the moment?'

'Yes, sir.'

'Right. Next case?'

'Same thing, sir. A woman—'

'Nationality, Sally. Nationality is vital.'

'Vietnamese.'

That was interesting. De Lisle pursed his lips. 'You get young Asians knifing each other, demanding protection money from their own kind, but you don't often get domestic violence. It's been my understanding that your Asian values the family.'

He looked inquiringly at his clerk and it was a while before she responded, picking her words carefully. 'I don't know if these things are necessarily culturally determined, sir. Men—'

De Lisle slammed his hand on his desk. 'Hah! Got you! I know where you're coming from, missy.'

She was confused. 'Sir, it just seems to me—'

'Seems? Forget seems. Use your eyes and your ears and look at the facts, that's my advice to you. I've been doing this for twenty years and I know the difference between what things *seem* to be and what they really are.'

'Yes, sir.'

'Look, Sally, we've got how many hearings on the slate today?'

'Ten.'

'Breakdown?'

She looked at her notes. 'Four intervention orders this morning, six thefts and assaults after lunch.'

'Jesus Christ. The same parade of trash day in, day out. Give me the ethnic breakdown of the intervention orders.'

'A Turkish, a Vietnamese: I told you those. Plus another Turkish woman and a name that looks like it could be Serb or Croat.'

'Lovely,' De Lisle muttered, scribbling on his pad. If it wasn't stupid everyday scum it was scum of a different kind, like the rock spiders, boy-fuckers, uncovered during that inquiry he'd worked on last year. Still, something had come out of that, and he'd be reaping the benefits for a long while to come. Meanwhile...

'You book the tickets?'

'I asked Julie—'

De Lisle had to lay down the law again. 'Typists do not make opera bookings for me. I asked you to do that and I expected you to do it. Same as it won't hurt you to make coffee now and then.' He held up his hand as if to stem a tide of protest. 'I know, I know. But just remember this—you're starting at the bottom and when you're at the bottom you have to expect to do some of the shitwork, pardon my French.'

Sally breathed in, swelling her chest, and breathed out again, a protracted sound of grim acceptance. Otherwise, she was silent.

'Speaking of French,' De Lisle said, 'some of my Vanuatuan cases have been very instructive.'

Sally tried to look interested.

De Lisle rubbed his hands together. 'Sometimes they have a nice tribal killing or two lined up for me, the occasional smuggling racket.' He sat back and grinned at her. 'I actually had a firebombing once, in New Guinea. So-called freedom fighters chucked a molotov cocktail through a Nestles depot in Port Moresby, saying what was wrong with milk from a mother's breast?' De Lisle laughed and his eyes dropped to a point below Sally's neck. 'I could do with an assistant,' he said, in a different tone of voice.

'Sir?'

'This circuit court caper through the Pacific. Life would be a whole lot more pleasant if I had an assistant along with me.'

'Yes, sir.'

There was a pause and then De Lisle pushed down on his desk, lifting up and out of his chair with a grunt. 'Well, the courtroom awaits.'

First up, as Sally had promised, was a Turkish woman requesting an intervention order against her violent husband. She was a Muslim and things got off to a bad start when she said she wouldn't swear on the Bible. De Lisle leaned over the bench at her. 'You must swear an oath. How can I accept your word if you don't?'

The woman's lawyer stepped forward. 'Sir—'

De Lisle rounded on him, snarling, 'If she won't swear on the Bible then I will not hear her case.'

The lawyer conferred with the woman. De Lisle watched in distaste. She was swaddled in cloth. Eventually the woman swore on the Bible, her eyes closed and averted. Her hand, he noticed, was a centimetre short of actually resting on the Bible. Still, he let it pass.

Then the evidence was presented. De Lisle had heard it all before. A husband, driven to distraction by something his wife has done or said, tries to sort her out and finds she's slapped a court order on him.

So De Lisle questioned the woman. 'How serious would you

166

say these punches were?'

She would not look at him. 'He broke two of my ribs.'

'Look at me when I'm asking you questions. Did your husband's punches break the ribs, or did you perhaps fall down the stairs?'

Still she would not look at him. It went on like that for ten minutes, a farce that De Lisle had to nip in the bud. He told the woman, told her lawyer:

'Your request for an intervention order is denied. I simply cannot accept the truth of testimony presented to me by a person who cannot maintain eye contact. It's shifty, meaning the testimony of such a person is shifty.' He lifted and dropped a handful of folders. 'I don't doubt that there was some violence involved but I urge you to seek a culturally appropriate remedy.' He looked hard at the woman's downcast face. 'Madam, surely you're aware of the powerfully patriarchal nature of your culture? Clearly violence is an expected outcome of the values of your particular society. There must be some more appropriate course of action you can take. Speak to the old women, the old men, cultural leaders who know what to do in cases like this. Application denied,' he concluded, and busied himself with making notations on the brief while the woman and her lawyer left the court and the murmurs in the background died away.

The hearings dragged on through the day and De Lisle found his attention wandering. Being around Sally all day had stirred something in him. Cassie Wintergreen. He'd go and see Cassie Wintergreen, maybe stay the night if she was amenable. He had a key, so he could let himself in if she wasn't there.

He went home, changed, and got to her house in Double Bay at six. He fixed himself a scotch. More news about the Asahi robbery on the six-thirty news.

She came storming in at seven-thirty, and she looked terrible.

'You bastard. You didn't tell me that gold butterfly was stolen.'

De Lisle waited a moment, spoke carefully. 'How do you mean?'

'How do I mean? I'll tell you how I mean. Last time you were away gallivanting in Vanuatu, it was stolen from my safe, and now I learn it was stolen to begin with.'

'Ah.'

'Yes, *ah*.'

'Cass, listen, did you report it?'

It was Wintergreen's turn to choose her words. 'I don't want to go into the reasons, but I had cause not to report it.'

Well, that was a relief. 'Cass, what makes you think it was stolen.'

'I was informed of the fact, wasn't I?'

De Lisle breathed out heavily, keeping a rein on his impatience. 'I'm listening.'

'There I was, in the office this evening, minding my own business, when who should come calling but the man who burgled me.'

'Huh,' De Lisle said.

'Is that all you can say? This fellow had a bit of style. Not your regular burglar. He wanted a chat, kind of thing. You know, where did I score the Tiffany, so on and so forth.'

Pause. 'Did you tell him?'

Nasty chuckle. 'I guess you'll soon know one way or the other.'

Whore. 'Cass, can I use your phone?'

'Why darling, you've gone all pale.'

De Lisle scowled, wheeled around, made for her study, rapidly mapping his way out of Australia. He'd need to keep the risk of detection and interception down. Ansett to Coffs, first thing in the morning, charter a small jet to Suva, bugger the cost, sail the *Pegasus* back to Vila, where the Asahi stones would be waiting for him.

Meanwhile, though, he couldn't risk going back to his apartment. De Lisle made his phone calls, wondering exactly how he could sweet-talk Cassandra Wintergreen into letting him stay the night.

30

After his run of piss-poor luck, things were beginning to look up, Baker could feel it. Things were beginning to fall into place.

He'd seen the Goldman bitch before lunch the previous day, and this time he'd quizzed her about De Lisle. Just casual, not making a big thing of it, just stuff like: was De Lisle Australian? Did he have a wife and kids? Did he live in a wealthy suburb? Was it true they called him the 'hanging judge'? Why 'hanging judge' when hanging wasn't allowed any more? Did he always have a go at people in court, their surnames and stuff, making them feel small? Maybe he lived on the North Shore? When was he next headed for the Pacific? Stuff like that.

Goldman had acted busy and abstracted again in her little partitioned office. A whole mob of ethnics going yap yap yap outside, waiting to see a duty lawyer, keyboards tapping in the background, printers whining, high heels up and down the corridors, phones ringing, clerks yelling out names and docket numbers and what court to go to. Plenty to distract the bitch but she went cagey on him and wouldn't give him a straight answer. Just, the surname was French but as far as she knew he was born in Australia; she didn't know about his private life; yes, he had a reputation for sternness; 'hanging judge' was just an expression; she was sorry, but she had no intention of discussing De Lisle's movements or where he lived.

She gave him a hard, level look. 'Terry, I hope you're not thinking of doing something stupid.'

'Like what?'

'Like having a go at him.'

'Give us a break,' he'd told her. 'What do you take me for?'

'A man with a grievance,' she said, 'just because another man called him a loafer. A man who was supposed to seek professional attention for a drug and alcohol problem but didn't.'

'Yeah, rub it in,' he said sourly. Then he brightened. 'Besides—' smirking, '—I can't find him in the phone book.'

She smirked back. There wasn't much humour in it.

Okay, if she wouldn't tell him where De Lisle lived, he'd follow the bastard. Baker walked right back down the corridor to the notice board, found the day's listings, saw which court De Lisle was in, and took a seat in the back corner where he couldn't be seen clearly.

He watched through the long afternoon. De Lisle seemed to be in a hurry, rushing through the hearings. He'd been in the sun, Baker guessed, taking in the man's mottled skin—unless it was due to his shitty personality. Entirely possible, Baker decided, watching De Lisle lean forward at one point, practically spitting in some poor bastard's face: 'Mr Patakis, why are you dressed like that?'

The Patakis geezer was about twenty, small, agile-looking, a gold stud in each ear, long black hair, a lot of hair on his bare arms, legs and chest. Probably what was getting to De Lisle were

171

the loose gold satin shorts, the perforated powder-blue workout singlet, the sockless high-top Nikes.

Patakis looked down at himself, briefly brushing one hand down the black hairs on his legs. He looked genuinely puzzled. 'This is top gear, judge. Three-fifty, four hundred bucks worth.' His mouth hung open. Baker knew he was handing De Lisle a line.

So did De Lisle. He snarled, 'It's an insult to come into my court dressed like that.'

Patakis took a different tack. 'I was in court six yesterday, judge—'

'Your worship, thank you.'

'—worship, and my best strides got too creased to wear today. They're at the cleaners.'

'Couldn't you have borrowed some clothes? Spent your ill-gotten gains on a decent wardrobe?'

Patakis' defence lawyer had been watching De Lisle and his client tiredly, amusedly, but in good conscience he couldn't let this go by unchallenged. Baker watched, grinning despite himself, as the lawyer bobbed up from his seat. 'Your worship, I really must—'

De Lisle waved a hand irritably over the courtroom. 'All right, all right. Mr Patakis, you are charged with…'

Baker had tuned the bastard out, thinking about how he'd fix him. An hour later he'd tailed De Lisle to Woollahra. De Lisle didn't stay long. He came out wearing a change of clothes and was in his car and gone before Baker could get the Holden started.

Frustrated, Baker had another look at De Lisle's apartment block. The place looked impenetrable: ground floor apartment, lock-up garage under the building, inside elevator, swipe-card access to the lobby. He tried something that he'd seen work on

TV, pushed all ten intercom buttons, but no one buzzed him in and when a woman said 'Yes?', all clipped and hoity-toity, Baker had gone tongue-tied and backed off.

The next day he'd gone back after breakfast, wearing overalls and carrying a bucket and a squeegee. He waited until a suit in a BMW drove out of the underground carpark, slipped inside the building before the door had closed, and made his way to De Lisle's patio. He knocked. No answer. Cunt, Baker thought. He's gone for the day already.

He lifted the sliding glass door experimentally. Piece of shit: it rose three centimetres out of the track and he had no trouble levering the bottom away and stacking the whole door against the wall.

De Lisle's apartment had the cool, restful air of a place that has been switched off while its owner is away. Baker roamed through the darkened rooms, pocketing a silver ashtray, a Walkman, a gold pen. The broad quilt in the main bedroom bore the impression of a suitcase and one or two shirts and items of underwear had been left behind.

Baker found De Lisle's study, got out the Yellow Pages and began to ring around the airlines, giving the name De Lisle, saying he was confirming his flight details.

He hit paydirt at Ansett.

'I don't understand, Mr De Lisle. We had you on our eight-thirty to Coffs Harbour this morning. That flight has already left.'

'My mistake,' Baker said hurriedly, breaking the connection.

Coffs?

He pressed the redial button, prepared to disguise his voice, but he was connected to a different booking clerk this time. 'You got any spare seats to Coffs today?'

'Let me check that for you.'

He could hear her tapping away. 'Nothing until tomorrow lunchtime, I'm afraid. Shall I confirm that for you?'

It would have to do. Baker told her yes, then asked how much.

'Return?'

'Yes.'

She told him and he wondered if his good luck was running out before it had begun. No way could he afford it. 'When do I have to pay?'

'When you collect the ticket, sir, an hour before departure if possible, otherwise the seat may be allocated to someone else.'

So Baker went to the Cross after dark to earn himself an airfare.

There was a back street where young blokes about thirteen or fourteen would hang out, hopping into the Jags, Mercs, Saabs that cruised by. A few quick blowjobs and they'd have enough to score themselves a virusy needle. But it wasn't the kids Baker was interested in, it was the perverts driving the expensive cars. Unlike normal blokes, who bought their fucks off women inside four walls, the blokes who cruised for kids were usually very rich, usually puny, usually feeling dirty and guilty after.

At least they were easy to roll. Baker simply waited until they were finished and the kid was getting out of the car, then shoved the kid aside, dived in, punched the guy in the guts. The first one he rolled thought Baker was a cop, actually offered two hundred bucks to keep it quiet. Baker accepted. He topped the two hundred up with a cash advance of four hundred from a hole in the wall using another guy's PIN number. The third one had a gold band on his ring finger so Baker threatened to tell the man's wife if he didn't pay up. Another four hundred from the automatic teller machine.

It was hard work and it was tricky and he had to deal with the dregs of humanity in the process. All in a good cause, but he'd hate to make a living out of it, not when there were easier ways to score some cash. Not this much cash though, or so quickly.

Baker went home to bed, feeling dirty, and had a shower. He woke Carol up, really wanting to wipe the evening from his mind. Apart from a bit of soppiness after, it was pretty good.

He got up early on Thursday morning, showered, shaved, told Carol he was going for a job interview, took the bus up to Shopping Town. He had a short back 'n' sides at Hair Today, bought a sports coat, strides, sunnies and an overnight bag from Target, joking 'Tarzhay' with the girl on the cash register, who looked at him with deep boredom. Then he went to the Edinburgh Castle to score some speed, and finally took a taxi to the airport, where he slapped cash on the counter at the Ansett desk and said, 'I believe you're holding a ticket in the name of Baker?'

He'd always wanted to say that.

31

Wyatt had spent all of Tuesday night staking out De Lisle's apartment in Woollahra. By dawn it was clear that the man wasn't coming back. That left the house on the coast.

As the first Coffs Harbour flight on Wednesday afternoon banked over the sea, wing tip angling at a thread of white sand between the breakers and the green hinterland, then levelling for the touchdown, Wyatt swallowed, and swallowed again, to clear his ears. He ran an internal gauge over himself, alighting again on the tooth. There was no pain there but his tongue would not let the jagged edges alone, automatically testing for sharpness and further erosion. He'd eaten fruitcake twenty minutes out of Sydney. The fleshy remnants of a raisin were lodged in the crevice and he knew he should take Liz Redding's advice and have the stump pulled.

These obsessions got him onto the ground and through the terminal building and into a taxi. Coffs Harbour straggled over the ranks of coastal hillocks that rose to the mountains behind, the buildings predominantly white in the sun. White stucco, with terracotta tiles, he noticed, as the taxi weaved through the outskirts of the town. Then the houses gave way to ochred-brick shopping precincts, flashy takeaway places, car yards and pylons, with only palms and spreading overblown tropical flowers to suggest that he was in a holiday paradise. The place had a swagger born of sun-dazed greed and hedonism, not intellect. It was all desperation underneath, as superannuated retirees from the south struggled to keep small businesses alive during the off-season. If you had money and sense you'd build yourself a gangster's fortress back in the hills. Exactly what De Lisle's house looked like, according to Cassandra Wintergreen.

Wyatt got out at a small rental car concession, no more than a transportable hut in the back corner of a Caltex station. He'd reserved the car by phone from Sydney and had documents and cash ready, giving the rental man the name of a motel on the Esplanade. He bought a map in the Caltex shop, drove half a kilometre to a shopping mall, checked De Lisle's address in a call-box phone book. The time was midday and the town was gearing up for the afternoon trade, cars and vans adding to the endless burden of the heavy traffic on the Pacific Highway which split the town from the hills.

On impulse then, Wyatt dialled De Lisle's number. He counted ten rings. He was wondering if that meant that De Lisle was still on his way to Coffs Harbour or had already left when a voice grunted, 'Yeah?'

Wyatt tried to read the voice. Someone unused to the phone? A driver, gardener, bodyguard? He didn't want to alarm the man by hanging up, so loaded breeziness into his tone and said, 'How are you today? My name's Jason, I'm calling from the Pacific Spa Fitness Centre and this month we're featuring—'

'The boss isn't here. Call back another day.'

The phone went dead. Wyatt replaced the receiver and returned to the car. The road he took inland from the coast passed steeply banked banana plantations, crossed a river and skirted a rainforest. There were roadside stalls around every bend, signalled by misspelt blackboards advertising *mangoe's, pineapple's, tomatoe's.*

After twenty minutes on the blacktop he turned onto a dirt road. Here the forest had been cleared a century ago, leaving stands of tall gums along the roadside and pockets of jacaranda and native pine along the creeks and gullies—the only vegetation apart from rich, close-cropped grass, cattle growing fat on it. Here and there Wyatt spotted big houses set into the hillsides, overlooking the Pacific.

The grounds of De Lisle's property suggested broad, cultivated parkland. The house itself sat far back from the road gate, a vast, softly gleaming slate roof showing above glossy trees and tangled, white-flowered creepers. It suggested new money and De Lisle clearly didn't want strangers coming in: a three-metre security fence topped with barbed wire ran around the property and the driveway was barred by a massive locked gate. It was an incongruous structure there in De Lisle's vulgarian landscape—thick twin wooden doors higher than the security fence and shaped to fit an archway. Very old and worn but sturdy enough to withstand a battering ram, they had probably come from a seventeenth-century Italian courtyard, admitting carriages, men on horseback.

Wyatt drove back to Coffs Harbour. In what remained of the afternoon he went shopping, paying over the odds for some items because he couldn't produce the necessary forms and authorisations. Then he slept.

By 5 a.m., one hour before dawn, he was back on De Lisle's

hillside, concealing the rental car behind an abandoned tin hut in the gully below the house, where the looping road forked.

He got out and began to climb the slope to De Lisle's perimeter fence. Dressed entirely in black, he'd also blackened his cheeks and forehead and the backs of his hands with greasepaint from a theatrical suppliers. He'd washed in plain water before leaving Coffs Harbour: no soap, shampoo or deodorant, no chemical odours or perfumes that might betray him. He carried twin oxy-acetylene tanks strapped to his back and a knapsack in one hand. When he reached the fence he stared up at the lumpy shadows that defined the house and the trees around it. A faint light was showing. It didn't mean anything. People burn lights in their garages and on verandahs every night of the year.

Power to the property came from a branch line that finished at a steel and cement pole adjacent to the fence. A smaller line ran from a transformer at the top of the pole to the house itself. If Wyatt could cut the power he'd throw De Lisle's house and grounds into darkness and cancel any alarms or traps the man might have set for someone like him. The dawn hour gave him an extra edge, for it was the hour when people were blurry with sleep. If there were guards, one would be coming off duty tired, his replacement coming on tired.

Wyatt used a thermite charge to destroy the transformer. Thermite burns, it doesn't explode, and he contained the fuse inside half a metre of two-centimetre PVC pipe to conceal the sparks. De Lisle would only know that his defences were being breached if he happened to be standing under the transformer. Nothing would be seen or heard from the house. For a while, at least, they'd assume there was a legitimate power cut.

It was a fifteen-minute fuse. Wyatt heard the transformer blow and saw De Lisle's light blink off among the black trees.

He was ready to cut through the steel fence now, the torch head attached to the tanks, welding glasses over his eyes, heavy gloves on his hands. As soon as the transformer blew he lit the torch head with a sparking tool, opened the valves on the tanks, and turned the petcock on the torch head, keeping the sparking tool in the thin stream of gas until with a whump he had a flame on the torch, cobalt blue in colour, tinged at the edges with yellow. He adjusted the valve on the oxygen slowly until the yellow disappeared. The flame was at its hottest now, and he applied it to the steel. One by one the bars turned orange, then cherry red, parting finally with a spray of molten sparks. Wyatt cut himself a hole big enough to escape through without having to duck or crawl, and went in.

For two minutes then, he rested his eyes. The goggles had protected them from damage but, until his vision cleared, the dawn seemed to consist of fiery red bars across the dark slopes and the darker trees beyond.

His breath, he realised, was wreathing around his head like smoke on each exhalation in the low dawn temperature. He got out a handkerchief, masked his nose and mouth with it, shrugged the knapsack onto his back and began to make his way across the grass to the outer edge of the trees.

Wyatt reached the house unchallenged. He climbed a set of steps to a broad verandah and heard only the softly rising wind clacking the palm fronds against the roof of the house. Then a sudden gaseous stench reached his nostrils and he heard the first heavy rush of urination. A man was standing where the verandah was darkest. In that same instant, he seemed to register that Wyatt was there. He cried out, fumbling at his crotch.

Wyatt head-butted the smear of face in the darkness and disappeared down the steps. Behind him, the man bellowed. Ahead of him were the trees. That's where he'd be expected to run. Instead, he ducked under the verandah and, when two men clattered like horses down the steps and into the trees after him, torches probing, Wyatt slipped back onto the verandah and in through the open door.

32

Wyatt went through the house, rapidly checking each room, automatically noting the gun cabinet bolted to a fieldstone feature wall in the study. De Lisle wasn't there. A short, soft, middle-aged man running to fat, the Wintergreen woman had described him. There'd been enough early light outside the house just now for Wyatt to see that neither of the men hunting for him had been De Lisle. They were the wrong age and size, more like athletes or cops who hadn't lost their fitness.

Bodyguards? It didn't seem likely. They'd made a makeshift camp of the sitting room, leaving cans of beer on the carpet and the smeared-foil remains of microwaved frozen dinners on the coffee table. Apparently they'd been taking turns to sleep on the sofa: cushions piled at one end, a blanket bundled at the other. They'd been waiting for De Lisle by the look of it.

Wyatt was armed only with Jardine's little .32. Otherwise all he had was a rope and a jemmy in the pack on his back. He needed to improve the odds a little, especially if the action moved out into the grounds of the property. He returned to the gun cabinet, splintered open the glass door with the jemmy. There was one shotgun, two rifles with telescopic sights, a little .22 for shooting at rabbits. He selected one of the rifles, a Steyr-Mannlicher SSG, .30 calibre, capable of planting a six-centimetre grouping in a target at five hundred metres, and was just pocketing a box of shells for it when he felt a faint vibration under his feet. The men were crossing the verandah.

'Look at the floor, Manse. I told you, he's in the house.'

Wyatt looked down. The grass had been dewy out there. He'd left the damp evidence of his presence on the carpets of the house. The men entered the hall, tracking him. He wiped the residue of moisture and sodden grass from his shoes, looked wildly for an exit, somewhere to hide until he knew where he could find De Lisle.

There was a place. The main bookcase reached almost to the ceiling. It was heavy, mahogany, with cupboards beneath the shelves and an elaborate carved facia about forty centimetres high across the top. Wyatt climbed the shelves, gently placed the rifle in the hollow space behind the facia board, tumbled in after it.

The men came in a few seconds later. Wyatt heard only a couple of whispers, a scrape of fabric as they moved, a soft swish of feet in the thick wool pile on the floor.

Then a murmur: 'See that? He's armed himself.'

'I don't like this, Riggs. Who the hell is he?'

The man called Riggs said heavily, 'We know it's not De Lisle, we know he's a threat, end of story.'

'Okay, keep your shirt on.'

They were gone again, whispering through the house like ghosts. Wyatt waited for ten minutes, staring at the ceiling as dawn light gathered in the room. When he heard them again they were not bothering to be silent.

'Grab yourself that shotgun. I'll take the rifle. He'll be outside somewhere and I don't intend to tackle him with a .38, not when he's got a rifle himself.'

'Where?'

'How the fuck do I know where? Jesus, Mansell, use your eyes. If he's gone back across the grass there'll be tracks.'

'Yeah, but what then? Have you thought about this?'

'Want me to pull the trigger for you?'

Wyatt gave them a minute to leave the house and enter the trees, then climbed down with the rifle and went hunting for them. Their natural inclination would be to spread out and head downhill toward the road and the gate. Wyatt went uphill, striking away from the house at a sharp angle. He had no intention of trapping himself in the house.

He kept to the trees where there was no dew to betray him, only the springy mulch of fallen leaves. He was looking for a high vantage point, one that gave him a wide-angled field of fire, taking in not only the house but also the lower belt of trees and the open grass stretching down to the gate. In the end he chose a tree. The lowest branches were three metres above his head. He could stand on them and not be seen; lean against the trunk or rest the rifle on a higher branch and pick off one man and then the other.

Wyatt slung the rifle across his back, the strap around his chest and shoulders, then weighted one end of the rope with the jemmy and slung it over the branch, throwing twice before the jemmied end looped over the branch, dragging one half of the rope with it. Using both halves then, Wyatt hauled himself into the tree. When he was comfortable he pulled the rope and jemmy up after him and folded them back into the knapsack.

Of course there was another way of doing it. He could go on

the offensive, running low, weaving wherever the ground was open, coming up on the flank of each man to kill him while he was in a state of surprise, still bringing his gun around.

But there were two men. Which one should he choose first? Which flank, left or right? What if one or both men had anticipated him and changed direction? These were the questions Wyatt had played with as he made his choice. They were remembered from his old training, a drill instructor drumming them into him, Wyatt his best pupil.

This was the better way. He would not let himself be drawn, not break cover. If your enemies don't see you move, they don't know if you've left the area, stayed put or are moving without being seen. It forces them to search in several directions, splitting their forces and their concentration. That's how Wyatt read it. Better to let them make the moves, the mistakes. Better to let them come across open ground than to cross such ground himself.

What he wanted was a clear shot at the man with the rifle, the man called Riggs. Riggs had to go first; he was the one to watch. It would mean giving away his hide in the tree to the man with the shotgun, but Wyatt was counting on the shotgun being out of close range.

He settled in to wait. Now and then he caught brief glimpses of each man at the lower reaches of the trees around the house, but lacked a clear shot at them. They were keeping to cover, not risking the open grass between the trees and the fence.

At other times they tended to disappear for minutes at a time. Wyatt guessed that when they found no return tracks across the grass they would begin to circle back, searching the grounds tree by tree before searching the house again. Wyatt did what he'd done in Vietnam, switched off his mind as if some aura of himself might be sensed by the men who were hunting him. It wasn't something he'd been trained to do; it was instinct and it had got him out of that foul place alive.

The sun was fully above the horizon now, casting long shadows, winking in the dew. Now and then Wyatt drew deep breaths to expel carbon dioxide from his system, to cut down on the natural trembling in his hands. He blinked, trying to distinguish human shapes in the tricky light.

In blinking he seemed to place an apparition in the landscape. He shook his head to clear it. Not an apparition but a man, stepping through the holed fence and hurrying at an absurd crouch up the slope toward the house. He was dressed curiously in a stiff new sports coat and polyester trousers. Wyatt put his eye to the rubber cup on the scope, cutting out extraneous light. The man's haircut looked new and raw and Wyatt could see the damage of cigarettes, alcohol and bad diet in his face. There were two rings in one ear lobe, tattoos on the backs of his hands. He had the nervy appearance of a burnt-out minor hoon dressed for church.

Wyatt pulled back from the scope. If he hadn't, he would not have seen a movement among the trees on the left flank, Riggs sighting the hunting rifle on the man coming across the grass.

Riggs fired and Wyatt fired. Wyatt's shot was clean and on target, punching into Riggs' back, between the shoulderblades. Riggs' shot caught the stranger in the stomach. The third man showed himself then, clearly panicked. Wyatt watched him make short, senseless runs left and right, weaving as he made for the house.

Wyatt let him go. He climbed down from the tree and set out at a lope across the back lawn, flattening against the back wall when he reached the house. He listened, tracking the man through the rooms. Then he went in.

He found the man called Mansell crouched at a window in

the study. He let Mansell hear the oily snap as he worked the slide of the rifle. 'Drop the gun and turn around.'

Mansell turned but he brought the shotgun around with him. Wyatt saw fear and confusion in him and didn't fire. He waited, letting the growing silence work for him. Mansell was mostly a bluffer but Wyatt knew it could be a mistake to push a bluffer too far, for he might then look at himself and become fatalistic or despairing about his inadequacies and decide to take a foolish risk, to cure himself of them.

But finally Mansell sulked and threw the shotgun down and told Wyatt most of the things he needed to know about the magnetic drill robberies. Wyatt locked him in the cellar. There had been a reason to kill Riggs; there was no reason to kill Mansell.

That still left De Lisle unaccounted for. Wyatt doubted that he was still in Australia. The Wintergreen woman had mentioned Suva, Port Vila, a yacht. Wyatt searched De Lisle's study. Rolodex, desk diary, silver-framed photograph of a lovely two-master, *Pegasus* stamped on her bow. Wyatt checked the Rolodex, lifted the handset of De Lisle's phone and tapped in the number for the yacht basin in Suva Harbour. Yes, sir, Mr De Lisle flew in yesterday evening. He immediately put to sea. Estimated sailing time to Port Vila? Two or three days, sir.

On the way out Wyatt went through the pockets of the stranger in the grass. He found an Ansett ticket in the name of Terence Baker. The name meant nothing to him at all.

33

The initial search had failed to find him, and so had a more thorough sweep of the building. Liz had felt time slipping through their hands. Springett had got out somehow, had got himself onto the street and away unobserved. She'd sent a divisional van to his house, waited impatiently for them to call back. 'Not here,' they said. 'The place is shut up.'

She shrugged. It had been a long shot. She went home. Nothing more she could do.

The next morning she gathered all the paperwork there was on Springett and read it in Montgomery's office, drumming her fingers on his desk as she read. Montgomery came in at nine, sporting a bandage and a black eye. 'Make yourself at home, Ms Redding.'

Said with a half smile. She blushed, gathered her files together. 'I think we've lost him, sir.'

Montgomery eased himself into his chair. 'If you were him, where would you go?'

'I wouldn't stay in Australia.'

'You've alerted the airlines?'

'For what good it will do. Rudimentary disguise, false passport, what's to stop him? He'll have an indirect route mapped out as well. France via New Zealand, for example.'

Montgomery nodded for a long time. 'I shouldn't have doubted you.'

'Boss, I want to search his house.'

'I'll come with you,' Montgomery said, enlivened suddenly.

Thirty minutes later, they stood looking around at the walls and furniture in Springett's Glen Iris house. 'No obvious signs that he's bent,' Montgomery said. 'No Merc in the carport, nothing funny inside.'

Liz ignored him. She didn't want Montgomery here with her. It was as though he wanted to atone somehow, be supportive, but he was ineffectual and he was in her way. She sat on the carpet and began to sort through paper scraps from Springett's rubbish bin and documents from drawers in his study, kitchen and sitting room.

His telephone bills seemed to be worth a closer look, several monthly bills from Optus, a quarterly from Telecom. Why the separate Optus account? As far as she could tell, it listed only a handful of interstate numbers. The same numbers cropped up on each bill, except for the most recent, which listed a new number. Liz went to the Touchfone on Springett's desk, called the most frequently called number. A recorded message told her that she had reached the residence of Vincent De Lisle and that he wasn't in right now. She was offered the choice of leaving a message or trying him at the North Sydney Magistrates' Court.

She tried the other number. A harsh, clipped, recorded voice said: 'Niekirk. Leave a message.'

So she had the names of the people Springett was dealing

189

with but not where he was hiding himself. She sighed, glanced around the room. There was something about the floorboards behind Springett's desk chair. One of them was a poor fit.

Then Montgomery broke in upon her thoughts. A heavy smoker, he was fidgeting. 'I'll see you back at the car.'

'Yes, sir.'

Liz stood for a moment. Then, on an impulse, she pressed the redial key and, as Niekirk's cruel voice unwound, pressed the #1 key. If Niekirk's answering machine had a remote access function, one of the keys would activate the messages his callers had recorded. She went through the numbers and it was the #6 key that switched the machine over. There were a couple of hangups, then this: 'It's all falling apart here, better make yourself scarce. I'm going after De Lisle in Vila, collect what's owing, if you want to meet me there.'

Liz grinned to herself. She didn't leave immediately but probed experimentally around the edge of the offending floorboard.

34

Wyatt caught a Pacific Rim flight originating in Brisbane. He could have made the connection in Sydney, but he wanted to minimise all risks, and the advantage of flight 204 was that Brisbane passengers were not required to disembark at Sydney while connecting passengers boarded the plane. If the authorities were circulating his description they'd be circulating it at Sydney airport.

He had a seat in first class, the only seat available on Pacific Rim. It had been a while since he'd been able to afford first class. There had been a time when he always flew first class, a time when the big jobs had been easier, netting him first-class spending power.

Twenty minutes later they were still sitting on the ground at Sydney. Maybe he'd been spotted flying to Brisbane from Coffs Harbour? He flipped through the in-flight magazine, unconsciously running the tip of his tongue over the hole in his tooth. He had a sudden sensation of himself as an ordinary man after all, small and afraid, trapped inside a thin metal skin. Then the pilot announced another fifteen minutes, saying that air traffic above Sydney was clogged and they were waiting for it to clear, and Wyatt felt the tension ebb a little.

In Port Vila Wyatt joined the passengers making for the front exit door of the Pacific Rim 747, stepped out into the air of Vanuatu, and was engulfed by old sensations. They were a compound of remembered people, places, sounds and bitter risks, encouraged into life by the smells of the tropics, the warm humid air blanketing his skin. He was in Indo-China again, a knife-edge time, on the run after snatching a base payroll in Long Tan, ten months before the Prime Minister brought the troops home. It was another four years before Wyatt had gone home. He had a new identity by then, his skills were sharper, and he was even less inclined to lead a straight life.

The passengers straggled across the tarmac to the immigration hall. Three queues formed, a small one for local residents returning to Vanuatu, two longer ones for the visitors, Australian and New Zealand tourists mostly, with a handful of others there on business of some kind.

Wyatt passed through immigration after ten minutes in the queue and collected his luggage. It was a collapsible leather suitcase which he'd bought at Melbourne airport and stuffed with T-shirts, paperbacks and pharmacy items from the shops scattered through the international and domestic terminals. He hoped it would pass inspection. He had nothing to declare but plenty to hide. The customs official who tried to imagine a life from the contents of Wyatt's case would end up with more questions than answers.

But he was waved through to the arrivals lounge. He stood uncertainly near the main terminal exits. It was a small place, consisting of no more than a bank, a duty-free shop and tourist information counter. Well, he'd need money before he could do anything. He crossed to the bank, changed a hundred dollars for small denomination vatu notes, and went in search of a telephone. De Lisle was listed: a number in the high thousands on Kumul Highway.

Wyatt left the terminal. Overhead signs listed various resort destinations: Le Lagon, White Sands, Radisson, Royal Palms, Reriki Island. He began to queue for a minibus but noticed the people ahead of him giving vouchers to the driver. He slipped away from the queue, walked back down the line of waiting buses, and caught a taxi.

It was a battered, newish blue Datsun. Left-hand drive, he noticed. He climbed into the back seat with his case and gave the driver an address twenty houses beyond De Lisle's.

The driver nodded. He didn't speak and Wyatt didn't try to encourage him. There was a small child in the front seat. She had coppery skin and a short, tight furze of red-blond hair. She wore a blue and yellow cotton dress and gazed at Wyatt solemnly as her father drove out of the airport and along the narrow, pitted six-kilometre stretch to Port Vila.

Wyatt had washed up in central and southern Africa when he left Indo-China, smuggling emeralds and De Beer diamonds. Something about the roadside commerce on the drive to Port Vila reminded him of Africa: the plain, flat-topped general stores painted white or left the colour of cement; the Coke signs, the palm trees and vines, the skin-and-bone dogs sniffing the dirt, the people themselves, bare-footed, dressed in bright simple cottons, watching the cars from shopfront verandah steps. But there was a torn, damaged look to some of the trees, a collapsed wall here and there, roofing iron weighed down with heavy stones as though frequent storms lashed the islands. Then the road climbed briefly and Wyatt found himself looking down into the cramped compound of the main prison. Meanwhile the taxi continued to brake and shudder on the broken road and Wyatt's tooth ached.

The road flattened again as it entered Port Vila. The taxi crawled along the narrow main street, past small banks, cafes and all-purpose stores. Wyatt glimpsed the harbour between the buildings, twenty or thirty moored yachts and Reriki Island farther out in the bay. A bloated, rusting shape at one end of the island materialised as a wrecked ship belly-up on the coral. Rusty inter-island cargo ships were moored at various points along the waterfront. For all the taxis, pedestrians, noise and colour it was a strangely still, flat-spirited place.

The taxi began to chug uphill, leaving the buildings and warehouses behind. The highway had been sliced into the hillside and Wyatt had a sensation of burial, the deep edges appearing to fold in on the taxi.

Then the road levelled again and ran parallel to a strip of costly cliff-top mansions overlooking the bay. The taxi drew into the kerb a minute later. The driver pointed. 'We are here, sir. One thousand vatu please.'

There was no footpath, only a track in the dirt. Wyatt saw high fences and hedges, tiled roofs squatting low behind them. He paid the driver, got out, and walked back to De Lisle's house, narrowing his eyes against the glare.

Three metres high, toughened steel, looped with razor wire, protected by alarms and sweep cameras, just like De Lisle's place in the hills behind Coffs Harbour. Wyatt checked both corners at the front of the property: the fence plunged downhill to the water on each side of the house. Midway along the road edge was a locked gate that led directly to a short driveway that looped past the front door.

There were three ways in: scale a ladder and throw a bag

over the razor wire, assuming he could find a ladder and a bag; cut his way through the steel mesh, assuming he could buy what he needed in Port Vila and do the cutting without being seen from the street; break open the lock on the gate, assuming he could get his hands on something like a tyre iron. And assuming he could evade alarms and cameras when he did get in. Wyatt prowled along the fenceline again, whistling softly, checking for dogs. There didn't appear to be any.

He crossed to the other side of the road to a bench along the main wall of a tiny market. Judging by the Suva harbour master's estimation, De Lisle wouldn't be arriving for another twenty-four hours. A quick check of this part of the Kumul Highway told Wyatt that there were no hotels or motels nearby, so where could he station himself to watch and wait?

The island. It faced across to Port Vila and the cliff-top mansions on the Kumul Highway. Wyatt hailed a passing taxi and two minutes later he was in a small dirt parking area near the wharves at the bottom of the hill.

He could see the island clearly, a humped shape in the centre of the harbour, fringed with tropical trees, cabins on stilts just above the waterline. Two more rows of cabins were set further back and there was a large complex at the centre which Wyatt guessed housed offices, bars and dining rooms. There was also a roof among the trees at the peak of the hump. He'd read in Pacific Rim's in-flight magazine that it had been the British Commissioner's residence during the period of Condominium Government.

The Reriki Resort minibus had already delivered its load of passengers from the airport. Wyatt joined them under the shelter at the edge of the wharf. One or two looked at him curiously. He nodded and half smiled, not because he wanted to and they had shared a flight together but because it was expected of him and he didn't want to draw attention to himself. Then the ferry drew in and they filed aboard.

The turnaround took thirty seconds, the crossing to the island two minutes. Wyatt examined the moored yachts keenly. Sydney, Southampton, Vancouver, Catalina Island. T-shirts, towels, shorts and underwear were pegged to dry on the rigging of the smaller yachts. One man was repairing a sail. Two couples were playing cards on a fast-looking red trimaran. The men wore shorts and beards, the women bikini tops and sarongs. There was an idle, easy assumption of privilege in the way they were indifferent to the ferry and the lives being led beyond the nearby harbour front.

Wyatt's case was collected and he climbed the steep path to the main building. There were a dozen people waiting to be checked in. Wyatt pushed through to the desk, smiling apologetically. 'I haven't booked. Are you full?'

The clerk smiled at him. 'Off season, sir. No problem.'

Wyatt slipped to the back of the line. A woman wearing a flower in her hair came out from behind the desk and showed him to a small waiting area. A minute later a waitress came by with a tray of drinks. It was the way things were done here, so Wyatt took a tall frosted glass of something and thanked her. He didn't drink it. His case, he noticed, sat with a stack of luggage at the porter's station, a tiny wooden stand like a pulpit in an impoverished church. Then he was called to the desk and he handed over his false passport and filled out the registration form and collected his key.

The porter showed him to number five, in the first row of cabins behind those at the waterline. Wyatt liked what he saw. The door opened onto a small alcove consisting of a wardrobe, refrigerator and handbasin. There was a bathroom off to the left. A doorway ahead of him led to a large main room furnished with a queen-size bed, cane lounge chairs and glass-topped coffee table, desk, television set, bedside phone and reading lamps, prints on the walls. The airconditioning hummed softly. A ceiling fan hung motionless above the bed. Wyatt turned the fan on, the airconditioning off, and checked under the bed, inside the wardrobe and behind the shower curtain.

Then he called room service and ordered a gin and tonic. He took it out to the balcony. A purple evening light was beginning to soften the edges of things. He eased his long trunk and legs into a cane chair and watched the ships' and harbour lights wink on, the water darken and finally go black. At De Lisle's house across the harbour there were no lights burning and the private dock was empty.

35

The resort was deceptive. When dawn broke the next morning, Wyatt set out along the paths that stitched the parts of the island together, and found orderly rows of cabins stretching back up the hillside, concealed from sight by coconut palms, canopies of flowering vines, and small, almost comical trees which resembled stick insects, their rows of exposed roots like flexing legs.

Then the path gave way to a walking track which led through dense tropical growth as high as houses on either side of him. The soil felt springy under his feet and Wyatt enjoyed the sensation of his solitary state, the only man alive to see the sky brighten and smell the air grow steadily warmer and sweeter. There were spiders the size of his hands spread in ambush in dewy webs along the smaller corridors between the trees. Wyatt was reminded by their patience of his chosen life and reminded by their task that he could not afford to sit and wait, he was here to attack.

It took him only thirty minutes to map the island in his mind. He wound his way back by the stony beach and up a crumbling cliff path to the dining room and ordered breakfast. He ate muesli for its bulk and energy, grinding only with the teeth on the right side of his face. But chips of nuts and grain caught in his broken tooth, the gum surrounding it seemed hot and swollen to his flickering tongue, and he resolved to have the tooth yanked.

Wyatt returned to his cabin with a handful of old newspapers and magazines. He sat in a cane chair, his feet on the rail, and read, and watched De Lisle's dock across the water. A rustbucket coastal steamer glided past at the midpoint of the morning. One of the island-hopping yachts put out to sea. The ferry ploughed unvaryingly between the island and the mainland, water taxis crisscrossed the harbour, directed by the random needs of their passengers, and tourists heaved back and forth in the water adjacent to the island's only strip of sand, skinny legs dipping and rising as they worked the paddleboats.

But no De Lisle. His house remained shut up, his dock empty.

A sensation of vulnerability crept through Wyatt. His tooth. He became convinced that pain existed and was growing worse. That and the helpless need of his tongue to explore the contours of the tooth stump and his engorged gum were dangerous distractions. He felt that he was not concentrating effectively. He told himself that even if the yacht were to dock now, De Lisle was unlikely to turn around and leave within minutes of arriving.

Wyatt sealed his cabin against the rising heat and walked down to the ferry. What he disliked about going up against an individual like De Lisle, for reasons of revenge as much as for gain, was a sense of slippery control over events. Wyatt never attempted anything that wasn't workable, but everything about this—from the foreign location to his lack of background intelligence on the man, his house and his habits—was too loosely assembled. On the other hand, Wyatt wanted some of De Lisle's accumulated cash, and he badly wanted to even the score for Jardine's death and the attempted shooting in the cafe in the hills. And, if he cared to admit it, even the most workable plans contained within them an addictive element of craziness.

The ferry docked. Wyatt clambered over the aluminium bow and onto the concrete steps of the wharf. A man rang a bell on the handlebars of a rental scooter. Wyatt smiled briefly, shook his head. He reached the main road and looked along it to the downtown shops. On the harbour side was a narrow tattered strip of parkland set with market stalls. On the opposite side a cracked footpath ran past dozens of small shops and cafes. Wyatt crossed the road. He knew he'd feel oddly exposed yet herd-like if he were to walk past the market stalls to get to where he was going.

It had been halfway acceptable, his arrangement with Jardine. His main doubt had been that it had a robbery-on-consignment aspect to it. Unless the take was hard cash, they both had to wait on someone else to get a cash return for them. In the old days, Wyatt had liked to use a 'banker' for his hits. The banker knew nothing about the job, who was pulling it, or how his money would be spent. Wyatt had absolute control of the investment, finding the best professionals each time, outfitting them, dividing the take afterwards, then paying back the banker twice what he'd invested. Wyatt had liked the security of that arrangement. But he was increasingly unable to control the quality of the men he worked with and the banker was eventually named in a Royal Commission and fled the country.

Wyatt glanced into each shop as he passed it. Behind the glass and neon and the global brand names the shelves were sparse, the goods costly, shopkeepers and shoppers a little defeated-looking. The air trapped between the buildings was heavy with diesel fumes.

Wyatt thought that if he could build up his fortunes again he should construct a new identity to go with it, paper by paper until it had the texture of reality—tax records, bank accounts, passport, income documents, property deeds, investment certificates. If he had genuine investments he could live off the income.

'And do what for the rest of the time?' he muttered, his eye caught by a sun-faded molar depicted on a dentist's sign down a narrow alley behind a cafe. An arrow pointed up a flight of rickety steps.

Wyatt took the stairs carefully. He'd been taught, and he believed, that a man is at his most vulnerable on stairs. The terrain is awkward, you're an easy target from above and below, the banister hems you in.

But it was only an ordinary staircase to a suite of small, airy rooms above a fishing tackle shop. The dentist was alone at a reception desk and she greeted Wyatt with a keen smile that went straight to his jaw. 'Poor, poor man,' she said, in softly accented English. She was round and sympathetic and took him by the arm.

'You can do me now?'

She gestured at the empty rooms, the open doors. 'Of course.'

She pushed him into the reclining chair and clicked on the silvery light above their heads. Then she drew on latex gloves. Wyatt told himself that he needed latex gloves for what was ahead of him.

'Open wide, mister.'

Her hands were swift with the pick and mirror. She smelt of coffee and mango; his shoulder merged with her pliant thigh. She stepped back, almost reluctantly. 'It must come out.'

'Yes.'

'I will inject you. You will have numbness for several hours afterwards, maybe a little swelling to spoil your beauty, but very little pain.' She touched his jaw lightly, grinning at him. 'I would not want to see you in pain, mister.'

His smile came easily. She was a balm to his risky life. Laughter bubbled from somewhere deep inside her. The University of Adelaide, according to a framed degree on the wall. Wyatt wondered what those dour Europeans had made of her.

At one point her telephone rang and she went into the other room. He pocketed a pair of latex gloves and returned to the seat, hearing her cajoling someone to come in and see her, don't delay.

When he left her twenty minutes later, Wyatt needed a hand on each banister to get down the steps. There was no pain and no real disorientation, only the sense that there should be. He started out for Reriki. After five minutes he doubled back and went into the tackle shop beneath the dental surgery. He pointed to a long, slender knife, not trusting himself to speak, and laid out money on the counter. He didn't touch the knife himself, but carried it out with him in a paper sack.

He was back in his cabin by four o'clock. De Lisle's yacht had berthed while he'd been away. Everything about the tiny fat figure going up and down the steps between the dock and the house on the cliff top suggested panic.

36

When De Lisle returned to the house after collecting the tartan suitcase on Reriki, Grace, his hi-Vanuatuan servant, was waiting for him at the top of the steps, holding a silver tray. She'd placed a white calling card in the centre of the tray. De Lisle had trained her in a thousand little rituals and courtesies. Today she was staring at him and something about it made him uneasy. For two years she'd refused to meet his eye, as though he were an unknown guest in the house, not the man who came into her room in the servants' quarters night after night. So why the sudden confidence?

De Lisle opened the card. It was from Walter Erakor and said simply, 'Meet me in Ma Kincaid's Eating House at five this afternoon'.

De Lisle dismissed Grace and fixed himself a drink. He wondered what Erakor wanted. Walter was a jungle bunny—born on the island, a law graduate of the Sorbonne, but still a jungle bunny. De Lisle worked with the man whenever he was in

Vanuatu, mainly routine circuit court cases, but he'd also called on Walter Erakor's help in getting around the kinds of legal loophole matters that required a greased palm in the local judiciary. Erakor had saved De Lisle time and trouble in setting up holding companies, bank accounts and real estate transfers. Did the man want a bigger slice of the pie? De Lisle hated dealing with the blacks. He wished he'd been in Vanuatu before Independence, when there'd been plenty of decent Frenchmen in the public service.

De Lisle checked his watch: almost five. Too late to deposit the Asahi Collection jewels in a safety-deposit box. He stashed the tartan suitcase temporarily in the safe in his bedroom and decided to walk to Ma Kincaid's. It was downhill all the way and it would help keep him fit. He could get a taxi back.

A ceaseless stream of badly tuned cars and vans passed him on the way down the hill, Port Vila's version of rush hour at the end of the working day. De Lisle felt safer at the bottom of the hill. The road began to level out at the diving school and soon he was walking on a proper footpath. Today was market day. One or two stallkeepers were selling cowrie shells, fresh coconuts and bright, flimsy, cotton dresses in the parking lot for the Reriki Island ferry. Most of the small businesses had shut their doors but the Vietnamese supermarket was still open, run by the descendants of plantation workers brought to Vanuatu by French planters in the 1920s.

De Lisle trudged through the humid late afternoon. There were more market stalls now, crowding the footpath. No one was buying and the only people looking were elderly tourists from a cruise ship moored in the harbour. De Lisle saw them picking over dyed coral, shell necklaces, carved animals. He supposed they'd buy something. They generally did. They would tip, despite what the guidebooks advised. Some of the locals would accept it, too, as though they hadn't read the guidebooks that claimed they'd be offended and embarrassed to be offered a tip.

It was dim and cool inside Ma Kincaid's. Ceiling fans stirred the air, a couple of tourists and sailors sat at the bar, some local Europeans ate at the tables. De Lisle nodded at one or two of them. They were French and had stayed on after Independence. A table of yachting types in the far corner were speaking English. De Lisle listened: Kiwis and Australians, five men and a woman. De Lisle was betting that they were on the run from something shady. They might stay here for a few months before moving on. One or two of them might even stay permanently and open the kind of import–export business that helped to launder cash and offered ways of smuggling anything from coconut soap to arms or New Guinea cannabis and pink rock heroin from Thailand.

Walter Erakor was waiting for him in a back room. De Lisle didn't like the look on the man's face. Erakor seemed to be suppressing glee at bad tidings and doing a poor job of it.

'Well?' De Lisle demanded.

It bubbled out of Erakor. '*Bonjour*, my friend. I'm afraid you must flee the island. Tonight, tomorrow, you must leave.'

De Lisle went still. He decided to play it straight. 'Leave? Why? I just got here. There's work to do.'

Walter tapped the side of his nose. 'A little bird tells me.'

'Tells you what?'

'You are under investigation.'

De Lisle didn't reply immediately. He continued to stare at Erakor. Surely the Australian authorities weren't onto him, requesting his extradition? Not so soon. And certainly not when the island was riddled with Australian con-men, thieves and dealers straight out of 'Australia's Most Wanted' on TV. He looked at his watch. He had time. Wheels would be turning slowly back home.

He said at last, 'Who's investigating me?'

'Vice police.'

'*Vice* police?'

'Your servant, Grace—her father has lodged a complaint against you.'

'She's an adult, for Christ's sake. She knows what she's doing.'

Walter Erakor leaned over the table and said very quietly, 'But she was under age when she first went to work for you.'

'I didn't know that. Besides, it's her word against mine.'

'Maybe so, my friend, but her father is a chief, you know.'

Chief, De Lisle thought. A man who ran a rusty Mazda minibus, that's all he was.

'A certain zeal has entered the investigation,' Erakor continued. 'The police have asked for warrants to search your bank records and other business dealings.'

De Lisle leaned forward, hissing. 'You bastard. Grace isn't the issue, you're just using her as an excuse. You want my money. You bastard.'

Erakor shrugged. 'I'm not in charge of the investigation.'

'But you told them about my bank holdings, right? You and your crooked cronies want to rip me off, seize my deposits, under-declare what was there and keep the rest for yourselves. I know how it works.'

Erakor gazed at him levelly. 'I'm giving you a chance to escape.'

De Lisle changed tack. 'Have you issued the warrants yet? Can't you do something to rescind them? Walter, old friend—'

Walter Erakor was flat and hard and there was no friendship in him. 'We issue them tomorrow, maybe the next day.'

Relief flooded De Lisle. 'I need twenty-four hours, maybe less. I need to be here when the banks open in the morning.'

Walter Erakor began to smile. It was a beam that said he could delay the warrants in return for a cash consideration. De Lisle groaned. He looked at his watch. Just as well the yacht was ready to put to sea. God, why hadn't he given the Tiffany to Grace instead of that Wintergreen slag? None of this would have happened.

He groaned again. Who was he kidding? Keeping Grace sweet wouldn't have stopped Erakor and his mates getting greedy. They must have loved it when Grace showed up with her nose out of joint, giving them the excuse they needed.

He looked at Erakor. 'How much?'

37

It had to do with context. If you see a workman among a slouch of workmen, that's all he is. Similarly, you don't look twice at an airline passenger aboard a plane-load of passengers, not when you've got your mind on more pressing matters. But when one of those passengers, standing alone in the Port Vila terminal building, held his head tilted at a certain angle, Niekirk knew that he'd seen him before. A minute later the answer came to him: Wyatt, meeting the fence on a park bench in Melbourne.

Where was Springett? On the island? Coming by a later flight, a different airline?

Niekirk, keeping well back in another taxi, tailed Wyatt to a cliff-top mansion on the other side of the harbour. He saw Wyatt get out and check casually for outside cameras and sensor alarms. Later he tailed Wyatt to the ferry stop for the island resort across the harbour.

He recalled that there had been a few passengers in first class when he boarded in Sydney, and the man had been among them.

The surveillance photograph had shown only the man's inclined head, animated by the woman's company, and his shoulders. Now Niekirk had a clearer image of him: hooked, pitiless kind of face, black hair pushed indifferently off his forehead, tall and loose in the frame, a habit of touching his jaw every few minutes. The guy had a poor dress sense for the tropics: trousers, shoes, long-sleeved shirt rolled back at the wrists. Niekirk was wearing yellow shorts, sandals and a 'Life's a bitch, then you die' T-shirt so that he'd melt in with the Australian yobbos who populated Asia and the Pacific.

Niekirk couldn't watch two places at once. He'd come here for De Lisle, so he went back to the house on the cliff top and slept fitfully through the night in the passenger seat of a rental car. He had a story ready, but no one came near him.

The first rattling diesel motors of the day woke him at five-thirty. He crossed the road. The house still had its shuttered look; the yacht still hadn't docked.

Niekirk drove down to the wharf, bought coffee and sandwiches, and returned to his watch over De Lisle's house. He wondered what Riggs and Mansell were doing. Maybe they'd shot each other by now. When told what De Lisle was up to and that there'd be no more jobs, Riggs had gone very still, dangerously quiet, and Mansell had blustered. Neither man felt ready to quit: 'Not when we're onto something good,' Mansell said. The only analogy Niekirk could think of was grief: it was as though a loved one had been snatched away and they wanted a sense of closure before they could put the grief to rest. He'd given them the address of De Lisle's house in the hills behind Coffs, told them they might pick up some goodies for themselves there, told them to keep De Lisle on ice if he happened to show up.

Niekirk saw the shutters open at three o'clock in the afternoon. He crossed the road and stood where he could see down between the houses to the water. The yacht had come in. As he watched, a water taxi called in at the dock and De Lisle stepped aboard. He saw it sweep among the moored yachts and tie up at Reriki Island. Certainty began to settle in Niekirk. Wyatt was here to meet De Lisle. Wyatt and Jardine had been fencing stuff on behalf of De Lisle all along.

He sweated it out, only relaxing when he saw the water taxi skimming back across the water, De Lisle upright in the back. When De Lisle got out, he had the tartan suitcase with him. So, the island was the drop-off point.

Niekirk went back to his car. But maybe Wyatt had been ripped off, too, and was here to even the score. Niekirk sat there for an hour, sticking to the vinyl seat, baking in his glass and metal cocoon. He was still there late in the afternoon when De Lisle appeared again, walking this time.

Niekirk began to hate it all. If he shadowed De Lisle on foot, he risked losing him if the little shit got picked up by a vehicle later on. If he took the car, there was the hassle of traffic and parking in the narrow streets. In the end he got out and tailed De Lisle on foot. De Lisle wasn't carrying anything, so at least he wasn't on the run with their stuff.

De Lisle made for a cafe called Ma Kincaid's. Niekirk was watching it from under a Cinzano umbrella across the road, face disguised by a straw stuck in a frosty glass of iced coffee, when Wyatt appeared from an alley behind Ma Kincaid's. He had his mouth open, his tongue apparently exploring the back of his mouth, and he was carrying a parcel and seemed pleased about something. Niekirk liked none of it.

38

Wyatt didn't hear anything until it was too late. He was on the narrow balcony, watching the cliff-top house across the water as the sun weakened behind the mountains, waiting for full dark so that he could cross to the mainland and tackle De Lisle, and heard nothing above the chopping blades of the ceiling fan in the room behind him, the mutter of the island's generator, the scrape and rattle of wind in the palm tree fronds, the band thumping in the dining room a short distance away, the men and women toiling up the path from the ferry, spectres with white teeth, shirts and dresses, drenched in duty-free lotions. And now and then his tongue flickered over the hole torn inside his upper jaw. Deep, raw, salty; a dull, receding ache; a huge relief. So all of Wyatt's senses were distracted and he was unprepared for an attack from behind.

Until he heard a slick, oiled, double click, the slide of an automatic pistol jacking a round into the firing chamber. The voice came from inside the room; just inside the open sliding door, was Wyatt's estimation. He stiffened his arms on the chair.

'Uh uh. Wrap your arms around yourself as if you were cold. That's it. Now stand, turn, come back here into the room, nice and easy, all the time in the world.'

Wyatt tracked the voice. The man was retreating farther into the room. He read the voice: arrogance, certainty, experience, wasting nothing.

Wyatt hadn't wanted a light behind him as he waited on the balcony and so the room was dark, illuminated only by the green LED time display of the bedside clock. It was reading 20:05 and picked out the man's face in a play of pallid cheeks and eye sockets and solid bones. The dark pistol gestured: 'On the bed. Now, place both pillows on the floor—I said place, not throw.'

There was a pause, the man satisfying himself that Wyatt hadn't secreted a weapon under the pillows. 'Now I want you flat on your back, head touching the bedhead, hands clasped under your head.'

Wyatt complied. It was not a position he'd want to maintain for long. He knew his arms would begin to ache. He was too rigid, too awkward, placed so that he'd signal any intention to go on the offensive long before it could do him any good, and the gunman was counting on that.

'What's your connection to De Lisle?'

'Nothing. Never met him.'

'You've been selling stuff for him.'

'No.'

'You were photographed with Frank Jardine and a fence back in Melbourne. You were trying to offload a Tiffany brooch for De Lisle.'

'Not for De Lisle. For myself.'

As Wyatt's eyes adjusted further to the dark, he saw a sinewy

212

frame, a thick tangle of nondescript hair, and dispassionate eyes set in a cold face, facial lines like cracks in cement. Was this the man who'd frightened Jardine to death? He imagined the man playing with Jardine, resting on his friend a set of dark eyes that would have seemed bottomless and unendurable.

'I stole the Tiffany,' Wyatt said. 'I found out later I'd stolen it from someone De Lisle was shagging.'

It was language he hoped the man would appreciate. The planes of the man's face shifted, became less controlled, and the voice lost its metallic edge as emotion moved it: 'He gave it to some sheila? Jesus Christ.'

As if he were talking to himself. Wyatt shifted a little, crossing his feet at the ankle, moving his hands until they clasped the back of his neck, not his head.

The man stiffened automatically, his gun arm tensed, but Wyatt could see that his attention was mostly inwards, on De Lisle.

'Now he's getting ready to run,' Wyatt said, keeping the focus away from himself. 'You do all the dirty work, he fucks up and still reaps all of the profit.'

The man laughed. 'Keep guessing, pal. You're history anyway. Reach one hand over and turn on the bedside light.'

Wyatt saw the man step back into the corner as the light came on, then pull on the drawstring that closed the curtains over the sliding insect-screen door leading to the balcony. Finally the man reached down dreamily, picked up a cushion, and advanced on the bed. There was no suppressor on the pistol, so a cushion, interspersed at point-blank range, was the next best thing. Wyatt said, to distract the man again:

'How did you get a gun into the country?'

'Had a permit, didn't I.'

A cop? The Niekirk character Mansell had told him about?

Wyatt said, 'I can help you get De Lisle.'

'Forget it,' Niekirk said, stepping forward.

Wyatt sidearmed his water glass across the space between them. Niekirk lifted the tip of his gun, let the glass sail by. That was his mistake; it granted Wyatt one more second of life. He used it to yank on the electric flex of the bedside lamp and in the sudden darkness he rolled away from the snapping pistol, over the side and onto the floor.

He scrabbled along the carpet to the end of the bed and waited a moment, letting his eyes adjust to the darkness again. Niekirk fired twice, placing his shots, keeping them low, but he didn't have a target, only intuition and hope.

Wyatt tensed. He had marked a passage between the cane armchairs to the balcony, where the glass door was open and only a curtain separated him from the night. He sprang from the gap between the bed and the wall, streaked low across the room.

Niekirk had him now. He snapped off three more shots. Too quick, too careless. Glass broke in the side window of the balcony. He paused, waiting for Wyatt to fumble at the curtains, to silhouette himself and present a solid target into which he could empty his clip.

Wyatt read his intentions. Staying low, he picked up the glass-topped coffee table and threw it, aiming at Niekirk's knees. Niekirk went down; there was another shot.

Lights and voices started in the darkness. 'I heard a gun.'

'Come away, dear.'

'I tell you, someone shot a hole through our window.'

Then there were other voices, other lights.

'Call security.'

'What number?'

'I don't know, do I? Use your brains, woman. Call reception.'

214

'There's no need to take that tone.'

Behind Wyatt, Niekirk was rolling onto one hip, patting the carpet for the gun. Wyatt reached one hand over his shoulder to the space beneath his collar, between his shoulderblades, and drew and threw the fishing knife. He wanted the throat and got it, the blade spearing Niekirk's windpipe, taking away his voice, leaving him with only the froth and rattle of his useless breathing to keep him company as he died.

Wyatt left through the balcony door and slipped over the side, a shadow among the shadows.

39

He edged down the terraced garden slope, dodging fleshy spurs, exposed root cages and stiff vine tendrils. The island's generator continued to throb through the night, the only calm point in a place of alarmed cries and running feet and jerking torch beams. Once or twice he froze; but there were security guards and paths and lighted areas to get around, so he moved again, showing himself this time.

Shouting, running, waving his arms to confound the searchers and witnesses: 'The shots came from that room…I saw someone over here…Careful, he's armed…He ran up the hill…'

The row of cabins at the water's edge sat on stilts. When he was clear of the confusion above him, Wyatt took shelter under the cabin closest to the ferry mooring, his feet ankle deep in seawater. The ferry wasn't there. He could see it across the harbour, waiting at the little wharf on the mainland. It wouldn't be in a hurry to return to the island. The traffic this late at night was all one-way, guests returning from the mainland casinos.

Wyatt considered his options. He didn't want to swim. His shoes would protect him from the spines of stonefish as he waded into the water but the island was ringed with coral and the guidebooks warned against sea snakes, cone shells and sea urchins. He imagined the coral tearing open his skin, his blood attracting sharks; he imagined the numbing pain as venom shut down his nervous system. These were fears he could only live with in the daylight, when he could see what was coming.

There were plenty of small boats on the island. Half a dozen aluminium dinghies powered by outboard motors were moored to the jetty. A paddleboat and snorkel hire concession operated from a shack at the edge of the only stretch of sand on the island, just beyond the jetty.

Wyatt slipped out of the sheltering cabin and ran half-crouched toward the jetty. Then he stopped, flattening himself on the mossy wetness of the stone shelf that led into the water. Figures were loping along the jetty. Wyatt watched as they peered into each dinghy. A moment later they were gone, leaving two men to continue the search of the hire boats. Finally a security guard growled a few orders, climbed into one of the dinghies and sped away across the black harbour, trailing phosphorescence and a high, small-motor whine.

Wyatt crouched ready to run again but was warned off a second time. Somebody had called the police. Three launches were approaching the island from the mainland, going fast, searchlights poking at the dead water.

Wyatt allowed himself half a minute's grace, mentally mapping the harbour and the high ground opposite, where the costly white houses sat on green lawns that stretched to private moorings on the water. There was a light burning above De Lisle's mooring.

Just then a searchlight swept erratically along the shoreline, highlighting cabins and mangroves. Wyatt ducked. People were gathering on the jetty, shouting, encouraging the police launches.

Wyatt's options were shrinking. The ferry was out of the question; so were the bulbous orange paddleboats the tourists played about in. He couldn't head inland, into finger-pointing chaos. That left only the rocky shoreline at the uninhabited corner of the island. He slipped under the first cabin again, then down the row away from the jetty. The world beyond the final cabin was dark, treacherous, and that's where he let himself be swallowed up by the night.

Away from the jetty and garden lights his eyes began to adjust to the gloom. He came upon cliffs first, limestone scored and fissured and sharp enough to tear open his hands and shoes. Then the cliffs dropped away and he was wading knee-deep in water and finally picking a path along a metre-wide band of coarse, corally sand. Mosquitoes swarmed around his head, and in the darkness and the urgency of his slapping hands he didn't see the object that spilled him onto his face.

He was out for a few seconds, all the breath driven from his body. When he could move again he climbed free of the trap and explored his ribs, hoping he hadn't cracked them. It hurt to breathe and his head swam dizzily.

He sat on the sand for a while, breathing shallowly, concentrating, reducing the pain to a size he could shape and channel. It wasn't a mangrove root that had caught his shins, and he hadn't pitched onto a sharp-edged log—it was something unchanged in centuries that had trapped him and it was also his salvation.

Wyatt got to his feet. The outrigger section had been fashioned from a sturdy branch about two metres long, pointed at both ends and shaped to slice through the water. It was separated from the body of the canoe itself by two bamboo poles about three metres long. The canoeist sat in a hacked-out tree trunk. Even in the darkness Wyatt could see that both the outrigged float and the main body had been daubed in bright paint. The only concession to the twentieth century was the binding: nylon rope instead of vines or raffia fibre.

Wyatt turned the canoe over. The paddle was underneath, fashioned from a machined board that had probably washed up after a storm. He tried to imagine the man or woman who owned the canoe: someone who had nowhere else to store it, someone who fished the dark side of the island, away from the eyes of the Europeans who still ran the little republic.

He hauled the canoe over the sand to the sea's edge, tugging it by the axe-fashioned bow. It was heavy, and sat low in the water. He waded out until he was waist deep, the water cold and sobering, erasing the clutter from his mind. For the next couple of minutes he eyed the narrow stretch of water between the island and the mainland. The police launches were concentrating their search around the international yachts and the two ferry stops. Wyatt had no need or intention of straying there. Where he wanted to cross, the harbour was black, impenetrable. If he set out now, he wouldn't be spotted.

He climbed in, began to paddle. His bruised ribs shot pain that made his eyes water, but the little outrigger was like an arrow, skimming him across the calm surface, past the wrecked steamer, between the rusty buoys, toward De Lisle on the other side.

40

The black water was not so black once he was upon it. Wyatt found a style with the paddle that would not swamp the canoe or waste energy in spurts and misdirections, and began to see phosphorescence boiling around him, shoreline reflections, and a low, sombre tone in the water itself, a colour he couldn't name. Far to his left there were shouts, incoherent above the restless ping of sail rigging slapping the masts of the big yachts as they gently tossed at anchor.

Wyatt recalled a heist he'd pulled off the northern Australian coast a decade earlier. Salvage divers had found a Dutch DC3 in forty metres of water near Broome. The DC3 had been there since 1942 and a member of the salvage team had made the mistake of telling a pub crowd that it had been carrying a handful of fleeing Dutch colonial officers from Java and a box full of diamonds. Wyatt and a professional diver had got to the wreckage first. At a little over thirty metres, burdened with an air tank, torch, hatchet and knife, Wyatt began to feel the first, subversive lightheadedness as nitrogen built up in his blood, brought on by water pressure. He'd heard the term 'rapture of the deep', and now it made sense to him. He felt loose, forgetful, in a state to be playful and take chances, dangerous attitudes at that sort of depth. Fortunately the professional diver with him had not taken chances but brought him back to the surface in five stages, waiting three minutes at each stage for him to decompress. At the surface they'd seen a salvage ship with a police escort, so that had been the end of that.

He steered in a wide half-circle around the yachts now, aware that people could be awake aboard them, curious about the commotion on the island. The crossing took ten minutes. When he was a few metres short of De Lisle's water frontage he stopped paddling, allowing the outrigger canoe to glide in against the little dock just aft of the yacht moored there. The area was dimly illuminated by the lights in the house above.

According to a nameplate bolted on the stern, above the rudder, the yacht was the *Stiletto*, home port Panama.

Wyatt needed a weapon. Perhaps there was one on board the yacht. He reached for the short chrome ladder on the starboard flank of the yacht and climbed aboard. He could just as easily have climbed the steps to the dock and stepped onto the yacht, but the risk of standing exposed under the light was greater that way.

There was no one on deck. He crouched at the steps that led below and listened. Nothing.

The cabin was empty. There was a light switch but he drew open the curtains rather than turn it on.

It was clear at once that De Lisle was intending to flee. The first thing Wyatt found was the original nameplate, *Pegasus*, home port Coffs Harbour.

The second thing he found was a Very pistol and a box of

221

signal flares. He loaded one flare and stuck a further two into his waistband and went looking for a knife.

The galley offered some cheap alloy cutlery but nothing sharper than a bread knife. Wyatt felt there had to be a decent knife somewhere. How did De Lisle cut rope or sailcloth? How would he clean fish?

Wyatt went through the boat quickly and systematically, tapping the bulkhead, checking inside sail lockers, cupboards, the space under the benches. The knife showed up in a door rack, along with a small axe and a handsaw. It had a thick rubber grip and a broad flat tempered steel blade with a short, curved, slicing edge and a sharp stabbing tip. But Wyatt felt that there had to be a handgun, too. He kept looking.

And that's how he found the safe. He tugged on the black glass door of a small wall oven, the whole unit slid out, and he found himself looking into the open space behind it. De Lisle had left the safe unlocked. That could mean he was still packing to go and didn't want to bother with unlocking the oven every time he came down to the yacht with a handful of whatever he was running with.

Wyatt rocked back on his heels. Rings, bracelets, necklaces, tiaras; diamonds, rubies, emeralds, pearls; platinum, gold. That was on the lower shelf. On the top shelf were a number of files and Wyatt saw that De Lisle had kept a record of every robbery his team had pulled, together with dirt on the men who had worked for him.

There was a garbage compactor under the sink in the galley. Wyatt fed the files into it, piece by piece, then left the yacht. He didn't lock the safe, just pushed the oven home so that it wouldn't excite attention. The jewels could wait: he didn't want to go up against De Lisle with his pockets weighing him down. And later, when he left on the run, he didn't want to waste time trying to force the safe open to get at what he now considered to be his property.

The final problem solved itself. De Lisle hadn't locked the gate. Wyatt propped it open with a rock, then ran up the steps to the house. There were no dogs. If there were guards, none came at him from the seaward side of the house.

The steps stopped at a coral-chip path that made a lazy loop left then right through the final stretch of terraced garden. It ended at a long, low verandah. The path wound through a ground cover of fleshy-leafed plants and Wyatt cut across that way, avoiding the noisy coral.

There were two doors and several windows along the verandah. Wyatt didn't go in but circled the house a couple of times quickly, once to locate other doors and windows, the second time to come back to a well-lighted room where he'd heard a voice that was pitched on the wrong side of reason.

41

The window was open. He looked in. Liz Redding had reached De Lisle before he had but it hadn't done her any good at all. She sat slumped in a chair, blood clogging her nose, while the magistrate quivered on the carpet a metre in front of her. There was more blood on her shirt, a spill of it that had none of the sheen of blood recently spilled. Her head lolled and once or twice she tipped it back and shuddered.

'Again, how did you get in?'

'Walked in.'

De Lisle reddened, a fat, easily aggravated man who welcomed anger as a natural condition. He sucked on an asthma spray and said: 'I haven't got time for this.' He darted forward, punching her inexpertly in the stomach and darting back out of reach.

Wyatt felt his hands clench. He wanted to slice through the flywire and wade among the fussy antiques between the window and where De Lisle was ranting, shove the flare pistol down the man's throat. The feeling came naturally, surprising him with its intensity.

He fought down the impulse and watched De Lisle slap at the cop's upper arms. It puzzled Wyatt. De Lisle had the vicious tendencies of a torturer but none of the technique.

'Tell me.'

Liz Redding controlled the slackness in her neck for long enough to say, 'The gate was open,' and spit blood at a point near De Lisle's shoes.

'Open? Grace, that bloody cow.'

De Lisle paced up and down. He looked at his watch. 'Why did you have to come here? Look what it's got you.'

'Mr De Lisle, if you cooperate, if you fly back with me now, I'll see to it that the court takes it into account.'

De Lisle put his face close to hers. 'There's no underestimating the stupidity of people like you, is there? Missy, you're in no position to bargain.'

She went on doggedly: 'Do you *want* to spend the rest of your life running and hiding?'

De Lisle was growing tired of playing with her. He looked at his watch, glanced at the window, seemed to listen for something. Suddenly he tipped back his head and bellowed: 'Come on, Springett. What's going on out there?'

Too late, Wyatt understood. He began to back away from the window. He stopped when the man whom De Lisle had been calling said softly: 'That'll do.'

Wyatt began to turn. The voice grew harsher. 'No you don't. Drop whatever it is you've got there, then straighten up and walk slowly around the corner. I don't want to discuss it, I don't want to see your face, just go on ahead of me into the house. If you don't, I'll shoot you, and there's a suppressor on the barrel, so I'm not worrying about noise.'

Wyatt dropped the flare pistol. Springett snorted. 'What good was that going to do you? Go on, get moving.'

Wyatt took three crushing steps along the coral-grit path before he heard the start of footsteps behind him. That put Springett three metres back, out of range for a spin and kick, in range for getting a bullet in the spine. He did as he'd been told and walked around the corner and onto a verandah, ducking under latticework choked with bougainvillea.

In along a broad, dark hallway, toward an open door spilling light at the end. Springett was moving stealthily; Wyatt listened but could not place him in the geography of floorboards, carpet runner and hallstand behind him.

Into the room where De Lisle was waiting. De Lisle looked at him with satisfaction, then past him to Springett. 'I told you I heard something.'

'Also your gate's open. The alarm system's off.'

'My servant, bloody cow. She thinks the local cops are coming for me, only I've paid them off for twenty-four hours.'

'You're a fuckup, De Lisle.'

Wyatt felt the gun for the first time, prodding him across the room. De Lisle danced out of his way. He stopped next to Liz Redding. He gazed curiously at her. It would look suspicious if he ignored her. She was breathing through her mouth; he saw a plug of blood in each nostril. The nose itself didn't look broken. 'Can I turn around?'

'Yeah, let's look at you.'

Wyatt had discounted De Lisle as the immediate threat. His eyes went straight to Springett. The gun was a Glock, mostly ceramic, maybe smuggled past the metal detectors. Springett himself stared back, full of forbearance and contemplation, taking Wyatt's measure. He made no movement, and Wyatt began to ready himself for a pointless contest of wills, but it was over before it had begun. Springett wore the ease of a man in charge. He said, 'All paths lead to Rome.'

Wyatt stayed neutral, limber, putting his weight on the balls of his feet. De Lisle said abruptly, jerking his head at Springett, 'Come on, mate. Help me get rid of them.'

Springett snarled, 'Fuckups like you, you invoke mateship whenever it suits, but you'd shop your own mother to stay out of gaol.'

The differences and tension between the two men became palpable to Wyatt. Some things united them—they were about to go on the run, there was desperation underneath the swagger, they'd swipe at threats—but they didn't trust each other and Springett clearly thought that De Lisle had been cheating him.

De Lisle flushed. He said stubbornly, 'We have to get rid of these two.'

'Like, leave a couple of bodies behind, kind of thing? Give the local cops an extra incentive to track us down?'

'Well, *you* sort something out.'

Springett gestured. 'Simple. We take them with us. Burial at sea.'

'We can't leave till the morning, not till after the banks open.'

Wyatt heard Liz Redding cough and spit again. She said, 'You won't get far. Why don't you just give yourselves over to my custody, fly back with me and we'll forget the assault. You don't want murder charges on top of everything else.'

She was going through the motions. Still, it would suit Wyatt if Springett and De Lisle did go back with her, leaving him behind to loot the yacht.

But it wasn't going to happen. Wyatt had only one thing in his favour—he knew about the concealed safe on the yacht and what was in it. Springett and Liz Redding clearly didn't. Springett was expecting to collect when the banks opened in the morning. For reasons of his own, De Lisle had chosen not to tell Springett that he hadn't got around to depositing the jewel collection in one of his safety-deposit boxes.

'Springett,' Liz Redding was saying, 'don't stuff up more than you have already.'

Springett said nothing. He stepped forward and smacked the edge of his hand on the bridge of her damaged nose. He knew what he was doing. He also sensed something in Wyatt, for he swung the gun around warningly: 'Don't even think about it.'

He turned to De Lisle. 'How much is in the house?'

'I told you, nothing. Walter Erakor cleaned me out.'

'You trust him?'

'We mistrust each other. The thing is, he wants the deeds to this house as well. He can't get them until the banks open in the morning, so meanwhile he's keeping the cops off my back.'

Springett mused on it. 'We'll take these two down to the boat now. Out of sight, out of mind.'

De Lisle spread his arms fatly. 'At last, movement at the station.'

With barely concealed fury, Springett moved behind Wyatt and Liz Redding. 'Let's go.'

They began the descent through the steeply terraced garden, stepping carefully in the light of the moon, De Lisle leading, then Wyatt, supporting Liz Redding, Springett in the rear. Wyatt had reached the halfway point when a voice screamed '*De Lisle!*' and a fiery light leapt at him from the shadowy house above.

42

Crystal had been halfway to the crew's quarters at the Palmtree Lodge after the latest delivery for Huntsman when on impulse he told the driver to turn around and go back. 'Reriki,' he said.

Thirty minutes later he was admiring how the other half lived. All he'd ever been able to see from his room at the Lodge were a smudgy coconut-oil soap factory at the rear and an ugly strip of corally beach at the front, but the Reriki cabins were something else. He turned switches: the ceiling fan came on, the aircon, the TV. The bed was queen-size. He went out onto the balcony. Cane chairs, not moulded plastic, and a stunning view of blue water, manicured lawns, the neat, shingled trunks of carefully tended palm trees. The air smelt sweet, clean, scented by tropical flowers and afternoon rains.

But De Lisle didn't arrive to pick up the case that day, or the next. Finally he rang De Lisle's house. 'He come in boat, tomorrow,' a woman said.

So he watched the house. He saw the yacht tie up midway

through the afternoon. Shortly after that, a water taxi collected De Lisle and headed across the harbour toward the island. Crystal left his cabin and made for a secluded alcove across from the reservations desk and the bar.

The management had placed a couple of armchairs there, flanking a coffee table stacked with back issues of *Readers' Digest*. There was also a small bookcase crammed with books left behind by resort guests. Crystal flipped through a New Age paperback while he waited. It told him how to own his own life and acquire guilt-free wealth and power as he did it. Well, the wealth would come soon enough. He wasn't stupid enough to run with De Lisle's jewels but he did intend to push the man from five grand a delivery to fifty, a fair enough amount considering what he was expected to carry, the risks involved, and being hassled by nameless cops in Melbourne.

De Lisle arrived dressed in tropical whites again, beaming at the staff, shouting *bonjour* and letting them cluster around and pat and hug him. All an act, Crystal decided. For the next thirty minutes, De Lisle held court at the bar, then eased away and walked on short, heavy legs to the door of the security office, his face damp with humidity and effort. He paid the man, collected the suitcase and disappeared.

Crystal waited a couple of minutes then sauntered down to the ferry. It was five o'clock, tourists flocking back to the island to have an early sundowner at the bar. On his way across to the mainland, Crystal watched De Lisle's water taxi steer a course among the ocean-going yachts.

At the other end, Crystal headed left, down to the cafes and restaurants of the little port. He had a coffee, took a stroll, filling in time until evening, when he would tackle De Lisle. A pleasant edginess animated him, a sense of having reached the final stage.

All that evaporated at six-thirty when he reached De Lisle's house and saw another taxi there, saw one of the Melbourne cops pay off the driver and press the intercom.

'Keep going, keep going,' Crystal urged, shaking his driver by the arm.

He got out two streets farther along, paid the driver and walked back, trying to grow into the shadows under the palms on the other side of the road. A cop. That changed things. There'd be no walking in and asking for fifty grand with that cop there.

Crystal watched De Lisle's house helplessly, his hands slipping in and out of his pockets, looking for somewhere to rest. He looked both ways along the street. Kumul Highway, what a laugh. In that spirit, Crystal noticed the open-air market and the low-slung cement block building next to it. In the late sun of the day it glowed the colour of strong tea. Otherwise it was riddled with salt damp; mangy dogs scratched in the packed dirt around it. Still, it said BAR over the front door and Crystal had worked up a thirst coming this far.

He went in. Not too bad. A few tables, booths, wooden floors. Clean-looking. Overhead fans kept the place cool. A few locals drinking. Hell, they even sold Fourex.

Crystal fronted up to the bar. He said, slowly, carefully, 'I don't want a beer, I don't want Bacardi and Coke, screwdriver, none of your tourist crap. Give me a kava.'

The local brew was served in small, deep-bowled shells. Crystal had never tried one in all the time he'd been flying in and out of Vanuatu. But it was never too late, and he tipped the kava down his throat. He gagged, coughed, lit up a smoke. Thick, vile, like muddy water mixed with castor oil. He wanted to throw up.

The barman was watching him with interest. Bugger you, Crystal thought. 'I'll have another.'

Then he had a third. The barman was wearing half a smile now. Crystal wondered why. He couldn't feel anything; there was only a bit of an aftertaste.

Following his fourth kava, Crystal went to the men's. Jesus, now he could feel it. His knees gave way for a moment. He came back from the men's and collapsed in a booth near the silent juke box in the rear of the place. Waves of euphoria and nausea swept through him. The euphoria was good, but he didn't trust it. The way he was feeling, he might just knock on De Lisle's door and apologise for thinking bad thoughts.

Time to get off the kava, though, that was for sure. Crystal switched to beer—Fourex. God knows what an un-Australian beer might do to him.

He left the bar. The moon was high and bright and he stood for a while under the palm trees, looking down the road at De Lisle's house. Bastards. Wrecking his life. He'd like to tie De Lisle to a chair and dance around him slicing off a piece here and there like that guy in *Reservoir Dogs*. He began to walk. At the gate he stopped, reached out a hand experimentally to the cold steel.

43

'De Lisle!'

A scream of hate and revolt from the head of the steps.

Then the flare snaking from out of the darkness, an eyeblink comet of oily smoke and flashpoint combustion.

Wyatt ducked, pulling Liz Redding down with him. Springett, surprised, stood where he was.

The flare arrowed over Springett, over Wyatt and Liz Redding, struck De Lisle in the flesh at his waist, and began to burn.

De Lisle went down soundlessly and Wyatt did two things: he threw his jacket over the flare, shutting off the giveaway spluttering light, and he went after Springett, flare-burn in his eyes.

Springett had his back to Wyatt, snapping off shots with the silenced Glock, spraying them over an arc, hunting for the man on the terrace above him. Wyatt heard the slap of impact, a grunt of surprise and pain, and heard Springett's triumph: 'Got you, you bastard.'

Ramming with both fists, Wyatt caught Springett behind each knee. Springett buckled, his arms windmilling as he toppled over backwards, flailing uselessly at the black air. Wyatt, crouching behind him, heaved upwards as Springett thumped onto his shoulders, flipping the man onto his head.

Wyatt stayed close to the ground, ready to uncoil and attack Springett, but Springett stirred, sighed, and lapsed into unconsciousness.

Liz found the gun. Wyatt saw the hard concentration in her. In a series of crouched jerks she swung the gun on De Lisle, Springett, the danger above, always covering Wyatt between moves.

'There's not,' Wyatt observed, 'all that much wrong with you.'

He saw her relax the gun arm a little, smile crookedly at him. 'I guess we're even. If we don't count your tying me up.'

Wyatt gestured, uncomprehending and irritated. He could never see the sense in weighing up this kind of profit and loss. 'Liz, we can't stay here.'

She let the gun fall to her side. 'What a mess. What a fucking mess.'

Wyatt looked out across the water to Reriki. The search party was winding down. Nothing was happening on the island itself and one by one the probing searchlights were blacking out on the patrol boats, letting the coral, cliffs and mangroves become shadows in the moonlight again. He could smell his jacket burning, but the flare was close to extinction now. There were no neighbours gathering on either side of De Lisle's fence.

Liz Redding was crouched over Springett, the fingers of one hand on his pulse. Wyatt made to step past her. 'I'm out of here.'

She swung the gun on him. 'You're under arrest, Wyatt.

234

Springett too, when he wakes up.'

Wyatt stopped. 'You don't have jurisdiction here, not over me, not over him. You shouldn't be here in the first place. Does your boss know you're here?'

A twist of hate: 'Springett's my boss. Wyatt, I'll put in a good word for you. You saved my life. You cooperated. You were not involved in the magnetic drill robberies.'

Then she swayed, put out her hands, found nothing to cling to and sank gratefully onto the terraced step. Wyatt unpicked her fingers one by one until he had the Glock pistol. She laughed a little wildly. 'It's Springett's. I found it at his house and smuggled it here in my luggage.'

Wyatt stepped away from her. He watched as she straightened her back, both arms holding her trunk upright, and cranked her face around to look at him. She was stubborn, fixed, angry.

'I need to get something out of this,' she said. 'Do you know what I was told? We couldn't touch De Lisle over here, no real evidence, respected magistrate, friends in high places, blah blah blah. I was told to take some leave, I'd exceeded my responsibilities. They said they'd put out an international alert for Springett but don't expect any joy in Vanuatu because last year an Australian priest here had his hands in the parish till and was fiddling with the choir boys but before they could arrest him he was tipped off by a bishop in Sydney and got away.'

'So you thought you'd just fly in and bring them back yourself.'

She looked away. 'Springett tried to have me killed. My own boss.'

Wyatt proferred the Glock silently. She recoiled. 'Is that how you work your life? I want to see him wriggling in court.'

Wyatt crouched there with her for a while. 'The yacht,' he said.

'What about it?'

'There's a dead man in my room over there on the island, two dead men here. I can't fly out. They're not likely to let you fly out. The yacht's our only chance.'

She was working herself into a spitting anger. 'I can't sail. Can you sail? It's all a big mess.'

'I know the basics, but I'll need your help.'

She shot out a foot, striking Springett, who groaned, stirred, tried to kneel. 'What about him?'

'Bring him with us. You'll have formal jurisdiction over him once we're in Australian waters.'

'His lawyers are going to just love that. What about De Lisle and the other man?'

Wyatt walked down the steps with the Glock, wiping it with his handkerchief. He wrapped De Lisle's fingers around the butt, the trigger, then shook it onto the grass near the outstretched hand.

He went back to Liz. 'Let the locals work it out.'

'Piece of cake,' she said.

They got Springett onto the yacht and roped him to a bunk. Then Wyatt remembered the false nameplate on the stern. 'I'll be back.'

Alarm showed on Liz Redding's face. 'Where are you going?'

Wyatt said it again: 'I'll be back.'

He found De Lisle's study in a corner of the house. The window overlooked the harbour. There was an open safe behind a painting on the wall. Empty. He went through De Lisle's desk. The papers for the yacht were in the bottom drawer, listing the new name and registration. De Lisle had put it all together so that he could run and hide. There's no reason, Wyatt thought, why it shouldn't work for me as well.

236

He returned to the yacht. He found Liz Redding in the little galley, swabbing the clotted blood from her nose, dabbing antiseptic cream onto her cuts, examining the bruises on her stomach. He touched her. As soon as she felt the contact, she sighed raggedly, as if he'd drained something bad from her.

She turned. 'I don't think I'm up to hauling on ropes.'

Wyatt pushed her down onto a bench seat. 'Rest.'

He cast off, fired up the auxiliary diesel, and eased the yacht away from the little dock. Then he steered for the open sea. He named the dangers, as he always did. If the waves didn't swallow them up or patrol boats intercept them in the light of the morning, there was finally the big land mass to the west, where he was a thief and a killer and Liz Redding a cop. They had that to work out between them. There were days to do it in. And days to separate himself and the Asahi jewels from her, if it came to that. In a snatch of light from the sea moon he caught her staring at him. No calculation, trust or gratitude, just acceptance that they needed one another just then, and that was pretty much how Wyatt saw it.

FALLOUT

By the fifth hold-up the papers are calling him the bush bandit. An inspector of police, flat, inexpressive, resistant to the pull of the cameras, is less colourful: 'We are looking for a male person who is armed and should be considered dangerous. His method of operation is essentially the same in every case. He targets a bank in a country town within an area covering west and south-western Victoria and east and south-eastern South Australia. He selects a quiet period when there are few if any customers, then menaces bank staff with a sawn-off shotgun, demanding cash from the tills. To date, we have no reports of an accomplice. I repeat, this person is armed. On no account should he be approached.'

There are things that the inspector doesn't say. He doesn't say that the police are at a loss to pinpoint an operating base for the man. Given the area he moves in, the bush bandit might be holed up in Mount Gambier, Bordertown, Horsham, even somewhere up on the River Murray. Or he might be operating from Adelaide, even Melbourne.

The inspector doesn't say how effective the bandit is. First, the shotgun, its blunt snout, those twin black staring mouths. Everyone knows about shotguns, knows the massive damage they inflict at close range, the spread of the pellets, scattering and cutting like hornets. The dull gleam of the metal, the worn stock, the smell of gun oil. A shotgun spells gaping death, and so you are quiescent before it. You spread yourself out on the floor, you empty the till, you forget about being a hero.

Then there is the bandit himself. Witness descriptions tally for each of the five hold-ups. The man is tall and slender and he moves well. 'Athletic,' one bank teller said. 'No wasted motions,' said another. Other than that there is no clear description of the bush bandit. He varies his dress from job to job—a suit, jeans and a check shirt, zip-up windproof jacket and trousers, overalls, tracksuit. And something always to divert attention away from his face—glasses, sunglasses, cap, wide-brimmed Akubra, a bandaid strip.

He also speaks in fragments, so that bank staff are never able to get a clear fix on his voice: 'Face down… fill the bag, please, no coins… foot off the alarm… don't move… don't follow.' It's a quiet voice, that's all they can say. Calm, patient, understanding—these are some of the words the witnesses use. And young. They agree that he can't be more than about twenty-five.

Although they don't say it, the police believe that he's probably not a junkie. First-timers and junkies, they barge in screaming, pistol-whipping staff and customers, generally encouraging a condition of panic and instability that can tip over into hostages and spilt blood.

It's agreed that the man rides a big Ducati. No, a Kawasaki. Maybe a Honda. Big, anyway. Plenty of guts and very fast. Hard to track. On a bike like that he can be miles away before the alarm is raised. You can put up a chopper, send out a pursuit car, but all the bush bandit has to do is simply wheel off the road and under a gum tree or behind a windmill until the danger blows over.

Where does he store the bike? The police have no answer. Could be anywhere. Maybe their man has a dozen bikes stashed away, all around the country.

'One thing we do know,' the inspector says, 'one day he'll slip up. And we'll be there when it happens.'

It was a wheat and wool town on a dusty plain. According to the local paper, the parade would pass down the main street between midday and half past twelve, turn left at the tractor dealership and wind its way on to the showgrounds next to the Elders-GM stockyards. This was the first anniversary of the Australia Day fire that had burnt out an area the size of Luxemburg and almost destroyed the town. In fact, the front actually licked at the edges of the high school, destroying a portable classsroom. Later the wind had changed, sweeping unseasonal rains in from the west, but not before Emergency Services personnel had lost one unit and two volunteer firemen. The shire president had wanted to run the parade on a Saturday, but feelings were still raw in the town and councillors voted for Australia Day itself, which this year fell on a Friday.

The man known as the bush bandit had never felt welling pride or sentiment for anything, but he knew how to read emotions. He walked down the main street, stopping to buy a newspaper, a half litre of milk, a packet of cigarettes that he would never smoke. A banner swayed in the wind, thanking the volunteer firemen. People were lining the footpaths, yarning and joking, cameras ready. Half of them were farmers and their families, and that's who the bush bandit was today, a pleasantly smiling farmer dressed in elastic-sided boots and clean pressed work shirt and trousers. He wore a stained felt hat pushed back on his head. He looked work-worn and weary. He wasn't alone in wearing sunglasses. It's

243

just that his were anachronistic, a flash narrow strip of mirrored glass across his eyes. They belonged on a roller-blading kid at St Kilda or Bondi or Glenelg. If anyone thought about it, they thought the man had eccentric taste. Certainly it was the only thing memorable about his face.

He watched the parade trumpet past: police, firemen, ambulance crews, the two widows in the back seat of a squatter's black Mercedes. It was over in ten minutes. In ten minutes the main street was deserted, the tail end of the spectators disappearing around the corner and away from the centre of the town. There was only one bank, and the bandit walked into it at 12.25, removed his sawn-off shotgun from his bag of shopping, and announced that he was robbing the place.

There were no customers, only two tellers. One said, 'Oh, no.' The other froze. The bush bandit trained the twin bores of the shotgun on the one who'd spoken. He'd picked her as the likely source of trouble, so he said, 'Face down. Not a sound.'

He watched her sink to the floor. She stretched out awkwardly, one hand holding her skirt from riding up.

The other teller watched the gun swing around until it was fixed on her stomach. The bandit placed a chaff bag on the counter. 'Fill it.'

Friday. There would be more cash than usual, though not enough to make him rich. But that was a thought for the edge of his mind, a why-am-I-doing-these-pissy-jobs? thought for the dark hours.

He watched the teller, the shotgun now back on the woman on the floor. The meaning was clear: She gets it if you stuff me around.

At one point, the teller hesitated.

'Move it,' the bandit said.

'Traveller's cheques,' she burst out. 'You want them?'

Hundreds of cheques, crisp, unsigned. The bush bandit could almost conjure up their new-paper-and-ink smell. He'd take them to Chaffey. Chaffey handled wills, property conveyancing and sentence appeals in his front office; in his rear office he'd pay twenty cents in the dollar for anything the bush bandit turned up that wasn't cash or easily negotiable.

'Yes,' the bush bandit told the teller.

When it was done, and both women were on the floor, he said, 'Remain there, please. Five minutes.'

One woman nodded. The talkative one said 'Yes,' but the man was already gone.

The motorbike was on the tray of a farm ute. He'd turned it into a farm bike with mud, dust, dents, a cracked headlamp. He drove the ute slowly away from the town, his elbow out the window, an irritating figure familiar to interstate coach drivers, truckies and travelling salesmen, and soon had faded into the landscape, faded from memory.

He ditched the ute on a dirt track and switched to the bike. This time it was a Honda and he'd stolen it in Preston. He ran into a storm, strong winds and driving rain, on the way back to the city, but by evening was in his balcony apartment, looking out over Southgate and the stretch of the Yarra River between the casino and Princes Bridge.

At eight o'clock he went out into the storm again and made his way to the casino, to see if he could improve on the twelve thousand bucks he'd taken today. By morning he'd have the early edition of the *Herald Sun*, another bush bandit story for his scrapbook.

The bush bandit, that was his public name. Ray, or Raymond, those were the names his mother and father—both now dead—had called him. What Raymond wanted was simply to be called Wyatt. He liked the whiplash quality of the word.

But his uncle was called Wyatt.

1

One hundred kilometres south-east of the city, the hold-up man called Wyatt brought a crippled yacht in from the storm-tossed seas of Bass Strait to the calmer waters of Westernport Bay, bringing to an end a seven-day voyage from Port Vila. It was 4.15, almost dawn. Just five hours earlier, the bent police inspector called Springett had been washed overboard. Wyatt's only other passenger, the woman who had arrested Springett in Port Vila, was asleep on her bunk. Wyatt furled the torn sails and switched to the auxiliary diesel. The yacht burbled quietly between the red and green markers, following the channel to the little jetty on the Hastings foreshore. Liz Redding didn't stir, not even when Wyatt dropped anchor, bundled his clothing inside a waterproof jacket and slipped over the side and away. She was too tired, too warm, too lost to the grains of Mogadon he'd fed her for that.

Wyatt dragged himself shivering from the water and wiped himself down with a handtowel from the yacht. He dressed rapidly in the shelter of a concrete retaining wall, occasionally poking his head above it, looking for fishermen, patrol cars, insomniacs. There were street lights behind a screen of foreshore trees; shire offices ghastly white in the sodium lamps; rows of slumbering small houses; a swimming pool and kiosk; a hut on the jetty that sold fish; and, to his left, a stiff forest of drydocked yacht masts behind a cyclone security fence.

What he wanted was a car.

If he left now, he would be in Melbourne by the time most people's alarm clocks were rattling them awake. If he were not so conspicuous—a stranger with wet hair appearing from the direction of the marina at the break of day—he'd take one of the town's taxis. Otherwise, there was the train, the local from Stony Point, connecting with the Melbourne express in Frankston, but that meant too many factors that he could not control, and which threatened to bring him unstuck—altered timetables, nosy ticket inspectors, faulty boom gates. Or he could hitchhike. But who would pick him up? Wyatt knew that the dark cast of his face and his fluid height and shape and his materialisation at the side of the road would spell prohibition and risk to any motorist.

And so his only option was to steal a car, one that would not be missed for the next couple of hours.

He ventured a short distance away from the little dock, into a region of humble side streets where the houses huddled together and the family car sat in the driveway or in the street outside it, straddling nature strip and gutter. But a dog barked. Wyatt backed out of there.

He couldn't see any service stations nearby. As he recalled it, they were mostly on the outskirts of Hastings. There are often cars parked outside service stations, keys on a hook somewhere inside.

He returned to the jetty. Wyatt had at first rejected the motley station wagons and utes parked there, fishermen's cars, rustbuckets all of them, with mismatched panels and doors and half a dozen registration stickers up and down the windscreens. He imagined their interiors, their snagging springs and crammed ashtrays and rolling UDL cans and faulty electrics. The Hastings police might turn a blind eye, allowing a local fisherman to drive between home and jetty and nowhere else, but Wyatt doubted that bald tyres, rust and cracked windscreens would pass in Melbourne.

But what choice did he have?

He could cut down on the risk, though, by driving to a place like Springvale, still well short of the city but a place where he wouldn't be looked at twice. Take a taxi from there.

Maybe three or four taxi journeys—angling north and south as he closed in on the city, so that anyone mapping his route would make little sense of it—and board a city tram at some big interchange like Kew Junction.

Wyatt checked his watch. 4.35. He hoped it was still too early for the first of the fishing boats to come in. He hoped its crew would have plenty to do when it did dock, leaving more time before one of them realised that his bomb was missing from the car park.

Wyatt went along the row of vehicles, testing drivers' doors and checking for keys left in the ignition. Most were unlocked—there was nothing worth stealing, after all—but no keys.

Then he checked behind bumper bars and inside wheel arches. He found plenty of rust, plenty of gritty mud. He also found a small metal container the size of a matchbox, held inside the wheel arch of a Valiant utility by a magnet.

There was nothing tight about the motor. It whirred freely and when it finally fired, Wyatt could hear piston slap and rattling tappets and smell the oily exhaust of poor combustion. The seat sagged, threatening backache and stiff neck and shoulders. Wyatt kept himself fit but he was in his forties now and on the lookout for things like the size and shape of the seats he sat in and the beds he lay in.

But the headlights worked, the left angled higher than the right, and he found reverse without tearing a cog in the gearbox. The fuel gauge showed empty. Either that or it's stuffed, he thought. He couldn't risk filling it locally. He'd put some distance behind him first.

Wyatt cut across country toward Frankston. In the cool dawn light, fog appeared, hanging in the roadside depressions and above the creeks and dams, and hovering in thin streaks across the road, making him blink, as though to clear a film over his eyes. He remembered the fogs of the Peninsula from his recent past. There was a time when he'd strike fog on his way back from some smoking bank or payroll van. That was before he'd been forced to go on the run. That was a long time ago.

The engine coughed, surged, coughed again. The fuel gauge was working after all. Wyatt limped through the confusing roundabout in Somerville and into the Shell station on the Frankston road. The fisherman deserved a good turn: Wyatt filled the tank and poured a litre of oil down the throat of the clapped-out motor.

He abandoned the ute in a side street next to the level crossing in Springvale. He took a taxi to Westfield shopping centre, a second to the taxi rank outside Myer in Chadstone, a third up to Northlands in Doncaster. He felt safer with each journey, as though he were shaking off the dogs and trackers of the past. The tram from Doncaster to the city was warm and quiet and full of early workers. If anyone looked at him it was incuriously.

There was a 24-hour cafe in Swanston Walk. Wyatt was bone-tired and hungry. They offered bottomless coffee and he downed three cups of it. He wanted something solid in his stomach and ordered muesli, scrambled eggs and wholemeal toast. He looked at his watch. Liz Redding should still be deeply asleep on her bunk aboard the yacht.

Revived, bouncy on his feet, he headed on foot along Little Lonsdale Street. At 8.30 he stepped into a call box at the Elizabeth Street corner and rang Heneker at Pacific Mutual Insurance.

In Wyatt's experience, all switchboard operators spoke with an upward inflection, as if framing every statement as a question, 'I'm sorry? Mr Heneker won't be in until nine?'

Wyatt hung up. He felt knots in his torso from his cooped-up days at sea. Thirty minutes to kill. He decided to walk, and as he stalked through the streets without seeing the shops, the cars, his fellow humans, he replayed his voyage across the Pacific with Liz Redding. But it all came down to one thing: he'd drugged her coffee and slipped away. He'd betrayed trust and desire. The fallout from something like that is often very simple: all bets are off.

At 9.05 he returned to the phone box and called the insurance company again. Heneker had the surging enthusiasm of his trade. 'Heneker here, Mr—'

He waited for a name. Wyatt didn't give him one. Instead, he said, 'I've got the Asahi jewels.'

He pictured the man, the white shirt and sombre suit and darting calculations. Heneker recovered quickly. 'Shall we discuss where and when and how?'

'And how much,' Wyatt said.

'How could I forget,' Heneker said.

2

It wasn't strictly true that Wyatt had the Asahi jewels. He had one piece with him, a white gold necklace set with a dozen chunky emeralds, but the remaining pieces—rings, necklaces, brooches, pendants, tiaras—were still locked away in a concealed safe on board the yacht. Taken together, they were too bulky to cart around and too valuable to dump if he found himself in trouble. At the same time, he was not interested in fencing the jewels piecemeal or removing the stones and melting down the settings. To do that involved time and too many middlemen. Wyatt wanted to offload the Asahi Collection quickly, for a lump sum, the reward offered by the insurance company. The emerald necklace was simply his hook. It was the most eye-catching piece, promising more, yet also an easy thing to dump if the deal went sour.

Wyatt headed down Elizabeth Street, musing upon the twists and turns of his life. The Asahi Collection, touring Australia and New Zealand, had been stolen from a Japanese superstore in

Melbourne. Wyatt wasn't the culprit—the actual raiders were policemen using security information supplied by Springett—but Liz Redding had suspected Wyatt. They'd both wound up in Port Vila, where Wyatt had discovered the hiding place of the Collection. He'd not revealed its location, not even when, on the voyage back, he and Liz had moved from being thief and thief-taker to being lovers.

Wyatt had almost been able to imagine a life with her. In the end, though, she was a cop, and Wyatt was a hold-up man with a long history that would not withstand close scrutiny, and so he was on the run again.

The meeting place was an undercover car park on Lonsdale Street. He went in, climbing to the third level, where he prowled among the shadows. The ceiling felt very low, the air sluggish, fumy and full of hard-to-place noises. The simplest sound was flat, hollow, booming.

He waited behind a concrete pillar. Heneker had described himself as 'tall, a bit on the thin side, wearing a blue suit, carrying a *Time* magazine'. When the insurance man finally appeared, Wyatt observed him for a couple of minutes. Heneker looked uneasy, the magazine held against his chest as though to ward off arrows. Wyatt supposed that he'd be nervous if he were in Heneker's shoes, and he stepped out into the weak light. 'Mr Heneker.'

Heneker turned to him with relief. 'Thought you weren't coming.' He coughed. 'What have you got for me?'

Wordlessly, Wyatt handed him the necklace. Heneker took it, wiped his sleeve across his face, and said, 'A fake.'

Wyatt faltered, just for a second. 'Maybe the light's not bright enough for you.'

Heneker looked around nervously, then said, his voice low and complicitous: 'You don't understand. It's a copy. They're all copies, the entire collection.'

Wyatt said nothing. He went onto his toes, ready to slip into the darkness.

'Good copies, mind you,' Heneker said, getting back some of his nerve. 'You'd need to be an expert. I mean, the settings are real enough, the white gold itself is worth a few bob, but the stones are all high-class fakes.' He shrugged in the gloom. 'The Asahi management got cold feet. Didn't want to pay the insurance premium for the real stones so we worked out a special deal for display copies. The collection toured right through New Zealand and Australia with no-one the wiser.'

'So why didn't you tell me to piss off on the phone?'

Heneker waved the necklace in the air. 'These aren't cheap copies. Cost twenty grand to have them made up. We still want them back.'

'How much?'

Heneker thought about it, swinging the necklace on his forefinger. 'I'm authorised to offer five.'

Wyatt smiled, like a shark, then laughed, a harsh bark in the slice of poisoned air between the concrete floors. 'Five? Is that hundred or thousand?'

'Thousand,' Heneker said, pocketing the necklace.

'Jesus Christ.'

Wyatt turned away and began to merge with the shadows.

'You'd turn your back on five thousand bucks?'

No response. Wyatt continued to walk away. Heneker said, a little desperately now, playing for time: 'I've got the five grand, here in my pocket.'

Wyatt paused, came back and said, with deadly calm, 'The deal is this: you give me the five, I tell you where the other pieces are.'

Heneker shook his head. 'Pal, you must be desperate. First you bring me the entire Asahi Collection, then you get your five thousand.'

The sounds when they came consisted of tyre squeals on the up-ramp and the snap of shoe leather. At once Wyatt dropped to one knee and kicked out, hard into Heneker's groin and then into the shins of the man who had run in screaming: 'Police! On the ground! Police! On the ground!'

Both men went down. Wyatt tackled the next cop. He heard a bone snap, heard a prolonged scream. And then in the noise and confusion, he ran.

3

Raymond thought that if these people had any idea, *any idea*, that he was the bush bandit, they'd piss in their pants, spill their drinks, lose their hairpieces, tremble so hard they'd knock over their roulette chips. They *talked* hard and tough—mergers, windfall profits, takeovers, injunctions, lawsuits, union bashing—but it was all hot air, the men pink and soft, the women wasted by sunlamps and starvation diets to the consistency of old bootleather. Sometimes Raymond was tempted to pull a stunt with his sawn-off shotgun, risk gaol for the pleasure of wiping the greed and satisfaction from their faces.

They weren't all like that. Raymond played at a big-stakes roulette table in the far left corner of one of the upper-level salons. It was a table that attracted your vulgarians, sure, but it also attracted the occasional cool, unblinking Asian gambler, who'd make and lose a fortune without feeling that he had to advertise it to the world, the occasional professional from Europe or the States, and the occasional middle-aged business type who'd looked after his health and didn't make a fuss about how big he was.

This particular roulette wheel brought luck to Raymond. Or rather, he knew it would be unlucky to switch to one of the other tables. On average, he was ahead—win twelve grand one night, lose eight or nine the next. A week ago he'd won twenty-five. Two nights later he was down thirty. It all meant that he lived a good life but there wasn't much hard cash in his pocket. Tonight he was behind, most of the cash from the bank raid gone down the drain.

It was a relative term, 'losing'. Raymond never had a sense of falling behind, not when he could simply go out and pull another job to top up his reserves. And there were the other positives: the women, the covetous glances, the contacts like Chaffey, whom he'd met playing craps, and the intoxicating dreamland of tuxedos, crisp white cotton, strapless dresses, his own lean jaw and sensitive hands in the muted 24-hours-a-day light.

A number of regulars played this table. Others liked to watch. Raymond was on nodding terms with all of them but in the past couple of weeks he'd found himself drawn to the company of a man called Brian Vallance and Vallance's girlfriend, Allie Roden.

He watched them now as he stacked his chips. Vallance was quick and compact looking, with olive skin and a closely trimmed grey beard on his neat chin. He had a healthy outdoors look, but Raymond wasn't sure that he liked Vallance. There was a sulkiness close to the surface, the mouth was too mean, Vallance's body language too buttoned-down. Vallance was about fifty, and that put him about twenty-five years older than the girlfriend.

Now there was a sight for sore eyes. Allie Roden had thick auburn hair like flames around a finely boned face, a kind of slow deep consuming fire in her green eyes, white skin, a beautiful shape, a readiness to toss back her head and laugh aloud. When she did that, Raymond wanted to bite her throat.

She came around the table while the croupier was making ready for the next spin of the wheel. Raymond felt her hand touch his wrist briefly, smelt her—a hint of plain soap and talc—as her lips brushed his ear and she murmured, 'Let's have a drink when you're ready.'

Raymond didn't take his eyes away from the croupier's hands. He nodded, sensed Allie step back, her fingers brushing his shoulder. When next he looked, she was standing behind Vallance. They both looked keenly at him and Vallance flashed a grin.

Raymond played on, losing, winning, pushing chips onto the board, pulling them toward him. Then he won five grand on one play and that was his signal to stop and have a drink with Vallance and Vallance's woman. He raised an eyebrow, inclined his head, and left the table.

'That was a daring play,' Allie said, coming around the table and winding her slim hand into the crook of his arm.

He liked the bouncy quality of her affection and generosity. No-one minded, least of all Vallance. Vallance wasn't possessive or jealous. Raymond couldn't see what she saw in him, though. There was the age factor, the hint of weakness in the man, her own energy and enthusiasm. She deserved better.

'You win some, you lose some,' Raymond said.

Vallance, at his other elbow as they walked to a secluded table in the lounge, said, 'You win more often than you lose, Ray. I've been watching. It's a real education. You're careful. You're not a man to throw his money away.'

Raymond played that coolly. He wasn't about to tell Vallance that he'd borrowed ten grand from his fence, the lawyer Chaffey, meaning that the five grand he'd just won was no longer his. With any luck, Chaffey would allow him a further five for the traveller's cheques and wipe out the debt completely.

They sat down, ordered champagne to celebrate. The talk circled around money and expert and inexpert gambling play. It emerged that Raymond was independently wealthy, from a good family, and gambled because he liked it. 'I can take it or leave it, though,' he said. He was no mug. Nothing desperate or pathetic about Raymond Wyatt.

They talked, they ordered a bottle next time, Dom Perignon, Raymond forking out the best part of two hundred bucks for it. And then, unmistakably, Allie's shoeless foot scratched his ankle and he felt the hot press of her thigh as she reached across him for the bottle. For the first time, Raymond thought that with a bit of skilful manoeuvring on his part he could extricate her from Vallance.

They relaxed, and into the warm glow of the endless night—it could have been a bright spring day outside for all Raymond knew or cared—Vallance slid a tin of shoe polish across the table. 'Take a gander inside that, young Raymond.'

The tin felt hefty in Raymond's hand. If it was shoe polish, it was very dense. He shook the tin and something shifted within it, a sense of heaviness and solidity transmitting itself to his fingers.

'Go on, it won't blow up on you.'

Raymond pressed where it said press and the lid popped open. He lifted it off, stared in and saw what accounted for the heaviness and the bulk.

'Gold guinea, dated 1799,' Vallance said. 'Silver florin, too worn by saltwater corrosion to establish the date but roughly the same vintage. Spanish silver dollar, dated 1810, and the one with the hole in it is a holey dollar, scarce as hen's teeth.'

He paused. 'I've got an airlines bag full of similar stuff at home. What's more, I'm the only man alive who knows where the rest is buried.'

Something stirred in Raymond, a kind of hunger, a hazy dream of adventure on the high seas, flintlock pistols and treasure chests. He looked up at Vallance uncomprehendingly.

'Why are you showing me?'

'You strike me as a man who knows how to keep his trap shut.'

'Maybe.'

'I won't bullshit you—you're in a position to help me and Allie.'

'You're the one with the story to tell,' Raymond said patiently.

He felt Allie's foot again. At the same time, she leaned over and slid an arm around Vallance. Raymond watched the man melt a little and rub his jaw over her skull. She said, 'Brian used to chart wrecks for a living.'

Vallance said defiantly, 'Until a year ago, Ray, I worked for the Maritime Heritage Unit. Our job was to locate wrecks from old documents, chart and excavate known wrecks, and safeguard others from scavengers. We even had a cop assigned to us full-time. Part of her job was checking Sotheby's and Christie's on the lookout for looted artefacts.'

Raymond waited.

A flush of anger filled Vallance's lined face. 'I was accused of stealing artefacts that hadn't yet been catalogued. Accused of selling to a private buyer. It was all bullshit. They couldn't prove anything, but I'd had enough so I quit rather than work for those bastards again.'

Sure you did, Raymond thought. You fucked up and almost got caught. It pleased him oddly to be listening to this desperado's story, almost as if Vallance could only be trusted because he was crooked.

He saw Allie pat Vallance's arm. In the dim light her features were soft and attentive. Raymond felt himself burning for her. He absently touched a finger to the coin with the hole in it.

'Tell you what, Ray,' Vallance said. 'That Spanish dollar is yours, whether you help us out or not. It's rated very fine, worth around a hundred and seventy-five bucks. All I want you to do at this stage is listen, no obligation to invest.'

'Invest?'

'Fifty grand could get you five million,' Vallance said.

4

The lawyer called Chaffey eased forward in his chair, the heat of effort rising on his broad, soft, clean, unhealthy face. He placed both hands on his desk and push-straightened his legs. Now he towered giddily against the window and, as he buttoned the vast folds of his suit coat together and prepared to show Denise Meickle out of his office, he glanced down upon the plane trees and tram tracks of St Kilda Road, the flashing chrome and foreshortened pedestrians, the park benches and rollerblading kids, trying to muster unfelt confidence into his voice.

'Leave it with me.'

The Meickle woman was a sorry-looking creature, small, mousy, belligerent. She was in love with a client of Chaffey's, a hold-up man and killer called Tony Steer, who was being held in the city watchhouse. He was about to be transferred to somewhere more permanent and Denise Meickle wanted Chaffey's help in springing him from gaol.

'First,' she said, reluctant to leave, though she'd been with him for an hour now and gone over everything a dozen times, 'you'll have to make sure he's transferred to the remand centre in Sunshine. Sometimes they're remanded in Pentridge, but we'll never spring him from there.'

Chaffey had doubts that Steer could be sprung from the remand centre, let alone Pentridge. 'Leave it with me,' he said again.

Meickle had been a prison psychologist attached to the gaol in Ararat when she first befriended Steer. Given the complex nature of a gaol environment, in which prison staff have to offer both welfare and custodial roles, it wasn't hard for someone like Meickle to blur or confuse these roles. It was especially hard for custodial staff who might find themselves comforting a bereaved prisoner one minute and strip-searching him the next. As a psychologist, Meickle hadn't had that kind of relationship with Steer, but the intimacy and role-confusion were no less compelling. 'We'll get your man out,' Chaffey said.

She didn't want to go. She numbered her fingers, so that Chaffey would get it straight. 'So this is the deal. New Zealand passports for both of us, a boat out of the country, and someone to help me spring Tony. For that we pay you fifty thousand dollars. Find someone good, someone who can drive and keep his nerve. Pay him out of your cut.' She poked Chaffey's huge midriff. 'Don't rip us off. We'll find you if you do.'

Chaffey nodded his massive head. He was Tony Steer's lawyer and minded Steer's money for him. He had more sense than to rob the man. Steer was bad news, a hard, fit man of flashing confidence and intelligence. Chaffey thought of the legions of women who befriended male prisoners. Lonely women, many of them, fired by good works, God or pity. Some of them married killers, waited for them to get out, and got killed for their pains. Maybe that's what awaited Denise Meickle.

263

He ushered her to the door. 'I'll get onto it straight away. The passports, the boat, no drama there. Finding a good man will require a bit of thought.'

'No junkies. No mugs. No-one with form.'

'Like I said, I'll get straight onto it.'

'He goes to trial in two weeks' time. We haven't got much time.'

When Meickle was gone, Chaffey ran through a mental checklist of names. None looked promising: dead, in gaol, feeding a habit or too narrow in their fields of expertise.

The phone rang.

'Chafe? Raymond here. How are you placed today?'

Here was someone he hadn't thought of. 'Raymond, old son.' Chaffey checked his watch. 'Meet you in thirty?'

'Usual place. I've got some paper for you.'

That could mean anything: bonds, numbered sequences of bills, cheques. 'See you then,' Chaffey said, cutting Raymond off before he compromised both of them on the line.

In the outer office he said, 'Back in an hour.'

'But you've got appointments.'

'Back in ninety minutes,' Chaffey said.

He put one foot after the other down the corridor. The lift gulped and clanked, dropping seven storeys with Chaffey braced, legs apart, at the midpoint of the floor, as though he were riding it to the ground. It hit the bottom, recovered, and Chaffey shouldered through the foyer to the street.

The 'usual place' was a booth in Bourke Street Mall that dispensed cheap theatre and concert tickets. Cursing, for there were no taxis in sight, Chaffey propelled himself toward the nearest tram stop.

Five minutes later he was strap-hanging in a draughty rattletrap along Swanston Street. It claimed to have the University as its destination, but that didn't mean it wouldn't reverse direction shortly or veer into Victoria Street. The seats looked minute and insupportable to Chaffey. He didn't trust them, or the conductor, or the other passengers. The students among them flashed their white teeth and clawed great arcs of gleaming hair away from their eyes as they spoke loudly, sub-literately, to one another. Otherwise there were pensioners, stunned and dazed, and women in suits with flying shoulders, snapping gum in their jaws.

Chaffey stood with his feet apart and tried to brace his solid legs in a counter-rhythm to the tram. His reflection in the glass revealed his bulk, a button nose, red lips, long pale lashes, damp acres of pink skin. It didn't reveal his vicious glee, for he was dreaming, of Raymond Wyatt saying that he would help Denise Meickle spring Tony Steer out of remand.

Chaffey alighted at Bourke Street, stepping down from the tram in careful stages, his movements as slow and ponderous as he could make them, thereby doing his bit to fuck up the timetable. Traffic braked for him as he heaved toward the foot-path.

He found himself face to face with the three bronze statues bolted to the footpath. They were tall, rubbery-looking caricatures of businessmen, their faces a little desperate in the swirling toxins. They were also painfully thin and Chaffey, spotting a swagger of body builders outside a nearby Sports Barn, wrapped his big arm around one of the statues and grinned. The body builders, all violet shellsuits and body hair, stopped chewing and posturing, looking about for the insult.

Chaffey steered a straight course down the mall. He did not have to dodge or weave or break his stride. As he walked his eyes darted left and right, hoping that Raymond was still unknown to the law.

Even so, Chaffey had to admit that the mall was a good place to meet. The centre mile of the city was as useful as a sieve to anyone trying to seal it off. It was made up of lanes and alleys and back streets, all leading away from the centre. Raymond could easily slip away, or hole up *inside* the centre mile, up in some men's lavatory along a dim corridor on the second or third floor of a seedy side-street building where the tenants gave singing lessons, altered suits, made dentures.

Chaffey reached the ticket booth. He spent a few minutes circling it, reading the posters, then he stood facing up the mall toward Parliament House, his hands seeking purchase on his soft hips.

Raymond materialised at Chaffey's shoulder, tall and fluid-looking in a tuxedo, very calm and still, yet clearly prepared to vanish into the shopping crowds if he felt threatened. 'Chafe, old son.'

Chaffey beamed, his mind ticking over. Raymond was a long streak of quiet menace to look at, a man with a hard, cautious mind. Most thieves that Chaffey dealt with were full of doubt and spite and contradictions, their minds tripping them up every minute of the day. Here was a man who registered, analysed, then acted, all of it manifested in extreme alertness.

He did like to play the tables, though. 'What's with the tux?'

Raymond grinned. 'Just finished an all-night session.'

'Win?'

'Got your five grand, plus the paper I was talking about.'

'Not here. Let's go.'

They walked up Bourke Street to Chaffey's club, on the corner of King Street. It was a cloaked and sombre warren of private rooms and alcoves, where lawyers met clients and other lawyers. It was a place where Chaffey's conversation with Raymond would go unremarked, even if it was overheard.

Raymond stretched his long legs. 'In the briefcase.'

Chaffey opened it. Traveller's cheques, crisp and new, and a roll of $100 bills. 'Twenty cents in the dollar,' he said.

Raymond shifted in his chair. The leather, old and cracked and friable, creaked under him. 'I was hoping the five grand plus the paper would cancel the ten I owe you.'

Chaffey closed the briefcase. He gave a short laugh. 'Fair enough, but I think you owe me in *spirit*, if nothing else. I can put two jobs your way, one pays fifteen grand, the other a hundred.'

Raymond watched him carefully. 'Hundred grand? What do I have to do for that?'

'I've got a client prepared to pay a hundred thousand dollars for a collection of paintings.'

'Where are these paintings?'

'At present they're hanging in the University of Technology in West Heidelberg,' Chaffey said.

For the next ten minutes, he described the job, explaining how lucrative art theft was. 'This job,' he concluded, 'will be a pushover. No alarms, no cameras.'

Raymond stroked his bony jaw. 'I don't know. What do I know about art? I'd need a partner, someone who knows that kind of thing.' He paused. 'What's the other job?'

Chaffey told him about Steer and Denise and the remand centre. 'You get fifteen grand—up front, how's that for a sweetener? All you have to do it spring Steer, hole up with him and his girlfriend for a couple of days, then deliver them both to a freighter anchored off Lakes Entrance.'

Raymond turned a little sulky then. It spoilt his looks. 'Spring some guy from remand? Bit downmarket isn't it?'

Chaffey shrugged. 'Quick, easy money. All you have to do is drive a car and babysit for a few days.'

'I'll think about it.'

'You do that,' Chaffey said.

Raymond stiffened, cocked his head. 'Sirens. Hear them?'

'Just so long as they haven't come for you, old son,' Chaffey said.

5

Wyatt ran and the cops ran, Wyatt's shoes snickering minutely across the prefabricated concrete levels of the parking station. The cops were noisier, shouting, grunting with exertion, their footwear heavy and booming. As he ran, Wyatt took a baseball cap from the pocket of his jacket, threw the jacket under a parked car and rolled the sleeves of his shirt to the elbows. It was not much, but a little was often all he needed.

Wyatt reasoned it through as he ran. If Heneker had warned the cops, then they'd have arranged a trap at the parking station. Instead, they arrived late, indicating that they'd followed Heneker without foreknowledge of the actual meeting place.

There was only one explanation: Liz Redding had shaken off the effects of the Mogadon and alerted the police in Melbourne to tail Heneker. And that meant she'd come to suspect that Wyatt had the jewels after all and wasn't simply making a run for it. She was a cop, and Wyatt was Wyatt, so it was only natural that she'd suspect further treachery beyond the obvious and assume that he'd attempt to strike a deal with the insurance company.

Wyatt ran to the top level, to a door marked EXIT. He pushed through and found himself in a department store cafeteria.

Better cover than he'd hoped for. The chunky white crockery smacked onto plastic trays, the stainless steel cutlery rattled in serving bins, hot quiche steamed behind glass, the chrome rails gleamed and he was swept into a clamorous queue at the servery. Morning tea. He lifted an abandoned *Herald Sun* from a corner table, loaded two pastries and black tea onto his tray, and went looking for someone who could turn him into a law-abiding citizen.

All of the tables were occupied, and most of the chairs. Wyatt's eyes passed over the tables where he'd stand out or invite irritation. He didn't want elderly couples, friends enjoying coffee together, solitary eaters or office workers snatching a break from work.

There, at the centre of the crammed area of tables—a woman with a pram and two fractious children. Wyatt edged through to the unoccupied chair, said, 'May I?' and unloaded his tray and opened his newspaper. The woman glanced at him tiredly and went back to juggling the competing needs of the baby and the two older children. The children ignored her. They were squabbling over a date scone.

'Here,' Wyatt said. He nudged his pastries across the little table. 'I haven't touched these. I don't really want them.'

The woman flashed him a cautious smile. Deciding that he wasn't a threat, she said, 'Say thank you to the nice man.'

The children stared at him, looked down, muttered aggrievedly.

'You're welcome,' Wyatt said.

He scanned the newspaper. He'd been living in Tasmania before events had taken him to Vanuatu, and was out of touch. A hold-up man called the bush bandit had been hitting banks in country towns. The reporter used words like 'cool' and 'unhurried' and 'well-planned' to describe the man and his actions. Wyatt wondered who it was. There was a time when he would have known something like that. Whoever the man was, he was part of a dying breed. Junkies had got into the game now. They were vicious and desperate and prone to taking stupid risks.

Wyatt became aware of a shift in the atmosphere. Police, at least four of them, two in uniform, taking care not to alarm anyone but still scanning the cafeteria. Their heat and eagerness and frustration were palpable. He said to the children, 'What do you recommend? Should I go and see the new James Bond film?'

They kneeled on their chairs, craning to see his finger on the cinema ads. And their mother looked, welcoming the diversion. If you didn't know it, Wyatt and the woman and her children were a family in town for the day—shopping, morning tea, a film for the kids before they went home.

A ripple passed across the room and then it was gone, replaced by crockery smack again, laughter, complaints, the sounds of the city feeding itself. Wyatt got the woman to talk. He did that by asking her questions about her children. After a while she began to notice him, faintly longing, faintly wary. She coloured a little, inclined her body toward him, switched from talking about her children to talking about herself. She had no hope or expectation of anything, just grateful that someone should take an interest.

In a little while, the cops came back, as Wyatt had supposed they would. They found the cafeteria essentially unchanged. There were husbands and fathers among the diners and one of them was Wyatt. They faded away again.

Wyatt got to his feet, showing reluctance. 'Afraid I have to go.'

'Yes.'

He took the escalators to the bargain basement, alert for

trained moves and involuntary gestures, anything that promised trouble—hands curling near pockets, eyes flicking with recognition, mouths turned away to lapel microphones or radios. He was in a crowded space but moved through it as though along a deserted street, jettisoning the clutter in his mind and limbering his body for the moment he'd need to think and act faster than those who were going up against him.

He saw cops on the way down. They didn't see him. They were abandoning the search. The hard scrutiny had gone out of their faces.

At the bottom he filled two logoed shopping bags with cheap, bulky kitchen goods. Bit by bit he was building up his credibility. On the way out he bought sunglasses and a straw hat. On the streets of the city he was one among the thronging thousands.

The city offered trains, buses and planes that would take him out of the state, but he knew that the police would be watching the major terminals. He had to take a less direct and obvious route out. There were flights across Bass Strait from Tyabb, near Westernport Bay. Westernport was also where all this had started, so no-one would be looking for him there.

He walked to Flinders Street station, stopping from time to time to listen to the spruikers spilling onto the footpath outside the discount stores. Wyatt had no interest in the cheap and useless bargains. He was looking for gestures and movements again.

He took the express to Frankston. Thirty minutes later he was on the train to Westernport Bay. When he got out at Hastings it was late morning and he did not look out of place among the handful of other shoppers returning from the city.

Wyatt wandered down the main street. There was an opportunity shop opposite the new library. He went in, stacked the kitchenware on the counter, nodded, went out again, toward the jetty.

As Wyatt saw it, Liz Redding would be questioning Heneker by now. It wouldn't occur to her that the jewels were still on the yacht. It was a long shot, but maybe they hadn't got around to impounding it yet. Maybe it still sat at anchor.

A long shot. What Wyatt found was the yacht tied to a jetty inside the marina with a yellow crime-scene tape all around it.

He walked back up the main street. At the library door he veered to avoid colliding with one of the librarians. She was young, fair, ready to smile, and glanced at him as he edged past her into the foyer and put coins in the public phone. Wyatt asked about flights to King Island. There was one at 4 p.m. He booked a seat, looked at his watch, and saw that he had four hours to kill.

6

Liz Redding hurried from the staff room at the police complex, coffee slopping over her fingers. They had Heneker in the interview room.

There were two men with him—her superintendent, Montgomery, looking slightly out of his depth, and Gosse, her new inspector. She didn't like Gosse. She'd never seen him smile; he reduced the civilian typists and filing clerks to tears three or four times a week; he'd look past you as though you were nothing to him while he spoke to you.

Montgomery climbed to his feet. 'Come in, Sergeant Redding.'

Gosse frowned, as though to argue, but then he shrugged and turned away from her. It's already started, Liz thought. Gosse will freeze me out and soon have Montgomery doing it too.

The room was small and bare. Liz glanced at Heneker. He'd been the last person to see or speak to Wyatt, and she felt a surprising need to be alone with him, ask him if Wyatt looked okay, even though Wyatt had doped her coffee last night and run from her. She'd awoken feeling thick in the head but known at once what had happened. She'd alerted Montgomery from a pay phone in Hastings, and Montgomery had alerted the insurance company.

Heneker looked nondescript, dishevelled by the struggle in the undercover car park. He brushed grit from the knees of his trousers, dabbed a damp handkerchief at an oil stain. His tie was crooked, his suit coat crumpled, the collar turned up.

'What more can I tell you?' he said, looking at Gosse.

Liz mentally framed a question, but suddenly was racked with yawns. They threatened to lay her across the table.

'Sergeant Redding?'

She gulped her coffee. 'I'm fine, sir.'

'Carry on, Inspector.'

'Mr Heneker—'

He looked up. 'This being taped? I want a lawyer.'

'You're not under arrest, for God's sake. A few more questions—'

'Then I can go home?'

'Of course,' Liz said.

Gosse twisted his mouth at the interruption and threw down his pen.

Heneker took advantage of it. He put his head on one side and narrowed his eyes at Liz. 'If I may say so, you don't look a hundred per cent.'

A basic rule was: Never let the bastards start to question *you*. Liz said, 'Let's start from the beginning. You got a phone call? A visit?'

'Phone call.'

'After we contacted you?'

'Yes.'

Gosse picked up his pen again. His knuckles were white around the barrel. This was *his* show. 'A man? Did he give his name?'

'Nope.'

'Didn't recognise his voice?'

'Nope.'

'When you saw him, did you recognise him?'

'Nope.'

Montgomery's chair creaked. Like a kindly uncle he said, 'Your firm ever encountered a man with the name of Wyatt before? He does this sort of thing, commits a robbery, negotiates a reward from the insurance company.'

Neither Liz nor Gosse could bring themselves to look at Montgomery. Montgomery would be better off back in Traffic, from whence he'd come. One, he'd given Heneker a name, if Heneker didn't already have it. Two, Heneker could start doing his own checking now. Three, by butting in he'd eased what little tension she and Gosse had been able to generate in the room, meaning they'd have to start all over again. It didn't seem that Heneker had anything to hide, but it wouldn't be the first time that a burglar and an insurance agent had worked hand in hand.

Heneker shrugged. 'Wyatt? Was that his name? Can't say I know it.'

Gosse said, 'Let's go back to the phone call. What did the caller say?'

'Wyatt? He—'

'Not necessarily Wyatt,' Montgomery said. 'There could be others.'

Gosse threw down his pen again. Heneker's eyes opened wide. 'You mean there's a gang?'

'Just tell us what the caller said.'

'He said straight out that he had the Asahi Collection.'

'And?'

'Well, naturally my ears pricked up. I mean, there was hell to pay when those stones got lifted. Phone calls from Japan all hours of the night and day. Quiet word from the Japanese consul. You name it, I had to take it.'

'Your company wanted the stones back.'

'Sure.'

'You told the caller that you'd meet him?'

'Yep.'

'Did you suggest the parking station?'

Heneker was getting agitated. 'He did. You know all this.'

'So you'd never seen this man before?'

'Never. I told you that.'

Liz leaned forward. 'What did he say?'

'Wasn't much of a talker.'

She knew the truth of that. She'd spent seven days with Wyatt and in that time had learnt almost nothing about him. His *body* had told her things, communicating desire, even affection and regard, and he'd relaxed enough to smile readily, if tiredly, but he had no small talk and he imparted no secrets, even though he was full of secrets. Time—a lot of it—might have helped. Time, and stepping over the line. What would it be like, leading his risky life with him? Would he have stepped over the line for her? She'd never know now.

'He must have said something to you. Didn't he offer proof that he had the stones, for example? Didn't he ask how much the reward would be?'

'Nope.'

Gosse snarled, 'He was observed handing you something, Mr Heneker.'

Heneker shifted in his chair. He reached inside his coat pocket.

277

'All right, all right, he gave me this.'

A necklace spilled onto the table. For a moment they were silent in the face of the soft glow, the winking hard stones.

Liz said, 'You're not a trustworthy man, are you, Mr Heneker? Do your superiors know that?'

'I get results.'

'What were you going to do with the necklace? Sell it?'

Montgomery looked pained. 'Mr Heneker is not suspected or accused of anything, Sergeant Redding. What we have to focus on is this man Wyatt.'

'Yes, sir.'

Gosse leaned forward. 'Did he have the other pieces with him?'

Heneker shook his head. 'Didn't see them.'

'Did he tell you where you could find them?'

'Nope.'

'You didn't warn him?'

'Inspector Gosse,' Montgomery began. 'Mr Heneker is—'

Gosse ignored him. 'You didn't arrange to meet this man later?'

Heneker was outraged. 'What do you take me for? You called and said he might contact me. He did, so I let you know. I've done my bit. If a dozen of you are not capable of catching one man, then that's your problem, not mine.'

'All right, all right, Mr Heneker. I'm sure Inspector Gosse doesn't mean any offence. Is there anything else you can tell us about the man? He didn't say where he was staying? Didn't give you a number to call? Didn't mention any names. Nothing like that?'

'Not a thing.'

'Then you may go.'

'What about the necklace?'

'We'll need to hang on to it for the time being,' Gosse said, 'pending further investigation.'

Heneker shuffled out, scowling, putting plenty of outrage into the tilt of his head. Heneker smelt wrong. Liz didn't know how, but knew that he'd held something back, some fiddle.

She was lost to these thoughts and didn't register the hard stares of Gosse and even Montgomery until it was too late. Gosse said, 'Nice tan, Liz.'

Liz stiffened. Here it comes, she thought.

'So, you decided to go to Vanuatu and arrest Inspector Springett.'

'Yes.'

'Yes, *sir*,' Gosse said.

Liz shrugged.

'An unauthorised trip to a country over which the Victoria Police have no jurisdiction. You came back with Springett and this man Wyatt, only Springett drowned in yesterday's storm and Wyatt gave you the slip, the Asahi jewels in his pocket. Correct, so far?'

'Sir, you have to take into account—'

'I hope to God the press don't get wind of this, Sergeant,' said Montgomery. 'They'd have a field day.'

Gosse said irritably, 'Sergeant, you can understand that we have a problem with your story. The jewels. Your relationship with this Wyatt character, Springett's convenient death.'

Liz struggled against the fog in her head. There was a blowfly buzzing against the glass above the chair in which Heneker had been sitting. Why had Wyatt thought it necessary to drug her? Why had he run? Such contempt and calculation after their seven days together. She felt incomplete and grubby, as if she'd had no say at all in their…encounter. As if he'd had all the power. And he'd had the Asahi jewels all along.

279

She felt muddled and dreamy. Montgomery and Gosse talked around her, talked about charging her, pending suspension and an inquiry. Liz let them talk.

She'd been seven days on the open sea in the stolen yacht before she saw the change in Wyatt. It had happened as they neared the eastern seaboard. She'd been expecting it. He was a hold-up man, after all. Their days together in the briny air and mild sun were simply a respite from the running that was mostly his life and the hunting that was mostly hers. Then the first land birds and rusty coastal freighters had appeared to remind her that she had a job to do, just as she supposed Wyatt was reminded that he had a fortune in jewels in his possession and a cop for a travelling companion.

God, was it only yesterday afternoon? She remembered that he had checked the compass bearing, referred to the chart, made a slight adjustment to the wheel. Rough seas had been forecast, and for Liz that was the precipitating factor.

She'd stood at his elbow, staring down at the chart, then used her finger to trace the coastline of Victoria from Wilsons Promontory to the rip at Port Philip Heads, and up into the bay toward Port Melbourne. 'How big a storm?' she'd asked.

'I wouldn't want to be tossing about in it.'

'So what do we do?'

'Put in somewhere until it blows over.'

'Where?'

She loved his hands. Wyatt had pointed with a finger as slender and worn as a twig weathered by the wind and the rain. 'Westernport marina at Hastings. We can be moored there by about four o'clock in the morning.'

Liz remembered saying, to gauge his reaction: 'I could call CIB detectives to come down and collect us in Hastings. No need to wait for the storm to blow itself out.'

Wyatt had said nothing, his face settling into an impassivity that he wore like a familiar shoe. He could not be read, and that annoyed her.

'Wyatt? We have to talk about this.'

But he stared out at the sea, sombre and cryptic, a hard alertness under it. Impatiently she said, 'Do you want to spend the rest of your life running and hiding? I'll bring you in. I doubt if you'll do any gaol time.'

She squirmed now, remembering this. He must have thought her either naive or devious. But she'd gone on, pestering, cajoling. 'Your testimony will help me clear everything up.'

'I had nothing to do with Springett or his operation.'

'Not directly, maybe, but—'

'So I can't help you.'

'You mean you won't help me.'

'I won't help you put me in gaol, certainly.'

A wave had heaved out of nowhere and they breasted it, tilted, hung there in space, and returned with a crash to the horizontal. Liz had felt her teeth snap together. Wyatt fought the wheel until they were pitching and butting through the surface chop again. They could see coastal towns in the muted light of the approaching dusk. Darkness fell rapidly after that; the sea grew rougher; their running lights burned in the seaspray.

Then the yacht yawed violently. When it was stable, Wyatt said, 'You'd better release Springett or the cuffs will break his wrist. Also he could be useful to us up here.'

She had done that, and Springett had stepped on deck and straight into a foaming wave that washed over the bow and took him with it. She'd been sad and appalled. Wyatt had registered no emotion at all and, once he'd found calmer waters in Westernport Bay, had gone below and laced her coffee with Mogadon.

'Did you hear me, Sergeant Redding? Your suspension will

281

take effect from Friday. In the meantime I want you available for further questioning.'

Liz blinked out of her daze. 'Yes, sir.'

They all left the room. Outside, in the corridor, cleaners had been splashing disinfectant around. Shoe-black streaked the floor and the bottoms of the walls. Liz's head felt heavy, heavy. Before she could stop herself, she veered toward Montgomery. Their shoulders touched. They sprang apart.

'Go home and rest, Sergeant.'

Liz made him stop and face her, in this building that was never still, phones ringing, doors opening and closing. 'But I stopped Springett, sir. I arrested him. A bent policeman, a senior officer. Surely that counts for something?'

Gosse was hovering behind them. He shoved forward. 'Sergeant, if we had the jewels, if we had Wyatt, we might be inclined to go along with your story.'

He shrugged. 'As things stand now, you're history.'

7

Steer's jaw dropped. 'Pentridge?'

'Yep.'

'How come?'

'Because you're a piece of shit,' the Correctional Services officer said.

They were waiting at a reception window in the new, privately operated remand centre in Sunshine. Steer had been remanded on a charge of aggravated burglary, bail denied, and as he understood it you got sent to one of the remand centres pending trial, so why was the system stuffing him around today, turning him away, sending him to Pentridge prison?

'You're joking, right?'

Someone came through from an inner room with a form on a clipboard. The Correctional Services officer signed it and turned to escort Steer out to the police van again. Steer said, 'I mean, how come? Tell me you're joking. I'm on remand, mate. I haven't been to trial yet.'

The officer said wearily, 'Can it, okay? The paperwork says Anthony Steer, remanded to Pentridge.'

'But it's a fucking gaol, mate. It's full of blokes that'd slit your throat because they only got one egg for breakfast.'

'You've done time before. You can handle it.'

Steer could handle it. The problem was, Denise and Chaffey were lining someone up to spring him out of remand. Escaping from Pentridge was a whole other ballgame. He'd have to get Chaffey to do some fancy footwork with Correctional Services, slip someone a few bucks to alter the paperwork.

They bundled Steer into the rear of the police van. Steel floor, walls and ceiling, tiny reinforced glass window, plenty of steel separating him from the driver and the driver's offsider. He was the only prisoner. He heard the bolt slide home on the door of the van. He heard the Correctional Services officer tell the driver, 'Remand's full. They've got room for him in Pentridge.'

'Doesn't make sense,' the driver said. 'You've got remanded guys in Pentridge and sentenced guys in remand. Doesn't make sense.'

'Tell it to the Minister.'

The van braked and spurted fitfully through the western suburbs of the city. At Pentridge, in Coburg, the world seemed to darken, all light and goodness swallowed up by the bluestone walls. They were waved through. Steer's escort parked the van against an inside wall and disappeared for an hour. Steer grew jumpy in his metal tomb. When the doors of the van were finally opened, he said, 'Morning tea, right? Your boss know you boys bludge on the job?'

'Shut it, arsehole.'

They took Steer in to be admitted. A prison officer said, 'Name?'

The driver of the van checked a sheaf of papers in his fist.

'Steer, first name Anthony.'

'*Anthony*, wacky doo,' the prison officer said, ticking something. 'Right, he's ours now.'

Steer watched his escort walk back across the industrial-grade carpet and out through the door to the van. He swung back to the prison officer. 'Look, I shouldn't be here. I should be in remand.'

'Every remand centre in the city is full, pal. That's why you're being remanded here, in D Divison.'

'That's better than H Division, right?'

Steer had spent gaol time in Long Bay, Beechworth, Ararat and Yatala. But he knew all about Pentridge. H Division was high security. It held killers, gunmen, escapers, men with a history of violence toward the prison guards, let alone other prisoners. Some inmates were handcuffed whenever they left their cells, even to have a shower. Others were kept in separation for months at a time, with only two hours out of the cell each day.

'Marginally,' the prison officer said. He handed Steer a stack of clothing. 'Put these on.'

The shirt was thin from repeated washing, the collar frayed. The trousers stopped at his ankles. Both knees had worn through at some stage and been mended with patches on the inside and a crosshatch of thick black cotton thread. The windcheater, once chocolate brown, barely came to his waist. The shoes needed reheeling.

Wearing these clothes would be like wearing the skin of every pathetic junkie and rock spider who had ever been incarcerated in Pentridge. 'No fucking way, mate.'

The officer stiffened. 'Come again?'

'I mean, give us a set of new gear and I'll make it worth your while.'

'Yeah? How much?'

'Fifty.'

'Make it seventy-five and you've got yourself a deal.'

'My lawyer will slip it to you tomorrow.'

'If he doesn't,' the officer said, 'then you go back to wearing cast-offs.'

'For seventy-five,' Steer countered, 'you can chuck in a decent set of bedding.'

Finally an officer escorted Steer out of the administration wing. One inmate whistled on the long walk to his cell. Others stopped to stare as he passed among them. They approached a door. An inmate who had been leaning on the wall, smoking, sprang forward and opened the door, making a big show of it, doing Steer a favour.

Steer knew what it was about. It was a test. If he said thanks, he'd be marked out as a soft target. Steer wasn't soft. He was hard and lithe and very fit. Tall, narrow through the hips but broad at the shoulder, with a flat stomach and big hands, the knuckles like pebbles under the skin. There was scar tissue on his face but it was a grinning, clever, likeable face with bright killer's eyes and bad teeth. He stared at the man, cold and unnerving, and saw him drop his gaze and step back.

The guard watched it happen. 'Piss off, Bence.'

'Right you are, Mr Loney, sir.'

They were in a corridor of simple cells and Steer could see two bunks in each. The cells were poorly lit, about three cubic metres, the walls exuding bitter cold and dampness. Two men were hovering at the open door to the cell at the end of the corridor. 'New bloke,' they said.

Steer gave them the stare. Like Bence, they fell back. So far so good.

The guard said, 'This is your cell, Steer. The charmer on the bottom bunk there is Monger. You'll show Steer here the ropes, won't you, Monger?'

'Sure, Mr Loney,' Monger said.

The guard left them to it. One of the men at the door wandered away. The other, leaning against the jamb, shook a cigarette from the packet in his top pocket. 'Welcome to D Division, matey. Smoke?'

Steer said, 'No thanks.' It might have been a genuine offer, it might also have been a test.

'Suit yourself,' the man said, wandering off.

Steer turned to Monger. Monger was young, nervy looking. 'Mate, you're in my bed.'

Monger sat up in the bunk. 'What?'

'Yours is the top bunk.'

Monger opened and closed his mouth. Finally he nodded, stripped the bedding from his bunk, and climbed onto the top bunk, far from the floor and the crapper, up where the farts gathered—all of which told Steer that this was Monger's first time.

Steer made himself comfortable. At lunchtime he saw Monger bend even further. He was at a scuffed table behind Monger, and watched as Bence and another man sat on either side of Monger and went to work.

First, Bence leaned forward. He fingered Monger's watch strap. 'Nice.'

Steer saw Monger jerk back his arm.

'Steady on,' Bence said. 'Just looking.'

Monger nodded warily.

'Wouldn't have any smokes, would you?' the other man said. 'I'm fresh out.'

Monger had been given his prison issue. He got them out but before he could offer one Bence grabbed the entire packet and slipped it into his top pocket.

'Hey, come on,' Monger said.

287

'Mate, you owe me.'

'Owe you? How come?'

The other man was looking at Monger's food. He reached across, helped himself to the pudding and started to spoon it into his mouth. 'Hungry,' he explained, catching Monger's eye.

Monger said, 'I suppose I owe you as well?'

Both men ignored him. Bence peered around him to the other man. 'What duties they got you on this arvo?'

'Cleaning the shithouse.'

'Get Monger to help you.'

Monger protested. 'I asked for the library.'

'I bet you did, but that's too good for a little shit like you. I'd hate for you to get bored in here. I mean,' Bence went on, 'do a bloke a favour, you expect one in return, right?'

'Absolutely,' the other man said.

Much later, back in the cell, Steer found Monger curled on the floor at the foot of the bunks, tired and dirty, his face streaked and miserable. 'Come on, don't chuck in the towel.'

Monger let himself be helped to his feet. Steer brushed him down, told him to change his clothes. 'Mate,' he said, 'I could see it happening a mile off. 'I watched it all'.

'So why didn't you give us a fucking hand?' Monger said, fighting down his self-disgust, his jitters.

'A few basic survival rules,' Steer said, 'all right? One, from now on, especially out in the yard, you're a marked man. The heavy boys like Bence will give you a hard time, stand in your way, shove you around, stuff like that. If you try and avoid them, go around them, you might as well curl up in a ball and die. You'd be theirs for good. Bum buddy in the shower. What you have to do is take them on. If you make eye contact, don't back down. Give them the old thousand yard stare. They'll beat the crap out of you, but at least you'll earn yourself some respect.'

He broke off to look Monger up and down. 'Jesus, you got it wrong from the start, didn't you?' He flicked his fingers at Monger's worn shirt, his patched trousers. 'Look at this gear they gave you. You shouldn't have accepted it. Same goes for smokes. In here you only accept the offer of something if it comes from a close mate, not some bloke you don't know. Marks you out as weak, accept anything, unable to stand up for yourself. Plus, you'd then owe the guy something in return. That's what that was all about with Bence this afternoon.'

'So why are you helping me?'

Steer said, 'Don't like to see a young bloke stuffed around.'

'I'm not a poofter. I tell you that right now.'

'Didn't say you were. I'm not either. But we got to pass the time away, right? Might as well give you a few pointers.'

In fact, Steer liked to lecture young crims. It was a side of him that could be irritating, but he couldn't help himself. He liked to point out where they'd gone wrong. Partly he got a kick out of it, partly he was reminding himself of where he'd stuffed up in the past, and partly it earned him respect—if he didn't push it.

The next day they called to say he had a visitor. He was escorted to a room that smelt of hopelessness. Denise was waiting for him. She gave him a watery smile, and a kind of sadness settled in Steer.

The visitors' room was like a cheap cafe, a place of scraping chairs, shouted conversations, coughing smokers and general defeat. Poverty, that was the word, poverty. This was a world of poor men and their poor families. Their clothes were cheap, their haircuts and shoes, their ambitions. Every man in the room had showered and shaved that morning, but most had used soap in place of shampoo, and wore bad shaves from blunt electric razors, and generally looked unwashed and unkempt. It was no place to be meeting your bird.

Steer shook off the sadness. He became vigorous and sharp. 'Great to see you, sweetheart.'

'Great to see you, too.'

'Chaffey's got to get me into remand.'

Denise touched the back of his hand. 'I saw him this morning. He's working on it.'

Steer gave her a loaded look. 'Any other news?'

'He rang before I left. He's confident.'

Steer snarled. 'Confident? What does he think I pay him for? I want results.'

8

Vallance and Allie said the Windsor Hotel, said could he pick them up and give them a lift to their place in Westernport. Maybe they didn't own a car, maybe they didn't drive—whatever, when Raymond left Chaffey he walked back to his apartment so that he could change and collect the keys to his XJ6, then he drove to the Windsor, parked outside and called up to their room on the courtesy phone.

'On our way,' Vallance said.

Raymond went back to the car and waited. There was still a lot of cop activity in the centre mile of the city. The Windsor. Clearly Vallance and Allie weren't short of a bob or two—unless it was all for show.

As he waited, he let himself think about Chaffey's proposal. A hundred grand for lifting a collection of paintings was better money at a lower risk factor than robbing a bank, so it was worth thinking about—if he were able to find himself a good partner.

According to Chaffey, art theft was the world's most lucrative crime after drug dealing. Stolen paintings found their way into private collections, were used as a stake in buying and selling arms and drugs, sold to crooked gallery owners and dealers for a third of their retail value or sold back to insurance companies or owners for the reward money. Police in Australia had only a twenty per cent clear-up rate. They were forced to sift through computerised records that listed stolen chainsaws and laptop computers alongside Picassos and Renoirs. Security was costly for most gallery owners and most private collectors kept inadequate records.

As Chaffey put it, there was only a 48-hour window of opportunity for lifting the paintings. The building where they were housed was undergoing a renovation, and for 48 hours—a Saturday and a Sunday—the power would be switched off and the paintings locked away in a storeroom. No cameras, no alarms, for 48 hours. Just a few locked doors and a nightwatchman every now and then through the night.

Twenty minutes later, Allie and Vallance appeared with their cases. They wore jeans and polo shirts, designer quality. Raymond found both of them hard to figure out. The jeans hung loosely on Vallance's bony hips and he looked all wrong, somehow too old for the picture he was presenting to the world. Allie didn't, so what was she doing with him? Raymond wanted to peel her open like a piece of fruit.

Vallance got into the back seat. Allie slid into the passenger seat and her long thighs filled Raymond's imagination. Vallance leaned into the gap between the seats. 'Now, this is a no-obligation trip, okay? You don't have to commit yourself. Spend the night at our summer place and we'll take a boat out in the morning, look at the wreck, then you think about it. But I'll ask you to keep this confidential. I think you understand.'

'No drama,' Raymond said.

He fired up the Jaguar and slid into traffic. Neither Allie nor

Vallance said anything about the car, as though they were born to luxury.

'You were talking about some old newspaper clipping,' Raymond prompted, watching Vallance in the rear-view mirror.

Satisfaction and passion mingled on the man's narrow face. 'Got it right here,' he said, opening a document wallet. 'You know, it can be like detective work, hunting down old wrecks. You accumulate apparently random fragments of information and look for the patterns and answers. Often what you get are false leads; you find yourself exercising your mind about the wrong problem.'

He paused, staring into space. Raymond groaned inwardly. He was about to learn more than he needed to know, but the world was full of Vallances, full of tidy, narrow, pointless passions.

'In 1827,' Vallance said, 'a barque called the *Eliza Dean* was reported missing between Sydney and Hobart. She'd sailed with a handful of passengers, plus provisions, plus fifty thousand quid's worth of gold, silver and copper coinage. Can you imagine what that would be worth today?'

Raymond allowed himself to look awed. He sensed Allie next to him, her secret, almost conniving smile.

'Gold and silver coins, mostly. Also bank notes, cheques and the royal mail. Most of the coins were bound for the garrison stationed in Hobart Town. The officers and soldiers hadn't been paid for some time.'

Raymond steered with one hand, fished out his Spanish dollar with the other. 'You think this came from the *Eliza Dean*?'

'I'm sure of it. The date is right, all the other wrecks and missing ships around that period have been accounted for, and none was carrying currency. You want to know how I worked it out?'

'Sure.'

'At first I thought Bass Strait pirates. What they'd do was build bonfires on the shores of King Island during fogs and lure ships ashore. They'd loot anything they could use—cutlasses, pistols, knives, clothing, food, tools—and store it all on Robbins Island. One story I heard, a woman was washed ashore wearing diamond rings. What did they do? They chopped off her fingers to get the rings. They'd fight amongst themselves. They'd drink, trade women, disappear without trace.'

'Charming,' Raymond said.

Allie turned to him, smiling her smile. 'Of course,' she said, 'we've come a long way since then in relations between men and women.'

Raymond thought: Maybe he hits her, the bastard. He coughed, glanced into the rear-view mirror. 'You thought pirates got the *Eliza Dean*?'

'I did,' Vallance said. 'Then I thought, no, why would she be sailing that far west? The Cornwall Group, islands about seventy k's south-east of Wilsons Promontory seemed like a better bet. A score of vessels have come to grief there. Thick sea fogs, howling gales, no lighthouse until the 1840s.'

'So we'll be diving in howling gales and thick fogs?' Raymond asked.

'Nope. Where I found the coins we can anchor in sheltered waters, safely spend weeks exploring the reefs there if we wanted to. Want to know how come I focused on the Cornwall Group and not Flinders Island or the east coast of Tassie?'

'Sure.' Raymond wound the big car past the Melbourne Cricket Ground. The big lights loomed coldly like spy cameras.

'Okay, listen to this. *Hobart Town Courier*, 1827. It's what I mean by piecing clues together.'

Vallance waved a photocopy between the seats, then settled back to read aloud. 'Blah, blah, blah...*Captain Whitby, master of the*

Government cutter, Swordfish, *was dispatched to make a search among the* Bass Strait Islands *for tidings or wreckage of the missing brig,* Mary May. *Captain Whitby reported on his return that considerable wreckage from the* Mary May *had been discovered on Clarke and Preservation Islands, but no trace of her passengers or crew.*

'*Nevertheless a curious but related fact has emerged as a result of Captain Whitby's search. Whilst at anchor under the Cornwall Group during the term of a powerful gale, Captain Whitby had occasion to take the ship's vessel to the nearest shore, where he came upon a sealer living with two native women. The sealer, Sydney Dan by name, was unable or unwilling to provide a satisfactory account for the presence in his hut of certain items, namely a sea chest, a snuff box, numerous pistols and a major's uniform. Furthermore, part of a deckhouse had been converted for use as a pigsty roof. Having ascertained that none of these items belonged to the* Mary May, *Captain Whitby questioned the man more closely. His answers appeared to be most evasive, and* Whitby *returned to the* Swordfish *with his curiosity and suspicion considerably aroused.*

'*Next morning Captain Whitby returned to the island and, taking the native women aside for questioning, discovered a cooked leg of mutton, a ham and a cushion. Pursuing his inquiries farther afield, among sealers, fishermen and sailors from diverse parts of the Bass Strait islands, Captain Whitby learned that numerous sealers had recently arrived in Launceston bearing cheques, gold coins and bank notes for which they could not give a clear accounting. One man possessed a ship's studding sail boom, with the sails still attached.*

'*The mystery has since deepened. The* Courier *has it on good authority that Captain Gibb, Port Officer at Hobart Town, last month received anonymously in the post the register and other papers from the* Eliza Dean, *a barque missing between Sydney Town and Hobart Town this past half year. Further to this, letters which could only have been carried by the* Eliza Dean *recently arrived at their destinations in Hobart Town, postmarked Launceston.*

'*Grave concern is held for the* Eliza Dean, *if indeed she was lost upon the reefs surrounding the Cornwall Group. There is a dereliction of duty on the part of the Government if immediate steps are not taken to unravel the mystery that enshrouds the fate of the thirty individuals on board. It is a matter of importance to know whether they were drowned or murdered, and whether they landed alive or if the bodies were plundered after being washed ashore.*'

Raymond frowned. 'Yeah, yeah, yeah, but how do we know the treasure is still on the wreck? It sounds as if she was looted before she broke up. The coins you found could have been a handful that got left behind.'

He saw Vallance smile complacently. 'Trust me, I know. I've already made several passes with a metal detector and accounted for all of the ferrous metals. The rest is gold, solid gold, and silver.'

Gold. The word lodged in Raymond's head. He found himself braking hard to avoid ramming the rear of a taxi on the approach to the south-eastern freeway at Hoddle Street.

As the endless suburbs slipped past their windows, Raymond asked questions. They were as hard and knowing as he could make them. He wasn't an easy catch. He didn't want them to *think* he was.

'You're looking for investors, fifty grand each. What does my fifty grand buy me?'

'A sixth share in the treasure. Me, Allie, you, and three others. Equal sixths.'

'I don't mean that. I mean, what kind of expedition are we mounting here?'

He sensed Allie shift in her seat. She was looking at him, her knees swivelled toward him. Raymond had read about that in a book on body language. If they cross one leg over the other or face away from you, they were unconsciously saying they didn't want to screw you. Allie wasn't saying that. She was saying she wanted him, clear as day. Raymond almost didn't hear Vallance say:

'We need a ship we can live on in comfort for a few days. Something with a winch and a fair-sized deck and hold area. We'll need different types of metal detectors, sonar gear, underwater video, an airlift, underwater scooters, maybe even a prop wash.'

Those were just words to Raymond. He was more interested in concealment. 'I get the impression you don't want anyone knowing about this expedition, so how do you propose to outfit it and spend a few days searching without being noticed?'

'You're right,' Vallance said smoothly. 'Why should we arouse the curiosity of others? I intend to hire a good boat in one port, the gear in a range of other ports around Victoria and Tasmania.'

'Do we need all that gear?'

'That coin you've got there is one of a handful I found on a quick dive. The rest have been buried by the action of the tides. They'll need some getting at. It's been a hundred and seventy years, after all.'

'I've scuba dived, but that's all,' Raymond said.

'That's good enough for tomorrow's dive. It's just exploratory. I guarantee you won't be disappointed. When the time comes to mount a salvage dive, I'll do the diving. I've got hours of experience.'

'How long?'

'The salvage itself?'

Raymond nodded.

'Several days, maybe a couple of weeks. We have to locate the wreck first—'

'I thought you already had.'

'What I found were loose coins shaken free by the tides. The actual wreck, where the majority of the treasure is, could be some distance away after all this time. It might have broken up and be

297

scattered over several hundred metres. So we locate the wreck, then make a plot chart of the overall site, then we start excavating, marking all our finds on the chart. That'll give us a better picture of the spread pattern.'

They were off the freeway now, heading south on the Dandenong–Hastings road, past waterlogged farmland. Raymond looked at his watch. Almost time for lunch.

'When do we go out?'

'First thing in the morning,' Allie said, her soft growl almost in his ear as she shifted to get comfortable.

Raymond liked her voice. 'So I stay the night at your summer place.'

'Be it ever so humble,' Vallance said.

'Do you have your own boat?'

'We have a friend who runs a charter operation. He'll take us out in the morning.'

'Good old Quincy,' Vallance said.

'Good old Quincy,' Allie agreed.

Raymond frowned. 'How many people are in on this?'

Allie's cool fingers touched his wrist. 'It's all right. Quincy's not involved. So far we've lined up three of the four investors.'

Raymond's draw dropped. '*Three* of the four? Already? Who are they?'

Vallance seemed to close down. 'You'll understand that they don't want their identities revealed. These are professional men. They've paid their fifty thousand.'

'What if I say no?'

'Then no hard feelings. We'll approach one of our other contacts. It's just that you appeal to us. These are old geezers we're talking about. To them it's just another investment. They've got no soul, no romance in their veins. Someone like you, likes to hear the stories, willing to come out and dive with us, willing to have an open mind and not tie us up with lawyers and accountants—that's what we want for our fourth investor.'

Raymond was silent. He felt a gut-clench of anxiety, a feeling that he might miss out entirely if he didn't act soon.

They drove over the railway tracks on the outskirts of Hastings, Vallance directing Raymond to a run-down flat in a block of four, several streets back from the waterfront. Again, Raymond couldn't work them out. It was an ugly little flat. They unpacked and drove to a cafe at the marina. One hour passed. Two. They made small talk. Raymond guessed that Allie and Vallance were maintaining a delicate silence around the topic of his investing with them, and so didn't want to pressure or confuse him. After a while they left him to think, saying they were going to make arrangements with their charter-captain friend, Quincy.

Raymond ordered another coffee and stretched his legs. Gulls wheeled above the cafe tables. Sail rigging pinged on the dry-docked yachts. He blinked, taking in the man who was staring moodily at the chalked menu.

'Uncle Wyatt?' he said, his old name for his father's brother.

9

A while since Wyatt had been called that. He knew of only one person in the world who'd called him that, but Wyatt distrusted coincidence and didn't turn around, not until he'd sought out the voice in the mirror behind the cash register. Still Wyatt didn't respond. He ran a checklist of his senses. They were a barometer of the town, the marina, the cafe itself. The place *seemed* all right: scratchy muzak, idle yachting types, tourists, the clank of cafe cutlery. Finally he said, 'Ray?' and turned to his nephew.

Raymond unfolded from a plastic chair and grinned awkwardly. 'Been a long time.'

Wyatt was shocked. It was as if his brother stood there, languid, graceful, knockabout, wearing a likeable grin. But in the case of Wyatt's brother there had always been sour grievances under the grin. A lot of people, like Ray's mother, hadn't seen that until it was too late.

Wyatt stepped forward and shook the boy's hand. 'Ray.'

Boy—hardly a boy. If this were a normal occasion and Wyatt a normal man he might have said something like, 'You've certainly shot up,' or 'The last time I saw you you were knee high to a grasshopper,' but Wyatt had nothing mindless to say.

Instead, he looked at his grown-up nephew and asked, aware of the suspicion in his voice: 'What brings you here?'

Raymond sensed it. 'Don't worry, I'm not tailing you if that's what you think. I'm here with some friends.' He searched for the term he wanted. 'Fishing trip. You? On holiday?'

It occurred to Wyatt that he hadn't had a holiday in his life, just long stretches of idle, recuperative time between heists, periods spent resting his body but not his head. There was always the next job to plan, for when the money ran out. He clapped a hand shyly on his nephew's shoulder. 'Good to see you,' he said.

Raymond seemed to fill with pleasure. 'Sit,' he said, signalling to the waitress. 'Beer? Something stronger?'

Wyatt shook his head. 'Not for me.'

At once Raymond went still. 'You're not working on something?' He looked around the marina, as though banks and payroll vans had materialised there.

Wyatt allowed himself to smile. He watched carefully as Raymond turned to signal the waitress again. The last time Wyatt had seen the boy was fifteen years ago, when they'd put his father in the ground—Wyatt's brother, a man weak and vicious enough to blacken the eyes and crack the ribs of his wife and kid whenever the world let him down. In the end the world had disappointed him all the way to the morgue. Raymond had been ten at the time, fine-boned and quick like his mother, laughter always close to the surface. He'd had a black eye at the funeral, Wyatt recalled, and it was clear how he'd got it. He'd shown no emotion when the family tossed dirt into the yawning grave, only satisfaction. The official story was that Wyatt's brother had pitched

301

head-first from a flight of steps, onto a concrete floor. He'd been drinking heavily. Wyatt had gone with the accident story—until he saw Raymond at the graveside. Then he'd known it wasn't an accident, or mostly not.

'More coffee here,' Raymond told the waitress.

Wyatt had known that his brother was no good. He'd tried to help, giving the family money, giving his own brother hard warnings to play it straight with his wife and son. It hadn't been enough, and later, after the funeral, they lost touch with one another. It seemed to be the best thing to do. Raymond had been getting too interested in the stories that surrounded Wyatt, making them add up to something more than the truth, until he'd asked, at the wake: 'Can I live with you, Uncle Wyatt?'

'What have you been doing?' Wyatt said now.

'This and that.' Then, slyly, 'Not checking up on me, are you?'

Wyatt said nothing. He searched deep behind the open face. If Raymond was a user, his body would betray him. The boy's eyes were clear. No twitches. If Raymond were somehow wrong inside, like the man who'd fathered him, that might reveal itself as well. Wyatt needed to know.

The waitress came with their coffees. For a moment, Wyatt wondered if he'd seen something in Raymond, but now it was gone. He blinked, and saw Raymond sitting across from him, cool, very collected.

For the next thirty minutes, they talked, Wyatt keeping the conversation away from himself, away from questions about the past, always shifting the focus back onto Raymond. He had no use for small talk and an abhorrence of the world knowing anything about him. If he had to be the focus, he stuck to an abbreviation of the present. But Raymond was equally withholding. To cover it, he sometimes made absurd wagers. 'Bet you five the woman

302

drives,' he said, nodding at an elderly couple crossing the car park to their car.

Finally he said, 'So, Uncle Wyatt, let's cut the crap. What are you doing here?'

'Going home.'

'Home? No point asking where that is?'

Wyatt didn't reply.

As if to say, 'I'm a better man than you are,' Raymond fished out a pen and scribbled on the back of a coaster. 'This here's my address and phone number. Look me up next time you're passing through Melbourne.'

Wyatt nodded.

'Look, no more bullshit,' Raymond said. Colour and embarrassment showed on his face. 'Those country banks? The bush bandit? That's me.'

Wyatt waited for it to sink in. He felt faintly shocked. After a moment, he said flatly, 'The bush bandit.'

He supposed that it could be true. Raymond wasn't boasting, just stating who he was now. Wyatt had no wish to offer advice or warnings to his nephew, and there was nothing at risk for himself, so he decided to leave it at that.

'Never been caught, never even been a suspect. I work alone. If I pick up something I can't offload, there's a guy who'll do it for me.'

'Maybe I know him.'

'Chaffey. Lawyer in the city.'

Wyatt shook his head. He was out of touch.

'Chaffey knows *you*,' Raymond said. 'I mean,' he said hastily, catching the stiffening of Wyatt's face, 'he knows you're my uncle, that's all, knows all the stories about you, knows we don't have anything to do with each other. He hasn't sent me to track you down, if that's what you're thinking.'

'Good.'

'Although,' Raymond said, 'he did mention a job to me.'

Wyatt waited. He could see now that Raymond had been working up to this. 'I see.'

'I more or less turned it down,' Raymond said. 'It's an art collection, outside my field, plus I'd need a partner and I don't know anyone I trust enough to work with.'

Wyatt felt a stir of interest, almost an itch. 'What sort of art collection?'

Raymond outlined the job swiftly. 'Worth a hundred grand,' he concluded. 'Chaffey's got a buyer already lined up.'

Wyatt kept stony-faced. A hundred thousand dollars, split two ways.

'Think about it, Uncle Wyatt. This is right up your alley. I wouldn't know a print from a poster.'

Wyatt felt his nerve endings stir. He looked around the marina, looking for the trap. 'You sure you're not following me?'

Raymond's face darkened. 'Fuck you. For fifteen years I haven't known where you were. How could I follow you? Pure coincidence.'

'Okay, okay.'

'So, you interested?'

'I'll let you know.'

Gloomily Raymond began to shred a paper napkin. 'Don't suppose you need the money. You must have stashed a fair bit away over the years.'

Wyatt couldn't tell his nephew about the big jobs that had gone wrong, the stuff he'd left behind, the pissy jobs in the past couple of years. A kind of sadness settled in him. If he'd stepped in all that time ago, he could have saved Raymond from a world in which the only men he had to model himself upon were brutes like his father and hold-up men like his uncle. Raymond had

304

grown up too quickly and seen too much too soon. Wyatt tried to name the source of his sadness. It was composed of many things, among them guilt, sadness for his brother's short, failed life, a renewed sense of responsibility for Raymond.

All of these things, but mostly his memory of that last meeting, when Raymond was ten and had seen his father into the ground and had turned to Wyatt and asked, 'Can I live with you, Uncle Wyatt?'

'Raymond, my boy, there you are.'

Wyatt felt his interest wane and his wariness return. A man and a woman, the man a skinny character in his fifties, the woman a lithe, pouting fluffball in her twenties.

'Um, meet my fishing mates,' Raymond said.

He named the man as Brian Vallance, the woman as Allie Roden, and told them that Wyatt was an old family friend. 'Known Macka since I was a kid,' he said.

Wyatt shook the woman's hand briefly, then the man's. The man held on, slowly squeezing, testing Wyatt.

A waste of time. Wyatt shook his head irritably and withdrew his hand. He didn't like the man or the woman, and watched them when they were all seated. Vallance wore the pout of a man convinced that he'd never exercised choice, that his failures were none of his doing but the result of the raw deals that life had thrown up for him—the bad luck, accidents and treachery of others. He wore costly jeans and Wyatt saw him tug the fabric away from his knees carefully and smooth it under his thighs whenever he shifted in his seat. The woman was playing some kind of game. She was with Vallance, but giving Raymond soulful looks. And once, when the other two men were not looking, Wyatt found her looking long and hard at him.

'You a fisherman, Macka?' she asked, a slow heat in her face and her voice.

Wyatt shook his head. He climbed to his feet. 'Not me.' She was slippery. He had to get away. Unaccountably, then, he thought of Liz Redding.

10

She was under orders from Gosse not to leave the building before five. He'd call her in every couple of hours for another bout of questioning, sometimes with Montgomery in attendance, sometimes with the faceless men from the Internal Investigations branch. It was always the same thing: they wanted times, dates, places, names, and they wanted her to account for her motives in going to Vanuatu and coming back with a known crook.

Liz chafed through the day. At one point a friend came by and whispered, 'Mate, they're searching your locker.'

Mate, Liz thought. Man or woman, you're everyone's mate in the police. It was a life built for mates, all differences levelled out, including gender. But one false step and they soon reminded you how different you were.

She found Gosse there, supervising. 'Go back to your desk, Sergeant.'

'You have no right—'

'I have every right.'

'You think I've got the jewels hidden in my tracksuit pants? Think I've got a valentine from Wyatt hidden in my tampon box?'

Gosse turned, snarling, 'Nothing about you would surprise me. Back to your desk, Sergeant.'

Liz went back. She felt the beginnings of a shift in the way she viewed the world. She wanted to find Wyatt but realised that she no longer wanted to find him on behalf of the Victoria Police. She hunted the files for an address. When Wyatt had first come to her attention he'd been trying to offload stolen goods. Liz had posed as a fence, and the man who'd led Wyatt to her was Jardine, a burnt-out thief and friend of Wyatt's. Jardine had since died, but his sister Nettie might know something.

At five o'clock Liz drove to a flat, depressed corner of Coburg, where small weatherboard and brick-veneer houses breathed into one another's mouths and old women and men broke their hips on the root-buckled footpaths. The paint was flaking on Nettie Jardine's house. One corner needed restumping and the external boards and frames harboured a deep, rotting dampness. It would be there even in mid-summer, like an exhalation of hopelessness.

Nettie opened the sticking main door to Liz but not the screen door. She wore the cares of the world in her thin frame, her limp pale hair, her narrow mouth. But a spark of something animated her sorrowing face when she saw Liz. 'You again.'

'Hello, Nettie.'

'That's the shot, first names. What do I get to call you, your majesty?'

'I don't mind if you call me Liz.'

Nettie Jardine sniffed. 'Thought I'd finished with you lot.'

'Just a couple of questions. Do you think I could—'

'Right here will do,' Nettie said, folding her arms firmly

behind the screen door.

'Right. About your brother—'

'He's dead.'

'I know. I'm sorry.'

'Sorry's not going to bring him back.'

'Nettie, we're more interested in a man your brother was involved with. Wyatt.'

'That bastard.'

Liz said mildly, 'I understand he was your brother's friend. Didn't he help out with rent, bills, living costs?'

'Guilt money.'

'Your brother blueprinted burglaries for him, Nettie. He wasn't forced into it.'

Nettie was stubborn. 'Wyatt had influence over Frank.'

Liz doubted that. She said, 'What I need to know is, how did Frank get in touch with Wyatt? When Frank put a burglary or a robbery together, how did he pass on the photographs, the floor plans, the briefing notes?'

'Mail drop.'

'You mean a holding address?'

'Call it what you want. He's paranoid. Doesn't like you to know where he lives.'

Liz nodded. She had an impression of the unreality of her life. Wyatt's life, a secretive, complicated parallel life, seemed suddenly clearer and more appealing to her than her own. 'So you've never seen his place.'

Nettie shrugged. 'Why would I?'

'Know anyone who has? His family, maybe?'

'Far as I know, there's only a nephew.'

Liz sharpened at that. 'Nephew?'

'Raymond Wyatt. Flash bugger.'

'Where would I find him?'

Nettie laughed. 'Try the bloody phone book.'

Fair enough, Liz thought. 'This mail drop. Where was it?'

'Hobart,' Nettie muttered.

Hobart. The mail drop was probably inoperative now, given Wyatt's caution, but a man can't live in total isolation. He has wants and needs that bring him into contact with the wider world. He has dealings with dentists, doctors, real-estate agents, local shopkeepers. Hobart was a small place. She could go down there, flash his photo around. It wasn't much of a likeness. It was a blurred, long-distance surveillance shot. Wyatt, eternally watchful, had never let himself be photographed clearly. Liz made a few impressionistic notes in her mind—tall, slender, graceful on his feet, big hands, rarely smiles, thin face, sharp lines with a dark cast to the skin.

'Where in Hobart?'

There was no humour in Nettie's smile. 'Couldn't say, really. All I know is, you're too far away and too late.'

'Nettie,' Liz said warningly, 'what's going on?'

'You wait and see. All I'm saying is, no-one hurts the Jardines and gets away with it.'

11

On the outskirts of Hastings the cab driver caught Wyatt's eye in the rear-view mirror. 'You got a yacht down here?'

He wants to discuss sailing with me, Wyatt thought. To forestall that, he said, 'Just been visiting for a few days.'

'Like it?'

'Sure.'

'People think this is a bit of a backwater, but we have our share of drama.'

'Yes,' Wyatt said.

'That kiddie abducted on the other side of the Peninsula, that killer up in Frankston. You'll even see in the marina a boat the police impounded. Something to do with smuggling from Vanuatu, one of them places.'

Wyatt glanced out of the window. The taxi was passing swampy flatland. Beyond it was the refinery. A big tanker was in dock.

He let the driver talk on. Once inside the terminal at Tyabb aerodrome, he stood at the glass, gazing across the airstrip. Suddenly a shadow washed over the field, cutting off the sun briefly, and a harsh motor swamped the ordinary human sounds behind him. Wyatt looked up. A plane was barrelling in, hard and fast. It was squat-looking with a high cockpit, and it wore US Navy markings. It dated from the Second World War and Wyatt hadn't seen it for a while. He'd forgotten it. It used to roll and flip in the sky above his house behind Shoreham. He watched it sideslip against the cross-wind and touch down, skipping a little before it settled into a fast run toward the hangars. It dwarfed the Cessnas and Pipers.

At four o'clock Wyatt and six other passengers boarded a twin-prop, ten-seater commuter plane. During the ascent, he watched the topography clarify into a school at a crossroads, a trucking firm, a motel, a sunflash in the distance from the refinery at Westernport, the wingless, snout-up DC3 in a corner of the airfield, then horse studs, wineries, small holdings, roads and fences. The plane held a course south-east. This was a part of the world that Wyatt had crossed and recrossed a thousand times, on foot, in a car, in the air, often on the run from the law. He had staked life and a degree of contentment on it, using the little farmhouse somewhere below as his bolthole, slipping away from time to time to knock over a bank or a payroll van. That life had failed him in the end. But he knew the place, it had mapped itself in his brain and on his nerve endings.

Inverloch and the Victorian coast slipped by beneath him. King Island was ahead, and a separate flight to Hobart. The water looked choppy.

Wyatt allowed himself to think of Liz Redding again, and of their voyage from Vanuatu in the stolen yacht. For six days they had managed to forget who they were, but when the coastline of Australia appeared, Wyatt had found himself planning the next stage, escaping with the jewels. He hadn't known how to include Liz in his plans, so convinced himself that she wasn't a factor.

Liz had been more forthright. Running with him was out, she didn't want to lose him, which left an impossible alternative.

'Wyatt,' she'd said, 'let me bring you in.'

Wyatt had shaken his head. Killings and millions of plundered dollars marked the years of his existence and the police of every state wanted a word with him.

'Out of the question,' he said.

There was distress in her voice. 'What about us?'

Wyatt had been unable to say anything. He'd stared at the sea, the rising chop on the surface of the water, the seabirds sideslipping above the white caps. The clouds had been scudding. There was plenty to be on guard against: the waves, iron shipping containers floating just beneath the surface, waiting to rip a hole in the hull.

And his feelings. Liz Redding was combative, bright, generous. She made him feel wanted, even loved. The word quivered there in his head, once he'd admitted it. Wyatt thought of her squirming naked energy, her wit and affection. But all that had become a complication. Old habits of preservation had kicked in.

'Wyatt? Are you deaf?' she'd demanded. 'Have you thought about us at all?'

Into the silence that followed, Wyatt had muttered, 'All the time.'

He realised now, far above Bass Strait, that he was unused to conversation, unused to the slipperiness of a conversation like the one he'd had with Liz Redding. His disposition was built upon layers of secrecy and preservation, a lifetime's habit of believing that no-one was dependable but himself. People found him resourceful and cautious, a man with a dark, rapid mind, who took nothing on trust and who could be trusted to place his safety before anything, but they always wanted more, a man with ordinary doubts and scruples and impulses. What they got was a man who shut himself down. They looked for the doors and windows in him but few ever found them. Liz Redding had come close, in those seven days. He liked that, but it scared him. He'd seen that a life with her might be possible. She was his way out, if he'd wanted that.

But he'd decided that he didn't want it. As the storm rose in intensity, he'd charted a course for Westernport Bay, a place he knew better than his own face in the mirror. It wasn't imperative that they dock in Westernport, but Wyatt hadn't told Liz Redding that. Old habits were kicking in and he was going to betray her.

He'd gone below, first to the packet of Mogadon in the medicine cabinet, then to the wall oven in the galley. It was set into the bulkhead and worked perfectly well as an oven, but it also slid out to reveal a small waterproof safe. Wyatt pocketed a roll of $100 notes, his .38 revolver and a distinctive necklace, and closed everything again, just as Liz Redding had called down to him, 'Wyatt? Is everything all right?'

'Coming now.'

He'd laced her coffee, then added a dash of Scotch, and carried it to her in the wheelhouse.

She let him take the wheel. She sipped her coffee. 'Ah, hot, foul and bracing.'

Wyatt said nothing. He watched the heaving sea. It was not a companionable silence. All of the topics between them had been pushed as far as he was able to take them, and he was waiting, with sadness, for his final act of betrayal to take effect. In a mood of disconnection and apathy, they had sailed through the night.

Someone had once accused him of working from an emotionless base. He mused on that now, as the plane banked above the Bass

Strait islands. He mused on it for half a minute, all it was worth, trying to picture the face he presented to the world. He knew it could be assertive, prohibitive, sometimes chilling, giving nothing away. Most people's faces were a barometer of their feelings. They bulged in all directions, chased by doubts, scruples and conflicts. But it was not true that Wyatt was emotionless. He had room only for the essential ones, that's all, and he kept those to himself. Up until now, that hadn't been a problem.

The pilot's voice broke in upon his melancholy. They were descending.

Ten minutes later, Wyatt discovered that he would have to spend the night on the island.

The next morning, he was on the first flight out. When the plane touched down at Hobart Airport, Wyatt climbed into a taxi. There was always the risk that a cab driver would remember his face one day, but Wyatt had no intention of taking the airport bus to the city. Wyatt knew all about that bus. He'd been caught before. A good ten years older than airport buses anywhere else in the world, it would hum along the freeway and over the bridge and into the tight, one-way streets of Hobart, encouraging a sense of mission accomplished in its passengers. But then, unaccountably, it would begin to stop at the hotels, the motels, the casino way to hell and gone down Sandy Bay Road, dropping off passengers, before finally winding its way back to the downtown bus station, scarcely emptier than when it had set out, the majority obliged to wait for the chosen few. There was nothing democratic about that bus.

He paid off the taxi at the wharf opposite Salamanca Place, leaving him with a ten-minute walk to his apartment building. He'd never taken a cab all the way to the door in his life. He always concealed his final destination and covered his tracks. That was second nature to Wyatt. It was part of an automatic checklist that had kept him alive and out of gaol and mostly ahead since the day he was born.

The Mawson base supply ship was in dock. He idled for a while, watching crated food and equipment being winched aboard. The bow looked scraped, freshly wounded, as though the ship had ploughed through ice recently, leaving paint smears in its wake.

Wyatt turned to go. He stood for some time on the footpath, waiting for the traffic to clear, and came close to witnessing a death. A boy had ambled onto the road from the opposite footpath. He was about ten, undernourished, cheaply dressed, hair cropped short as though for fashion's sake but probably to control head lice. He was cramming a hamburger into his mouth, and the car that braked to avoid him, snout dipping with the raw, smoking bite of its tyres, skewed violently and finally stopped, its front bumper gently knocking the boy's knees.

The world held its breath. One second. Two seconds. There was something wrong about the boy's reaction time. Then suddenly he spasmed with fright. One hand jerked involuntarily, scattering the hamburger. A kind of sulky defiance and embarrassment showed on his face. He sniggered. Wyatt knew exactly what it meant. The boy was saying, *'Missed me—but I wouldn't have minded if you'd run me down. Death—or food and a warm bed in hospital—would be better than the life I've got.'* Wyatt felt that he knew the boy. His home was a place where you got smacked about the head and thrown across the room. Where a belt buckle drew your blood for no reason at all. It was a pathology Wyatt recognised.

Grief settled in him, dull and dark. Wyatt and his brother had had 'uncles' when they were kids. One after the other. Those men hadn't stayed for long. They didn't want a couple of kids hanging around. They were bitter and afraid and their only solace was to witness fear in the two boys. Wyatt had made sure that they never saw it in him. His brother hadn't been so lucky. Wyatt's brother

316

had absorbed all of that bitterness and it had erupted when he had a son of his own, Raymond.

Wyatt glanced at his watch. Almost lunchtime. He decided to call in at his mail drop, a dingy barbershop on the other side of the downtown area of the little city. When he got there, the barber said, almost relishing it, 'Nothing.' Wyatt shrugged. He hadn't really been expecting mail or messages. He crossed back to the waterfront, climbed the Kelly Steps into Battery Point.

Wyatt lived on the ground floor of a squat, tan brick and white stucco block of flats overlooking the Derwent. He'd been there for a year, in this city where no-one knew him, where no-one cared that he came and went once a month or so, where no-one connected his movements with a rifled office safe in Toorak, a hallway stripped of Streetons in Vaucluse, an empty jewellery box on the Gold Coast.

A man called Frank Jardine had put these jobs together for him, but Jardine was dead now, and Wyatt would have to go back to putting his own jobs together.

He turned left at the top of Kelly Street, crossed over and began to wind his way through the little streets, over the hump of Battery Point, toward the down slope on the other side. Wyatt was a good burglar, but only if he had a shopping list, and was acting on information supplied by someone like Jardine. His chief talent lay in hitting banks and payroll vans, hitting hard and fast with a team of experts. A wasted talent now, for all of the experts were gone. He still got 'sweet' invitations from time to time, but knew that it was better to stay put than to make a mistake; better to reject the 'sweet' money than risk his life or his freedom.

So, how 'sweet' was Raymond's art heist?

Wyatt unpacked his bag and rested. That evening he made his way back to a bistro in Salamanca Place. He ordered wine and pasta, then coffee. In the old days there had been experts he could

317

work with, men who could drive, bypass a security system, crack a safe, all without a shot being fired. Now there were only youngsters with jumpy eyes and muscle twitches, in need of a fix, their brains fried, as likely to shoot dead a cop or a nun as Wyatt himself if they felt mean enough, or paranoid enough, or heard enough voices telling them to do it. Or they talked too much before the job, boasting in the pub to their mates or their girlfriends, who then whispered it to the law.

He finished eating and walked back, misty rain blurring the street lights. As a potential partner, Raymond looked pretty good to Wyatt. It was in this frame of mind, assessing, reflective, that Wyatt let himself into his flat and into trouble.

12

He should have taken a moment to clear his head before going in. He should have looked, waited, thought, had a back-up plan ready, a way out.

For when he let the door close behind him, flicking on the light as he did so, all he got was the sound of the switch. The darkness was absolute.

Then an arm went around his neck and the twin barrels of a shotgun, apparently cut short with a hacksaw, tore the skin at the hinge of his jaw.

'Not a sound. Not a fucking *move*, mate.'

Wyatt remained still, loose and relaxed on his feet. His flat smelt ripe, lived in, an odour compounded of grievances and shot nerves and perspiration breaking through cheap talc; the odour of a man with the jitters.

'Bastard. Where you been?'

It was a rhetorical question. Wyatt said nothing.

'I'm going to search you.'

'Okay.'

At the moment the arm relaxed its hold on his neck and felt for and found the .38 in his waistband, Wyatt drove the heel of his shoe down the man's shinbone, then dropped like a rock from the man's grasp. The .38 fell to the carpet. Wyatt patted the carpet uselessly for a few seconds, then scooted away in the darkness. He sensed opposing inclinations in the man—the tearing pain, Wyatt at large and dangerous to him. 'I'm gonna fucking kill you,' the man said.

Wyatt heard a chair fall. He didn't search for another light switch, guessing that the power was off at the fuse box—the gunman's mistake, for now they were both blind. The man should simply have removed the bulb.

Wyatt listened, backed into a corner, straining his eyes to pick up stray light from the curtained windows. Unfortunately they faced the water; there were no street lights out there. But no-one could get behind him, no-one could see him, and he had a measure of control over the doors and windows if the man had friends with him.

'Bastard. I'll have you.'

Wyatt was silent.

'Frank's dead because of you.'

He's talking about Frank Jardine, Wyatt thought. He must be the younger brother. He risked a reply:

'Frank knew the score.'

Frank Jardine had worked with Wyatt in the old days, hitting banks and security vans, before retiring to become a blueprinter, planning high-level burglaries for Wyatt from information supplied by croupiers, insurance clerks, taxi drivers, builders, tradesmen who installed alarms and safes, shop assistants. Then, while coming out of retirement to pull one more job with Wyatt, he'd been head-shot and suffered a series of strokes, and now was dead.

Wyatt had given money to the Jardines for his convalescence, but clearly that wasn't enough for the family.

Sometimes, late at night, it wasn't enough for Wyatt.

'He's dead because of you,' the brother repeated now.

Wyatt had no intention of speaking again. Jardine's brother had made up his mind. Wyatt waited. After a period of cursing and carpet scraping, the man abruptly ceased moving, as though sharper instincts were finally kicking in. He was listening, just as Wyatt was listening, and he wasn't giving his position away.

Wyatt eased himself onto his back. It was pointless looking for the .38. He felt with his right hand until he found the old armchair that sat against the wall next to him. It wore a fussy beaded fringe around its base and Wyatt slipped his hand in and found the knife he'd taped to the lower frame.

The man heard him. A spurt of flame erupted from the shotgun and a wad of pellets tore through the armchair. Wyatt placed him. He uncoiled from the floor and plunged blade-first across the room.

The blade missed. Their shoulders collided but the blade slipped past, slicing the empty air.

They grappled. Jardine's brother was unused to close fighting. His instinct was to spring away from Wyatt and level the shotgun at him; Wyatt's was to hold him close, trapping the gun between them. Then, punctuated by the man's sobbing exertion and panic, Wyatt began to pull him onto the blade. He felt the initial resistance of cloth, skin, bone, then the blade was slipping between the bones of the ribcage. Jardine's brother uttered a soft 'oh' of surprise. He released the shotgun. Wyatt felt him sway. A moment later he was lowering him to the carpet. There was a weakening pulse when he felt for it.

Wyatt found the fuse box and turned on the lights. He worked it out. The family knew about the mail drop. The brother had

321

simply come to Hobart and staked it out, then followed Wyatt home. Now Wyatt had a body in his flat, pooling blood on his carpet and neighbours who might have heard the shotgun. It had all been unnecessary, but he supposed that he couldn't blame the Jardines. In Wyatt's game, there was always a simple accounting for people's actions. What mattered now was, he had to find himself another bolthole.

13

For Raymond it was a form of hell, sharing quarters with other people, getting up when they got up, sitting around a kitchen table with them, eating toast and eggs and drinking coffee, then waiting around through the long hours, waiting for them to do something, enduring their small talk. But he wasn't working solo now. He was working with other people and they had to be kept happy. It was necessary for the job, but he looked forward to that time after the job, when caring about the happiness of other people no longer meant anything and they could be jettisoned.

Or not quite. Maybe Vallance could be jettisoned. Allie was a different matter.

He watched them eat breakfast and it was hell. Allie and Vallance moved in a comfortable stale fog, jaws grinding, their faces puffy with sleep. Allie wore loose satin pyjamas that somehow, where they clung to her breasts and buttocks, suggested hot pliant skin. She was stunning. Vallance wasn't. He wore a towelling robe and looked creased and shambling and inert. Raymond tried to imagine the nature of their passion. He couldn't.

They had given Raymond the couch to sleep on. The sloping pitch of the base had threatened to stuff up his back for days, so at midnight he'd moved the cushions to the floor. He still slept badly. At 4.20 he'd awoken and seen, in the light of a digital clock, that Allie was crouched nearby, gravely watching him. He didn't think she'd been there long, for somewhere along the corridor the toilet stopped flushing. Raymond had breathed in audibly, ready to speak, but Allie had silenced him, kissing her fingers and laying them on his lips. He now wondered if he'd dreamt the whole thing. It had been erotic, sure, but somehow also tender, and he'd not had much of that in his life.

An hour later, fully showered and dressed, Vallance showed him a red vinyl Thomas Cook bag. 'Told you I had a whole heap of coins,' he said.

Raymond unzipped the bag, whistled at the sight of so many gold, silver and bronze coins, plus small ingots, some of it melded together by a hard sediment. 'Nice,' he said.

'That it is,' Vallance said. 'Right, shall we go?'

Raymond drove the short distance back to the marina. Quincy was waiting for them, a grizzled character with an alcoholic's broken blood vessels in his face. He seemed incurious about Raymond, incurious about the purpose of the voyage. Raymond guessed he was paid to keep his trap shut.

Their passage out of Westernport Bay, toward the Cornwall Group of islands, induced in Raymond a sense of anticipation. He fingered the silver dollar in his pocket. It wasn't eagerness, hunger or greed. He'd be hard pushed to define any extreme of feelings. But he couldn't deny that all of his senses were alert, that the blood ticked in him inexorably, that he felt the prickling awareness of the hunter closing in. Hidden treasure. Buried treasure. His skin tingled. His mother had once said, 'You're my treasure.' Queer that he'd think of that now. He wasn't a man who had much time for looking back. The world was full of people crippled by regret for past actions and inactions. It got them nowhere. They didn't know how to forgive or accept themselves. Then again, the world was full of monsters who remained monsters exactly because they had no trouble forgiving themselves at all.

Raymond blinked, shaking off the trance, putting himself firmly in the here and now again, on the deck of a trawler, sailing in mild sunlight. Bass Strait was calm. Raymond was glad: his guts would have acted up on him otherwise. Five hours later, the islands appeared. Quincy steered toward a narrow boiling passage between reefs, heading for sheltered water beyond.

Raymond and Allie stood on the port side, Vallance on the starboard, reef-spotting while Quincy throttled back and picked a way through the gap. The boat pitched and jawed a little in the rougher water. It felt dangerous to Raymond, a gut-lurching sensation, but Vallance and Allie rode the twisting deck comfortably so he told himself it was nothing. The air felt cool and damp on his face, briny in his nostrils, and seabirds slipped in the air currents above him.

Then they were through, gliding across still water. Grey cliffs, a tiny pebbly beach set with large rounded boulders, a muttonbird rookery, a glimpse of treeless vivid grassland above the cliffs. Raymond tipped back his head and breathed the air. He felt alive, and then Allie was standing next to him. Her arms circled his waist briefly and her chin pressed him between the shoulderblades.

She released him. 'Isn't this great?'

Her eyes were bright, keen, full of curiosity and simple happiness. It was infectious. Raymond felt an absurd need to reach out and dab at some poorly applied zinc cream on her nose. He allowed a brief glint of teeth. 'Great.'

Vallance dropped anchor and joined them. He was grinning, his thin face and wiry frame revelling in the moment. 'Piece of cake.'

'Lucky with the weather,' Raymond said.

Vallance sobered. 'I agree. I also have to say that time is a factor here. The wreck's in about twenty metres of water on the other side of the reef. In a few weeks' time what we're doing today won't be possible. Gale-force winds, heavy seas, you name it.'

'In other words, if I'm going to put up the money for this it'll have to be soon.'

Vallance coughed, looked embarrassed. 'Well, yeah. That's why this'll be a quick visit. Take you out to the site, let you run the metal detector over the area, maybe dig up a few more coins, then head back to Westernport. Mate, we want you to see that this is a goer.'

Raymond still had plenty of questions. He looked away from the island to the other islands in the group, small, barren humps in the sea. 'Couple of boats anchored out there,' he said.

'Fishermen.'

'You haven't encountered other treasure seekers?'

'No.'

'What about official visitors? I'm thinking of inspectors from that crowd you used to work for, the Maritime Heritage Unit.'

'Nope.'

Raymond stared at Vallance for a while. Gulls wheeled above the yacht. The air was fresh and sharp, bracing to breathe. Raymond couldn't let the air distract him, lead him away from his natural state, which was suspicion and scepticism. 'Are there other wrecks here?'

'A score of them. They've all been charted.'

'Excavated?'

'Those that matter. A big convict vessel went down in 1813,

for example. That had the historians interested. Most of the other ships were small intercolonial traders. Livestock, timber, stuff like that.'

'So no-one knows the *Eliza Dean* is here?'

'Not yet. But they will. Someone will stumble on her by accident sooner or later. That's why it's imperative we go in now.'

'Why hasn't she been found?'

Vallance said impatiently, 'You dive with me, you'll see why. When she hit the reef, the hull would've gone straight to the bottom, weighed down by ballast, crates of coins, other heavy stuff. It'll be under a few metres of sand by now. The rigging, masts, upper decking, anchors, general superstructure, well that would have been strewn over a wide area by tides and storms. We're talking about a hundred and seventy years, you know. From what I know about the tides here, the smaller stuff, including the few coins that worked loose or were grabbed by the crew, will have been scattered in a particular way.'

He squatted on the deck, wet a finger, sketched two reefs and then a cone shape abutting one of them. Tapping the widest arc of the cone, he said, 'Where I found the coins, plus a tin plate and a couple of buttons and spoons, approximates to here. What we have to do is crisscross back in this direction.' He indicated the pointed end of the cone. 'That's where the wreck itself will be.'

'The mother lode.'

'Exactly.'

'You weren't so specific the first time you told me this.'

'You weren't so interested.'

Raymond looked out to sea, then back at the rapidly drying diagram. 'You're saying it's between those two reefs?'

'Yes. The outer one is deeper. The *Eliza Dean* passed right over it, then struck the inner one. That's why no-one's found her before.'

327

'What if we do have an unexpected visitor, either now or when and if we mount an expedition? They'll know something is going on.'

'I'm confident we won't have visitors, not this late in the season. But I can always dive at night or anchor some distance away and swim to the wreck from there. You're thinking telltale bubbles in the water? Simple. I'll use a rebreather.'

'You're the expert,' Raymond said.

'That he is,' Allie agreed, embracing Vallance, resting her temple on his shoulder.

A kind of hatred flooded through Raymond. 'One last question.'

'Fire away. You're the man with the money.'

'That's just it,' Raymond said. 'The world is full of fools with money to throw away. Why me? Why me and only three others? Why not a big consortium?'

From anyone else, these would have been first questions, but Raymond wanted Vallance with his hopes running high before he asked it. He wanted to see if Vallance would stumble or blanch or spin him a story.

What Vallance did under the wheeling sky, the wind in his sparse hair, was say, 'I won't lie to you. It's a protected area. No diving allowed.'

'Uh huh.'

'That convict ship? It's pretty close to where I found the coins. It's fragile, excavation is going to take years. The government doesn't want looters, they don't want amateurs, they don't want anyone doing anything to disturb the wreck.'

'So we'll be inviting arrest,' Raymond said flatly.

Vallance nodded.

'That's why everything about this will have to be kept secret,' Allie put in.

'With any luck,' Vallance said, 'the actual search will be quick. I did a preliminary survey the time I found the coins. Another survey today and tomorrow should help narrow the search area. Then when we come here with all the gear we simply vacuum up the sand, gather the coins, get away quick.'

He paused. 'Like I said, we need two hundred grand to get the show on the road. The return from your fifty grand will be in the millions. I'm not asking for fifty right away. If you can get twenty to me by the end of the week, that will secure your fifty grand stake in the syndicate.'

After a while, Raymond nodded. 'Okay.'

Vallance clapped his hands together. 'Time to get togged up, ladies and gentlemen.'

Raymond went below, changed, reappeared on deck again. He found Allie and Vallance, in colourful wetsuits, checking the air tanks and regulators. They were both slight in build and in their vivid costumes reminded Raymond of glossy tropical frogs. Vallance handed him lead weights on a belt and a sheathed, chrome-plated knife. 'Strap these on.'

And then they slipped over the side and into the water. Vallance led the way, over the inner reef to deeper water. As they angled toward the bottom, a strange fear gripped Raymond, a sense of a fist closing over his lungs. He knew that his lungs were contracting. The water grew colder. He found himself sipping at the air. It seemed to be thick, weighty air, as though a liquid were pouring down into his lungs. He found that he was losing red from the colour spectrum. A brand name stamped on the wristband of his wetsuit was being leached of redness. His heart pounded.

He looked about for Vallance and Allie. He couldn't see them. For several minutes he was suspended in murky water, then suddenly Allie was beside him, winking, pointing downwards. Seeing her gave him back his nerve.

329

He gazed around after that, enjoying himself, and when he saw Vallance again the older man was standing on the bed of the sea, scooping his arms for balance, his flippers stirring the sand, and Raymond saw an old coin of the realm appear, then another, stamped with the king's name and a Latin script and a date more than 170 years before he was born.

14

The coins—their tragic history, their weight and substance, their *goldness*—lodged in Raymond's head. He could feel want and fascination stirring inside him. In his mind's eye he saw the spill of gold on the seabed, and traced it back to the rotting hull and the laden chests. His share would make him a wealthy man. He hungered—for the hunt, the discovery, the division of the spoils, the addictive element of risk. He met these needs whenever he robbed a bank, but this time the take was buried treasure. Treasure. It was enough to make him dream.

But all he had in the world was a lifestyle and a promise. The lifestyle boiled down to clothes, a car, an apartment—but no money; and the promise boiled down to lingering fingertips, a brilliant smile, auburn hair like flames—but no warm flank pressed against him in his bed at night.

Occupied with these thoughts the next day, Raymond used false papers to buy himself a Kawasaki. It was one he could use on a job sooner or later, but right now he needed it as a scout vehicle.

The Western District of Victoria, home to small towns, prime ministers and old and new money living in National Trust homesteads, lay wide open to the bush bandit. Raymond intended to scout around for a few days, note the banks and the building societies, then strike quickly. He might get lucky. He might earn Vallance's fifty thousand from the first place he hit.

In Geelong he bought maps, then drove south-west, intending to follow the coast to Warrnambool before heading north, then east at Mortlake—a large circle, with plenty of diversions off the beaten track. He'd map the best targets, routes in and out, roadworks, the location of the police stations, areas of traffic congestion, hairpin bends, narrow bridges, school buses. It was painstaking, it was probably obsessive, but Raymond liked to know more than he needed to know before any job.

If he'd not met Vallance, would he have been able to function for much longer as the bush bandit? He knew of only four ways of getting at a bank's holdings—embezzlement, going in with a gang to intercept a large cash transfer, breaking in during a weekend and drilling through to the vault or the safety deposit boxes, or going in alone and armed when the bank was open. Only this last option was open to Raymond. But the banks were getting canny. One day he'd find himself in a trap.

By the fourth day, Raymond was ready to strike.

Biniguy was a small town, no more than a stretch of nondescript public buildings and old, verandahed shops on a country highway that narrowed to form the main street for an eyeblink on the way from Victoria to south-eastern South Australia. A small shopping centre—with a boutique, a Coles, a bank, a Mitre-10 and a furniture barn built around two sides of a car park—sat behind the main street. From the bank's security point of view, it was a bad location. Raymond listed what was good about it from his point of view: several exits; a public car park right outside; plenty of distracted shoppers around; half a minute from the highway.

He parked the Kawasaki next to an exit at the corner of the supermarket and dismounted. He set off in the opposite direction from the bank, the shotgun stuffed inside the pack on his back. He was interested in the buildings that overlooked the shopping centre, in particular a side-street block of flats and the rear of a hall and a public library on the main street. He was looking for a stake-out. There was a good chance of one, after all the outrage he'd precipitated in the past few weeks.

He crossed the street at an angle and entered the flats. All the sounds of the town were cut off inside the foyer. Only his muted breathing sounded in the still, stale air of the stairwell. He listened. He was listening for a cough, the staticky scratch of a hand radio, the rattle of a venetian blind.

Raymond waited for ten minutes, then left the flats and cut across to the external wooden steps behind the hall and adjoining library. He climbed, went in. The windows were opaque, ancient white paint over them. He poked his head around a few doors and along a few dim corridors.

Nothing.

As he descended the stairs he cast about over the car park, looking for other likely police stake-out posts. There was one, an electrician's van near the front door of the bank. But the rear windows were clear, and all he could see in there, a minute later, were tool boxes, switches and coils of insulated wire. The electrician himself was on a ladder propped against the facia of the boutique, fixing a new neon sign into place. He looked genuine. No radio apparent; no mike or earpiece on a wire. Finally Raymond wandered idly past the shops a couple of times. Still nothing. That left the rooftops, but he couldn't check everything.

Raymond went in. There was one customer, a woman with a sleeping new baby swaddled to the chin in a pale blanket. He knew that she didn't have to be a woman with a baby but a cop with a doll, but the baby snuffled and bleated so he relaxed by half a degree and marked time with a pen and a withdrawal form.

Three staff: a teller, a young woman standing at a keyboard at the rear, the manager inside a glass booth, tapping the keys of a desk calculator as he flipped through a stack of receipts.

When the woman was gone, Raymond approached the teller. All she could see of his face were his teeth, bared in a distorting grimace, dark glasses and bike helmet. She was about to point to a sign that told motorcyclists to remove their helmets when her eyes were drawn to the yawning mouth of the shotgun and she whimpered a little.

Raymond said nothing, merely pushed an airlines bag across the counter to her. She began to fill it, from her own till, then used a key to open the neighbouring tills. Raymond wondered briefly if she had been held up before. The others hadn't noticed him yet. The keyboard rattled; the manager continued to count his money. Raymond collected the bag from the teller, held his finger to his lips, and saw her eyes look past him and widen in surprise.

He turned. It was a silent world beyond the plate glass, a world where a reversal could appear out of nowhere and you wouldn't know it. A security guard had stationed himself near the door. He was sipping coffee and had his head cranked up to yarn with the electrician.

Raymond said gruffly, 'Wasn't here yesterday.'

'We have him on rotation with our other branches in the region,' the teller said.

Raymond moved quickly. He abandoned the money and the shotgun, stripped off his leather bike jacket and helmet, and walked whistling from the bank. He guessed that he had about thirty seconds before the bank staff gathered their wits. The guard glanced incuriously at him. Raymond left the shopping centre on foot and walked to the hospital. He stole an ambulance and drove as far as the next town before entering a system of side roads that would take him east. There were no road blocks and no pursuit cars. There would be soon, but he'd be well out of the area by then.

Later he stole a community bus and drove it to Geelong. There he rented a car. On the drive north to Melbourne, his heart stopped hammering and he said goodbye to the bush bandit. It was done in a second, and in that same second he defined the aims and limitations of his new life. One, he'd no longer hit small targets. No more country towns and their modest banks. Two, he needed one big score that would bankroll his share of the *Eliza Dean* syndicate. Three, he needed a good accomplice.

This time he met Chaffey on a park bench near the Exhibition Building. The glass wall extension gave crisp, out-of-true reflections of the main hall and the gardens, the strolling lovers seemed to yaw and bend like figures in funhouse mirrors.

'I'll do both,' Raymond said. 'Spring your bloke from remand and lift that collection of paintings.'

The fat lawyer tossed a pebble at a pigeon. 'Pleased to hear that, son. Steer comes up for trial soon, so he has to be sprung some time in the next few days.'

'You said fifteen thousand? Not much for the risk involved.'

'Take it or leave it, son. This isn't a cheap operation. Your role is only part of it. There's also his new ID, a safe passage out of the country, the dosh to tide him over till he's settled. There's whatever gear you and his girlfriend decide is needed. There's a new ID and a ticket out for her as well.'

'All right, all right, I get the picture, I'll do it for the fifteen. You said up front?'

'Up front, but only for this job.'

It was a step down in Raymond's career and he felt obscurely

335

ashamed. It wasn't the kind of job Wyatt would line up for.

'These paintings,' he said.

'Time's running out for that, too. Not this weekend but the weekend after. Two days when the collection will be off the walls and in storage and the alarm system turned off while they renovate.' Chaffey turned his massive head to watch a girl walk by. 'Like I said, it's a two-man job. You found someone?'

'My uncle comes to mind.'

Chaffey went still. Then he tossed another pebble. 'Heard something about him during the week that doesn't exactly inspire confidence.'

'Like what?'

'He tried to flog some precious stones back to an insurance company and almost got caught by the cops.'

Raymond felt the pull of conflicting emotions. He could picture his uncle's nerve and style, but why hadn't Wyatt told him about the botched handover, had a laugh about it with him, if nothing else? They were family, after all.

And did Wyatt still have the stones?

'But he didn't get caught.'

'True, true,' Chaffey said.

'Plus he's stolen paintings before,' Raymond said. 'Art, stuff like that, it's not my thing.'

He recreated his apartment in his head. Half a dozen prints he'd rented, along with the furniture.

'See if you can arrange a meeting,' Chaffey said.

Have to find him first, Raymond thought. He coughed and said, 'About the prison break.'

'Yes?'

'Keep it between you and me. My uncle doesn't need to know about it.'

Chaffey swung his huge head around. Raymond felt the force

of the man's hard gaze. Men like Chaffey saw corruption every day. It corrupted them, gave a corrupt spin to their insights.

'You mean he wouldn't approve,' Chaffey said finally, and Raymond would quite happily have strangled Chaffey then.

15

Chaffey called in favours and made promises and when Steer was finally moved to the remand centre in Sunshine he made the trip out there by taxi. The place was privately run and tried to kid itself that plenty of bright fresh paint and natural light, and its situation alongside other public buildings, placed it at the cutting edge of modern incarceration practice, but Chaffey wasn't fooled. There was no concealing the rifles and batons, the commerce in drugs, phonecards and cigarettes, the stench of hopelessness and hate the moment you got through the main door.

Still, he'd rather have a consultation with Steer in the remand centre than in Pentridge, where the interview rooms were grim and spare, the walls always cold to the touch, the high windows too smeared and deep-set to catch the light, the air always ringing with the smack of metal against metal.

Steer, they said, was helping the maintenance crew. There'd be a thirty-minute wait. Chaffey mentally added another thirty to that and asked to see the paperwork on his client.

The clerk sighed elaborately. 'You want it now?'

Chaffey was used to grudging prison staff. One, he was a lawyer, he had it easy. He didn't have to be shut up with the dregs of society for hours at a time. Two, lawyers, like cops, kept things to themselves. They looked at a bloke's file and their little minds ticked over and they went off and did important things. They were right up themselves. Three, Chaffey looked rich and fat. Four, he didn't wear a uniform. Chaffey read all of these things in the sour face of the clerk, not necessarily in that order.

The man put him in a smoky side room. A transistor radio vibrated on a window shelf, a poorly tuned talkback host encouraging every vicious prejudice ever thought or uttered. Two guards came in, made coffee, stared at Chaffey, yelled above the racketing radio, went out again. Chaffey knew that he was being put in his place. He didn't care. It was all in their heads, not his.

The officer came back with Steer's file. Apparently Steer was behaving himself. Well, he would be, given that he intended to escape on the one hand and was looking at long gaol time if that fell through on the other.

Fifty minutes later, Chaffey was taken to an interview room. Steer sat on a plastic chair at a plastic table, blowing smoke rings at the ceiling.

Chaffey turned to the guard. 'My client and I would like some privacy, if you don't mind.'

The man flushed. 'No skin off my nose.'

He left. Chaffey said, 'Are we okay in here?'

Steer nodded. 'Cost me fifty smackers. No-one's listening.'

'Good,' Chaffey said.

He made a rapid assessment of his client. Steer was watchful, careful, apparently relaxed and self-contained. 'Keeps to himself,' the report said. 'The hard men of the yard leave him alone.' Chaffey could see why. You sensed the glittering danger in him, just as you sensed it in certain dogs.

'I've seen Denise,' Chaffey began.

Steer nodded. He tipped back his throat and huffed three smoke rings at the spitting fluorescent tube.

Chaffey saw his teeth then: gaol-rotted teeth, full of stumps and black cavities. 'We're ready to roll, our end,' he said. 'New Zealand passports and driver's licences, a boat from Lakes Entrance to a freighter, a guy to drive you.'

'Who?'

'His name is Ray Wyatt. The police don't know him. Good nerve, cautious, he won't let you down. Denise has been working on your shopping list. The rest is up to you.'

'Things are jake my end,' Steer said. 'Back up a bit. This guy, you say his name is Wyatt?'

Chaffey nodded, adding a chin to the chins that hung over the knot of his tie. 'You know him?'

Steer shook his head. 'Has he got a father, a nasty piece of work, knocks over payroll vans and that?'

Chaffey thought that 'nasty piece of work' pretty well described Steer. 'The lad's uncle. Is that a problem?'

Steer smiled. There was no humour or good will in it. 'Just asking.'

'Now, about your money,' Chaffey said.

Two hundred thousand dollars, in a fireproof steel floor-safe at his house, cemented into a hole in the corner of his basement. Steer's money, and Steer knew the combination, just in case, but that two hundred grand still burnt a hole in Chaffey's head. He was not mug enough to touch it, though. Steer would slice him open and whistle 'Waltzing Matilda' while he did it.

'What about my money? You fucking lost it at the casino?'

'Keep your shirt on,' Chaffey said. 'It's in the basement where it's always been. As soon as you're settled somewhere,

340

I'll wire it to you.'

'That you will,' Steer said, reaching to stub out his cigarette on the table, just millimetres away from Chaffey's soft, fat, pink, well-tended hand.

16

Wyatt always kept an emergency bag packed. Within minutes of killing Frank Jardine's brother, he'd left another stage of his life behind him.

A new bolthole. He couldn't stay in Hobart. There was the mainland, but too many people knew him there, too many wanted him dead. He'd risk short, hit-and-run visits to the capital cities, but it would be inviting trouble to base himself in one of them.

And so Wyatt drove north, in a Magna rented using a false set of papers. He took the Midland Highway. Wind gusts rocked the car in the high country after Hobart, where the road narrowed and levelled out for the dreary stretch up through the centre of the state. Traffic was sparse and slow and inclined to be careless. Wyatt found himself tensing at the wheel. The long hours and the strain of his life brought sharp aches to his neck and shoulders.

A new bolthole, and a big score to build up his cash reserves. That meant working with someone again. Wyatt thought about his nephew's proposition. He counted the advantages again. One,

Raymond was family and seemed to look up to him. Two, Raymond had successfully planned and pulled a number of armed hold-ups. Three, he'd never been caught. Four, he wasn't a junkie. The boy probably had vices and weaknesses, but they weren't apparent, and they hadn't got in the way of his bank raids.

Something else was prompting Wyatt, a feeling that lacked clear definition but connected Raymond with the child who had stepped into the traffic, inviting death. His brother's son. Raymond was the son of a weak, vicious man, and Wyatt had done nothing to make things better.

The road wound through valleys and rich farmland. The headlights flared over roadsigns that portrayed fat sheep and historic towns. He saw convict-built stonewall fences and imposing gates that indicated fine homesteads set back amongst English trees. He was in Tasmania's conservative heartland. The seat of government was in the south but the old money was in the north and it ruled the upper house of government.

At one o'clock he pulled off the road and slept until dawn. He was no more than thirty minutes from Devonport, but he knew that he'd attract suspicion if he tried to rent a room this early in the morning.

He drove to the next town, locked the car and walked to a cafe. Smells of toast and coffee inside; a couple of bleary farmers and truckies at a corner table. He ate, walked for an hour, drove on.

Later that morning he rented a holiday flat in Devonport. It was a depressing place. The window of the main room overlooked a block of similar flats—the Astor Apartments, pale yellow brick, rusting wrought iron, rotted window sills—and leaked a weak grey light into the place. Low, pebbled ceiling, wiry carpets the consistency of a kitchen scourer, Aborigines on black velvet in wooden frames on the walls. Frayed, burnt-orange armchairs and sofa. Parents came here exhausted with their tribes of children every summer and found little rest. They existed on fish and chips and videos. Humankind herded together in disappointment and conflict until death, Wyatt thought. He thought of Liz Redding and wondered at his own fate.

That afternoon he went out for maps, tourist brochures and real-estate listings. He spent the afternoon poring over them and making phone calls. He gave himself a week. When he stared out of the window, early that evening, he saw the running lights of the ferry as it set out for Melbourne, sliding massively down the channel toward the open sea, its superstructure dwarfing the little houses and cheap holiday flats.

In the end, he didn't need a week. Three days later, Wyatt moved to a remote wooden house near Flowerdale on the north coast, with a view across abrupt small hills to a slice of Bass Strait. It was a region of orchards, tree nurseries, dairy farms, creeks, gorges and muddy tracks. No-one was likely to question him in such a place. It was a rental house and renters had always stayed a while there, working or not working, maybe bludging on the welfare system, maybe teaching in the local school for a few terms. Wyatt was just another one of them.

17

Liz Redding didn't get to Hobart. Her suspension was made official, and she was obliged to report every day, pending an inquiry. She might have slipped away regardless of that, but Gosse called her into his office and told her that they'd had a call from the Tasmania Police.

He drummed his fingers on his desk. 'The name Jardine mean anything to you?'

'You've read my report, sir.'

'Indeed I have. Your friend Wyatt worked with a man called Frank Jardine.'

'Not my friend, sir.'

Gosse ignored her. 'This Jardine has—or rather, *had*—a brother.'

'I wouldn't know, sir.'

'Wouldn't you? Well, the brother has turned up dead—stabbed—in a flat in Battery Point, down in Hobart. Needless to say, being a resident of Melbourne, it wasn't his flat.'

So that's what Nettie meant, Liz thought. 'Whose flat was it, sir?'

'That's the interesting part, Sergeant. The tenant was a man, no-one knew him, the name probably false, nothing left to identify him, no prints, wiped clean.'

Liz sat stonily watching Gosse.

'That photograph we have of Wyatt. It's not very clear, but the real estate agent who let the flat to this man positively identifies him.'

What did Gosse want from her? He was playing some kind of game, loading a lot of meaning between the lines. Liz said, 'So, he's on the run, sir. I hope you catch him.'

Gosse snapped forward across the empty desk. She smelt toothpaste and coffee. He said, 'Did you warn him, Sergeant?'

She stared at a point above his shoulder. 'Sir, I've talked to the Association lawyer. If you want to charge me, charge me. If you want to find evidence against me, go out and find it. Meanwhile, all I'm guilty of is being too dedicated to my job, working outside of regulations in the interest of bringing a crooked copper to justice. That's all I'm admitting to, that's all I've done. Either throw the book at me or sack me or reinstate me. Until then, I've said all I'm obliged to say.'

Gosse rubbed his ring finger vigorously over his forehead. The movement made him grimace, as though he were screaming silently. Liz thought of Wyatt, who had probably been the killer. Self-defence? She hoped so. Wyatt didn't have the empty moral centre of a thrill killer. Anyway, not the Wyatt she'd known on the yacht.

'Fuck this,' Gosse said. He hunted in his side drawer, slid a form across the desk toward her. 'A warrant to search your house.'

Liz let the anger burn coldly. 'You won't find anything. Plenty of knickers, in case you want to have a sniff.'

'You may accompany us. You may even have the Association rep present if you so desire.'

'That won't be necessary. But I'll be watching you, you bastard, every step of the way.'

An hour later she was sitting, seething, in an armchair by the window, as Gosse, two other detectives and two uniformed constables searched her flat. She knew there was nothing to find. There was also nothing they could plant, unless Gosse had somehow got hold of the remaining rings and necklaces from the Asahi Collection, or something that belonged to Wyatt.

A third constable stayed in the room with her, standing uncomfortably by the door.

'Sit down,' Liz said.

He blushed. He was young and pimpled. 'I'm right, thanks.'

'Suit yourself.'

She watched gloomily as one of the detectives searched the room. He looked inside the CD cases and magazines, shook vases, tapped the fireplace tiles with his knuckles. He even took a screwdriver to the gas heater. It was dusty. He rocked back on his heels, sneezing.

Where would you hide a fortune in rings, bracelets, necklaces and tiaras if you were Wyatt and on the run and needing to travel light? Her thinking brought her by degrees to the yacht. Where on the yacht had the jewels been hidden in the first place, before Wyatt ran with them?

She straightened involuntarily, coughed to mask it, relaxed again. Three o'clock. Gosse would want to question her again at ten the next morning. Plenty of time.

At 3.30 Gosse said, 'That's all for now, Sergeant. Thank you.'

Liz said, putting on the sweetness, 'Find anything? That

347

earring I lost last year? A ten cent piece down the back of the sofa? Maybe a letter from my old Gran I forgot to answer?'

'Tomorrow morning, ten sharp,' Gosse said.

When they were gone, Liz left through her back door, climbed the fence into the alley, and made her way to a taxi stand two blocks away. She told the driver to take her to the Budget place in Elizabeth Street, where she rented a Corolla, and by 5.15 she was on the foreshore at Hastings.

It looked different. Then again, everything had been distorted the first time—dawn, the aftermath of a storm, her groggy head.

She found the yacht tied to a berth amongst a lot of small, flashy weekend yachts. There was a crime-scene tape around the rail. She looked about her. The place was closing for the day. She stepped over the tape and climbed down the steps to the area beneath the deck.

The yacht had been baking in the sun for days. The air below smelt of vinyl and glue, close and stale.

She started with the cabins, and worked her way along. By the time she got to the galley her hands were dirty, her fingernails torn.

She found the safe by accident. She was leaning her weight on the wall oven, resting, thinking, and when she stepped back she heard the soft click of a spring lock. The oven had moved a little, the edge jutting out a few millimetres from the wall. Liz hooked her sore fingers on the lip and pulled.

The oven slid out silently on well-greased channels, rather like a drawer in a modern kitchen. There was a space behind it. Liz reached into the wall cavity and the bulky, black felt bundle she brought into the light fell open and poured a stream of vivid stones and cool gold settings onto the carpet at her feet. The gold gleamed, the faceted stones flashed the colours of the spectrum. 'Oh,' she said aloud.

Liz Redding dated the permanent seal on the shift in her view of the world, and of herself, to this moment. She felt the tug of the stones. Her head filled with risky impulses. Her heart beat. Her mouth was dry. She wanted to walk further into the edgy darkness enjoyed by a man like Wyatt.

18

The safe house was a boxy weatherboard perched on a steep slope above a creek in Warrandyte, in the ranges north of Melbourne. Raymond felt claustrophobic, shut in by the dense overhang of trees, the squabbling birds, the gullies and hills. You could see for miles from his balcony in the city. Here all you could see was the fence through the trees in the garden, then more trees. If you were lucky you got a glimpse of the sky. Otherwise there was only the house and the driveway and his Jag.

And Denise Meickle, waiting stonily outside the front door. Raymond nodded, approached, not liking what he saw. He was supposed to spend a few days with her, help her bloke get out of remand, hang around afterwards and help both of them get out of the country? For fifteen thousand bucks? Jesus. He wouldn't be listing this on his CV.

Raymond got closer. Denise Meickle was a real sadsack, okay clothes but gloomy in the face, with the kind of skin that is permanently red and chapped around the mouth and nostrils.

Hefty jaw, broad forehead, slight body, as though her head and her trunk belonged to different people. It was inevitable that Raymond would think about Allie Roden and begin to count his luck. Steer had to be really hard-up.

'Made it,' he said.

The Meickle woman looked at her watch. 'I was expecting you an hour ago.'

No wonder Chaffey hadn't wanted to be in on their first meeting. 'I got lost,' Raymond said.

He'd taken a winding route through Doncaster and Templestowe, gazing unbelievingly at the crass houses, the evidence of vulgar new wealth, a lot of it acquired dishonestly. There'd been a story going around a few years ago that Wyatt had tangled with a crime family out here, raided their compound for the money they owed him. Nerve and vision. Raymond felt a kind of envy and resentment stir inside him. Why would Wyatt want to help him lift a collection of paintings, especially if he had a million bucks' worth of stolen jewels hidden away? There had to be cash stowed away, too, over the years. Wyatt could pick and choose as he liked. One day they'll say the same about me, Raymond thought.

'Tricky place to find,' he said now, 'tucked away back here in the hills.'

Meickle grunted. 'You might as well come inside. Bring your bag with you.'

Raymond followed her into the house. It smelt of treated baltic pine, wood stain and a stale trace of cat. It belonged to friends of Denise Meickle. They were overseas for a year. Meickle had a key, but wasn't expected to do more than water the garden every few days.

They came to a poky loungeroom with a glass wall that faced a stand of spindly tall gums. Raymond waited, content to let

351

Meickle take the lead. According to Chaffey, she used to be a Correctional Services psychologist at Ararat prison, where she met Steer. She might be a gloomy, box-faced cow but Raymond knew that a psychologist is someone who reads your mind, so he intended to keep his trap shut as much as possible.

'Sleeping arrangements,' she said. 'I'm in the main bedroom, you're through here.'

She led him to a tiny bedroom. There was a single bed, a nursery frieze around three of the walls, a zoo poster taped to an inbuilt wardrobe, a window that looked upon more fucking trees. 'Uh huh,' he said.

'If you don't like it, there's the sofa.'

'This will do.'

'When you're ready, we can start work.'

Raymond unpacked. He found her in the kitchen, watching moodily as an electric kettle boiled. She poured weak coffee and they sat at a chrome and laminex kitchen table, 1960s kitsch. Raymond stretched the kinks out of his back and shoulders, yawned, and said, 'I suggest we start with—'

It was clear that Denise harboured all of the disappointments of her thirty years in her face and her voice. The face was pinched and disapproving, the voice, too: 'You start by getting a few things straight. First, you're here to help out, not take charge, not do your own thing, just do as you're told, okay?'

'That's cool.'

'The plan is Tony's and mine. We—'

It was odd hearing Steer's first name. 'Big Tone,' Raymond said, then wondered why he'd said it.

'None of this is a joke. You come recommended by Chaffey, but I've yet to be convinced. You don't impress me. You don't make me laugh. You don't turn me on. I'm not going to cook or clean for you. Got all that?'

352

Delivered with a low, uninflected voice full of authority. Raymond saluted. 'Yes, sir, ma'am, sir.'

She waited. She might have been counting to ten. This is an awfully small house, Raymond thought, to be holed up in with a whaddaya call it, femo-nazi.

'The plan,' Denise Meickle said, 'is that we get him out on Sunday.'

'Bit soonish,' Raymond said.

'It happens to be a long weekend. The benefits are as follows. First, the remand centre in Sunshine is understaffed anyway, but even more so when we factor in the long weekend. Secondly, he's in a unit looked after by female officers.'

Raymond clicked his tongue approvingly. 'They're not likely to try it on. Pushovers.'

'In other circumstances,' Denise said, 'I'd take exception to that. But you're right, they'll be easier to control if anything goes wrong for Tony on the inside. Just two female officers in charge of a unit of twenty inmates.'

'What time?'

'Six in the evening. Just getting dark out. Inside they'll be finishing dinner, heading off to watch TV. Everyone milling around, relaxed, a fair bit of noise and orderly confusion.'

Raymond gazed out at the thick trees. Trees for miles. Houses and towns, too, and hills and paddocks, but this house was set fair in the middle of a fucking forest, it seemed like. He'd go mad if he didn't go out occasionally. But what really burned him up was the thought that if he didn't come up with some big money as a deposit soon, Vallance would sell the last syndicate share to someone else. The fifteen grand from this job would only appease Vallance for a while. What he really needed was to find Wyatt and convince him to help out with Chaffey's art theft.

He turned to Denise. 'You haven't said how.'

'Wait here.'

She came back with an architect's drawing, which she rolled out on the table, weighing both ends down with their empty cups. She had short fingers with unflattering nails—white flecked, poorly trimmed. Raymond liked a woman who looked after her hands. Allie's slim hands on his back, Denise Meickle's little hands on Steer's back. He shook the image away and tried to concentrate.

'This is the wall facing the alley that runs off Craigie Street. It's all administration here on the first floor. This—' she tapped a small rectangular shape '—is an air-conditioning unit set in the wall. It looks as if it can't be moved but in fact it will slide right out once Tony undoes a bolt holding it to the wall.'

'How's he going to do that?'

'Every air-conditioner in the building was serviced recently. Tony was on the work detail because he's good with machinery and electrics. When he replaced this particular unit he made sure it looked finished off but in reality it will slide right away from the wall, leaving a gap he can climb through.'

'So we park in the alley and pick him up.'

'Yes.'

'Stolen car?'

'We steal two cars, and two sets of plates for them. One car to pick him up. We drive it a short distance to the first change-over car, somewhere near the start of the Hume Freeway, then somewhere half an hour out of Melbourne we change cars again, using my car to head across back here to Warrandyte. They'll think we're heading north, into New South Wales.'

'I steal the cars, I drive?'

'It's one of the things you're supposed to be good at.'

'I'm good,' Raymond said simply. 'Where do you come into the picture?'

'I'll pick you up on the Hume. I've also been shopping for the gear.'

'What gear?'

Denise slid a sheet of notepaper across the table. 'Shopping list.'

'Jesus Christ,' Raymond said.

Stun gun, mobile phones, camping gear, camouflage net, police scanners, Victoria Police radio codes, handcuffs, bolt cutters, three pistols, three shotguns, ammunition, food, petrol and water.

'How we supposed to get all this stuff?'

'Most of it I've taken care of already.'

'Stun gun?'

'Mail order from the States. Arrived a couple of days ago.'

'Jesus.'

Raymond thought: This is how the hard boys operate. Look and learn, Raymond, old son. 'Why all the outdoor stuff?'

'If something goes wrong we'll head for the bush.'

Christ, Raymond thought. Mosquitoes, rabbits, foxes, sleeping with a rock in the small of your back, wiping your arse with a bunch of leaves. 'A lot of stuff to buy.'

'I need you to buy some of it, like the phones, camping equipment, etcetera. The rest is taken care of.'

'Must have some cluey mates.'

'You'll be told what you need to know, Ray. Don't worry about it.'

For all her mousy ways, she was pretty confident. 'I'm not worried,' Raymond said.

'Good.' She looked at him, and he could see that she was looking for a way to make him feel that he was just as much at the centre of the operation as she was. 'Um, how will you get the cars?'

Raymond thought, stupid bitch, then leaned back in his chair. 'We want cars that won't be missed until several hours after we break Steer out. We're looking at people who take a train to the city mid-Sunday afternoon—off to a movie, maybe a part-time job, concert, whatever.'

'Good thinking.'

Raymond nodded.

'Make sure one of them is a four-wheel-drive. Tough. Good tyres.'

'How come?'

'In case we have to leave the Hume and head into the bush.'

Always a step ahead of him. Raymond pushed back from the table. 'No time like the present. Got any cash?'

Meickle frowned. 'Chaffey's given you fifteen thousand.'

'My fee,' Raymond said. 'It doesn't go on expenses.'

Grumbling, she counted five hundred dollars into his hand. 'I want receipts.'

Raymond took the Ruger automatic and a suppressor, stowed them in the glove box of the Jag and headed down to the city to go shopping. He started with the camping shops in Elizabeth Street. It felt good buying the best, peeling off fifties and hundreds of Denise Meickle's hard-earned cash.

By six o'clock he'd bought everything on the list. Meickle was expecting him back at the safe house, but she could wait. Raymond let himself into his flat at 6.15, showered and shaved, and was ready for the voice on the intercom at 6.30.

'Come on up.'

He opened the door naked. It wasn't something you could do with every bird, but somehow he knew that Allie Roden wasn't likely to scream and run.

She didn't.

19

By six o'clock on the eighteenth, the two escape vehicles were in place. Raymond, armed with an automatic pistol for himself and another for Steer, and wearing gloves and a balaclava, nosed a stolen Fairmont into the alley next to the remand centre and waited. Shortly after six o'clock, Steer came feet-first through the wall and dropped lightly to the ground.

Those aspects of the plan were faultless. The first thing to come unravelled was the drive away from the remand centre. Raymond was barrelling the Fairmont out of the alley, braking for Craigie Street, when a taxi drew in to drop off a passenger and he braked but slid smack into the side of the cab.

'Get out,' Steer said, waving his revolver at Raymond. '*Move.*'

The Fairmont was undrivable, the bumper and wing folded in against the right front tyre.

'The taxi,' Steer said.

Raymond followed him. The Fairmont had smashed in both

passenger-side doors of the taxi, so Steer headed around to the driver's side. Raymond found himself matching Steer move for move. Steer opened the driver's door and hauled out the cabbie; Raymond opened the rear door and hauled out the passenger, who waved a wallet at him angrily.

'Stop daydreaming,' Steer screamed. 'Get in, for Christ's sake, and drive like the clappers.'

Raymond followed Steer into the front of the taxi. He felt a kind of elation, a kind of decisive, get-out-of-my-way competence. It was the feeling he got when he walked into a bank with the shotgun. He yanked the lever into drive and peeled away.

Raymond was soaring now. He slipped the taxi rapidly through the sluggish Sunday traffic and onto a broad, deserted avenue. Here his exhilaration broke. 'Ha!' he shouted, punching the wheel. 'Yes!'

Steer's big hand seemed to float free of his lap and suddenly swing like an axe against Raymond's upper lip. His head rocked back. The pain was intense and blood spurted from his mouth.

'There's a certain bone in the nose. Hit a certain way, it gets driven into the brain. Not a good way to die. So don't fuck up again. Fuck up again and you're history.'

Raymond eyed Steer bitterly. The guy was like Wyatt, a bit long in the tooth but coldly dedicated, efficient in the way he moved, full of power like a coiled spring. 'How was I to know—'

'You didn't look,' Steer said. 'You just barged through.'

Raymond fished for a handkerchief and spat into it. Street lights slipped past outside and he wondered what he was doing here with this psychopath. Steer seemed to fill the car, heavy and accusatory, so that Raymond couldn't help himself. He had to appease the man. 'Go all right inside?'

'Just drive.'

They switched to the Range Rover at Thomastown. Raymond

felt rattled, and at the entrance to the Hume Freeway accelerated ahead of a truck. He sensed the driver behind them pushing his brakes to the floor. Headlights flooded them and a horn sounded, mournful in the night.

'Easy, pal,' Steer said. 'No sense getting us killed.'

Raymond relaxed. The bastard seemed easier with him now. He drove on into the black night. After a while Steer muttered, 'I hear you're Wyatt's nephew.'

Raymond said hastily, 'He doesn't know about this.'

'Good,' Steer said. 'The fewer the better. You'll be sticking around for a couple of days, right?'

'Yes.'

Steer seemed to relax, stretching his legs and settling his shoulder against the door. 'Not many of us around any more. The old school, me and your uncle. It's all drugs with the youngsters now. No finesse. Too impatient to plan. It's a skill. You take each job slowly, meticulously. You have to think it through.'

'Right,' Raymond said.

'Like, never set up a base in the same town as the target. If you're working with others, you each make a solo reconnaissance of the target. Stay in motels or overnight vans in caravan parks. Never let yourself get boxed in. Make sure your alternative escape routes are clear—no roadworks, no rubbish bins. If it's going to help, tie up emergency services with a fire or an explosion somewhere.'

Steer was on automatic pilot, lecturing, maybe out of nervousness. Still, Raymond told himself, why the fuck do I have to listen to it? He said sharply, 'You're not telling me anything I don't already know.'

Steer shrugged. 'Chill out, Sunshine. No offence. Only you'd be surprised at the number of amateurs, addicts and ego merchants there are in this game.'

359

Raymond could almost taste the dislike in his mouth. 'So, how do you know I'm not one of them?'

Steer went very still, very concentrated, a chill in his soft voice: 'You come recommended, but if you fuck me around, remember that I've got a lot of favours owing. I know things. I network. The moment I walk into a nick, I run it. I know things or can find them out, and I'd track you down and not even your famous uncle could save you.'

They drove into the night. After a while, Steer rubbed his hands together. 'How'd you get on with my bird?'

'Fine,' Raymond said warily. Had the bastard been stewing away in remand, wondering if Denise was screwing around on him? He waved a reassuring hand. 'I mean, we were pretty busy doing our own thing, putting this together.'

Steer breathed in and out heavily. 'She's an ace chick. I've really been looking forward to this.'

Christ, Raymond thought. The bastard's actually keen on her.

Half an hour later they met Denise in a shadowy parking bay on the Hume Freeway. Denise flung herself onto Steer and Raymond had to stand back for a while, his head averted, while they kissed and murmured.

When they were finished, he said, 'Don't want to be hanging around here much longer.'

'Time for a quick snap?' Denise asked.

Raymond frowned. 'What are you on about?'

Denise pulled a small camera from her bag and said, self-consciously, 'A record of this historic moment.'

'Jesus,' Raymond said.

But he was taken with the idea. First he snapped Denise and Steer with their arms around each other, then Denise snapped Raymond with Steer.

Then the job unravelled again. 'People,' Steer announced, 'I've got things I need to do. I'll see you at the house sometime tomorrow morning.'

Denise had been hanging onto his arm, dopey with love, but stiffened when she heard this. 'What things?'

'I'll explain later. Just till lunchtime tomorrow. I want both of you to stay put at the safe house till I get there.'

Raymond said, 'This wasn't part of the original plan.'

Steer began to advance on him. Raymond stood his ground, trying not to flinch from the chest pressing against his, the hot breath gusting into his face. 'I said, I'll be back, okay?' A finger jabbed him. 'You got that? You're paid to see it through to the end.'

Raymond said nothing, just watched coldly as Steer climbed into the Range Rover, but Denise disintegrated. She cried out, even clawed at Steer's door as he drove away. When he was gone, she fell to her knees, shoulders heaving. 'Where's he going? Why's he doing this to me?'

Raymond walked across to her and helped her to stand. 'Come on, we have to get out of here.'

'What will I do? What if he never comes back? I can't go back to work. I can't go home. They'll arrest me. What will I do?'

Drive me fucking nuts for a start, Raymond thought.

20

Information was everything. Whenever Steer found himself in new environments or unknown company he put out feelers, made bargains, traded and exerted influence and pressure. Within hours of being arrested, he'd known who had sold him to the jacks. It was an outfitter called Phil Gent. You needed guns, explosives and detonators, a car, mobile phone, walkie talkies? Speak to Gent. Well, Gent had outfitted Steer's latest job, a warehouse load of Scotch, only one nightwatchman to deal with, then gone and spilled it to the jacks, who'd been waiting when Steer came out.

Steer had never met Gent at home. It was always on neutral ground such as a pub, a motel room or the docks. Within a couple of hours of his admission to Pentridge, he'd learnt where Gent lived: in a farmhouse near Colac in the Western District.

Steer headed there after leaving Raymond and Denise. Wyatt's nephew had looked pissed off, Denise heartbroken. It wasn't a betrayal, Steer intended to come back again, but it must have looked odd.

He thought about betrayal as he drove through the night. He'd been stiffed by Wyatt once, but right now he was more interested in Gent. What was it that made Gent sell him to the cops? For that matter, why had blokes in prison sold Gent to him?

To dog, to grass, to inform, to dob in. Steer tried to analyse it as the white line unfolded ahead of his headlights and darkness held him alone in the night. You'd do it for gain, like money, influence, power, advantage. You'd do it for revenge. You'd do it to get someone off your back. You'd do it to stop something happening.

Steer wondered about the other side of the equation. Take the cop who gave his ear to Gent: he'd have to reward Gent in some way, like give him money or turn a blind eye. There was dependency in that kind of relationship. Did the cop hate it? Not that he could afford to pin all his hopes on one informant. Someone like Gent might get cold feet or want more out of the deal or stop hearing good information if whispers about his reliability got about.

Or, Steer thought, smirking, someone like Gent might simply stop breathing.

It was a puzzle to Steer how Gent was able to live with himself. Money and favours would help, but he'd still have to come to terms with the fact that he was a dog. Did the shame and guilt get to him, or did he make the treachery acceptable to himself with a bit of fancy rationalising?—like: 'I'm doing this to those who deserve it. I'm not hurting those who haven't hurt me.'

On and on, the black road renewed itself in the light of the moon and the headlights. There was another form of treachery that could not be rationalised. It boiled down to abandoning your partners on a job, letting them take the risks and get caught by the law. Mostly it could be explained by greed, impulse or cowardice, but when a man like Wyatt does it to you it's cold and hard and calculated and unforgivable.

On the approach road to Gent's farmhouse, Steer turned off his headlights and kept the engine revs down. Gent might be naturally jumpy, or he might have heard about the prison break on the evening news. Either way, Steer didn't want Gent to know he was there until it was too late. The house came into view, an old weatherboard set well back from the road, looking grey and unlovely in the poor light of the moon. Steer pulled to the grass verge, switched off, and got out.

There was a kelpie on a mat outside the back door. It bared its teeth, it might even have attacked, but it didn't bark. Steer shot it through the head.

A light came on inside the house. Then a shape appeared at the window, Gent leaning to peer into the darkness. Steer shot him through the glass.

Steer stood where he was for a while, blinking, trying to encourage vision back into his eyes. Shows what a man can forget. His old training—unless you want to blind yourself for a couple of minutes, never look at the muzzle flash of a gun at night.

The darkness around him remained still and silent. When he could see again, Steer walked to the broken window and looked in.

Gent lay dying on his back. Typical gut-shot symptoms—grey face, glassy eyes, laboured breathing, a pleading grimace that heralded death. Then Gent retched violently, a froth of dark blood spilling from his mouth. His eyes widened. His tongue protruded. Steer turned away. He knew the final stage well enough. Gent would turn blue-grey, the cast of death.

Steer considered hiding the body. Kick in the teeth first, burn the hands, dump the body in a gorge somewhere. Unidentifiable remains, the papers would say. But the time, the trouble, the cleaning up the house first, the removal of the kelpie—stuff that for a joke.

Instead, Steer went into the house and ransacked it, making it look like an aggravated burglary. And he found five hundred bucks in an envelope taped to the bottom of a drawer, so that was all right, plus four grand and a passport in a cavity behind a false power point in a skirting board in the bedroom. The passport was no good to him, for Gent had the squashed features and jowls of a bulldog, and Chaffey had supplied him with a new ID, but the cash would come in handy.

Finally Steer concealed the Range Rover in a barn at the rear of the house. Gent owned a Kombi, parked under a tree in the yard. It needed plenty of choke and was low on fuel. Steer thought about that.

What stopped him thinking was the torch, a finger of light coming slowly across the flat ground behind the house, and an elderly woman's voice quavering, 'Mr Gent? Are you all right?'

Steer started the Kombi and drove slowly out of the yard. He hadn't seen another house nearby, but clearly there was one. Maybe the old dear would turn around and go home again, thinking she'd heard a backfire, but he couldn't take that chance. He'd have to find another car, and he'd have to take a different route out, a longer one, deep into the Western District then maybe north to the goldfield country. He'd allow himself two days, otherwise he'd be too late to meet the freighter off Lakes Entrance.

As he weaved through the Western District he thought about Denise. She loved him. It was gratifying. There hadn't been much love in his life. Denise wasn't exactly an oil painting, a bit pink and dampish and sour at the world, but she had a good brain. In fact, she made him feel obscurely inadequate. He wanted her to admire him; otherwise there would be that niggling doubt—was she just another female getting her kicks from screwing a hard man?

And Steer thought about Raymond Wyatt, a bit of luck that had just fallen into his lap.

At dawn the next morning he watched a farmer wave goodbye to his wife outside a log-cabin kit house and drive off in a dual-cab ute. There was a barrelly Falcon in the carport attached to the house, and no kids' clothing on the Hill's Hoist in the backyard. Steer gave the woman a concussive blow to the temple, concealed the Kombi and drove off in the Falcon ute. At lunchtime he stole a Holden, that evening another Falcon. All the time he was heading west, toward South Australia. At Dimboola he stole a Mazda, fitted it with plates from a scrapyard, and doubled back, driving through the night in heavy rain until he was in the Western District again, closing in on Geelong.

He wasn't expecting the roadblock. He was on a rain-lashed plain and saw brake lights ahead of him through the wash of the wiper blades. Pulling in behind a line of cars and farm vehicles, he thought *roadworks*, but when a muddy ute ahead of him U-turned out of the line and two motorcycle cops flashed past to intercept, he knew that this was no roadworks. He ran a mental eye over himself, over the car. The pistol was in the glove box, in a small tool kit.

He watched his wing mirror. The cops had stopped the ute. The driver, an elderly woman in overalls and rubber boots, climbed out, a kelpie butting through to the ground ahead of her. The woman began to berate the cops. One of them laughed. The other walked to the rear of her ute and searched under the tonneau cover. He apparently found nothing, but noted her plate number and a moment later waved her off.

Why here? Steer thought. Are they looking for me all over the state? The van ahead of him moved forward a car length, then stopped. Steer moved with it. The car behind him moved.

He looked at his watch. 9.20. He'd missed the nine o'clock

news and would have to wait until ten.

Five minutes later he reached the roadblock, which consisted of three pursuit cars angled so that quick acceleration forward was impossible. Half a dozen cops. Two further motorcycles.

A face filled his window; eyes the colour of slate gazed hard at him. Steer tensed, but there was no change in the man's expression, nothing to betray recognition or action. 'Your licence and registration, please, sir.'

'What's going on?' Steer asked, knowing that everyone would ask it.

'Your papers, sir, if you please.'

Steer fished the papers Chaffey had given him out of the glove box. He itched to bring out the pistol.

The cop passed the false papers back to him. 'Would you open the boot, please, sir?'

Steer leaned down and operated the boot release. There was a faint clunk as the lock disengaged. He turned to watch the cop, who stood to one side and gingerly, with his forefinger, raised the lid. An overnight bag of nondescript clothing, that's all.

The cop shut the boot and returned to the driver's window. 'On holiday, are we, sir? From New Zealand?'

'Lousy weather,' Steer said. 'Might as well be back home.'

The cop stood back from the window. 'I wonder if you would mind pulling off the road, sir, over there where those other drivers have parked.'

'What for?'

'Just routine, sir, if you don't mind.'

Steer saw two cars in the mud behind the pursuit cars. He guessed that he shared physical characteristics with both drivers. He started the car, moved forward off the road, switched off. The rain bucketed down. It was miserable, drenching rain, that seemed to reduce the world to the dimensions of a phone box. Figures blurred in the drifting curtain of water, and Steer removed the interior light bulb, pocketed the pistol, opened the passenger door and walked into the rain and out of the police net.

21

His overnight bag lay packed ready to go on the bed. Wyatt stripped off his clothes and went into the bathroom. He prepared the way by hacking the hair from the crown of his head with a pair of scissors. When the bulk was gone he took up the razor, a cheap gadget with a high whine that seemed to cut at the nerves behind his eyeballs. Facing the mirror with a hand mirror angled behind him, Wyatt made long careful swipes until he was left with a bald dome and tightly trimmed hair above his ears and at the back of his head. He looked thinner, sharper, like a man who lived a life of the mind. Finally he put on a pair of prescription glasses. He hadn't needed glasses, according to the one-hour dispensing optician, and so the lens adjustment was mild, but what the optician hadn't known was that Wyatt didn't want anyone to wonder why he had plain glass in his lenses and that Wyatt's real purpose in getting glasses was the heavy black frame. It altered his face completely.

It was a one-hour drive to Devonport. The ferry's departure

time was 6 p.m., but the company asked passengers to be on board well before that, and the hire car had to be returned, so Wyatt left Flowerdale at three o'clock in the afternoon. He wore light cotton trousers, a polo shirt and a lined woollen windproof jacket. He looked like a teacher or a priest in civvies. The heavy glasses transformed the cast of his face, from prohibition and wariness to internal musing and melancholy.

At five o'clock Wyatt found himself being swept by a crowd of people past drink machines, video games, slot machines and knots of smokers around barrelly chrome ashtrays, into corridors that led to the staircase at the midpoint of the ship. It linked all of the floors, and he plunged down to D deck. Here the air rushed in the vents and he bumped shoulders with passengers who had nowhere better to go. His cabin when he got to it was like a tomb, pinkish grey, as disagreeable as the holiday flat in Devonport. He went in carefully, checking corners, checking the shadows. Wyatt lived in corners and shadows and that's where the end would come for him.

He ate upstairs, at a table next to a window, only the black night and the waves outside the salt-scummed glass. Inside the glass it was a world of scratchy muzak, kids erupting through doors, overweight men and women, smoke, and the mulish, quickly combustible emotions of the herd.

He slept badly. The ferry shuddered through the night. The next morning he made his way to the dining room but, realising that he was to be penned like a sheep again and expected to eat like a pig at a trough, he grabbed an apple and a banana and made his way out onto the upper deck, where the wind was cold and clean and empty.

When the public-address system crackled into life, asking drivers to go to their cars, Wyatt went below, retrieved his overnight bag, and waited at the lifts. He chose an elderly couple. They were tottering toward the lifts, fighting a clutter of string bags and cases and each other.

'May I help you?'

'Help the wife throw some of this junk overboard,' the man said.

'Charlie, shut up,' the woman said. She smiled at Wyatt. 'That would be most kind.'

The man looked Wyatt up and down. 'You going to your car?'

Wyatt laughed. 'I don't drive. I'm on foot. I just thought you might need a hand.' He reached for a case. 'These look heavy.'

He saw that he'd disarmed them. The woman gave up a case and a shoulder bag to him, the man a second shoulder bag.

'Most kind of you.'

They stepped out of the lift into a claustrophobic iron shelf, the air full of fumes and echoes, the cars lined up like capsules in a pillbox. The elderly couple's car was a small blue Golf.

'If you'd care to squeeze in with a couple of doddery old fools,' the woman said, 'we'd be pleased to drop you somewhere, wouldn't we, Charlie?'

'Of course.'

Wyatt rubbed his bald patch, feigning embarrassment. 'Oh, I'm sure you don't want to—'

'Don't be silly,' the old woman said. 'We live in Hawthorn. We could drop you right in the centre of the city.'

'In that case,' Wyatt said, 'I'd be glad to take you up on your kind offer.'

By 8.30 they were leaving the dockland. Wyatt felt safe. He wouldn't have felt so safe on foot, eyes watching him file off the ferry.

Wyatt didn't know what sort of hours his nephew kept. Besides, he wanted to approach Raymond with better information than the boy had provided at Hastings a week ago. Wyatt waved

371

goodbye to the elderly couple on Bourke Street and caught a taxi to the University of Technology in West Heidelberg.

Twenty minutes later he was walking through to a broad lawn at the centre of the campus. According to the map displayed at the main gate, the R.J.L. Hawke School of Burmese Studies was the building facing the lawn from the west. He found a bench near a pond and stretched in the sun. There were few students about, fewer staff. The university had once merely called itself an institute of technology, and it appeared that the word 'technology' had determined the creative hand of the architects, for the place was universally ugly and pragmatic. No imaginative spark could ever be nourished in its stolid buildings. They dated from the 1960s and squatted among untidy eucalypts like grey bunkers. Here and there an external wall was pebble-dashed or set with glazed pink and grey tiles in outdated attempts at a stylistic flourish, but the general effect was depressing. No-one ran or whistled or walked with a bounce or conferred earnestly with a friend. Wyatt imagined the humourless lectures and tutorials, the staff down at the mouth because of budget cuts and job uncertainty and the ever-present jibe: 'It's not a real university. It's just a tech.'

He eyed the School of Burmese Studies. It had a look of temporary flashness, an effect encouraged by a new roof and plenty of smoky glass. Workmen were still renovating the interior; Wyatt could see them coming and going with electrical flex, plasterboard, tins of paint and ladders from a makeshift depot behind a cyclone security fence adjacent to the side entrance. Power to the building itself had been turned off. The workmen were relying on an external cable from the mains, looped like a thick black snake to a wooden pole staked temporarily in the lawn outside the security fence.

Chaos and clutter. He liked that. He looked more closely at the building. There were half a dozen trades represented by the workmen. Along with everyday tools they surrounded themselves with specialist equipment, supplies and vehicles. In one corner of the makeshift depot was a stack of plasterboard under a tarpaulin. In another was a portable tin shed. Through the open door Wyatt could see buckets of paint. The air-conditioning subcontractor had claimed a third corner, his lengths of galvanised conduits, angle bends, grilles and ducts scattered as though to help the earth exhale. There were ladders, copper and PVC tubing, reels of flex. In the fourth corner was a rubbish skip, overflowing with broken plasterboard, strips of wood, glass, aluminium window frames, tubes and hosing and empty paint tins. Vans and small trucks and utilities came and went through the morning. They bore stains and rust and crumpled panels, and they leaked unburnt exhaust gases into the atmosphere. Some of these vehicles would be locked in overnight, Wyatt guessed.

He began to formulate questions and answers. At midday he strolled through to a cafeteria, bought a sandwich, and prowled the perimeter of the university, mentally mapping the configuration of roads and buildings. The campus wore a kind of down-at-heel, blue-collar innocence. It wasn't geared to anticipating hold-ups, burglaries or heists of any kind, only pilfering from the union building shops and theft from the library.

By two o'clock Wyatt was on a different bench at a different point of the main lawn. He watched, read a newspaper, sometimes ambled across to the men's in the library basement. The newspaper carried an update on Steer's break from prison. He'd first caught the story from a discarded *Mercury* on the ferry. Since then a man matching Steer's description had disappeared near a roadblock in the Western District. Wyatt had no thoughts on the matter of Steer other than that, no matter where Steer went to ground, he'd be difficult to find. He'd once trained with Steer, and could attest to the man's gifts.

373

22

Ninety minutes after breaking Steer from the remand prison, they had been back at the house in Warrandyte. The drive in darkness across from the Hume Freeway had been hell for Raymond. He had nothing in common with the Meickle woman and all she could talk about was Steer, carrying on about how she'd given up everything for him, would walk through fire and water, so what was going on? Why had he cleared out like that? Where was he going? When would he be back? Would he be back? On and on.

They had left the car at the rear of the little house and gone inside. There she had clutched Raymond's arm. 'Ray? He will be back, won't he?'

Raymond shook her off. 'How the hell would I know? I'm going to bed.'

Wait with Denise until I get back, that had been Steer's instruction. One thing was for sure, Raymond was earning his money on this particular job.

The next day had been hell, rained all day, and now a new

day was dawning, hell all the way, cooped up together, no topic in common except Steer. The Meickle woman was all pink and damp, from two days of bawling her eyes out. She looked like some small, hairless albino dog, Raymond thought.

'I gave up my career for him,' she said.

Raymond flicked through his Jaguar Car Club magazine. He didn't know why he'd joined. Okay if you wanted to wear a tweed sports coat and go on a fun run through the Dandenong Ranges, stop in a picnic spot and have your picture taken for the magazine. Okay if you wanted to be buttonholed by some little twerp from the social committee. Okay if you wanted to read a blow-by-blow description in jokey prose about changing the diff oil in a '68 S-type. He yawned massively. The sun was pouring through the glass wall at the rear of the house. He'd slept well, had toast and coffee, and here it was, only 9 in the morning. The long hours lay ahead like a sentence. Couldn't even call anyone on the phone; it had been cut off while the owners were away. Raymond had the patience to stake out a country bank for a day or more, no problem, but he didn't know if he could just sit around like this for much longer. Casing a bank was different. There you had something to aim for, to look forward to. Here it was all up in the air.

'We could be waiting for nothing,' Denise said. 'He just used me.'

Raymond stood, prowled the perimeter of the little room, looked out upon the forest with his fists crammed into the back pockets of his Levis. 'Look, he's probably got some dough stashed away somewhere. Gone to get it.'

Denise Meickle shook her head emphatically behind him. He saw it like a moon reflected in the glass. 'Chaffey takes care of Tony's money matters.'

That was interesting. Raymond turned. 'Chaffey is Steer's banker?'

375

'It's safer that way.'

'Huh.'

Raymond sank into an armchair, hunted in the cane magazine rack for something better to read. He turned to the back of the *New Idea*, looked at the candid shots of the rich and famous. Fergie's tits, Richard Gere shopping incognito, Australia's own Nicole Kidman on a beach with her sister and a heap of kids.

Still only 9.30. 'Want another coffee, Denise?'

'I mean, how long do we wait? When do we know there's no point in waiting for him?'

'Got me there, Denise.'

He found the Maxwell House and spooned coffee and sugar into a mug. Turned on the kettle, then discovered it was switched off at the wall. Lunch. At least there was that to look forward to. He peered in the refrigerator. They had to shop. Get him out of the house at least.

Denise had trailed after him into the kitchen. She climbed onto a stool at the bench. 'Or what if he's had an accident? What then? He'll be arrested. If he's hurt, he'll need me, he'll call for me. I'll have to come, even if it means I'll be arrested as well.'

'Are you mad? There's no fucking way that *I'm* going to gaol for your boyfriend.'

Raymond slammed the cutlery drawer. Jesus Christ, what a stupid bitch. 'We need some things at the shop,' he said finally.

'I'll stay here,' Denise said complacently. 'He may come back.'

Raymond hadn't intended to take her with him in the first place. 'Anything you need in particular?'

'A paper,' she said. She gave a coy little shiver. 'I want to see if they spelt my name right. They could even have pictures.'

Raymond went cold. Pictures. He forced himself to relax. Sure, they'd have pictures of Steer and Denise; no reason why they'd have a picture of him.

'And orange juice and vodka,' she said.

Good. Drink yourself into a stupor. 'Got any cash?'

Denise turned sourly and went to her room. She came back, carelessly shoved a folded fifty at him, as if offering a tip to an undeserving waiter. 'I want change.'

'You're a sweetheart, Denise. I'd go for you myself if you weren't already taken.'

The reply strangled in her throat and the tears spilled. She turned away from him and Raymond shrugged and left the house.

In a shopping centre over the next ridge he bought a *Herald Sun*, groceries and vodka. Steer and Denise were on page three. The photo of Denise was ten years out of date. Her aunt in Cranbourne begged her to notify the police that she was still alive. There was no-one who wanted Steer back. Raymond found himself referred to simply as 'the getaway driver'.

He sat in the Jag and used the car phone. Got the answering machine at Vallance's flat in Hastings; no Vallance or Roden registered at the Windsor. Raymond felt frustration begin to settle in his bones. If Allie had been around he could have slipped down to the city this afternoon, fucked her brains out for a couple of hours, been back in time to babysit Denise before it got dark. He looked at his watch. Only another eight hours of daylight to get through.

Raymond drove back to the house, Allie stirring in his mind's eye. There would be time, if he could find her. He had until midnight before he was supposed to take Steer to meet the coastal freighter—that's if Steer was going to show up. Raymond had his doubts. Steer was probably well away by now. He'd done a runner, had his own agenda, wanted to dump old Denise without having to listen to a lot of crap first.

At one o'clock Denise said, two vodkas under her belt, 'Where are you going?'

'Out,' Raymond said.

'Where? Tony might come.'

'Face it Denise, he's long gone.'

Her face dissolved again. 'Don't say that. Wait with me, please?'

He unhooked her stumpy fingers from his sleeve. 'I'll be back early evening, okay? I can't hang around here all day. Got things to do. Got a life of my own, you know.'

'You've been paid to look after me.'

Raymond pointed at the vodka bottle. 'Suck more piss. Dull the pain.'

He left her crumpling behind him and whisked the Jag down into the city. Called at his flat, slipped on his good gear, went to the casino, feeling as eager as a kid at school who had the hots for someone.

But Allie wasn't there. Nor was Vallance.

And so he sat at his table and, in a cold rage, gambled away a third of the fifteen thousand dollar fee that Chaffey had given him to spring Steer from gaol, leaving him short for the deposit he'd promised Vallance.

The Warrandyte house was in darkness when he got back. Raymond's mood by now was *fuck this for a joke*, and he went in with Denise's shopping-list Ruger in his hand, jacking a round into the chamber, screwing on the suppressor.

The place stank, as if she'd been drinking all day, shut away in misery, too depressed to turn the lights on when the sun went down.

Unless the cops had been. Unless Steer had some little surprise lined up for him.

Raymond edged through the dark house, letting the bitter

disappointments of his afternoon give way to hair-trigger nerve and preparedness. He heard the floorboards, saw the shape poised against the moonlit window, and raised the Ruger to fire.

But it was Denise, foggy with booze. She slurred her lover's name. 'Tony?'

Raymond scraped his hand over the wall, looking for the light switch. He couldn't find it, so let his eyes adjust to the tricky light of the moon filtering through the crowding trees outside the house. 'No such luck.'

She came across the room, only half comprehending him. 'Ray? You brought Tony with you?'

'Face it, Denise, he's done a runner.'

She wailed. Raymond had never heard anyone wail before. It acted on him like a migraine, like fingernails screeching down a blackboard, and he put both hands to his head to make it go away. The Ruger knocked his skull. 'Ouch. Will you fucking quit that?'

She stopped a metre away, her mouth wide, tears glistening on her face. 'He's hurt somewhere, I just know it.'

'Get your act together, Denise.'

She made to turn away. 'I should ring the hospitals.'

Raymond yanked her around by the arm. 'Yeah, right, ring the cops as well while you're at it.'

She stood miserably then gathered herself and said, with drunken cunning: 'You've got a phone in your car.'

'Forget it.'

She came chest to chest with him. 'Just a couple of calls. I won't give our names. Please? Pretty please?'

Revulsion welled in Raymond. He pushed her hands away. 'You disgust me.'

She changed again, fierce and concentrated now, intent on prising the Ruger away from him. 'You can't talk to me like that.'

They seemed to perform a kind of shuffling dance across the floorboards. At one point the suppressor on the barrel of the Ruger flipped up and smacked bruisingly against Raymond's cheek. 'Christ, will you bloody well—'

He should have switched the gun to safety when he had the chance. He should have shoved it away in his waistband. It went *phut* in the tangle of their hands and Denise's head snapped back. Her fingers clenched, relaxed, and she dropped to the carpet like a stone.

He found the light switch and with the return of his senses, Raymond saw that Denise had been shot smack bang in the centre of her face. His first reaction was to swallow, once, again. He opened his mouth to speak. He shivered, looked around for help.

A moment later he shook off his attack of nerves. He thought, serve the bitch right, she was redundant anyway.

The more he thought about it, the more he realised that what they didn't know wouldn't hurt them—Chaffey, Steer, the police. Yeah, she'd simply decided she couldn't hack the pressure any longer and shot through, caught the first bus to Queensland.

He wondered if he was losing his edge a little. He'd always felt in control before. Allie Roden, the treasure—they were doing something to him.

The jitters came when he wiped the place clean, buried Denise with her stuff and drove back to his flat. The jitters threatened to shake him apart when, as he turned the key in his front door, a hand clamped on his arm and a voice growled, 'Raymond.'

23

'Take it easy, son,' Wyatt said. 'Didn't mean to scare you.'

Raymond breathed out heavily. 'You're a sight for sore eyes. Come in.'

They walked through to the kitchen, where Wyatt peered keenly at his nephew under the unremitting fluorescent light. 'Are you okay?'

There was a bruise on Raymond's face. He wore a distracted air, an edge of hysteria under it. He gathered himself. 'I'm fine. Rough night, that's all.'

'Six o'clock in the morning. A long night.'

'Yeah, well, you know,' Raymond said.

'There's blood on your sleeve.'

Wyatt saw his nephew start violently, turn his shirtsleeve this way and that. 'This guy tried to mug me.'

'Where?'

Raymond blinked, grew more concentrated. 'King Street, outside one of the clubs. I fought the bastard off. Anyhow, what about you? What gives with the haircut?'

Wyatt rubbed his shaven dome. 'I'm a known face in this city.'

Raymond shrugged, losing interest. Then he yawned widely and stretched his back. 'Rough night.'

Wyatt said, 'I want you to take a shower, then have something to eat, then we'll talk.'

'I'm right.'

'No you're not.'

Raymond weaved out of the room. The shower, food and coffee gave him the sharp edge that Wyatt was looking for. Half an hour later they sat at a table in the harsh kitchen light, Wyatt with a pad and a pen at his elbow.

'Right. I went to look at the building where the paintings are stored. It can be done.' He drew rapidly. 'These are possible exits. As you can see, the place is like a sieve.'

Raymond gulped a second cup of coffee. 'Chaffey mentioned nightwatchmen.'

'I'd rather deal with a nightwatchman than cameras and alarms,' Wyatt said.

'What do we do if it goes wrong?'

Wyatt looked at him. 'Let's say you walk into one of your bush banks to rob it. There's a cop at the counter, paying his mortgage. What do you do?'

Raymond shrugged. 'Turn around and walk away from it.'

'Exactly.'

There was a pause.

'What's on your mind, Ray?'

'Just going through the scenarios. We could shoot through, not bother with Chaffey. I mean, fifty grand each, it's not much. We'd get more selling the collection ourselves. Or,' he said, grinning, 'I could shoot through on you, take the collection with me.'

Wyatt didn't take the joke. 'I'd hunt you down. Never cheat your partners. They have very long memories. When it's an institution there's nothing personal at stake. With a partner there is, and if he's like me, he'll hunt you down.'

Raymond shrugged. He was full of sulky gestures, like a teenager out to stir an adult. 'Why not invest the paintings in some coke, some pink rock from Thailand? Cut it, sell it, we'd get a million back easy, maybe more.'

Wyatt seemed to snap like a coiled spring. His expression was direct and unnerving as he grabbed Raymond by the throat. 'No drugs.'

'Lighten up, Unc. Just a joke.'

'I never deal with that stuff.'

'Maybe you should go with the flow. You're out of date.'

Wyatt knew that his nephew was stirring. Even so, a rare feeling welled up in him. He wanted to slap some sense into his nephew. If Raymond were anyone else he'd have walked away.

But he said nothing, just let the heat dissipate.

Raymond felt the force of Wyatt's stare. He said uneasily, 'It's okay. I was only joking. I'm not a user or anything.'

'Good.'

After another pause, Raymond asked, genuinely wanting to know: 'How come you don't pull the big jobs any more? You loaded or something, just keeping your hand in for the fun of it? These paintings, for fifty grand, hardly your style.'

The answer rose unbidden in Wyatt. 'I'm tired.'

Raymond stared at him, his brow creasing. He seemed to be touched a little with panic and confusion, as though Wyatt had identified a hard, necessary and inescapable fact of existence. 'You? No way known.'

Wyatt said, 'All right. Not tired. But there are two things going against me: technology and time. It's getting harder to break into places, and the people I used to trust are all dead and gone.'

As if to bolster Wyatt's spirits, Raymond clapped his hands together and said, 'I won't let you down.'

'Good. Time to let this Chaffey character know.'

Raymond stared at the wall, grimaced as if swamped by bad thoughts. 'Chaffey?'

'It's his job,' Wyatt said, frowning. 'Don't you want to see him?'

Raymond said vaguely, 'She's jake, no worries.'

Raymond phoned, and Wyatt noticed that he leapt right in, choking Chaffey off, only letting him suggest somewhere to meet.

It was the grounds of Montsalvat, the artist's colony in Eltham. Chaffey had a ticket to an afternoon jazz concert, and met them on a grassy slope above the hall. It was a good place for a meeting, Wyatt thought, but Raymond's mood had changed again as they'd driven deeper into the hills, a reversal to his nervy distracted state, as if the trees and folds and gullies were populated by demons.

But all that mattered was the job, and Chaffey. Wyatt assessed the big man, noting the unhealthy skin, his wheezing chest and damp neck and brow, then looked for what the face and eyes might reveal, some predisposition that told Wyatt he should walk away from this.

He was startled to find that Chaffey was returning the intense scrutiny. 'Heard you were at the centre of a ruckus in the city the other day.'

Wyatt waited a beat, then said, 'The police know it was me?'

'Yes.'

'That's all they know?'

'Yes.'

'How did you hear about it?'

'Pal,' the big man said, 'I'm a lawyer. I hear things.'

'I'm here,' Wyatt said. 'They're no closer to finding me.'

'Glad to hear it,' Chaffey said. He moved decisively, placing a briefcase on the grass between them, patting it. 'Take this when you leave here. It contains a list of the works my client wants, their dimensions, and floor plans of the building.'

'Your client wants only some of the paintings?'

'A big Whiteley, two Tuckers, two Booths, three Lloyd Rees drawings, a Dobell and four Heysen watercolours.'

'You say you've got floor plans. I hope they can't be traced back to you.'

Chaffey shook his head. 'I applied for them in the name of the firm renovating the building.'

'Who's your client?'

Chaffey laughed. 'The wife of the man who put the collection together. According to her, the paintings were a present, but the husband pissed off overseas with his secretary, owing a few million to his creditors, so the collection was sold off and the wife got nothing. She's understandably upset, wants her paintings back.'

'What makes you think the cops won't look closely at her?'

'They will, but she's no longer around. The paintings are going straight to New York, where she lives now. You deliver the paintings to me, you get paid, I crate them up and courier them to her, that's how it works.'

Raymond stretched out in the sun. He'd shaken off his mood. 'You're her lawyer?'

'No.'

'How do you know her?'

'Our kids went to the same school.'

If often happened that unimaginable lives were revealed to Wyatt. They were lives lived parallel to his, defined by money and respectability, private schools and skiing holidays, Volvo station wagons and horse-riding teenage daughters, divorces and charity functions. Now and then his life and theirs veered course sufficiently to intersect. Whose life was the most honest or the least unrealistic, he couldn't say.

He followed the exchange between Chaffey and his nephew. Raymond was asking all the right questions. 'The same school? So there's no other connection between you? The cops won't come looking at you?'

'No.'

'Good. Because I don't want to sit on these paintings while the air clears. I need my fifty grand the moment we hand you the pictures.'

Chaffey said nothing while a woman wheeling a pram passed close behind them. When it was safe, he cocked his head. 'Gambling debt, young Raymond?'

'Business deal,' Raymond said, and Wyatt and Chaffey looked at him, waiting, but Raymond didn't elaborate.

'How about things in general?' Chaffey asked. 'Everything going according to plan, Ray? No hiccups?'

There was something about this, some sort of private communication. Wyatt watched and listened, but all Raymond said was, 'No dramas my end, Chafe, no worries.'

'Glad to hear it,' Chaffey said. He climbed in painful stages to his feet. 'Keep me posted.'

Wyatt shook his head. 'We're dropping out of sight till this is over.'

24

Back at Raymond's flat, Wyatt felt himself switching gears, taking in his surroundings as he retreated mentally from matters of escape routes and the unknown. He had a few days up his sleeve for planning the job. Right now there was Raymond and Raymond's flat.

Wyatt didn't feel comfortable. Unless the apartment was being watched, he was safe enough staying there, but he hated not having control. Nothing here belonged to him, he liked to have his feet at ground level, not ten floors above the street, and he had to wear a public face.

Perhaps that's why he scribbled down his Tasmanian address for Raymond. 'Treat it strictly as a way out if you're in trouble,' he said. 'Somewhere to go if you can't come back here.'

Raymond held the slip of notepaper in both hands, examined it, made to slip it into his wallet. 'Thanks.'

Wyatt's fingers clamped on his wrist. 'Memorise it,' he said.

Raymond sighed raggedly. He looked bad to Wyatt, the

demons still chasing around in his head. Wyatt saw his nephew mouth the address silently, close his eyes in concentration, blink open again.

'Got it. Where the hell is Flowerdale?'

'Between Burnie and Stanley on the north coast.'

'Yeah, right, lots of cafe society, nightclubs,' Raymond said, screwing the paper scrap into a ball and tossing it into an ashtray. They both looked at it. 'Suppose you want me to swallow it now?' he said sourly.

Wyatt said nothing, simply put a match to the paper and crossed to the window to stare down at the river and the city.

He liked to know that he was close to water. Water was alive. It meant contradictory things to him: stealth, power, restlessness, an endless calm.

He heard a groan and turned to see Raymond clutch himself, his face white. 'My guts have been playing up.'

'Food poisoning?'

'Maybe nerves,' Raymond said, grinning weakly. 'No, don't worry, nerves of steel.'

'There's a chemist downstairs.'

'Good idea.'

Raymond left the flat. Wyatt stood for some time, staring at the river, seeing the job ahead of them. He became conscious of the open door to Ray's room, and wandered across to the door and went in. The boy was untidy. Wyatt knew that he employed a cleaning lady, so presumably there was no incentive for him to be tidy.

The cash box sat in darkness on a high shelf, under an empty nylon overnight bag. The key was in it. It surprised Wyatt, seeing Steer there, gazing coldly at the camera. Raymond stood next to him, grinning. The photograph had been taken at night, near trees. He found Steer in another photograph, his arms around a short, broad-faced unhappy woman, the woman close to him as though she wanted to meld herself with him.

Wyatt hunted deeper into the cashbox. Newspaper clippings, going back several years. He recognised some of the headlines: 'Airport Bullion Heist' was an old one, one of his own. More recently there were clippings about the bush bandit, highlighted here and there with strokes from a yellow pen.

And clippings about Steer's escape from gaol.

When Raymond returned to the flat, Wyatt forearmed him across the throat, propelling him backwards and pinning him to the wall. He said, in a low, dangerous rasp: 'I'm going to remove my arm now. I will ask you some questions. You will answer them.'

Raymond's eyes were wide and aggrieved. He forced a nod.

Wyatt let him go. 'Good. Did you help Steer escape?'

'Me?'

Wyatt's forearm went back across his nephew's windpipe. He relaxed it again.

Raymond gasped, 'Yeah, it was me.'

'The papers say the woman was involved.'

'Her and me.'

'Where is Steer now?'

Raymond swallowed. 'Overseas. That was the deal. Boat from Lakes Entrance.'

'The woman too?'

'Her, too.'

'Raymond, Steer was seen running from a roadblock recently.'

'Well, yeah, then he turned up as planned where I was minding the girlfriend and I took both of them to the boat. I swear.'

Wyatt stepped back. He took Raymond into the bedroom and forced his head onto the cashbox, then off again, as if Raymond were a dog who'd fouled the carpet. 'This is what an amateur does. He keeps all his little mementos with him, letters from his pals, photos, clippings, stuff that will tie him to everything he's ever done or come near. It's stupid, stupid. It'll get you gaol time. It's sentimental and there's no room for sentiment in this game. Burn this crap.'

'Fuck you—'

In a cold rage, Wyatt gathered the spill and took it into the bathroom. He made a bonfire of it in the bath, and when it was reduced to ashes he sluiced it all away with the shower nozzle, his own long career and his nephew's shorter one.

He went out to Raymond. 'Your life starts over again,' he said, as if the past had had nothing to do with anything.

'You bastard.'

'Ray, you're on your own now. I'm out of this. You're on your own.'

Wyatt said it heatedly, a new sensation for him, almost as if he hadn't decided on the words but let them pop out.

Raymond grew passionate in the face of them. 'Haven't I always been alone? You dumped me and my mum. You dumped family. I thought I'd at least see you when she died, but you couldn't give a stuff, couldn't even come to the funeral.'

Wyatt had been on the run when it happened. He'd heard the news weeks later. Seeing the fretfulness, frustration and sore feelings in his nephew now, he allowed his expression to soften. It was intended to be a look of compassion, but Wyatt was not good at compassion and something—his habitual scepticism, his permanently unimpressed view of the world—made itself known to Raymond. Raymond swung away and left the room.

Wyatt followed him. 'Tell me about the break-out.'

Raymond said, 'You still here? I thought you were pissing off on me again.'

Wyatt said, 'I was too hasty. I apologise. But I don't like surprises. Did Chaffey put the escape together?'

Raymond nodded.

'You did it for a fee?'

'Yes.'

'What do you know about Steer?'

Wyatt saw his nephew shrug. 'What's there to know? Chaffey's his lawyer.'

'You don't know anything of Steer's history? Chaffey didn't tell you anything about that?'

'No. Why should he? What's Steer to you?'

'An old grievance, that's all,' Wyatt said. Steer was a loose end, like a live power line snaking around on the ground nearby, but one that could be attended to later. He made for his room and packed his bag.

'So, this is it?' Raymond said.

'The job's still on. But we both need to find somewhere else to stay. Separate places.'

'You must be joking.'

'I never joke.'

'You ought to try it sometime,' Raymond said.

25

From the driver's seat of her car, Liz Redding watched Raymond Wyatt stride down the slope toward her, into the underground residents' garage. The location was a pricey motel in Parkville, and Raymond was whistling, swinging a key ring around his index finger. He passed right by her. Two days earlier she'd followed him here from his apartment block on the other side of the city, but this was her first close look at him. A more sullen version of his uncle's hooked face and hooded eyes. The same black hair, only worn longer, so long that it hung greasily about his face, meaning he was forever clawing it back with his left hand. The hands: not shapely and nimble. Shorter, thicker. And while Raymond was built like Wyatt—tall, sinuous, compact, with a quickness under the still surface—he lacked strength and vigour. Liz Redding formed an impression of unfocused courage and grand, frustrated ambitions.

His Jaguar was in the far corner. Liz started her car and ploughed up the ramp and onto the street, where she slowed down, as though looking for an address, one eye on the rear-view mirror. She wanted to be moving when the Jaguar appeared behind her. If Raymond saw a parked car turn on its lights and pull in behind him, he'd know he was being tailed and he'd try to lose her. Of course he might turn left out of the driveway, in which case she'd switch off her headlights, U-turn, and follow him for a distance before switching on again, but she doubted that he would turn left. Twice now she'd followed him right, down to Gatehouse Street, then around by the cemetery to north Carlton, before losing him.

She inched along, whistling impatiently. A moment later, headlights rose and dipped behind her as the Jaguar entered the street. The car accelerated, coming up behind her, and Liz turned on her indicator and steered into the kerb, letting him pass. She saw his brake lights flare at the corner. He turned right, then was gone from sight. Liz pulled out again and put her foot down.

She relaxed when she was on the Parade, settling in three car lengths behind the Jaguar. Even if he veered onto an unfamiliar route or tried to be evasive, she was reasonably confident of staying with him. The XJ6 was a distinctive car, but, even so, earlier in the day she'd detailed the rear of the big car with small strips of reflective tape. They were under the bumper and not immediately apparent to someone standing close to the car, but clearly visible to anyone farther back in a car at night, showing as an irregular red pattern in the headlights. Raymond's car was unmistakeable. He could merge with a freeway of similar cars and Liz would know him.

The minutes passed. Raymond followed the cemetery around and headed toward Princes Street. Now and then he altered speed or skipped lanes, as though to shake off a tail, but Liz didn't let herself be drawn. He was simply going through the motions. He probably imagined a tail even when he went out for bread and milk. She stayed where she was, in the left lane, at the speed limit, more or less.

Liz followed the XJ6 to Alexander Parade and onto the Doncaster Freeway. Raymond wasn't so tricky now. He kept to one lane and to the speed limit, a young blade tooling along in his glossy big car. Liz drifted close to him from time to time and had a clear view through the rear window of the casual way he draped himself in the car, one shoulder against the door, one hand on the wheel, the other along the top of the passenger seat.

Raymond took the Bourke Road exit, winding through the cuttings in the little hills of Ivanhoe and down into West Heidelberg. He surprised her by parking in a side street and strolling into the grounds of the University of Technology. Liz parked, got out, removed the reflective tape from the XJ6, and hurried after him, into a world of lighted footpaths between clumps of shrubbery and a hotchpotch of blockish buildings, many of them well lit. Even so, the place seemed dark and creepy, and she thought of the female students braving the shadows at night, on their way to a lecture or back to their cars in the vast car parks.

Raymond came to a bench seat near a pond. Here there was plenty of light, even a couple of smooching students on the grass, and then, for the first time in two weeks, she saw Wyatt. He wore a dark cap and a dark zippered jacket and was standing rock still, watching from the corner of a nearby building. She knew that look: dark, sceptical, wary as a cat. He didn't spot her. He began to approach his nephew, moving with an easy fluid lope that could have turned into an attack or flight in an eyeblink. Part of her stirred, transforming the loose grace of his walk into the more concentrated grace of his hands and his body as he'd touched and flowed with her on their narrow bunk aboard the yacht. Despite the distance, she noted tight lines of exhaustion, even of sadness, on Wyatt's narrow, hooked face. She was reminded of a prowling creature aware of its needs and the hunter's weaknesses.

What broke the spell for her was Wyatt lifting his cap to scratch his head. He'd shaved off most of his hair. He looked monkish, like a grim recluse in an old painting.

Liz watched them for an hour. They could pass as mature-age students, she realised, taking a break from the library stacks. One of them went for takeaway coffee from a machine. They talked, strolled, sat again. Once when a nightwatchman went by she saw a subtle stiffening of their spines, and after a while it occurred to her that Wyatt and his nephew were watching a particular building. She would have to find out why. It had a shut-down look about it, a cyclone security fence around an area of building supplies against one wall.

She wondered what Vallance had to do with it. Twice she'd seen Vallance and a young woman arrive at Raymond's flat. She'd also seen the woman visit Raymond alone, at the motel in Parkville. Liz had had dealings with Vallance before and couldn't see someone like Wyatt getting involved with him. Maybe Raymond had his own agenda. It might be worth tipping the wink to her friends in CIB. They could pull Vallance and the woman. If nothing else, it might scare Raymond and Wyatt into walking away from this job, whatever it was. She hated to think of Wyatt in gaol. She'd crossed a line and was walking with him, now.

Wyatt parted from his nephew at nine, when the late lectures and tutorials broke. Liz knew where Raymond lived. Time to learn where Wyatt had his bolthole.

26

'Okay, Raymond,' Vallance said, 'just so you know I haven't been twiddling my thumbs.'

For this meeting, Raymond was back in his apartment. Fuck Wyatt. He watched as Vallance cleared a space on the coffee table and stacked it with brochures and photocopied price lists. 'I can get this stuff in Geelong, Williamstown, Devonport, Port Melbourne.'

He spread the documents over the table and tapped with a bony finger. 'This here's your up-market scuba gear and tanks. Tough, good air capacity. Okay, this is an underwater scooter.'

The brochure showed a clumsy machine trailing a diver. Raymond leaned over the table for a better look. Allie was next to him on the couch. That was good, heat from her long thigh.

'I know it looks like a handful of buckets and tubes welded together,' Vallance said, 'but you can cover a lot of ground quickly. Plus it's fitted with a metal detector. A scooter's good for backing up a visual search in clearish water less than fifteen metres, which part of our area is.'

Vallance slid another brochure across the table. 'This here's your proton magnetometer.'

Raymond saw a diver in murky water, holding the centre point of a transverse bar to which two sensor heads, shaped like small torpedoes, had been fitted. 'How does it work?'

'See this cable? It connects with a monitor in the boat. The boat tows you in a predetermined search pattern over the seabed. The sensors pick up anything made of iron or steel, like cannon or anchors, even if they're a hundred and fifty metres under. One of these babies will pick up a large steel ship up to a quarter of a mile away.'

Raymond leaned forward and indicated a different brochure. 'What about this? Looks like a vacuum cleaner.'

'Good one,' Vallance said. 'That's more or less what it is and how it works. Depending where you come from it's called a dredger or an airlift. Operated by a compressor on the surface. We'll have a lot of sand and sediment to clear away.'

Where Vallance couldn't see it, Allie was scratching her bare toes against Raymond's ankle again. He returned the pressure. 'Pretty impressive.'

Vallance nodded. 'So you can see how it all mounts up. Equipment, plus a boat with plenty of deck and hold area, doesn't take long to eat up a quarter of a million bucks in this game.'

Raymond was fascinated by the machines. 'What's this?'

He indicated a photograph of a diver dwarfed by two massive hollow tubes, suspended on either side of him at the rear of a ship.

'It's a prop wash,' Vallance said. 'You anchor your salvage vessel thoroughly fore and aft, so she doesn't move, place these tubes over each propeller, then run the motors. The wash effect gets directed downwards, like a whirlpool, and it blows away the bottom sediment. Clears a large area *molto* quickly. Not much good in water over fifteen metres, but I thought we should get one, given that we can't afford to hang around the wreck for too long.'

Raymond said, 'But if it's just lying there, like the stuff we saw the other day, why all the bother?'

'It's not just lying there. If you took the trouble you might pick up twenty or thirty grand's worth of gold coins just wearing scuba gear, but the bulk of it will be intact, buried deep somewhere.'

Raymond nodded. 'So all this equipment's available now?'

'It is.'

'None of it's cheap?'

'Not if it's top grade.' Vallance numbered his fingers. 'You've got your hiring fee, insurance, transport costs, incidentals like our accommodation and ferry charges. I won't lie to you, it's going to cost. But consider the return. Jesus Christ, unimaginable.'

Raymond felt more alive than he'd ever been. Part of him wondered if his judgement was shot, but mostly he itched for Allie Roden, itched for the treasure. 'Need a big boat for all this stuff.'

'That's right.'

'So have you got one lined up?'

'Down in Geelong,' Vallance said. 'Look, Raymond, I won't bullshit you, we have to move fast on this. Most of the syndicate's money is already accounted for. Plus, one guy pulled out at the last minute, putting more pressure on us. I'll need at least a deposit from you, as soon as possible. I mean, no offence, but I'll have to look elsewhere for funding if you decide you can't—'

'I can pay.'

'Sorry, put it another way—if you don't wish to get involved.'

'You said someone pulled out?'

Allie spoke for the first time, rolling her eyes in exasperation at what fate had delivered. 'We were *this close* to finalising the deal, and he pulled the plug. Now we have to start again, put out feelers, make approaches...'

'So there's nothing to stop me buying *two* syndicate shares?' Raymond asked.

She looked at him doubtfully, mouth open, thinking about it. 'No reason why not,' she said slowly. 'What do you think, Brian?'

Vallance was sharper. 'When I see some hard cash, Ray, then we can discuss whether or not you buy one share, two shares or none at all.'

Raymond swallowed. Denise Meickle swam into his thoughts again, her unappealing face, her slack body flipping into the hole he'd dug for her. He tried to shrug her away. He was a few days away from fifty grand. Hundred grand, if he had Wyatt's share. Fucking Wyatt, big man with a reputation, sneaks a look at his private things and puts a match to his memories. What did Wyatt want with fifty grand, anyway, considering he had the jewels and God knows what else stashed away in his house across Bass Strait. Wyatt, a bully and a coward, just like his brother, Raymond's father.

'You'll get your money,' Raymond said.

There was another scenario—pay Vallance with a million bucks' worth of paintings.

Vallance was staring at him disbelievingly, but then smiled and folded away the brochures. 'I know you will. I have every faith.'

'Not all my assets are liquid at the moment,' Raymond said. 'Like, a lot of it's tied up in art.'

Vallance peered doubtfully at Raymond's walls: a Formula 1 racing car, a Ken Done print.

'Not this crap,' Raymond said. 'The real thing, stored in a

vault. Family heirlooms.' He named the artists Chaffey had listed.

Vallance looked interested. 'Dinkum?'

'My Dobell,' Raymond said, 'could fucking *buy* you a boat, let alone rent it.'

'Well,' Vallance said, climbing to his feet, 'I'm certainly interested, but, like I said, I need cash.' He looked at his watch. 'Be back in a couple of hours. There's some other people I want to show these brochures to.'

Allie showed him to the door, kissed him on his leathery cheek, closed the door and leaned her long back against it, smiling a languid smile at Raymond. 'Two hours.'

She uncoiled from the door. She loped across the carpet on her bare feet and pulled his head to hers, periodically laughing with pleasure, a dark laugh deep in her throat. They undressed. She breathed, 'What would you like me to do?' and Raymond stroked her, feeling her moist heat. 'Wash me with your cunt,' he said, and heard the laugh again, her sheer delight in him. He gave himself up to the sensations, a kind of floating. She was good for him. She had the power to drive Denise Meickle from his head.

At the end of it she propped herself on her elbow and moodily traced his ribcage. 'I wish I could see you all the time, instead of snatching an hour here and there.'

'Me too.'

She laughed shyly. 'For the first time in a long while I've been thinking more than one week ahead, you know?'

'Do I figure in your plans?'

She said simply, 'Yes.'

'Dump old Brian?'

She sighed. 'It's run its course anyway.'

'He won't like it.'

She shrugged. 'So? It happens all the time.'

'Make sure you dump him *after* he pays me,' Raymond said.

She looked at him. He tried to fathom it. 'Or dump him permanently at the site, if you know what I mean.'

Raymond found himself saying, 'You know the paintings I said I owned?'

'Yes.'

Raymond told her about the university, the R.J.L. Hawke School of Burmese Studies. He told her about Wyatt and the bush bandit and the prison break, not bragging, just wanting her to know.

Awe and excitement settled in her face. 'Is *that* who you are?' she said.

27

'Why a van?' Raymond wanted to know. 'Why not something fast?'

'We're going to attract attention if we walk out with a heap of paintings and try to stuff them into the boot of your Jag. Not that they'd fit in the boot.'

'So concealment is the issue.'

'Yes.'

They were sitting across from the R.J.L. Hawke building again, ham sandwiches and cans of mineral water between them on the grass, talking it through. Seagulls wanted their crusts. Students sauntered past, the women with books clasped to their chests, the men with no books at all.

Raymond concentrated, biting his lower lip. 'You know when you stole that Picasso?'

Wyatt nodded.

'The word is you hid in the building overnight, walked out with it the next day.'

'Yes.'

In 1986 a bent art dealer from Prahran had hired Wyatt to steal *Weeping Woman* from the National Gallery on St Kilda Road. His story was that a rich man with a grudge was putting up the money. The painting was bound for Europe. Wyatt had got the painting out, concealed as a folio purchased from the Gallery's bookshop, but the job had gone sour after that and the painting had found its way back to the gallery.

'We could do the same,' Raymond said.

Wyatt wanted his nephew to think it through. 'But in this case we'll have on our hands fifteen paintings, some the size of the top of a kitchen table. For that we need a van, whether we stay on the premises overnight or not.'

Raymond mused glumly for a while. 'Is there anything to say the paintings have to stay in their frames?'

'You're on the right track.'

'We roll them up in something.'

'Yes.'

'Plumbers, electricians, they carry stuff around in long PVC cylinders.'

'You're getting there,' Wyatt said.

Raymond flung a crust to the gulls. 'How come we have to go through this rigmarole? If you already know what you want, how come you don't just tell me and I'll do it.'

'I'm not telling you anything. You're arriving at the answers yourself.'

'Am I a kid? Is this school? Arsehole.'

Wyatt looked away. He was learning how young Raymond was, after all. He wanted, by asking questions, to encourage thought. He wanted Raymond to identify problems and offer solutions, to inquire and speculate. In Wyatt's game, working well was at once thinking well, perceiving well and acting well.

And he couldn't deny that Raymond had badly unsettled him. That box of photographs, letters and clippings—amateurish and oddly human and ordinary. It was an aspect of human nature that Wyatt could not understand. But the boy's most damaging bombshell concerned Steer. Steer was a problem, and, because he'd helped Steer to escape, so was Raymond. Wyatt wondered if, even now, as he sat watching workmen come in and out of the target building, the police had a firm idea who was behind Steer's escape. When this job was over, he'd cut all ties with the boy.

He watched the ducks among the reeds, watched the students, watched a pigeon settle on the temporary power cable at the building site. 'Okay, when would you do it?'

'Overnight Saturday.'

'Why?'

'Not many people around.'

'And?'

'The robbery wouldn't be discovered till the Monday morning.'

'True. Though we could also go in on Friday night.'

'I wouldn't.'

'Why not?'

Raymond indicated the workmen. 'Those blokes will be working there the next morning.'

Wyatt nodded. 'On the other hand, there won't be any students or staff around on Saturday, not when they'd have to endure drills and hammers and transistor radios all day, and that means there'd be no-one to spot that the paintings were gone. The workmen are unlikely to notice or care one way or the other.'

'So there's no reason for anyone to go into the library storeroom until Monday.'

'Exactly.'

'What it boils down to, how do we get them out, and when?'

Raymond shrugged. 'At least we don't have to think about alarms and cameras.'

'But we do have to think about nightwatchmen.'

'Concealment,' Raymond muttered. 'Conceal the paintings in the PVC cylinders, conceal who we are.'

'Yes.'

They fell into silence. Eventually Raymond said, 'We need to look like we belong.'

'Clearly.'

Silence.

'Cleaning staff?' Raymond suggested.

Wyatt shook his head. 'Not in a building that's still being renovated.'

Irritation came quickly over Wyatt's nephew. 'Chaffey should have thought of all this.'

Wyatt sensed that the irritation owed itself more to the palpable sense of competition and resentment that had developed between them than to Chaffey's lack of solid information. He said nothing. If he put things right for the people he dealt with, then he'd never get any work done, that's how he saw it.

Besides, Raymond had to learn: the job came first. He had to curb his impulses. Wyatt tried to look back along the years. Had he ever been impatient? Had he ever been young? It sometimes seemed to him that he'd landed on the earth fully formed and always this age, always this careful. If there had been a time when he was a child, a youth, it was according to the calendar, not character. He supposed that that was a shame.

Now he did say something. 'Ray, ultimately it's up to us.'

But Raymond wasn't listening. His eyes were narrow and sharp. 'When I was at school we had an asbestos scare.'

'Asbestos?'

'These blokes came and looked in the ceilings. Nothing

happened, the place was clean, but it scared the shit out of everyone.'

'Go on.'

Raymond rubbed his hands together, thinking. 'Right. Let's say we pose as electricians. We run the risk of meeting the real ones. If we go in as asbestos inspectors, not only will we be alone in that, we'll look as if we belong and everyone will avoid us.'

Wyatt turned, smiled a snatched smile. It was his way of praising Raymond, but Raymond misread it.

'So? You do better.'

'It's good, Ray.'

The heat subsided in Raymond. He turned away, muttering, 'Let's go get that van.'

28

Raymond took them to a multi-level car park in Chadstone. They had the number plates, from a wrecked Volkswagen gathering dust outside a crash repairers in Altona—now all they needed was the vehicle.

'Check that panel van,' Raymond said, some time later.

A white Falcon, with a roof rack and windows in the rear compartment. It wasn't a commercial vehicle, but could be adapted without much trouble. They tailed it to the upper level and watched the driver, an elderly man, park, lock up and shuffle across to the lift.

When the man was gone, Raymond approached the driver's door with a tyre iron. He levered a gap between the door frame and the pillar, then slid a loop of stiff plastic binding tape behind the glass. Wyatt looked intently both ways along the sloping ramp. Wednesday, early afternoon. They needed to be in the campus grounds by four on Friday, giving them two days in which to alter the van.

He turned back, just as Raymond caught the latch with the plastic hook and pulled upwards. There was a click. 'You little beauty.'

Raymond slipped behind the wheel. Wyatt had stiffened, expecting an alarm, but there was silence. Raymond broke it. Suddenly all elbows and clenched teeth, he wrenched at the ignition with the tyre iron, splintering the plastic casing and laying bare the electronics behind it. He fired up the motor, grinning at Wyatt from amidst the wreckage. 'Piece of cake.'

'And obvious to anyone who takes a gander through the window,' Wyatt said. 'Wait there.'

He went to the front of the van and then to the rear, hooking the stolen plates over the originals. He ran his hand inside the rear wheel arch. The box was small, metal, with a sliding lid and a magnetised base. The elderly man's spare house and van keys nestled inside the box and Wyatt dropped them in his nephew's lap as he slid into the passenger seat. He said nothing, just buckled his seat belt, but his silence was hard and cold.

Raymond stared at the keys. There was always a smile close to the surface and it broke out over his sulky face now. 'Ahh,' he scoffed, 'more fun this way.'

That afternoon they repaired the ignition lock and took the panel van to be resprayed green at a place in Richmond—$999 of Wyatt's dwindling reserves. On Thursday they stencilled the sides of the van with the words 'Asbestos Removal Services', and filled the rear compartment with empty boxes, a stepladder and several lengths of PVC tubing.

They went in on Friday afternoon at four o'clock. They wore overalls and Wyatt carried a clipboard and an aluminium document case. They parked the van inside the enclosure as though they belonged to the place, got out, and asked around for the foreman.

'That's me.'

He was a large, loosely built man with a face mapped by broken capillaries. Friday, four o'clock. Wyatt was betting that all the man wanted to do was knock off and head for the pub.

'EPA sent us,' he said, flashing his clipboard.

The foreman was looking in alarm at the van. 'Didn't know we was working around asbestos. Bastards didn't tell us that.'

'You may not be. This is routine, that's all.'

'I mean, fuck, you been inside the place? Blokes have been breathing dust for days.'

'There's dust and there's dust,' Wyatt said.

The foreman looked at his watch. 'It's nearly knocking-off time. I'm out of here in ten minutes myself. Locking the gate and I'm gone.'

'I understand.'

'So you can't park your van here. I'm locking up.'

'That's all right,' Raymond said. 'We'll leave it overnight, catch a bus home.'

'His wife,' Wyatt explained. 'She doesn't want the van parked out the front of the house. Nor does mine. Can't say I blame them.'

The foreman licked dry lips. 'Do what you like. It's no skin off my nose.'

'The van's clean,' Wyatt said. 'No contamination. It's just the idea that gets to people.'

'You can say that again.'

Men began to stream from the work site. The foreman forgot about Wyatt and Raymond, and under the cover of men shouting, stripping off their overalls and cleaning brushes and rolling up flex, they loaded their arms with lengths of PVC tubing and entered the building.

According to the floor plans supplied by Chaffey, the

409

departmental library was on the first floor. They went up the stairs, whistling, ready to discuss the football if they encountered anyone, and found the first floor deserted and quiet, heavy with the smell of paint, plaster and sealant. They drew on latex gloves and made their way into the gloom, Wyatt counting the doors.

'This one.'

He tried the handle. It was locked. He took a set of picks from his overalls and leaned over the lock. Holding the tension pick at an angle, he teased with the raking pick, turning the tumblers. When it was done he breathed out, straightened and pushed open the door.

They went in, locking the door behind them. It was close and comfortable in the library. The carpet was thick, the shelves crammed with textbooks, folios and theses. A few small desks, a table and chairs, a sofa. 'Somewhere to sleep,' Wyatt murmured.

'Together?'

'One sleeps, one keeps watch.'

'Lighten up. I was only joking.'

There was more light here than in the corridor. The outside wall was mostly glass, and let in the lowering sun.

Wyatt crossed the room to a door set into the end wall, between two bookcases. He heard a rustle and scrape behind him and dropped to the floor.

'Quit that.'

Raymond was in the act of closing the curtains. 'We'll be seen.'

'We'll be seen from outside drawing the curtains when this room should be empty,' Wyatt said.

'Now we can't turn the lights on.'

'The power's been disconnected, remember?'

Raymond flung himself onto a sofa. 'You talk to me like I was a kid in school. Fucking well tell me what to do, then.'

Wyatt felt complicated emotions for his nephew, composed of love, hate and frustration. But some of the fire had gone out of Raymond, leaving him edgy and cautious, and that was a good thing as far as Wyatt was concerned. Keeping his voice mild, he clicked open the aluminium case and said, 'We work by natural light, there'll be a moon tonight, plus these.' He indicated a pair of torches, their lenses all but taped over. 'They give a narrow band. Just don't flash them toward the window.'

Raymond shrugged. It was a shrug of tiredness, of a short, spluttering fuse. 'One thing I've learned, I work better alone.'

'Come on, son, help me with the storeroom lock.'

'Son' was as close to love as Wyatt could get, but saw by the twist of his nephew's face that he'd chosen the wrong word.

Time for that later. He opened the storeroom door and they went in. 'If you hold one of the torches, I'll start sorting.'

The storeroom was small and windowless. Shelves started at waist height and were crammed with books, journals, binding boards and gluepots. The paintings were under the bottom shelves, leaning against two of the walls.

'So far so good,' Wyatt said.

29

Wyatt began to sort through the paintings, choosing those on Chaffey's shopping list. He saw that he was effectively gutting the collection. At least half of the works were worthless, minor drawings and prints. The collection's value lay in the big name oils and watercolours.

Darkness fell over the city. They cleared an area of carpet in the library and began painstakingly to remove each painting from its frame. Wyatt knew that it was necessary, but hated doing it. Each canvas, taut and humming, became lifeless the moment the tension was gone from it. Rolling it into a cylinder and sliding it into a PVC tube was a final barbarity. But it happened. It was what art thieves did. I can't afford, Wyatt told himself, to get sentimental over a few paintings. It hadn't always been like that for him. He'd once burnt a painting rather than let possession of it earn him a gaol sentence.

The long night was ahead of them. Wyatt was used to the waiting game and he'd supposed his nephew would be, given his experience with staking out and robbing banks, but Raymond's jiggling foot and pacing betrayed him.

Tiring of Raymond creaking out of an armchair for another prowl of the little library, he hissed, 'It's nine hours until morning. Get some sleep.'

Raymond dropped to the carpet and stretched out. He sighed, he rolled onto his back and made shapes with his fingers against the moonlight. 'How come you never been caught? Pure fluke?'

It irritated Wyatt to hear his life boiled down to notions of luck and chance. 'I've made mistakes. Things happened that shouldn't have happened, but because I hadn't thought through everything, not because my luck was bad. And if the cops didn't nab me then it wasn't because my luck was good—I made sure they didn't nab me.'

'You shot to kill.'

Wyatt hated this. 'I go into a job knowing that the gun in my pocket is going to add ten years to the sentence if I get caught, but also knowing it's there to save my life, not take someone else's.'

Wyatt saw a shadow, a kind of inwards look or memory or emotional trace, pass across his nephew's face. He pursued it. 'Have you used a gun? Do you want to?'

Raymond shook his head violently. 'No, no. Just saw someone get shot once, that's all.'

'Not a pretty sight?'

Raymond wouldn't look at his uncle. 'No.'

Wyatt let the silence mount. Then he went on. 'Let's say you get stopped by a cop or a guard tomorrow morning. Weigh up the situation. If you can shut him up just by talking to him, do it. Tap him on the head if necessary, but not so hard you'll cause a brain injury. Better to render him unconscious by cutting off his air, one hand over the mouth, the other squeezing the throat. He'll thrash around, but that uses up energy and sooner or later he'll be out cold. Anything in preference to shooting or seriously hurting someone.'

'You've shot people.'

'I've shot people who have crossed me or threatened to kill me or left me no other choice. Never a panic shooting, never a thrill shooting, never a shooting because I had a sore head that day and was easily irritated, never a shooting because it was the easy way out.'

Raymond draped an arm over his eyes.

Wyatt watched his nephew. 'You're feeling the pressure. So am I. It's normal. I'd be worried if you weren't.'

'What if it looks wrong when we go out the door in the morning?'

'Then drop everything, walk away, hang the time and effort and expense. In fact, I always expect the worst. That way I won't be surprised or caught off guard.'

'They could have plainclothes out there in the morning, seeing where the paintings are going to.'

Wyatt shrugged. 'Check for what's not obvious. Look at body language, the way someone's holding himself or walking. The way he's dressed. If everyone else is in shirtsleeves but one man is wearing a jacket, maybe he's also wearing a concealed gun.'

Raymond laughed harshly. 'Aim at a cop, hit a uni student.'

'You could try running at the cop.'

'*At* him?'

'It will rattle his nerves, stop him aiming properly.'

Raymond still lay stretched out on the carpet. He crossed his feet at the ankles and laced his fingers behind his head. 'I'll be glad when we're in the van. Downhill all the way after that.'

'There's a big difference between getting away and staying away. There's burning our clothes so we can't be tied to the scene, all those carpet fibres collecting on your back, for example. There's wiping down and dumping the van. There's the changeover with Chaffey. A long way to go.'

'Sometimes, Uncle Wyatt, you're a sanctimonious fucking pain in the neck.'

Wyatt felt obscurely hurt. He said nothing.

'I mean,' Raymond said, 'don't you ever *enjoy* what you're doing?'

To his own surprise, the words spilled out of Wyatt: 'Ray, if you've got the nerve and the ability, there's nothing like it on earth. I know I said drop a job if there's the slightest doubt, but I also know there's something addictive about testing the odds, being your own boss, making enough from one strike that would take a nine-to-fiver ten years to amass. But the money's not it, not even ten per cent of it.' He paused, searching for the words he wanted, then said, 'I like using my head and body well, doing what comes naturally to me in a risky game.'

There was silence. Then Raymond whistled ironically, raised one fist like a winning athlete, said '*Fucking A!*'

The wrong tone to use with Wyatt. Wyatt turned away, wondering what he was doing here, with this kid. Raymond was a distraction. When Wyatt worked with another man he didn't want to have him always at the back of his mind, having to think of his safety, wondering if he'd do his side of the job properly.

A dull flash in the corner of his eye. Raymond was sitting with his back to a filing cabinet now, spinning a coin. It caught the moonlight as it rose from his thumb, reached an apex, fell into his palm again. It seemed clear to Wyatt that he was expected to notice the coin. He said, 'Where did you get that?'

Raymond lifted his chin defiantly. 'My mate Vallance. He's a diver, found this wreck. Been there a hundred and seventy years.'

He went on to explain about the *Eliza Dean*. When he was

finished, Wyatt reached out a hand. 'May I?'

He caught the coin. He recognised it as a Spanish dollar. There had been one in a coin collection he'd once stolen from a house in Toorak.

'This is quite valuable.'

'Vallance reckons a hundred and seventy-five dollars. And there's more where it came from.'

Wyatt let the silence gather around them. 'Are you and Vallance mounting a salvage operation? Is that why you need the money so badly, the business matter you mentioned the other day?'

'So what if I am?'

'How do you know it's not a rip-off?'

Raymond flared, 'Give me some credit. I'm not naive. I dived on the wreck myself, saw the coins there with my own eyes. Plus, this is a proper syndicate.'

'If you say so.'

'Fuck you. I tell you what, keep the fucking coin. I won't need it.'

The boy was a bundle of nerves. Wyatt pocketed the silver dollar—for the time being, to keep him happy—and said gently, 'It's late. Get some sleep. I'll wake you at two, you wake me again at six.'

And so they passed the long night. At six o'clock on Saturday morning they shared a flask of coffee and a couple of fruit pies. At 7.30 the first workmen arrived. By mid morning the R.J.L. Hawke building rang to hammers, jigsaws, whistled tunes and radios tuned to weekend sports talkback programs.

Wyatt and Raymond slipped out of the library just before ten o'clock. They walked along the corridor, down the stairs and out to the panel van with the PVC cylinders under their arms. Some of the workmen were outside the building, smoking, yarning,

416

tipping the dregs of their morning tea onto the ground. They saw Wyatt and Raymond and went quiet and still.

'Morning,' Wyatt said. He read their hostility. It was all focused on that word 'asbestos'. With any luck, he thought, after a weekend of football replays and the pub and squabbling kids, asbestos will be all they remember.

The foreman scowled. 'Didn't see you arrive. You blokes find anything?'

'Clean as a whistle,' Wyatt said, and felt them relax around him.

Wyatt and his nephew loaded the stolen paintings into the rear of the panel van and drove slowly through the university grounds and out onto the depressed streets of West Heidelberg. Wyatt turned on the radio, fiddled with it, found the ten o'clock news.

The first item was the discovery of the body of Steer's girlfriend, Denise Meickle, in a shallow grave in Warrandyte. She had been shot in the head.

30

Wyatt yanked hard on the wheel, bringing the panel van in a skewing slide across the path of an oncoming bus and onto the forecourt of an abandoned Mobil station. He steered down the side of the service bay and braked nose to nose with a wheelless Cortina.

'You useless little shit.'

He turned, looked at his nephew. The movement was slow and deliberate, his expression carrying a chill. He took in one aspect of Raymond after another, quartering him, finally resting on Raymond's face. 'You shot her.'

'No way. Probably Steer, not me.'

Wyatt sidearmed his nephew in the throat, a chop with the side of his hand that rocked Raymond's head like a punching bag.

Raymond screamed once, a choked, liquid cry of pain and fear, his eyes wild. 'Don't hit me. Just don't hit me. All my life I've been hit.'

For just an instant, Wyatt stood apart from himself and didn't like the man he saw there, sitting cold and clenched, ready to strike out again. He wished that Raymond was a stranger to him. He was linked to Raymond by blood, and that was the complicating factor. He put his arm down, relaxed his fist. 'I won't hit you, but I want you to tell me about it.'

Raymond croaked, 'It wasn't me killed the bitch. Steer.'

Wyatt aimed for Raymond's stomach this time, a hard jab that drove the breath from his body. 'You were in a mess when I found you outside the door of your flat. A rough night out, you said, but there was blood on your sleeve and you looked bad. You shot her and it made you sick to the stomach.'

There was a tearing sob. 'She wouldn't shut up. Always snivelling on about Steer, had he run out on her, would she see him again, what should she do—it drove me nuts. I had to get out. When I came back the place was dark and I shot her by accident. Hey, what are you doing?'

Wyatt removed the keys from the ignition. The story sounded more or less right. But even if Raymond hadn't shot Steer's girlfriend, the complication was more than Wyatt was prepared to stand. He cranked down his window and tossed the keys over the dividing fence into an overgrown garden.

'What the fuck?'

Wyatt reached for his door handle. 'We abandon. We walk away from this like it never happened.'

Hysteria crept into Raymond's voice. He clutched Wyatt's arm. 'We can't abandon. We got out safely, we got the paintings. There's no need.'

'It all feels wrong now. Instinct tells me to get out. You shot her—you've probably still got the gun in your possession—and that means double the heat. How do I know what other ways you've fucked up? Maybe you were seen shopping in Warrandyte.

Maybe she was found a few days ago and all this time they've been moving against you. We're walking away from this, Ray. You go your way, I'll go mine. That's it.'

As Wyatt reached for the door, Raymond tugged the Ruger automatic from an inside pocket of his overalls. He ground the muzzle against the hinge of Wyatt's jaw, hissed: 'We take the paintings to Chaffey, now. We get our money. Then we split.'

'Too dangerous.'

'I need that money.'

'Walk away from it Ray,' Wyatt said, reaching up idly to push the gun away, then leaning under the dash and ripping hard on the wiring.

Sobbing, 'You bastard,' Raymond smacked the butt of the Ruger down on Wyatt's bare scalp, full force, several times. Wyatt felt a disabling blackness. Raymond's sobs receded behind a foggy wall of pain, blood pooled in the hollow of his collarbone, and all he wanted to do was curl up and nurse the pain. He had no inclination for fighting or flight.

Much later, Wyatt awoke, an island of misery behind the steering wheel of a stolen panel van. He shivered. He could not control his teeth, feverish and unquiet in his mouth. He remembered Liz Redding's warm hands on his poor skull. They had been two days out of Vanuatu when a rogue wave knocked him off his feet and he clipped his forehead on the mast. Sometimes she came back to him like that.

When he felt strong enough to move, he eased onto the ground and around to the rear doors of the van. He looked in. One of the PVC cylinders was missing. Wyatt supposed that that made sense, if you were Raymond. The cylinders were long and awkward. You'd be able to carry one on foot on a suburban street, not four. And you would take one; you wouldn't leave it and save your skin.

There was a water tap against the back wall of the service station. Wyatt washed away the blood, stripped off his overalls, put the cap over his injured skull and walked to the nearest set of traffic lights. A cruising cab picked him up. He gave the address of his motel in Preston.

Some procedures were automatic for Wyatt. He paid off the driver two blocks from the motel, then walked past the place a couple of times, on the opposite side of the street. Finally he crossed to the motel and followed the path around the car park to his room. He stood for a while, watching. He wondered if they'd be waiting for him.

At that moment a cleaner appeared around the corner, pushing a cart crammed with brooms, buckets and plastic bottles. A small transistor radio swung by its strap on the chrome handle. Wyatt changed direction until he was a metre away from her and murmured, 'I'm checking out of fourteen. The room's clear, if you want to start there.'

She peered doubtfully at the first door in the row. He saw that she liked routine. You started at the end and worked your way along. But the first door and two others wore 'Don't Disturb' signs, so the pattern was broken anyway. 'No skin off my nose.'

'Thanks.'

Wyatt walked away. He stationed himself behind a potted ornamental tree near the pump shed of the motel's swimming pool and watched the cleaner. She inserted the key in the lock, swung open the door to his room, pushed the cart in. Nothing. No surprises or shouts or backpedalling feet.

It took her ten minutes, and when she was done and in the next room, Wyatt went in. He moved carefully, stationing a chair under the bathroom ceiling fan, climbing onto it in stages, and taking his time to unscrew the fan. No sudden movements. He had a few hundred dollars there, a new set of papers.

Wyatt put an end to his hard, unravelling morning with a shower. He should have run, but just then he was too bone-weary, too dazed, too swamped by scalding, comforting water to care.

He towelled himself dry at the window, looking out onto the courtyard, keeping his movements slow, containing the pain. He blinked away the water from his eyelashes. It was Liz Redding, standing perfectly still and contemplative in the weird green light of the swimming pool awning, watching his room, watching his shape in the window. When he blinked again, she'd turned away and the last he saw of her was the long slope of her back and the tilt of her hips as she bent to fit a key into the lock of a small white Corolla.

But it was the wrong key. She straightened to examine the others on the keyring. Wyatt thought there was time. This didn't have to be the last that he saw of her.

31

Raymond's hand was sticky. He looked down: blood gouts, from when he'd smacked Wyatt in the head with the butt of his Ruger. Shifting casually, leaning forward and down as if to scratch his leg, he wiped his fingers on his sock, hoping the driver hadn't noticed the blood or the concealment. He straightened again, looked over into the back seat. Red palm prints on the PVC cylinder. Raymond drew in a ragged breath, whistled to calm his nerves.

They stopped at a light. The cab driver punched a thick finger at the keys of his dispatch screen, cursing softly. 'Hate this fucking thing.'

Raymond grunted.

A message came up. The driver peered at it. 'Call Mr Atkins at Thomastown Legal Aid? Christ in hell, what's she done now?'

Raymond figured that the cab driver was not so likely to remember him or smeared blood if he had troubles of his own. 'What's the problem?'

The driver glanced in the rear-view mirror. He was late for the green light and had been tooted from behind. 'Up yours, arsehole,' he said, giving the finger to the other driver. The cab streaked away across the intersection. 'The daughter,' he explained. 'She wags school, goes shoplifting with a gang.' Both hands lifted from the wheel, slammed down again in a gesture of hopelessness. 'I mean, what can you do? They don't teach them anything at school any more. You try to do the right thing at home, teach them what's right and wrong, and some pinko prick from the teachers' college undoes it all or they get in with some gang and skip school. I blame the drugs myself. The economy. Who cares about the family, these days? It's dog eat dog out there.'

Raymond wanted to say, 'Back up a step, you've lost me,' but mention of family and school gangs and shoplifting reminded him of his own high school years, reminded him of Wyatt, of Wyatt not being around for him. He wet the index finger of his left hand, rubbed where Wyatt's blood clung stubbornly to the palm and wrist of his right hand. He couldn't understand why he hadn't popped the bastard. Pow, centre of the fucking head.

Raymond didn't want to think that he wasn't up to it a second time.

'What's in the tube?'

Raymond stiffened. 'What?'

The driver jerked his head toward the back seat. 'You got plans there? You know, blueprints?'

Raymond coughed. 'Got it in one.'

'What, you a builder?'

'Work for one,' Raymond said.

Inside he was screaming, *Come on, come on, get me home.*

Where he'd shower, put on good clean daks, phone Chaffey with the news that Wyatt had fucked up.

'You wouldn't like to run an eye over my place? House needs restumping, salt damp coming up the chimney, thinking of putting in one of them pergolas out the back.'

Raymond squeezed his eyes shut. His head ached. He saw the endless blighted suburbs, populated by blokes like this driver, their wives and kids, from cradle to grave worried about money. That wasn't *his* career path, no way known. He opened his eyes. 'Sorry. We specialise in shithouses for government schools.'

'Fair enough,' the cab driver said. 'Just thought I'd ask, you never know.'

They lapsed into silence. Raymond watched the city skyline fill the windscreen as they trundled along Nicholson and down into streets that saw little of the sun. On the other side of the city the driver said, 'You'll have to guide me. Southbank's changing that quickly, I can't keep up.'

Raymond paid him off outside the ABC studios, then cut through a side street to his apartment building.

Upstairs he sponged away the blood from the cylinder then stood for ten minutes in a lacerating stream of hot water in his bathroom. It occurred to him then that he was stupid, coming back to the flat. He threw on some clothes, packed a bag and took the stairwell down to the car park beneath the building.

When he was on the move again, well clear of the concrete bunker, aiming the Jag for the south-eastern freeway, he dialled Chaffey on his car phone.

'Chafe? Guess who?' he said, when Chaffey answered.

Chaffey was quick. He didn't use Raymond's name. 'Why are you calling?'

'We have a problem.'

A pause. 'Our mutual friend?'

Raymond's brow furrowed. 'Pardon?'

'Your work colleague,' said Chaffey heavily.

'Oh, right, I'm with you now,' Raymond said. 'He's…got a sore head.'

The agitation was clear in Chaffey's voice. 'Permanent?'

'Wish it was,' Raymond said.

Chaffey left that alone. 'So the deal fell through?'

Raymond tried to think how to put this. 'We got about a third of what we budgeted for.'

'A third? All or nothing, that was the understanding. Otherwise the contract is null and void.'

Raymond swallowed. Just lately he'd been subject to panic attacks, swamping out of nowhere, making his heart race, his mouth go dry. He related the attacks to his obsession with the treasure, his anxiety about missing out. The attacks had been worse since the shooting in Warrandyte. He said to Chaffey, trying to control the hysteria in his voice:

'Chafe, I successfully completed part of the job and I deserve part payment. Not my fault our mutual friend dipped out.'

'You say he dipped out, he decided it was a no goer?'

Raymond barrelled the big car along the Hoddle Street overpass. Football traffic choked Hoddle Street and the inbound lanes of the freeway. 'That's what I'm saying. Blame him it went wrong, not me.'

Chaffey was clipped and certain. 'One, he must have had a good reason. Two, a third of the goods is no good to me. No payment. Nothing. Zero. Three, I've been trying to contact you all week. The goods from that other deal failed to arrive in New Zealand. I'd like to know why.' He paused. 'There's a knock on the door. Call me in a couple of days.'

The line went dead.

That didn't stop Raymond. He drove on, thinking about the cash in Chaffey's house: his lawyer's fortune, the payment for the paintings, the money he kept stashed there for the crooks he represented. Chaffey and Wyatt were probably similar in that way, never spent on the here and now, always had a stash hidden away somewhere.

32

'I liked you better when you had a head of hair.'

'It'll grow back.'

Her fingers explored his scalp. 'Nasty gash he gave you.'

Wyatt swayed a little, let her change the dressing. It was the next morning and he felt clean and calm. He was fully dressed, but hadn't spent the night fully dressed. Nor had Liz Redding. There hadn't been an erotic charge in their shared nakedness through the night, only comfort and an essential, restorative warmth. He closed his eyes and leaned against her. In a sense he was surrendering. The emotion was alien, oddly welcome. He'd lived a life built upon vigilance and sharp edges. It would be good to let go once in a while.

Liz smoothed a strip of sterile tape over the cleaned gash on his head and sat back to look at him, her hands in her lap. She looked fine and flashing to Wyatt—in good humour and ready to do combat with the world, using her head and her hands. He said, 'Anything on the news?'

'Some kids were caught looting the van. The police are trying to track down where the paintings came from.'

'They'll know soon enough. All you have to do is pick up that phone.'

'I told you, I've been suspended. They're going to chuck the book at me. I don't care. I've had enough. Anyway, I'm a woman. There's nowhere for me to go. The boys have got the force sewn up.'

Wyatt grunted. 'Do yourself a favour then. Impress them. Bring me in.'

'You came to me, remember.'

Wyatt remembered. He had seen it as a private communication, a warning perhaps, Liz standing outside his motel like that. He could have slipped away. Instead, he'd stepped outside and crossed the car park and tapped her on the shoulder. She'd taken him to a different motel. Said she expected to be arrested if she went home.

There was the soft beat of her body next to him. He wasn't interested in her career, only her impulses. 'Once a cop, always a cop,' he said, more harshly than he'd intended.

She said miserably, the words springing from nowhere, 'I love you.'

Wyatt breathed in. Then he breathed out.

'What I mean is, you're in my thoughts all the time. I don't want anything to happen to you.' She shrugged. 'If that's what love is.'

Wyatt looked around the room. It held no answers for him.

'I suppose,' she said, 'you want to run from me now that's out in the open?'

Wyatt thought of the unwanted clutter in his life and he thought about the absence of love in it. It was not an ordinary life. He liked it streamlined, but right now it was loaded with complications: Raymond, Chaffey, the dead woman in Warrandyte, Liz Redding, the paintings. As for love, that was another complication. Was it better than none at all? Meanwhile he could settle for an expression of it. He felt cold and ill. He picked her hands out of her lap, chafed them, placed them over his shoulders. 'Make me warm again.'

He saw that he'd put a foot wrong. A subtle change passed across Liz's face, as though a deep-seated pain were reasserting itself, drawing out her features, thinning and contracting her face in a kind of recoil. She pulled away from him and sat straight-backed, her chin lifted.

'Didn't you hear what I said? All this is momentous for me. You, my job. But everything with you is one way. I haven't a clue what you want or think.'

Wyatt tried haltingly to discover, from speech, what it was he thought and felt and wanted. The effort exhausted him, bringing on a kind of electric blackness. His head buzzed and dizziness racked him briefly, and pain. When he came out of it he felt her hands on his cheeks. 'You okay? You're very pale.'

'Please, I feel cold.'

She took him to the bed, removed his clothes, then her own, and the warmth revived him. 'Gently does it,' she said, easing him into her.

Later she curled up with him, murmured for a while, breathing against his neck, then fell heavily asleep. She was slack, heavy, peaceful and close against him. Wyatt drew his arm out by degrees, swung his legs to the floor and stood. The room swayed and tilted. He closed his eyes, sat, and when the room righted itself, dressed carefully. His shoes presented a problem. He stood above them, clasped the back of a chair, wound his toes in, forced the heel down. The laces could wait; he needed to keep his head up.

The keys to her car were in a leather shoulder-bag. He found a purse, a small box of tissues, tampons, moisturising cream and a mobile phone. Wyatt pocketed the keys, two hundred dollars and the phone. He glanced at the bed. She was sleeping. He closed the door quietly behind him and pressed the gadget on the key ring to disengage the locks on her car.

They sprang open with a strangled electronic yelp, the driver's door creaked when he opened it, and Liz Redding, wrapped in a motel blanket, was at his window before he could start the car and drive away.

He sighed, wound down the window and heard her fury and disappointment. 'You bastard. Not again, I don't believe it.'

Wyatt showed no embarrassment, no anger, no haste—only deliberation. 'Liz, you belong here.'

She stood away from him, suddenly exhausted, looking cold and vulnerable and insubstantial beneath the blanket. 'I'm tired of this, Wyatt.'

The pause was awkward. Wyatt thought: I've constructed a life out of moving on. It's easy, all you do is turn your back and put one foot after the other down the road. Would she stop him or wish him luck? It came down to disappointment. He'd disappointed her. But she was not vindictive. Wyatt suddenly felt obscurely grubby for trying to sneak away. His head boomed, a spike of pain behind his eyes. He leaned back and closed his eyes.

'You're not fit enough yet.'

'You could be right,' he said.

Some of Liz Redding's combativeness came back to her. 'I want you.'

'We're different.'

'No we're not. I've got the Asahi jewels.'

He opened his eyes. 'Where?'

She jerked her head. 'In my case. I went back to the yacht and found them. I intend to keep them, Wyatt. I intend to melt down the settings and sell the stones.'

'They're fakes.'

She laughed. 'Is that what Heneker told you? I knew he smelt wrong. He was playing it both ways. If you get arrested, his firm gets the Asahi Collection back. If you don't, and he can deal with you again, he'd pay you some minimal reward for the so-called fakes and pocket the rest.' She paused. 'Wyatt, join me.'

In the gathering silence they were both stubborn, waiting for a way out. Wyatt thought: How calculated are her moves? Does she resemble me, or have the things I've done, the evasions, made her wary? When doubts set in, you fix on what is known. Wyatt knew himself, he didn't know her. But he was beginning to, and that hadn't happened to him for a long time. He said, attempting a grin, 'We can't stay here.'

33

The drive to Belgrave took fifty minutes, but when Raymond got there he found that Chaffey's house was shut up tight, curtains drawn, no car, no sign of life. He searched under flowerpots and mossy garden stones, but found no spare key. The door was deadlocked; there were bars over the windows and security company stickers on the glass. Surely Chaffey wouldn't have panicked and done a runner because the job went sour?

After that he tried Chaffey's office. The whole building was shut. Saturday.

Raymond felt spooked. He drove to Hastings with a sensation of guns at his back, of dogs at his heels, expecting to be pinned to the ground by lights and clubs, but he completed the journey intact.

He wondered how he was going to play it with Vallance. Hold out for more time? Offer the paintings as collatoral? Offer to come on board as an employee? Holding out for more time seemed to be the best bet. He knew he couldn't get hard cash for the paintings in the PVC cylinder for weeks, maybe months.

Then again, he did have access to money. Wyatt would have heavy cash put away somewhere, maybe under the floorboards of his place in Tasmania. Plus he had things to settle with Wyatt, the old festering sore and now this more recent cunt act: the whole collection is in their hands and Wyatt walks out on the job as if the risks and rewards and hard work meant nothing at all.

In a slow pass along the street front outside Vallance's flat, Raymond noticed that the venetian blinds were closed and the front step was piled with newspapers. He felt the beginnings of another panic attack. Vallance had found other investors. Right now he was out diving on the wreck, stripping it bare. Leaving the Jag two blocks away, Raymond returned on foot and knocked on Vallance's door.

When there was no answer, he stepped back and examined the neighbouring flats. They looked as mute and unlived in as Vallance's, and there was only a seagull watching him, so he lifted his foot and kicked at the lock until the flimsy wood splintered and he could push through into the stale interior.

Within a few minutes it occurred to him how temporary the flat was. A few days earlier, when he'd stayed the night here, his mind had been on his prick and the gold coin, so he hadn't noticed the bareness. Now the flat looked what it was, a dingy place, probably rented furnished for a short term, the kind of place you walked away from.

Yet there were clothes in the closet and toiletries in the bathroom. Some eggs in the fridge. The answering machine was turned on.

Raymond thought his way into Vallance's skin. He'd fear burglars, a high unemployment place like this. Burglars headed for your usual places: cupboards, drawers, coat pockets, freezer compartment, under the lid of the cistern. Where wouldn't they

434

look? Raymond started with the exhaust fans, one in the kitchen, the other in the bathroom. Nothing. But he kicked a tile on the bath and it clattered to the floor. Behind it were gold sovereigns, silver florins and gold and silver ingots, and it all fitted nicely into a red vinyl Thomas Cook bag.

The next step was Quincy. Raymond found the captain listed in the local phone book, a weatherboard house near the waterfront. Again parking the Jag some distance away, he returned on foot to scout around outside the back fence. It appeared to him that Quincy was out. His only impression was of silence and dashed hopes.

He vaulted the fence. A patch of buckled asphalt outside the back door told him something about Quincy's past couple of days. Empty gin and beer bottles, leaking their dregs into a cardboard box; a lumpish garbage bag slumped against the wall, ribbed and jointed within by tins, cigarette packets, chicken bones.

He had a clear view through the window to a greasy sink and an overflowing ashtray on the table. At the end of the kitchen was an archway, and beyond that, in the curtained gloom of the living area, Raymond saw the body of the sea captain.

He tried the rear door. It wasn't locked. He went through to Quincy expecting to encounter the odour of death, but only alcohol fumes and cigarette smoke thickened the air and Quincy stirred when he prodded him.

'Where's Vallance and his bird?'

Quincy propped himself on an elbow, looked at Raymond, collapsed again. 'Gone out for smokes, what do you reckon?'

Raymond opened the blinds and returned to Quincy, hauling roughly on his arms, pushing him into a chair, slapping his face left and right. 'Are they out at the wreck? Are they stripping it?'

Quincy shook his head and pushed at Raymond's hands.

'What do I know? They never told me nothing. They're all the fucking same, these city jokers.'

Raymond wanted Quincy's intellect applied to this, not his feelings. He went into the kitchen and filled the electric kettle. A jar of instant coffee lay on its side in the cupboard above the sink. He spooned large quantities of coffee and sugar into a mug, added boiling water and milk, and made a weaker cup for himself.

He turned to find Quincy leaning in the archway, regarding him bleakly. 'Just clear out, okay?'

He ignored him. 'Drink this.'

'Fuck off.'

A memory boiled up in Raymond's head, of Denise Meickle and what he'd done about it. His vision went black for a few seconds. When it cleared he was still at the sink and Quincy was still alive, though pale and alarmed.

'Look, I don't know nothing,' Quincy said, backing away. 'The pair of them owe me six hundred flaming bucks, that's all I know.'

'Have they been here in the past forty-eight hours?'

'Haven't seen them for days.'

Raymond thought it over. 'I want you to take me out to the wreck.'

Quincy cocked his head. 'It'll cost you.'

Contempt and satisfaction clear on his face, Raymond slapped the red Thomas Cook bag into Quincy's hands and said, 'Take a look in there.'

Quincy peered in. He whistled.

'There's more where that lot came from,' Raymond said. 'Take me out, now, today, and you can have what's in the bag.'

'It's a deal.'

'Give me the bag,' Raymond said. 'You get to keep it later.'

They walked out into the bright sun, where children rode

bicycles and teenage boys tinkered with cars and women walked home from the supermarket. It was hot in the Jag. Raymond wound down his window, for cool air, for air that was not saturated with Quincy's pungent, boozy perspiration.

The marina was quiet under the wheeling sky. It seemed to Raymond that no-one saw them prepare Quincy's rustbucket for the open sea, not until a voice heavy with authority said, '*Freeze.*'

34

It had started with an anonymous phone call to CIB. The caller
had been very specific, CIB had swooped outside the casino, and
now it was paying off. As soon as Vallance and the girlfriend—and
Christou, the poor sod they were putting the hard word on—arrived
at the police complex, Gosse separated them and began by
questioning Christou.

Then he went to Vallance and said, without preamble: 'Mr
Christou said that you offered to show him a shipwreck site.'

'Might have done. What's it to you? It's business, private,
between me and him.'

Gosse stared at Vallance. The man was a clothes horse: dark
suit, expensive aftershave, a high gloss on his black shoes.

'He said that you were forming a syndicate and did he wish
to invest.'

'So? Nothing wrong with that.'

'Is that where you find your suckers? The gaming tables?'

Gosse agreed with the Opposition that the casino was a blight on society. Certain crime statistics had skyrocketed because of it. Good people—including coppers—were blowing all they had on a throw of the dice or the fall of the cards. It made mugs of a lot of people, and attracted mugs, like this Christou character, who owned a cluster of market gardens and had more money than sense.

'Mr Christou has given us a statement. In it he says that you showed him items of treasure from a wreck. Is that correct?'

Vallance's fingers went *tock, tock* on the interview table. He shrugged.

'Mr Vallance, for the sake of the microphone, please answer yes or no.'

'Yes.'

'Coins, in fact. Are these the coins you showed him?'

Gosse poked a shoe-polish tin toward Vallance. The lid was off. There were two florins and a bronze token nestling in tissue paper. 'Could be,' Vallance said.

'No "could be" about it. We found these in your possession. Now, where did you get them?'

'A shipwreck. Nothing wrong with that.'

'I can think of several things wrong with it. For a start, you are obliged to inform the authorities. Have you done that?'

'Paperwork, bureaucrats,' Vallance said. 'All takes a while.'

Gosse pressed on. 'It's also a problem if the coins have been looted from a protected wreck. See what I mean?'

'It's not protected. I found it fair and square. It's not even on the register.'

'So you don't mind if we have an expert look at these coins, Mr Vallance?'

Vallance cracked a little. He wiped a bony finger across his upper lip. 'Do what you like.'

Gosse got up to leave the room, saying 'Interview suspended' and the time for the tape, and pressing the pause button. As he got to the door, Vallance called out, 'I asked for a lawyer. Where's my lawyer?'

'Legal Aid is stretched to the limit. There'll be a solicitor here to see you as soon as one's available.'

Gosse stalked down the corridor. The sergeants' room was almost empty. A tired detective, rubbing his face, was yawning into the phone on his desk. Another detective was at the bank of filing cabinets.

'Where's Liz Redding?'

Both looked up. 'Haven't seen her.'

'I need her to look at some old coins. Tell her to contact me the minute she comes in.'

Then Gosse went still, his eyes far away. 'Get her on the blower.'

'Sir?'

'Do it, ring her home number. *Now!*'

Shrugging, rolling his eyes at the other sergeant, the man at the desk referred to a list and punched in Liz Redding's number. They waited. The seconds mounted.

'Answering machine.'

'She's done a runner,' Gosse said. 'I can feel it. Right. Find her. I want her brought in. Quick as you can.'

'Right, sir.'

Gosse was high in colour now, the blood pounding in his head. 'You,' he said, pointing to the other sergeant. 'Get hold of whoever we've got attached to that shipwreck protection outfit, get him or her over here at the double.'

'Yes, boss.'

Then Gosse gathered himself, counting slowly, and made his way to the interview room where Allie Roden was being held.

He stepped in quickly, pleasantly, a busy, efficient man with a job to do. He studied her file, letting the silence work on her, then looked up. 'Well, you're in the poo, wouldn't you say?'

She was bored. 'Would I?'

There were times when Gosse hated the games you had to play. They played their side of the game, you played yours. His head started to pound again. He decided to fight dirty. 'We're filing a procurement charge. Mr Christou said that he was being offered sex as an incentive to invest in a shipwreck syndicate.'

She flared. 'That's not true!'

'By far the more serious charge is theft from a shipwreck. According to Vallance, you have him in tow so that he can impress the mugs with his knowledge of diving and shipwreck history. It's your scheme, though, all the way, he says. You do all the heavy talking. And heavy breathing, if we're to believe Mr Christou. And, frankly, I do.'

'I don't know anything. I'm just along for the ride.'

Gosse pushed his face close to hers. 'Mr Christou said that four investors were involved, fifty thousand each. Did you have sex with the other three? We'll find them soon enough. They have security videotapes at the casino. All we have to do is identify who you've been seen with.'

She pouted. 'Don't know anything.'

She pronounced it *anythink*. The pout spoiled her looks. Her hair was dank and smelt of cigarettes, alcohol and expensive perfume soured by sweat. Breathing shallowly, Gosse sat back in his chair. He regarded her for some time, then went back along the corridor to Vallance.

'Miss Roden is quite upset. She says you made her have sex with these investors and one of them gave her herpes.'

Vallance went white. His hands flashed to his groin. 'That bitch.'

'Is it true? Did you make her have sex with them?'

'There was only one guy interested in investing. Young bloke. Not Christou, whatever his name is.'

Gosse said patiently, 'Okay, only one prospective investor. I'll ask again, did you or did you not oblige Miss Roden to have sex with this investor so that he'd fork out fifty thousand dollars?'

Vallance snarled, 'No. Look, I asked the bitch to be friendly, okay? Make the coffee, be around to answer questions, make hotel bookings, that type of thing. I certainly didn't ask her to sleep with this guy. Bloody hell, she's my bird. I'd like to throttle the bitch.'

'You didn't know?'

'I had my suspicions.' Vallance wriggled in his seat, as though his trousers were tight. 'She could have taken better care, got him to wear a rubber at least.'

'You're infected for life if it's herpes.'

Vallance began to scratch and tug. 'Fucking moll.'

Gosse said, 'Look at it this way. You'll do time, two, maybe three years, but the herpes will protect you from the hard men of the yard, keep them off you in the shower. You know, tell them you're infectious and they'll leave you alone. Of course, some of these guys have AIDS, so they won't care one way or the other.'

'You lousy bastard.'

'Make it easy on yourself. Get a load off your chest. Maybe the judge'll be lenient.'

Vallance was staring at his hands, wiping them on his suit coat and tie. The tie was glossy black silk, patterned with tiny silver diamonds. A lovely tie, now yanked free of the neck, the knot as tight as an almond, bunched up in Vallance's fist.

'This young bloke who was going to invest,' he began.

'What about him?'

'He told Allie a few things. Boasted about them.'

'What things?'

Vallance smoothed the tie. Still his hands offended him. He

rubbed them on his thighs. 'Understand that we'd decided we weren't going to have any more to do with him. I mean, this salvage thing is legitimate, I don't want some crim investing in it.'

Gosse was interested. 'He's a crim? What's his name?'

35

As they drove west from the airport at Wynyard, something she said penetrated the recurring fog in Wyatt's head. 'You tipped off CIB?'

'Yes.'

'About me? About Raymond?'

Liz Redding wound down the window a little. 'Some fresh air for your poor head. I said I tipped them off about Vallance.'

'Oh.'

'I saw Vallance and his lady friend with your nephew a couple of times. It didn't look right to me. I thought with Vallance removed from the scene, you and Raymond would abandon whatever it was you were up to. I wanted to save you from getting caught.'

'Vallance had nothing to do with the paintings.'

'I know that now. I didn't at the time.'

There was Bass Strait on the right, a range of mountains on the left, but here the country was featureless, the kind of place where you nodded at the wheel and your speed crept up to 130,

140. Liz, Wyatt noticed, was driving at the limit, her eyes flickering between the road ahead and the rear-view mirrors. She didn't once look at him.

'How do you know about Vallance?'

'I was attached to the Maritime Heritage Unit for a while. My job was to safeguard shipwreck sites from looters and track down looted goods. Vallance was working there, doing research, charting wrecks, that type of thing. He was given the sack. We couldn't prove anything, but we think he was stealing artefacts that were awaiting classification.'

Wyatt was silent for a long time. He fished out the silver dollar that Raymond had given him. 'Artefacts like this?'

Liz slowed the car, pulled on to the shoulder of the road. A semitrailer-load of wood ploughed past, storming the little rental car with a gust of wind.

'Let me see.'

She turned the coin over and over in her slender fingers. 'Did Vallance give you this?'

'He gave it to Raymond, Raymond gave it to me.'

'Did he say where it came from?'

Wyatt said wearily, 'Apparently from a wrecked ship called the *Eliza Dean*. Vallance had found the ship. It was carrying garrison pay to Hobart when it went down some time in the late 1820s. Raymond went out to the site with Vallance. Said he saw coins just lying on the seabed.'

Liz shook her head. 'I remember when Vallance found that ship. He really did find it, it does exist, but there was never any garrison pay. A cargo of timber and sheep, from memory. It's not an important site. It's tucked out of the way and not even scuba divers or looters are interested.'

Wyatt was putting a picture together in his head. 'This coin— could it have come from another shipwreck?'

445

'Yes.'

'It could be one of the things Vallance stole from the Heritage Unit?'

'Yes.'

Wyatt took the coin from her fingers. A traffic policeman slowed, stopped adjacent to them, but nodded and sped off when Liz smiled and waved a road map at him.

'We'd better move on,' she said.

'This is a Spanish dollar, right?'

'On its own it's proof that Vallance was lying to Raymond about the *Eliza Dean*,' Liz said.

'How?'

'In 1813 the English government shipped forty thousand Spanish dollar coins to New South Wales. The Governor knew they wouldn't last, there was a coin shortage, so he stamped out the centre portion of each Spanish dollar and created two coins from one. The holey dollar, and a coin of lesser value called a dump.'

'I know all this.'

'What you may not know is that by the 1820s the coin shortage was over and in 1825 the British government passed a law that only English sterling currency could be legal tender in the colony—two years before the *Eliza Dean* was sunk. Foreign coins, holey dollars and dumps were recalled from circulation. That coin you've got there is unlikely to have come from the *Eliza Dean*.'

'So what about the coins Raymond saw?'

'Vallance must have dived ahead of Raymond and salted the wreck. It's a not uncommon scam in the Caribbean, involving Spanish Main vessels.'

'Salted' was an unfamiliar term to Wyatt but he guessed what Liz Redding meant by it. There was no treasure on the *Eliza Dean*. Vallance had stolen old coins and scattered them near the wreck in order to attract cash investors, and Raymond had fallen for it.

He groaned. 'Bloody fool.'

'Raymond?'

'Yes.'

'What will happen when he finds out?'

Wyatt shrugged. 'Right now he's probably desperate because he doesn't have the cash he promised Vallance, and Chaffey is unlikely to give him any. He probably thinks he can use the paintings to buy into Vallance's syndicate, but if Vallance's under arrest and Raymond can't find him, he could do anything.'

'You think Raymond's in danger?'

Wyatt said, 'He was in danger from the moment he was born.'

'How do you mean?'

'Look at the family he was born into.'

'You're being too hard on yourself. He had choices.'

Wyatt thought about Raymond's choices: Whether he should burgle houses or steal cars. Whether or not he should betray his uncle. Whether he should shoot Denise Meickle or slap her face to shut her up.

'Wyatt, will he come after you?'

Wyatt said, 'I would put money on it.'

36

It was an odd sensation, knowing that she was in the house. Wyatt went for a prowl of the creek and nearby gullies and trees, tracing in his mind the useful landmarks: traps, places where they could hide, places of ambush. All the while he felt the pull of her, back there in his house.

When Wyatt walked back through his door a wall of heat enveloped him. Coals glowed in the open grate and freshly split logs had been tumbled on to the hearth. He looked around. He was not an untidy man, so he'd not left much that needed attention, but it was clear to him, from the aligned edges of an old newspaper and footprints showing against the raised weave of the carpet, that Liz Redding had cleaned and vacuumed the house.

Finally, as he advanced on the open fire, Wyatt made a swift appraisal of Liz herself. She was sprawled in an armchair, looking well-scrubbed and serene in a black tracksuit, with thick socks on her feet, her hair bright in the firelight, alive with static electricity. A cup and saucer on the end of the hearth held the dregs of weak black tea. He bent to kiss her.

Her cheek was cool. She made a sound in her throat. But, as he straightened, her composure cracked a little. She shifted self-consciously in the armchair, as though aware that she'd created a warm domestic cocoon but was in fact far from home and far from secure.

She turned away, fixed her gaze on the grate. Wyatt crossed to an ancient sideboard and cracked the seal on a bottle of Scotch. He poured a couple of fingers into a glass and left it on the mantelpiece while he swung the two-seater sofa to the opposite side of the hearth. But he stumbled, the room yawed, the sofa tipped with him to the floor.

All he wanted to do was lie there, in warmth and security, until the buzz and fog was gone from his head, but Liz was cupping his face in her warm hands. 'You shouldn't make sudden movements. Do you want a doctor?' Her palms tensed. She began to slap his cheeks. 'Wake up!'

Wyatt rolled onto his side, levered himself to his feet and righted the sofa. He collapsed into it, then remembered his Scotch.

Liz pushed him back. 'Stay there. I'll get it.'

Wyatt let the Scotch burn him into a state of relief from his trials. Liz, hovering uncertainly, sank into her armchair when she saw him smile thinly at her, saw the vulnerability rather than the customary chill in his hooded eyes.

She stared at his head. 'You need a doctor.' When he didn't respond she sighed. 'At least get some rest.'

'Right.'

After a while she said, a little sadly, 'I can't see you wanting me here with you.'

Wyatt said nothing. Beyond sleep, he didn't know what he wanted. He felt secure and warm, another chapter over. Then, as the Scotch burned a little more, the thought came unbidden into his head that he did want her there.

Then he felt her sit beside him, her thigh warm against his. In the light and warmth of the fire, Wyatt shifted position on the sofa and saw that Liz was watching him. Surprised by desire, the intensity and suddenness of it, he hooked his hand behind her neck. She shuddered. When they fell to the carpet, they made a clawing kind of love, Wyatt giving and getting back, finding a deep relief.

But when it was over, so was the pleasure. Wyatt didn't know Liz Redding, nor she him. They had desire and regard for each other, and were both in flight from the law, but that wasn't yet enough. He realised from her face that she shared his detachment, his drawing away. Her sadness matched his own. When the feeling passed they moved to the bed together for sleep. Wyatt wondered if he would wake in the morning and find her gone.

That was sad, too.

But if she *was* there—if he hadn't driven her away or allowed her to feel that she must go—then he would have to find a way of saying that he wanted her to stay. He wondered how people did that. Did they state it baldly? That's how he normally communicated his feelings, but surely that wasn't enough?

She was still there when he awoke at four in the morning. Moonlight streamed into the house, so he didn't bother with lights. He padded naked to the kitchen, downed a glass of tap water and mused at the window. That probably saved his life, for he was gazing unfocusedly across the moon-drenched open ground and otherwise might not have detected a flicker at the far end of the belt of trees that screened the house from the road. It was slight, and it was not repeated, but although stealthy it was not the movement of an animal of the night.

Wyatt drew back from the window and moved swiftly back

to the bedroom. He clamped his hand over Liz's mouth, watched as she woke, struggled and subsided, before he whispered, 'We have visitors.'

She heaved against his hand. He released her. 'Who?' she demanded.

'Keep your voice down. I don't know if they're after you or after me. They're not showing themselves.'

Somewhere nearby the house creaked. Wyatt hissed, 'Get into the wardrobe.'

Liz pushed the bedclothes away and slipped across the room. She didn't question or argue further, and Wyatt saw that she had dressed again while he'd been asleep.

He thought of his nakedness then and pulled on jeans, hiking boots and a cotton sweater. He kept a .38 revolver strapped to the underside of the bedframe, and hurriedly dropped to the floor now and reached in and retrieved it. After a moment's thought, he shoved spare pillows under the bedclothes to suggest sleeping forms and placed a dark handkerchief on one of the pillows at the head of the bed.

Wyatt wished that he'd had more time to imagine his house defensively. He knew how to *escape* from it—he had a mental map of the rooms, doors and windows, their positions and dimensions—but what he needed to know was how to *use* the house. He concentrated for a moment, identifying the areas where light, natural or artificial, didn't fully penetrate. There were several: between the door to the kitchen and the refrigerator, the space behind the couch...

He ran out of time. He heard a footfall in the hall outside the bedroom and he rolled across the carpet until he lay flush where the wall met the floor. From this position he put his weight on his stomach and elbows and trained the .38 at the open door.

That might have worked if the shooter had been careless.

Wyatt willed him into the doorway, even into the room, but all he got was a glimpse of a barrel. He was up against an assault rifle and a man who was too careful to frame himself as a target. Wyatt saw the barrel appear, squeezed off a shot from his .38, then all hell broke loose and he found himself deafened by the stutter of automatic fire. But he'd seen a face in the muzzle flash. It was Steer come to get him, not Raymond.

37

When Steer had stepped onto the steel deck of Quincy's boat and shouted 'Freeze!' he had the satisfaction of watching Raymond spasm in fright, almost piss himself with it.

Then, a few hours later, he watched Raymond all doubled over with seasickness, and that was pretty satisfying, too. Not the ultimate satisfaction—that was still to come—but still pretty good.

The trawler had ploughed on into choppy seas. Steer could have taken Raymond out in Melbourne, a clear shot to the brainbox while the little shit was trying to get into Chaffey's house, but a neighbour had been pottering around in the garden next door and Steer had decided to tail Raymond instead, hoping he'd lead him to the uncle.

Instead, it was to a one-horse town on the coast and Quincy and Quincy's boat.

Raymond had got his nerve back pretty quickly after the 'Freeze'. He'd swallowed, screwed a look of relief and apology onto his face and said, 'Steer? Tony? Jesus Christ, man, I thought you'd be out of the country by now. I mean, when you didn't come back, me and Denise—'

Steer had broken in calmly: 'You and Denise what?'

'Well, we figured that was it, you'd decided to go it alone.'

'Did you just?'

Raymond had swallowed again. Quincy stood off to one side, bleary, a fag in the corner of his mouth, holding a rope. He'd swung his head, trying to follow the conversation.

'Yep,' Raymond said. 'Denise was that upset. She thought, that's it, I'll never see him again, he's walked out on me.'

'I got delayed,' Steer said.

Raymond managed a laugh. 'Good to know you're okay.'

Steer had watched Raymond without expression for a few long seconds, wondering how the little shit would play it.

'She was upset?'

Raymond nodded vigorously. 'I'll say. Inconsolable. In the end she just cleared out.'

'Is that a fact?'

'Yeah. She knew she'd be arrested if she went home. Said something about dropping out of sight up north somewhere.'

'You don't say?'

Raymond had found encouragement in Steer's indifference. He took charge. 'Mate, you can't stick around here. Plus you're too late for that boat Chaffey had lined up for you. I don't know what to suggest.'

'*This* is a boat,' Steer said.

'Forgetting my manners,' Raymond said. He indicated the other man. 'This here's Quincy. It's his boat.'

'Quincy.'

'Like the TV show,' the bleary captain said.

Raymond frowned, clearly puzzled by the reference, but Steer

454

knew it. Re-runs of 'Quincy, M.E.' had always been popular in the places Steer had been—Long Bay gaol, Bathurst, Yatala. All those men hoping the medical examiner would find the killer yet also hoping they'd learn how to make a murder look like a suicide or an accident.

'How about it, Quince? This tub make it to New Zealand for my mate here?'

Quincy contrived to look cunning. 'It'll cost him.'

'No problem,' Steer said. 'In the meantime, where are you two off to?'

Raymond had zipped open a red Thomas Cook bag. 'Take a gander at this.'

Old coins and ingots, worn by the tides, encrusted with the sediments of the sea.

'This stuff comes from a wreck out on the Cornwall Islands. Quincy's taking me there. Let's hope we're not too late. You want to get in on the deal?'

As transparent as glass. Steer saw it from Raymond's perspective: distract Steer from the question of Denise *and* get him out on the high seas where it was two against one. 'Sure,' he said.

And now he was in the bow, getting on for three hours out of Westernport, his head tipped back slightly, sniffing the wind, while Quincy stood in the wheelhouse and Raymond chucked his guts out over the side.

From the alignment of the bow with the coastline and the still clouds on the horizon, Steer judged that Quincy had turned a few degrees to starboard. Quincy seemed incurious enough about everything; probably did a spot of illegal abalone diving or was paid to go out and pick up bales of cannabis from the odd ocean-going yacht, but no doubt some internal head-scratching was going on.

Steer looked back. The Victorian coastline was receding in the afternoon light. Ahead of them lay choppier water. It wasn't bad; Steer had seen worse in his time. According to Quincy, there were no gale warnings, no storms expected. It was just surface chop, but it had got young Raymond in the guts. Steer smiled again.

Quincy caught his eye and winked comically. Steer nodded. Quincy wasn't a man who shaved or wore fresh clothes. Steer had spent a lot of time in gaol, a lot of time in cramped conditions, and a man soon learnt to value cleanliness. There was little toleration for the inmate who didn't wash, didn't make an effort. Just as well Quincy was downwind, in his wheelhouse. Steer took in the man's greasy overalls and towelling cap, his fuckwit's eyes in a nest of wrinkles, and turned back to his contemplation of the sea and fate.

He supposed that the treasure would be a bonus—if there was any. It would top up his two hundred grand, which had still been sitting in Chaffey's safe, wonder of wonders. Steer had felt certain that it wouldn't have been there, given the rip-off that Chaffey and Raymond were working on Denise and himself.

At his elbow, Quincy said, 'Wouldn't have a smoke on you by any chance?'

Steer gazed past him involuntarily to the wheelhouse.

'Oh don't worry about this old darling,' Quincy said. 'I've set a course and she'll more or less keep to it for the time being. I mean, what are we going to hit out here? An iceberg? Fucking nuclear warship?'

A gurgling cough started deep inside Quincy and Steer realised that the man was laughing. He recoiled, stepped back a couple of paces, but Quincy followed. Quincy was a crowder. That was another thing you soon learnt not to do in the places Steer had been. To stall the sailor, Steer got out his Stuyvesants.

'Ta muchly,' Quincy said.

Where Steer came from, a complex pattern of human intercourse revolved around cigarettes. It wasn't like being on the outside, where you simply walked into a shop and bought smokes and smoked them. In gaol they were an item of currency. You bartered with them, accumulated and bought favours with them. They soothed you when you burned inside. You didn't, on any account, offer them without expecting something back. Quincy, puffing contentedly now, wasn't to know that, but that didn't lessen Steer's contempt for the man.

'Your little mate's puking his guts up.'

They gazed at Raymond, who lay on his side near the starboard safety rail, both arms around his head. He must be wrung dry by now, Steer thought.

'Is there calm water around the islands?'

Quincy said that there was.

'He'll be okay when we get there.'

Quincy looked at the sky, the deck, a point past Steer's shoulder. 'I don't want no funny business.'

Steer looked at him. Did the man mean sex? Does he think Raymond and I have a thing for each other?

'I don't want no shipwreck inspector arseholes breathing down my neck.'

'Right,' Steer said.

'Not worth the aggravation, know what I mean? They could seize this boat, fine us, slap us in gaol. Not worth it.'

'I understand,' Steer said.

They watched as Raymond rolled onto his other side.

'There's a thin blue line between fossicking and scavenging.'

'I guess there is.'

'Anything you find belongs to the government, by rights.'

Now Steer had a fix on him. Seabirds sideslipped above their

457

heads and the air hummed with a heady, briny ozone freshness. It was good to be alive. 'We'll cut you in,' Steer said.

Quincy's whiskery face contorted into an expression of cunning. 'Nice to know we're on the same wavelength. Those other bastards your mate was partners with were paying me by the hour, only they skipped, owing me six hundred bucks.'

'What other bastards?'

'Your mate's partners,' Quincy said.

'Where are they?'

'Scarpered, most probably. They didn't smell right to me.'

They gazed at Raymond. 'So we work something out, okay?' Quincy said. 'I'll see you don't get disturbed. If anyone shows, I'll have a good story ready, fishing rods over the side, stuff like that. We split whatever you find, no questions asked.'

'Fair enough,' Steer said.

Moron.

Quincy went back to the wheelhouse. They butted on through the swell and eventually Steer lost interest in the sea and Raymond and Quincy. He went below, found a paperback and stretched out with it on his bunk. Later he took a chart up to Quincy, breathed shallowly while Quincy indicated the location of the *Eliza Dean*.

They anchored late in the day in a sheltered cove on the eastern side of the main island in the Cornwall Group. Steer stared at the little land mass and thought it a fitting place for a wreck, for tragedy, for the end of the line. He saw eroded red stone peaks, ferns, a tidal river between prongs of granite, wind-stunted sheoaks, Cape Barren geese, a few muttonbirds, oystercatchers and sandpipers, bare shoreline rocks, even a fur seal. There was a chill in the air.

Raymond had hauled himself to his feet as Quincy manoeuvred the boat through the reef. He clasped the rail, pale and blurry. 'This it?'

'This is it.'

Quincy had taken another Stuyvesant from Steer. He ground it into the deck and winked. 'Over the yard arm, boys.'

Raymond stared at him suspiciously.

'Time for a drink, son,' Quincy said.

Raymond groaned. 'Not for me.'

Quincy turned to Steer. 'How about you? Game for a swig of something?'

Steer shook his head. 'I'll pass. You go on and have one.'

'Don't mind if I do,' said Quincy delicately, and he waited, and he waited.

Steer understood. 'Sorry, didn't bring anything with me.'

'Oh, mate,' Quincy said. 'First rule, a bottle for the captain.'

'Didn't know I'd be sailing with you,' Steer said. He moved off. He was tired of this joker. 'I need the bathroom.'

He went below. When he appeared on deck again he was carrying canvas carryalls from the house in Warrandyte. Raymond was leaning tiredly on the rail. Quincy was waving his arms about, giving Raymond a history lesson.

Steer unzipped one of the canvas cases and pulled out the stun gun. As described in the mail order catalogue, it fired a disabling jolt of electricity, useful for crowd control and subduing violent men and animals. Steer walked up to Quincy, fired it at his head and saw him drop, stunned, into the icy sea.

Raymond's jaw sagged. 'Jesus. Mate. Steady on.'

'She's been found, Ray. You think I don't listen to the news?'

'Who's been found?'

'You thought you could knock Denise and get away with it? I mean, what do you take me for?'

'Denise? I put her on a bus—'

'What happened, you try to race her off and she turned you down?'

459

Raymond backed away, eyes wide in pure fright. 'I didn't kill her. She was, you know, suicidal. I came back one day and found her. Or maybe she was cleaning her gun and it went off. Anyway, I panicked and dug—'

'Or how about this,' Steer said. 'You and Chaffey cooked the whole thing up. Get rid of me, get rid of Denise, pocket my dough. Only it went wrong, I didn't come back to the house with you.'

'I swear. Ask Chaffey. He—'

'Chaffey's dead in his basement.' Steer grinned then, a glittering cold grin of arrogance and vigour. Raymond looked away.

'Hey, Raymond, why so long in the face? Forget Denise. You tell me where Wyatt is and we're quits.'

Raymond turned, relieved. He started to blabber out an address in northern Tasmania, then said, 'Mate, if you want to waste him, be my guest. What'd he do?'

Steer stroked his chin, let the stun gun hang loose at his side. 'You would've been a gleam in your old man's eye at the time. Wyatt set up this job, an American base payroll near Saigon. We'd done it before. Spent weeks putting this one together, a real perfectionist. I couldn't see any holes in the job, but at the last minute he pulled out, said it felt wrong. So me and a couple of others done it. The MPs were waiting for us. A set-up, clear as the nose on your face. He wanted me out of the way. I think he struck a deal with the MPs, something like that.'

'Bastard.'

Steer saw the heat of strong emotions rise in Raymond, as though the little shit shared his sense of betrayal. Raymond shook his head in disgust and said, 'You reckon that's how come he's stayed out of gaol so long? He makes deals with cops?'

'Bank on it.'

'Anyway he—'

'Anyway, this is for Denise,' Steer said, and he zapped Raymond three or four times, backing him up to the rail, propelling him over the side. Steer watched for a while. Like Quincy, Raymond drowned quietly, his limbs feeble in the darkening water, as though stirring molasses.

There was some daylight left. Steer stripped, climbed into a wet suit, and contemplated the bottom of the sea. He didn't find anything on the seabed, but among Raymond's things on board the boat he did find a red vinyl Thomas Cook bag and a PVC cylinder with a couple of paintings in it. He spent the night anchored in the calm waters inside the reef. At dawn the next morning he sailed through the gap and headed south-west, across Bass Strait to the northern coast of Tasmania.

38

Wyatt fired again, snapping off a shot through the open door as he rolled toward it. For some reason, Steer was firing high, spraying the room, and there was something unprofessional about that.

And then he realised why. As ejected casings from the automatic rifle spun to the floor, Steer stumbled on them, his feet threatening to slide away beneath him. Wyatt kept firing, more wildly now to take advantage of Steer's carelessness.

But he was also counting. With one cartridge left in the cylinder, he stopped firing. He was listening now, and through all of his faulty senses he heard a door bang shut, heard footsteps boom on the verandah, then silence.

He lay there for a short time, trying to blink away the muzzle flash on his retina, swallowing to clear the ringing in his ears. Steer's presence here told him that Raymond was dead. He also knew that Steer would want to finish what he'd started. He had run, but probably to a safe place so that he could work out how to try again. The house was isolated, the target a man wanted by the law, so he had no reason to fear neighbours or that Wyatt would call the police.

But it didn't seem likely that Steer would try again before daybreak, not when he'd lost the advantage. Daylight was a different matter. Steer could move more freely then, shoot with greater certainty, place the house under siege.

Wyatt had no intention of allowing that to happen. He would let Steer know that he was the hunter now, even though he had only the patchy moonlight to work with.

He fumbled in the darkness for a box of cartridges, whispered 'Stay there,' at the wardrobe door, then hurried to the window, pushed open the insect screen and dropped to the verandah. For a moment he clutched the railing, waited for a wave of dizziness to pass, then ran at a crouch to the corner of the verandah. He saw from the dewy grass that Steer had returned to the clump of blackwoods, peppermint gums and manferns below the house.

Wyatt guessed that he was about a minute behind Steer. Yet he also had all the time in the world. It was 4.30, and in the two hours before daylight broke over northern Tasmania, Wyatt went on the offensive.

He began by letting Steer know that he was in pursuit. His boots thudded on the open ground; once among the trees, he tore through the undergrowth, his sleeves and trousers snagging on blackberry bushes. He drew ragged breaths. He shouted a couple of times.

And then he would freeze for ten minutes, letting the silence build, letting it work on Steer's nerves. Panic levels rise at night in the bush. You lose track of your quarry, lose track of your own position, yet—absurdly, given the darkness—you feel that you are under a spotlight, that all guns are trained on you. That's how Wyatt read the psychology of the man he was up against and he hoped for a careless rush through the trees, or wild shots, but Steer

463

refused to be drawn. He didn't even slap himself against the swarming mosquitoes.

Wyatt sniffed the air, trying to pinpoint Steer by smell, but got nothing. Steer knew all that Wyatt knew about tracking and hunting. They had trained together as snipers, after all, and no sniper will let himself be betrayed by insect repellant, dry-cleaning fluid, tobacco, shampoo, soap, deodorant, aftershave or any other chemical.

Wyatt tried to recreate his own odours. Sweat and tangled sheets and Liz Redding.

And in the act of recreating his past few hours he saw the bedroom again, saw the spray of automatic fire criss-crossing the bed and stitching the walls.

Stitching across the wardrobe door, across Liz Redding's lovely torso? He wished that he could remember. He started to reload the .38—but something was wrong. The spare cartridges: they wouldn't fit. In his haste he'd grabbed 9mm ammunition for his Browning. A chill crept over his skin.

He shook it off. He waited in perfect stillness, like a fox, thinking about his next move. His mind flicked down the years to his youth, the army, Steer, trying to focus on Steer's weak points. Reluctantly he admitted that Steer matched him. Steer's only weakness was that he was fixed on getting even with Wyatt, and that wasn't a weakness unless he let his feelings get in the way of his intellect. Wyatt's flickering thoughts brought him to the present again, to the shot-up bedroom, and it occurred to him that Steer had outfitted himself with the wrong weapon for a cat-and-mouse game.

Wyatt hated automatic weapons. They jammed, they were sensitive to dirt and knocks, they required no skill other than to pull the trigger. Steer had simply stood back from the door, extended the barrel into the room and fired. The natural kick of the weapon had done the rest. The bullets, spraying at the rate of thirty per second, had striped the room. It was an inefficient, noisy, careless way to kill someone, and it was the wrong weapon for a stalking game. Wyatt would have fired only once and it would have been a kill shot. He wondered if his .38, with one shot left in the chamber, was the right weapon. But it wasn't his only weapon. He had his hands and his head, after all.

His hands and his head. They were not as efficient as they could be. His hands were no good if his head gave way to blackouts.

He moved. He'd been still for long enough. The daylight was coming and he needed to blend with the trees and the grass and a variety of earthen colours. He drew closer toward the creek, startling a bandicoot. Once or twice he mistakenly snapped a twig or brushed against bark, but waited for several minutes before moving on again, hoping that Steer would dismiss the noise as a random one.

At the creek's edge he found wallaby and potoroo tracks in mud that was the consistency of axle grease. He scooped palmfuls of the mud over his jeans and sweater, daubed it onto his face, scalp and the backs of his hands. The clay seemed to bind itself to him like an outer skin. It would be slow to dry, slow to flake away. He finished with leaves and stalks of grass, distributing them over his body until he wore mud and flora like a kind of gillie suit, as if he were a Scottish poacher or gamekeeper, not a manhunter.

In full daylight, Wyatt began to hunt Steer. The creek wandered through a gully several kilometres long, here and there concealed by thickets of dense trees, bracken and manfern fronds but mostly running through a trench across open ground with sloping grassland for dairy cattle on either side. Starting at one end of the trees at the bottom of the slope below his house, Wyatt passed silently and swiftly to the other. Steer was no longer there.

At the western edge he stopped and peered through a fine, stubborn mist at the open ground, scanning quickly, not letting his eyes rest for long, for fear that he might miss spotting a movement or a shape that didn't belong there. The creek tumbled over stones; birds greeted the morning: a grey thrush, crescent honeyeaters, satin flycatchers.

As Wyatt saw it, Steer had three choices: to follow the creek across open ground to the next belt of trees; to head left or right up a grassy slope to either rim of the little gully, where he'd be among trees again and have a clear shot downhill; or somehow conceal himself and let Wyatt get ahead of him, so that he could become the hunter and Wyatt the quarry.

Wyatt investigated this last option first. The only shelter outside of the trees was a clump of bulrushes. Breaking cover at a run, he weaved until he reached it. He saw at a glance that Steer hadn't stopped here. The bulrushes sat undisturbed and there were no tracks in the mud.

He crouched and stared out across the grassland on either side of the creek. There were plenty of ways of playing this. He could wait, letting Steer make the moves, the mistakes. If he kept moving, on the other hand, he'd maintain the advantage and maybe rattle Steer. He'd broken cover to get to the bulrushes, something he'd rather not have done. But Steer hadn't fired. Did that mean Steer hadn't seen him? It could be that he was on high ground, keeping watch on several locations at once, meaning that his concentration was split. Wyatt would make Steer break cover if he could, but why should Steer want to do that? Much better to stage an ambush.

Wyatt guessed that Steer was either on the run now or intending to set a trap away from the creek. He peered at the ridge on either side. Steer was up there somewhere.

He returned to the shelter of a peppermint gum and began to

think his way into the soil. He crouched and looked along the grass, letting the slanting light of early morning tell him where Steer had been. After a while, he found the signs: a bruised grass stem; disturbed pebbles, their moisture-darkened undersides revealed to the light; a patch of bruised lichen on a rock.

Wyatt began to track Steer, out of the trees and parallel to the creek. He found more signs: an indentation where Steer had knelt briefly; tiny grains of soil pressed to the bottom of a dead leaf; the crust broken on a cow pat; finally a footprint, the heel deeper than the sole, indicating haste.

Wyatt tracked more surely and swiftly now. He began to listen and watch for larger signs such as quail disturbed from the grass, black cockatooos screeching from the treetops. It was clear that Steer had not climbed to the rim of the gully but was heading parallel to the creek, making for the next thicket of stringy-bark and blackwood. Wyatt noticed dark, kicked-up soil; the lighter underside of grass revealed among the darker surface that faces the sun. He encountered obstacles—a quartz reef, fallen logs and a tributary of the creek—where he lost the trail and had to gauge how Steer would reason his way past. He'd find the trail again, press on, knowing that he couldn't afford to take short cuts or try outguessing Steer, for backtracking would waste precious time.

Fifty metres short of the next thicket, he came to a depression in the ground and saw that Steer had rested there. Something gleamed wetly. He bent to look. Blood spots. Was Steer wounded? Had he cut himself? Wyatt climbed out, preparing to follow Steer's tracks into the trees, and noticed that Steer had changed direction. He was heading up and out of the gully after all.

Wyatt thought it through. He was wasting time following Steer like this. Steer might keep running, he might stop and set a trap because he was wounded, but either way he'd be expecting

Wyatt to come in behind him. As Wyatt saw it, he had to get ahead of Steer and ambush him.

He broke cover and weaved along the creek toward the trees. He ran through them, dodging branches and leaping rotten logs, and found himself at a culvert on a muddy backroad. The road told him where he was. If he went right he'd eventually reach the coast highway. If he went left, he'd climb out of the gully to the top of the ridge somewhere behind his house. He knew he'd find Steer there. If Steer had come by vehicle, that would be there too.

Still running, Wyatt scrabbled through a fence and up the embankment to the road itself and followed it uphill. It was a road subject to poor water drainage and he stumbled often on the deep red ruts and washaways. At the top the going was easier, and he came upon an old F100 ambulance parked under a screen of trees, low branches touching the roof. Wyatt watched, and when he was satisfied that the van was unoccupied, he ran to the glass in the rear doors and peered in. Empty but for a red vinyl bag and a PVC cylinder. *That* has come a long way, he thought. When he peered through the driver's window he saw torn wires around the ignition.

He straightened from the window, formulating an ambush. Steer would be hyper-cautious as he approached the van. He'd search the trees, then the interior of the van itself.

Suddenly Wyatt heard a footscrape, heard Steer slide free of the tangling branches down onto the van roof, swinging the assault rifle at him like a club. That explained Steer's failure to shoot. His clip was empty or the firing mechanism had jammed. Wyatt fired his last bullet uselessly at the sky as he thought these things and then Steer's rifle smashed against his temple and compounded all the hurt and damage of the years.

Later, when he stirred again, blinking at the light and daring to move, he saw that the sun was high in the sky. He turned onto his side. After a while, he levered himself to a sitting position, letting the front wheel of the van hold him upright.

'Bang, bang,' Steer said. 'You're dead.'

Wyatt waited for the tilting world to right itself. He felt too weak to stand. It occurred to him that this was how he might die one day, his backside in the dirt, at the hands of a man like Steer.

What was Steer waiting for? Did he want to spell out his grievances first? Unprofessional, Wyatt thought.

He blinked and focused. Steer was opposite him, almost his mirror image, seated on the ground, his back to a tree. He had Wyatt's empty .38 in his lap, and when he saw sharpening intelligence in Wyatt's eyes, he raised the .38 and pulled the trigger, once, twice, a third time, a series of dry clicks. 'Bang, bang,' he said, as if he'd been playing this game all through Wyatt's blackness, wanting him to wake up. 'Bang, bang,' he said. 'You're dead,' and he coughed blood and began to fall.

Wyatt watched. He saw Steer topple onto his side, stretch, arch his back, and apparently die. He'd been gut shot. The blood had seeped into his clothing, darkening a huge area around his waist. Wyatt wondered about that. He put it down to a lucky shot through the bedroom door. He felt tired. He heard whispering footfalls in the grass, possibly the wind, and lay himself on the damp, rotting leaves to wait for Liz Redding, or possibly sleep, to claim him.